Jacob's Dangerous Birthright

GAINING HIS *inheritance* MAY COST HIM HIS *life*

BONNEVILLE BOOKS

An Imprint of Cedar Fort, Inc.
Springville, Utah

© 2017 Doc Terrance M. Cooper
All rights reserved.

Horse photo by T&C Pet Photography.
Used with permission.

No part of this book may be reproduced in any form whatsoever, whether by graphic, visual, electronic, film, microfilm, tape recording, or any other means, without prior written permission of the publisher, except in the case of brief passages embodied in critical reviews and articles.

This is a work of fiction. The characters, names, incidents, places, and dialogue are products of the author's imagination and are not to be construed as real. The opinions and views expressed herein belong solely to the author and do not necessarily represent the opinions or views of Cedar Fort, Inc. Permission for the use of sources, graphics, and photos is also solely the responsibility of the author.

ISBN 13: 978-1-4621-2017-8

Published by Bonneville Books, an imprint of Cedar Fort, Inc.
2373 W. 700 S., Springville, UT 84663
Distributed by Cedar Fort, Inc., www.cedarfort.com

LIBRARY OF CONGRESS CATALOGING-IN-PUBLICATION DATA

Names: Cooper, Terrance, 1941–author.
Title: Jacob's dangerous birthright: a novel / Doc Terrance Cooper.
Description: Springville, Utah : Bonneville Books, an imprint of Cedar Fort, Inc., [2017]
Identifiers: LCCN 2016059009 (print)
ISBN 9781462120178 (perfect bound : alk. paper)
Subjects: LCSH: nephews-- fiction; uncles-- death-- fiction; inheritance and succession-- fiction; front and pioneer life-- fiction; Utah-- fiction.
Classification: LCC PS3603.O5843 J33 2017 (print) | 813/.6 | dc23
LC record available at https://lccn.loc.gov/2016059009

Cover design by Rebecca J. Greenwood
Cover design © 2017 by Cedar Fort, Inc.
Edited and typeset by Casey Nealon and Jessica Romrell

Printed in the United States of America

10 9 8 7 6 5 4 3 2 1

Printed on acid-free paper

Jacob's Dangerous Birthright

Gaining his inheritance may cost him his life

Doc Terrance M. Cooper

Acknowledgments

I want to thank my wife for her patience and long hours in helping me with editing this novel and her helpful suggestions. I also want to thank Becky Young Faucett for her hours in correcting and editing my manuscript. I am grateful for Blaine Yorgason for his encouragement and also Clair Poulson for his help in editing my first manuscript and for his patience as I asked many questions. And most of all I thank my kind Heavenly Father for blessing me with the ideas and the inspiration for this novel.

Foreword

In 1985, I moved my family to Hornbrook, California, to an eight-hundred-acre ranch, where we raised quarter horses and kids. I had opened a chiropractic office in Yreka, and became fascinated by the early history of Siskiyou County.

Gold was discovered in 1851 in Yreka and the surrounding areas. Names such as Horse Creek, Etna, and Fort Jones are still known today for their gold mines.

While living on our ranch, the idea of writing a book about the rich history in northern California and including the majestic Tetons came to my mind. While riding on horseback for over eighty miles through the Tetons and Yellowstone, I imagined what the Sioux Indians must have seen. I camped where they would have camped, I dreamed about the lives they lived, and I became a part of the area.

I learned how to train horses from my father and grandfather in Michigan. Over the years I have broken and trained many of my own horses. Throughout my career as a chiropractor, I have also been a part-time rancher. I actually had three buckskin horses, and one was a beautiful stallion named Buck.

In my novel, I have used actual names and places from the history I gleaned while researching at the library and traveling to the different mining towns in the area. There are still many active mines in the area, and claims are still being worked. Gold nuggets can be purchased from miners, if you know the right people.

One resident of Yreka told me that there were over one thousand Chinese workers in the mining fields. This I found documented in old newspapers from the early 1850s. I have used that information in my book. It was also known that the Chinese dug tunnels under their living quarters. Some people say that was not true. However, one of my patients asked me to come to his home and see the underground tunnel under his foundation. Its entrance was through one of their closets. I could kick myself now, because I never took him up on his offer.

Chapter 1
Preparation

The silence of the early morning was broken only by the whisper of moccasin-clad feet as the lone runner ran quietly and briskly along a dark cobblestone street of Boston. The cool, early-morning air in April 1854 was scented with the smell of fresh rain, which helped to soften the stagnant stench of open sewers, rotting garbage, and raw animal waste. Occasionally, the tempting aroma of burning wood and frying bacon drifted to the street from some of the early risers in this congested and dirty section of the old city. The smell reminded Jacob Morgan that a hefty breakfast would be waiting for him at the end of his three-hour run.

Jacob's strides were long and confident, carrying him quickly beyond the rows of old houses and hidden side roads into the open countryside. Every rut, rock, and pothole was familiar to Jacob Morgan as his long legs ate up the miles ahead of him. His breathing was effortless as he inhaled deeply and savored the freshness of the cool, country air.

Thoughts crowded his head as the rhythm of his running settled him into his familiar mile-eating pace. Memories and imagination ran free and easy, like his dark lone figure gliding through the silence of the still-sleeping world.

Jacob felt the soft wind against his face in the stillness of the early breaking dawn. His mind raced into dreams harbored in his mind, imagining himself amidst the pines and spruces of the western mountains. His dream turned to longing.

Why was I born in the East, in a city where I'm corralled in? he thought. *Why couldn't I have been born in the West? That is where I really belong.*

At seventeen, Jacob was well educated, strong, and ambitious, but he always felt like something was lacking in his life. He felt confined, like he was tied to his mother's apron strings that needed to be severed. He wanted freedom and the chance to experience adventures of his own choosing. In a nutshell, he craved to be a man in his own right, like his Uncle Zachariah Sherwood was.

Jacob had considered going west to join his Uncle Zac. How many years had it been since his mother's older brother had left Boston? Not that it really mattered. What did matter was that Uncle Zac had followed his dreams, despite what anyone else advised him to do.

Maybe someday, Jacob thought, *I will head west myself.*

Jacob's Uncle Zac was a mountain man who dressed in buckskins with moccasins laced up to his knees. Not that Jacob actually knew him that well. Jacob had only met Uncle Zac three times when he had come east to visit their family. The first time he remembered meeting him was when he was fascinated by the buckskin clothing his uncle wore. He remembered when his uncle would pick him up and set him on his shoulders and they would go on long memorable walks. Uncle Zac had told him stories of the Indians and how he had lived with them in the wilderness. Since hearing those stories, Jacob wanted to live that life and he felt connected with his uncle.

There was another time Jacob remembered when his uncle had visited him. Uncle Zac had told him of when he was on a ship sailing over the vast ocean and visiting other faraway lands. Jacob already loved the Sioux Indians and that was where his Uncle Zac lived. Then for some reason unknown to him, the visits stopped and his Uncle Zac no longer visited him or his family, and he longed to be with him.

Jacob's mother often scolded Jacob about his dreams, telling him that it was Uncle Zac who had put the crazy wandering ideas in his head. That wasn't really so; all Uncle Zac had done was reinforce his yearnings to go west and be with his uncle. However, his parents were dead set against his going, and they already had his life planned out for him.

Jacob imagined himself dressed in buckskins and carrying his rifle while running through the forest. The thought brought a smile to Jacob's face as he ran.

The sharp barking of several dogs brought him back from his thoughts. A light twinkled ahead and a door opened. A man stared out into the cold, early morning. Seeing nothing, a rough, harsh voice cursed the dogs, quieting them almost instantly. As Jacob lengthened his stride, the cabin swiftly vanished behind him into the predawn darkness. Ahead in the distance, lights winked on as more oil lamps were lit and the farmers of the area prepared for another day of toil.

As the dim gray morning light slowly emerged on the eastern horizon, Jacob was one hour away from the city. He turned around and headed back east, gradually closing back in on the city. He was invigorated and full of energy. He had run this course several times a week for the past two years. The muscles of his body were toned to a high pitch. He was in superb condition, and he told himself that he could handle the West and its challenges.

Jacob felt like he had been born a hundred years too late to belong in Boston. It was 1854, and by this time the settling and wildness of Boston were gone. There was no adventure left here for him.

However, the West was a hundred years behind the East. Revolutions were still going on there, and it was a land that needed to be tamed.

Nearing the end of his run, Jacob purposely turned off from his normal course and entered the forbidden, rough area of old Boston. He had not gone more than three blocks before he was exactly where he wanted to be.

A pair of ruffians blocked the street ahead of him.

"Hey, it's old Professor Morgan's kid," one of them taunted.

"You lost, Morgan?" His companion asked with a sneer.

Jacob said nothing, but just kept on running. As he went to pass, one of the men latched onto his shirt and jerked him roughly about.

The same thing had happened nearly six months earlier when Jacob had taken a sound thrashing. Isaiah, a constable, was one of Jacob's older brothers and had seen Jacob when he returned home with black eyes and a bloody nose.

"What happened to you?" Isaiah asked.

Jacob hung his head down as if ashamed, and said, "I got trounced."

"Little brother, you didn't get trounced. You got beat," Isaiah laughed. He then started helping Jacob clean his wounds. Isaiah seriously looked at Jacob and said, "I promise you, little brother, this will never happen to you again."

For the last six months, Isaiah had schooled Jacob in the art of boxing. Isaiah also felt that Jacob would need to know as much about self-defense as possible so he introduced him to a Mr. Jock Montclair, who was a swordsman and instructor from France. Jacob studied and practiced fencing every opportunity he had, and at the end of five months Jacob became an excellent swordsman. Mr. Montclair said, "Mr. Morgan, you are my finest pupil. Never have I seen anyone excel as fast as you have. You make me feel like you are my instructor."

Jacob was a fast learner and was becoming a good boxer and fighter. It had been a well-kept secret between Isaiah and Jacob; however, he had not yet tested his skills in the street.

That was about to change.

Jacob had purposely planned for this moment. He clearly remembered the beating he had received and it seemed as if it were yesterday.

The two thugs that blocked his way were the same bullies that had thrashed him six months ago. Because of their size and reputation, they intimidated everyone and anyone in the area. After learning self-defense, it was now his turn to show them some manners.

Jacob faced the lanky, flat-faced large young man who gripped Jacob's shirt with grimy hands. "Let go," Jacob said calmly. After nearly three hours of running, he still felt fresh, and his breathing was even and controlled.

The two bullies used any excuse to cause trouble to anyone in the area because this was their territory.

"Jest 'cause yer old man's a professor and yer big brother's a constable, you think you can run through anybody's neighborhood before they've even had their breakfast, is that it, Morgan?"

"I mean no harm," Jacob said, trying to look apprehensively into the narrowed eyes of his tormentor.

"Thought we told you months ago that you weren't never to come 'round here," the man said. "I guess we gotta teach you another lesson, eh?"

"You seem to know me, and I do vaguely remember your face," Jacob said calmly, wondering how many fights this man had been in to squash his nose so thoroughly against his face. "But, I don't know your name. If you plan to teach me a lesson, the least you could do is share your name first."

"His name's Sal," the second ruffian said.

"So, you are Sal," Jacob replied slowly.

Sal's friend had circled behind him, but Jacob was aware of where he was. Isaiah had taught him well; Jacob sensed when the punch was thrown. He twisted like a cat, tearing free of Sal's grip on his shirt, and threw a punch of his own. While the ruffian's fist behind him sailed by harmlessly, Jacob's fist connected with a solid smack on the nose of the ruffian, and the man slowly sunk to the cobbled street.

Sal hadn't expected this. The two bullies thought this would be another easy innocent victim of theirs, but suddenly Sal feared that he was going to become the victim.

Sal swung his boulder-sized fist, but Jacob ducked and delivered a solid blow to his midsection, and then a right jab to the large man's face. Sal still had a lot in him, so Jacob again delivered a left punch to the man's midsection and followed with a right upper cut to his chin. Sal staggered back. Jacob rotated on the ball of his left foot, and with another snap of his right arm, his fist connected with the Sal's jaw. The man was down for the count.

Jacob looked at the two thugs and hoped this would be a lesson to them for the countless people they had hurt in the past.

Jacob turned his back on the two moaning figures and was off running again. Except for a spot of grime on his sweat-soaked shirt from Sal's dirty hands, Jacob didn't have a mark on him.

Isaiah will be right proud of me, he thought with satisfaction.

Chapter 2
The Letter

It was six thirty by the time Jacob had cleaned up for breakfast. His mother greeted him in the kitchen with a somber expression on her otherwise pleasant face.

"What's wrong, Mother?" Jacob asked, as he sat at the table beside his father and looked hungrily at the plates his mother had already heaped with bacon, eggs, and potatoes.

She sat opposite of Jacob at the long wooden table, fidgeting nervously with her hands. "Reuben brought some bad news while you were cleaning up."

Reuben was the second of Jacob's two older brothers. He was a clerk in the mercantile a few blocks away. He was an early riser and often brought the mail to give to his folks. Jacob leaned forward, waiting for the bad news.

His mother wiped at her eyes, took a deep breath, and said, "Jacob, it was about my brother, Zachariah."

"What about Uncle Zac?" Jacob said with a sickening feeling in his stomach. Suddenly, the food in front of him had lost its appeal. His mother paused to choke back a sob.

"He's . . . he's . . ." she stammered.

"Your uncle is dead." Jacob's father interrupted bluntly.

"Oh!" Jacob said with a gasp. He couldn't help the tears that suddenly formed in his eyes. "What happened? He was healthy enough the last time he wrote."

"I guess he kept it from us, Jacob," his mother said sadly. "He died of consumption." Mrs. Morgan picked up a thick envelope that had been lying on the table. "This is the letter Reuben brought. There's another sealed envelope inside. It has your name on it." As she spoke, Jacob's mother extracted the envelope and handed it to Jacob.

His name was scrawled across the front of it in bold cursive: Mr. Jacob Morgan, Boston, USA.

With shaking fingers, he carefully tore the envelope open and extracted two yellowed sheets of paper. As Jacob glanced at the date on the top of the first sheet, he arose from the table. It was dated 21 March, 1854—over eight months earlier.

"Eat your breakfast, son." His mother urged. But despite his long, early-morning run, he'd lost his appetite. He felt his stomach turn inside out.

"No thanks, Mother. I can't. Not now. I'll just slip outside and read this letter."

She nodded in an understanding way. Jacob sought his privacy in the apple orchard at the back of their home. Seated on a narrow wooden bench, he looked at the letter again. With an ache in his heart, he slowly read. As he read, his eyes grew wide and his chin quivered. Upon completing the second sheet, he reread it over again thinking that perhaps his eyes had deceived him. *If you are not willing, then another recipient will be chosen.* After reading it a fourth time, he tucked the sheets back into the envelope and returned to the house. His father was just cleaning up the last of his eggs when Jacob entered the kitchen. "Well, Son, what did it say?"

"Was it something from Zachariah before his death?" Mrs. Morgan asked anxiously. "Had he intended to tell us of his illness?"

"No, Mother. It is from a Mr. Clarence Weatherbee."

"And who is Mr. Weatherbee?"

"Uncle Zac's attorney in San Francisco."

"Oh my! And what on earth did he want from you?" Mrs. Morgan exclaimed.

Jacob excitably said, "Mother, Uncle Zac left his entire estate to me."

"Oh, well that can't be much," Professor Morgan said condescendingly with a shrug.

Professor Morgan had never thought anything of Zac; he had always considered Zac just a worthless mountain man that lived with the Indians.

His wife agreed. "I'm afraid your father is right, Son, so don't get your hopes up for a lot of riches or some such thing. Why, Zachariah was always on the go. He never did settle down and make anything of himself. Anyway, what could he possibly have acquired clear back there in the wild Utah Territory? After, all he was just a mountain man."

Jacob nodded, and then trying to contain his excitement, said, "That's not all."

"Oh? So what else did it say, Son?" the professor inquired.

Taking a deep breath, Jacob continued, "It . . . ah . . . it says in Uncle Zac's will that I get his entire estate and his most prized possession—whatever that is—if I follow his instructions exactly."

"I see," Mrs. Morgan chuckled and softly said, "That sounds like my brother. What are his instructions?"

Jacob read on. "After I receive this letter, I am to contact a banker by the name of—let's see . . ." Jacob again extracted the faded yellow papers from the envelope and scanned the first page. "A Mr. Galloway here in Boston at the Massachusetts Bank. I am to meet with him, and if I accept Uncle Zac's proposal, he will advance sufficient funds from Uncle Zac's estate so I can secure passage on a ship to San Francisco."

"What!" Jacob's mother said with an astonished gush of air.

"That's right, Mother. I have to go to San Francisco and meet with Mr. Weatherbee, the attorney."

The professor's face grew hard, and his eyes narrowed as they rested heavily on Jacob's face. "So if—and only if—you were to go to San Francisco and meet with this so-called attorney. What could that be about?" he asked with his jaw set.

Jacob said, "We'll go over the will and find out what I inherited."

Jacob felt excited, and he was ready for this. He realized his parents were concerned for him, but sometime and some place he would have to make decisions for himself and perhaps this was the time.

"Well, I just don't know what to think about that," Mrs. Morgan said. "Zac always was telling Jacob stories and building him up about his adventures in the West."

"He did indeed," Professor Morgan said, and Jacob noted a distinct change in his tone of voice. Almost dreamy, he thought.

Mrs. Morgan noticed it, too. "Now listen here, Father," she said sternly, "don't you be getting any crazy ideas in that thick head of yours."

She was too late.

Jacob could see that his father had a faraway look in his eyes. They settled again on Jacob, ignoring his wife as though he had not even heard her. "Son, I could use a few months away from—"

Jacob was exasperated and shook the letter as he interrupted. "Father, the letter is very explicit and it says that I must go alone."

"Oh, that Zac!" Mrs. Morgan said in disgust. "It sounds just like him. But, that is out of the question. It just wouldn't be safe for you to travel alone clear across the country."

"Mother, I will go by ship." Jacob vaguely remembered the stories his Uncle Zac had told him about sailing, and the few years he had spent at sea before becoming a mountain man.

"You won't go at all unless I come," Jacob's father said sternly. "I'm sure that he didn't really mean alone."

"That's what it says!" Jacob argued.

"Well, we'll see what this Mr. Galloway has to say when we visit him," Jacob's father said. "I'm sure we can work things out."

Two days later, the professor, Mrs. Morgan, and Jacob sat in Mr. Galloway's office at the Massachusetts Bank in Boston waiting to hear what he had to say. He was firm when Jacob's parents began to argue. "I am very sorry," he said. "But my instructions are very explicit; I am to forbid anyone to accompany your son to San Francisco."

"Well, in that case, he just won't go," Mrs. Morgan said. "Not that there is any real purpose anyway, for my brother could not possibly have anything of enough value to justify the trip."

"Mrs. Morgan, I do not know the value of Mr. Sherwood's estate. However, I have received more than sufficient funds for your son to travel to San Francisco alone. It is his decision to make," the banker said, peering down through his thick glasses at Jacob.

How could he turn down this opportunity? Finally a chance to go west and live the life he had dreamed of.

"Well, Jacob—" his mother began.

"I'm going," Jacob said firmly.

His mother turned to his father for support, but, tenderly, Professor Morgan said, "Dear, Jacob is seventeen years old. It is time he determined the course of his own life. If he wants to go, then maybe we should let him. Who knows, maybe he'll come back with a little something."

Jacob's mother blurted out, "But he's only a boy, he doesn't have any experience of traveling, he needs someone to go with him." Though Mrs. Morgan thought of every reason she could why Jacob should not go chasing the dreams of her adventurous, dead brother, the professor finally prevailed. After signing the required documents, Mr. Galloway turned all the funds over to Jacob for the long ocean voyage. Jacob now looked forward with great anticipation for the adventure that lay ahead. The least of his concerns was the size of his inheritance, but he wondered what was his Uncle's most prized possession could be.

Chapter 3
Adventure at Sea

Jacob stood on the pier at the Boston harbor and stared in awe at the massive bulk of the ship *Brooklyn* with its stark mast outlined against the blue of the eastern sky. Despite his longing to begin the voyage, he was nervous.

Not every ship that departed this harbor over the years had reached the port for which it was bound. The sea, he had been told, was fraught with danger. Everything from fierce storms to bloodthirsty pirates had ended many voyages at the bottom of the sea. Each began with as much hope for others as this one would for him. His mother's tears did nothing to calm Jacob as they spent the last few minutes together.

"Son," she began in one last, earnest attempt to keep him home, "I fear that you are making a terrible mistake. I realize that you were fond of your Uncle Zac, but he was a wanderer. You hardly knew him at all. There will be nothing for you to inherit, and when you discover that, you will be eight months away from us. Please, Son, stay home. You can—"

Jacob firmly, but lovingly, cut her off. "Thank you for your concern, Mother, but I am going. There may not be much of an inheritance, but I need to leave. I need an adventure. I just wish that Uncle Zac could be there with me."

He could not tell her that he had let his hopes build these past few days as he waited the time that the ship *Brooklyn* would sail. He dreamed of riches and adventure. Deep down he was sure she was right about the inheritance. However, inheritance or not, this was an adventure of a lifetime, and Jacob was ready to begin his life.

The professor smiled and said, "Mother, he's going." The professor stood in front of Jacob. Looking deeply into his eyes, he put his hands on Jacob's shoulders and said, "Son, I know you have made up your mind, and I know the good Lord will protect you. However, remember who you are and the family name you carry throughout your travels. We love you and only want the best for you. God be with you." He tenderly embraced Jacob for a long, lingering moment before releasing him.

With tears in his eyes, Jacob reached over to his mother and embraced her. "Mother, I know what I'm doing, and I will make you proud of me." Holding her tightly, he whispered softly, "Mother, I love you," and misty tears filled his eyes.

As he turned toward the gangplank, a loud shout stopped him.

"Jacob! Wait for me!" Jacob turned back to see Isaiah running toward him, his arms extended for a full embrace. Something silver hung from his arm. Breathing heavily, Isaiah gasped, "I couldn't let my favorite brother go without saying good-bye!" He fiercely pulled Jacob into a bear hug that nearly took his breath away.

Before Jacob could respond, Isaiah whispered, "Remember what I taught you and learn all you can. You must always be on guard. There are unseen enemies, even those who are close, so don't trust anyone. If you trust your heart, then you will feel when danger is near."

Reluctantly releasing him from the hug, Isaiah held out a small tin pail to Jacob. "A gift for you. I have a feeling that soon it will be your dearest friend. Keep it near you at all times until you get used to sailing." The pail was small enough that Jacob could easily carry it around with him, but large enough to be useful should he need it.

"I promise I will form a close bond with my new friend, if I can stomach him," Jacob said. Everyone chuckled.

Jacob looked longingly at his family one last time before boarding the ship. Even Isaiah had tears in his eyes as he helped escort Jacob up the gangplank onto the *Brooklyn*.

As the ship set sail from the harbor, Jacob found himself waving from the deck and choking back a sob, as his family disappeared into the past.

As Jacob stood on the ship's deck, everything was new to him. He felt the salty breeze on his face as the ship cut through the waves on the open sea. The deck was well worn and the flapping of the sails engaged his ears and the sound of seagulls were heard overhead, yet he felt some apprehension of the unknown that lay before him.

That night, as he began the journal that would record the tales of his great adventure, Jacob was already experiencing a touch of the dreaded disease of the high seas: seasickness. Isaiah's gift was handier than Jacob realized it would be. His head was light and his stomach rolled and pitched with each movement of the ship. With an effort, he dipped his pen in ink and wrote the date at the top of the first page: 30 November 1854. This day marked the beginning of something that Jacob knew could well change the course of his life forever.

The next few days passed slowly. The weather on the vast Atlantic Ocean was cold at the beginning of their voyage, but as they steadily made their way south, it began to change. Jacob gradually grew accustomed to the constant motion of the great ship and his fear of sailing subsided.

Jacob spent many long hours gazing over the broad expanse of sea. Breathing in the salty spray, Jacob became invigorated; to keep in shape, he jogged back and forth on the deck every day. One day after his run, Jacob approached the ship's captain, Captain Richardson, and asked if he had ever met his Uncle Zac. The Captain said he hadn't had the pleasure. Jacob explained to Captain Richardson that his uncle had sailed the sea for a few years. Then Jacob asked if he could learn about ships as his uncle had.

"With pleasure," replied the Captain. "I could use the extra help with the crew." The captain yelled for Jeremy, motioning for one of the passing sailors to come over.

The sailor came as directed, waiting and ready to obey whatever order the captain had for him.

"Jeremy, this is Jacob. He wants to join us in manning the ship. Can you teach him the ropes and keep him busy?"

"Aye, aye, Captain," Jeremy said. Then turning to Jacob, he added, "Welcome to the crew."

Jeremy taught Jacob the responsibilities and work of a cabin boy, which wasn't as exciting as Jacob had thought it would be. He was given all the dirty jobs, and Jacob started to wish that he hadn't made the request at all.

However, after two months of scrubbing the deck, Jacob felt sure it was clean enough to eat off of. He learned how to tie knots, which were used to secure the sails.

Jacob loved sailing on the sea. He could not help smiling as he thought that his Uncle Zac would be proud of him. They were kindred spirits, and he loved what his uncle loved.

That evening as Jacob sat in his bunk, he reread his Uncle's letter. He wondered again what his Uncle's most prized possession was.

Within the next few days, the ship turned northward for two weeks and then, after rounding Cape Horn, the seas began to heave beyond their bounds because of a fierce gale. Jacob, for the first time in his life, learned what it was like to be deathly sick, and he regretted not following his mother's counsel to stay in Boston. At times, with the slightest movement of his body, Jacob was violently sick and he even thought it might be better to die, so great was his misery. The fierce crashing of waves against the ship caused him to wretch constantly throughout the day.

The terrible storm drove the ship back for several days, the unrelenting winds breaking the ship's mast. To make matters worse, Jacob—along with the rest of the passengers and crew—had to eat food that was moldy and rotten.

It didn't take long before Jacob and many of the other passengers developed scurvy. The sores from the horrid disease covered Jacob's mouth and other areas of his body. After a few days of suffering from these sores, Jacob began bleeding under his skin and from his gums.

Jacob and other passengers became so weak that they could scarcely climb the stairs or leave their quarters to the main deck. Many of the passengers just stayed in their small sleeping quarters, waiting for a friend or family member to bring them something to eat from the galley.

Even the water was dirty and stale tasting. When it was raining, Jacob mustered all the energy he had and went to the upper deck to drink the rainwater that had pooled in the tops of barrels or other containers filled from the storm.

Finally the storm abated, and the captain was forced to land the ship on Juan Fernandez Island, located southwest of Chile. The ship needed to be repaired before they could sail again, and the passengers needed a rest.

Stepping on dry land again brought life back into Jacob. He had almost forgotten what it felt like to have solid ground beneath his feet. And though he was still feeble from the weeks of sickness, he was relieved to have fresh air and fresh food. The fruit, Jacob was told, would help combat the scurvy, so Jacob ate as much as he could while they were on shore.

When Jacob was feeling stronger, he helped gather the needed food, including goats, pigs, peaches, and figs. He then helped replenish the firewood and water for the rest of the journey. The work helped his muscles regain strength. After two weeks on the island, Jacob, along with the rest of the passengers, boarded the ship and resumed their journey.

By the time the ship reached the San Francisco harbor, Jacob was in high spirits. All the miseries he had experienced during the journey over the past eight months had magically disappeared, and he looked forward to his new adventure.

The *Brooklyn* anchored on the first of July 1855, and the crew went to work making preparations to transport the passengers to land on a large boat. There were dozens of ships all anchored in the bay.

As Jacob stood on the ship's deck waiting to head to shore, he saw men in uniform riding their horses along the shore and soldiers marching. Jacob remembered learning that a treaty had been signed in 1848 after a war with Mexico, making California the possession of the United States. In 1850, it had become a state.

Jacob gathered his belongings and prepared to disembark from the ship. He stood last in line, as the adults and children boarded the waiting seacraft. Jacob felt a hand gently rest on his shoulder and turned to see Captain Richardson extending his other hand. "Jacob, if you ever want to explore the sea like your Uncle Zac, you are welcome aboard my ship any day. I would be proud to be your captain."

Shaking his hand, Jacob thanked the captain for his kindness, and soon found himself standing on the shores of California.

Chapter 4
The Attorney and the Mountain Man

The fog was beginning to clear as Jacob walked into the bustling town of San Francisco. He stumbled a few times as he went along, trying to find his land legs. All Jacob could think about was finding a room with a hot bath and a solid, tasty meal.

Jacob found an inn not far from where he landed and had his trunks retrieved. After bathing and having his hair trimmed and his clothing cleaned and pressed, he spent a night in deep slumber.

The following morning, Jacob looked and felt like a gentleman for the first time in months, and he went in search of Mr. Weatherbee's office. Walking along the dusty streets, he saw the rolling hills in the distance and buildings springing up in all directions. With the Gold Rush of 1848, San Francisco was no longer a small town. In a short time, the gold fever helped build the town to over twenty-five thousand residents who crowded the city, each wanting to make their fortunes.

Jacob, to avoid being stepped on by horses, carefully made his way across the main street, maneuvering around and between the horse-drawn wagons and buggies.

All alone in a new land, a foreboding feeling slowly came over Jacob. At first, Jacob brushed the feeling off as nothing more than loneliness. However, as he continued into the city, he became more and more uneasy and cast frequent glances over his shoulder. The hair on the back of his neck suddenly stood up, and he stopped and quickly turned and scanned the area looking for someone or something.

He cast his eyes carefully over the streets he had just traversed, and saw no one that seemed even vaguely interested in him, but he couldn't shake the feeling that someone was following him. As Jacob continued on, his steps quickened. He wondered if someone had been watching for him, even expecting him.

Glancing again in all directions, Jacob suddenly remembered something from the letter that his Uncle Zac's attorney had sent to him. It stated that there would be others who would be willing to inherit his uncle's estate. He now wondered if there was someone who didn't want him to meet with Mr. Weatherbee. After all, he was told there were other worthy recipients. Did they know he was coming?

Uneasiness turned to fear, and sweat trickled down his forehead into his eyes. Wiping his face with a kerchief, Jacob again looked in all directions, and still he saw nothing that looked suspicious.

Jacob ducked into the nearest alley, dashed up another street, and walked into the back door of a mercantile. Carefully glancing around from inside, he searched for several minutes out the front window, but no one appeared. In fact, everyone seemed so intent on going about their own business they didn't even notice him. He began to feel foolish.

Angry with himself, Jacob stormed across the street, and read a crudely painted street sign indicating the direction he needed to go; up the boardwalk and after a couple of blocks, the feeling seemed to leave. Surely, no one could possibly know him in this strange city, so far from his home. Shaking off the fear and concern of the past few minutes, Jacob finally located the office of Mr. Weatherbee.

The office was situated at the top of a hill in a two-story brick building. A weathered piece of wood hung from two small chains above the door that faced the street. It read, Clarence Weatherbee, Attorney at Law.

Jacob heaved a sigh of relief, walked up the stone steps, and reached for the doorknob. Once again, a vague feeling of uneasiness swept over him, and he glanced quickly behind him, looking to his right and then left. Jacob had never felt this feeling before. It was real and yet he felt he should give heed to his feelings. Seeing no one who appeared to be watching him, Jacob pulled the heavy wooden door open, stepped through, closing it quickly behind him.

"May I be of assistance?" someone asked.

Turning around, Jacob saw standing behind a desk a thin austere woman who appeared to be in her late fifties. She wore a white blouse and a long black skirt. She peered through small round glasses perched on her long thin nose. "I said, young man, may I be of assistance?"

Jacob shoved his hands nervously in the pockets of his trousers, then jerked them quickly out again and replied, "I . . . ah . . . excuse me, ma'am, I'm ah . . . looking for Mr. Weatherbee."

"This is his office, but he is rather busy. Would you like to make an appointment for another day?"

"No, ma'am. Ah . . . I mean, I hoped I could see him now. I've come a long way and—"

"Maybe if you could state your name and the nature of your business, I could tell you if Mr. Weatherbee can be of assistance to you."

"I'm Jacob Morgan. I . . . ah . . . well. I think Mr. Weatherbee has been expecting me." Before the stern lady could reply, he reached into his coat pocket and brought out the letter he had received so many months ago. "This is from Mr. Weatherbee," he said, waving the faded yellow envelope timidly in the air.

"I see. And what business would he have with one so young and from the East?" she demanded, as she looked at his clothing.

"Well, Mrs. . . . ah . . ."

"Miss!" she said with a hiss.

"Yes, ma'am, Miss . . . ah . . ."

"Miss Pitchford," she said.

He grinned despite his nervousness and said, "He wanted to go over my uncle's will."

"Your uncle's name?"

"Ah, Uncle Zac."

Miss Pitchford snorted primly and said, "There are a hundred Uncle Zac's in the world. Could you be a little more specific?"

Jacob blushed in embarrassment.

"His name is Zachariah Sherwood, Miss Pitchford."

"Oh, why didn't you say so?" she said with a sudden smile. "That Uncle Zac. I will tell Mr. Weatherbee you are here."

As she vanished through the door, Jacob wondered why she had suddenly smiled. He wondered even more when he then heard laughter from behind the door she had just entered. When she reappeared a moment later, her face was as stony and cold as it had been earlier. Very businesslike, she ushered Jacob though the door and into a large, unoccupied office.

Framed paintings of brightly dressed Indians and magnificent horses hung from the walls. There were rich woven rugs on the polished wooden floor. A large set of elk antlers loomed over the door above him. At the far end of the room was a huge, polished oak desk cluttered with papers.

Behind the desk was a large, black leather chair with arms that appeared to have seen many hours of use. Two small tables sat in the far corners of the room, each holding a large, unlit oil lamp. Jacob's eyes lifted to the wall directly behind the imposing desk. A .75-caliber English Brown Bess rifle was balanced on two wooden pegs. Hanging next to it was a powder horn, a small leather bag, and a matching set of .60-caliber Black Watch pistols.

From the door behind the desk came a murmur of voices and occasional light laughter. When the door opened, only one man appeared, a short potbellied fellow with huge black suspenders that protruded from beneath a black vest. The suspenders held up a pair of equally black wool trousers. What hair the man had was gray and was slicked across the top of his bald head in a vain attempt to hide the loss of a once full head of hair. A smile spread across his pudgy face that seemed to say to Jacob that he knew something that Jacob did not.

When he spoke, the fellow's voice was rich and mellow, "Jacob Morgan, it is a pleasure to see you!" He extended a wide, soft palm. Jacob reached out and shook the man's hand as the man continued to talk. "I am Clarence Weatherbee. Please, won't you sit down?"

Jacob sank into a deep padded leather chair in front of the desk. "Thank you," he said, feeling strangely overwhelmed. For the first time, Jacob actually believed that he was about to receive a rich inheritance. Before, he had only dreamed of it.

"Well, Jacob, how was your journey? Long?"

"Yes, it was long. I didn't think I'd ever get here."

"Well, you did, so we might as well get right down to business. As I told you in that letter you are holding, I am the executor of your, ah, late uncle's will," he said, and again smiled mysteriously.

Jacob glanced down at the envelope. He lifted the envelope and pulled out the letter.

"Yes, that letter," Mr. Weatherbee said. "Now, here is another. I will leave you to read it in private."

Confused, Jacob reached for the letter extended to him. The envelope, though less yellow, was very much like the one he had received many months ago. "Go ahead, open it," Mr. Weatherbee said as he rose from the chair he had only barely sat down in. "I'll be back in a few minutes." He exited the room without another word.

Again, the indistinguishable murmur of voices and light laughter drifted through the closed door. Jacob shut out the sounds and concentrated on the letter he had just removed from the new envelope. It was dated 21 March 1854, almost eight months before the one he had received from Mr. Weatherbee in Boston.

It began, "Well, howdy, nephew. Just like hearing from the dead, huh? If you are reading this, it means that you have arrived safely from Boston and are expecting to take back a fortune."

Jacob read the entire letter four times and even pinched himself to make sure he was not dreaming before the murmur of voices in the next room faded and Mr. Weatherbee propelled his short, heavy frame into the room once more.

After lowering himself into his chair with a groan, Mr. Weatherbee leaned forward as far as his ample belly would allow him. He pointed his fat finger at Jacob, and said, "Did you read that letter very carefully, young man?"

"Yes, sir. I did," Jacob replied.

"Good, because your uncle said a lot in a few pages." Mr. Weatherbee paused and allowed himself a hearty, chuckle before going on. "Jacob, it is my duty to acquire your signature before allowing you to proceed with your uncle's instructions, if you still desire to do so,"

Jacob realized that this was his only real chance to live the life that he had always dreamed of, and he would be wealthy beyond his imagination. "Yes, sir. Where do I sign, sir?" Jacob asked, his head still spinning from the intoxicating effects of the fantastic letter.

"Not so fast, young man. I want to go over the letter with you. I must be absolutely sure that you are willing to do everything your late Uncle Zac requires of you. I must see to it that you understand fully the dangers involved."

Jacob nodded, and Mr. Weatherbee continued, "Now let's see that letter a moment."

Jacob handed it over, and the attorney read quietly for a minute or two. Then he looked up and said, "You probably wondered if there was really an inheritance at all?"

"Well, I thought there must be something, but I had—"

"I suppose you were surprised to learn that your late Uncle Zac was worth over one hundred thousand dollars."

"Yes," Jacob said.

"Well, it's a fact, young man. Your Uncle Zac owned some ships and invested in other things that I will cover in a moment. And it's all yours if you do as he requests. Now mind you, if you fail—or if you decide not to try at all—there are others who would be more than willing to take your place, and the inheritance will go to another worthy recipient," Mr. Weatherbee said, as he again settled back into his chair and folded his arms over his enormous stomach.

"Yes, sir," Jacob answered meekly.

"He favors, or rather, favored you because you were so full of questions, and at a young age you reminded him of a son he had always wanted."

Jacob nodded in agreement. "As your Uncle Zac stated in the letter, the rest of the family all figured him to be a worthless mountain man and Indian lover. Not one of them, not even his sister, could accept Zachariah's having lived with the Indians for five years. They were especially disgusted by the tales he told of his Indian wife. And you, Jacob, on the other hand, had been enthralled by it all.

"All right, let's cover the things your Uncle Zac required . . . ah, expects me to have you do," Mr. Weatherbee said. "First, you must spend two years with a mountain man."

Jacob felt a shudder of pleasure pass over him. Wow! He would spend two full years with a real mountain man. It was always what he had wanted since he had known his Uncle Zac.

The attorney continued, "Zed Hafenbrack was like a brother to your uncle. As it says in the letter, the two of them spent nigh unto fifteen years as partners in the mountains. You must not only spend two years with him, but you must learn from him if you want your uncle's fortune. Is that clear, Jacob?"

"Yes, sir."

"Very well. Next, you must spend at least one year among the Sioux Indians. You are to learn their ways and their language. Your Uncle Zac had many friends among the Indians, and he loved them. He also learned their ways and was trusted by them and he wants you to do the same, if you can, that is."

Jacob withered at that request. It frightened him, but if Uncle Zac had been able to do it, then he supposed, he could. "I'll try," he said weakly.

"If you fail, you lose your inheritance" Mr. Weatherbee reminded him firmly.

"I understand, sir."

"As you read in the letter, your uncle not only owned ships, but he had lucrative gold mine investments in Yreka, California. Jacob, those things will be all yours after you have met the conditions he outlined. Following your two years with Zed Hafenbrack and one year with the Sioux Indians, you will return here and receive further information on your Uncle Zac's holdings." The attorney smiled and rubbed his bald head for a moment while he studied Jacob.

Jacob squirmed. His mother would have a fit when she learned what he was about to do. He could just imagine her calling her brother back from the dead and letting him know how angry she was for leading her son astray. He had every intention of doing exactly what Uncle Zac had required of him. Of course, if he wrote his family now, it would be at least eight months before they even received the letter. By then it would be too late.

Mr. Weatherbee interrupted his thoughts. "This is a great challenge for you, Jacob. You could be killed, or you could get sick and die out in the wilderness. Not all of the Indians like white men, and there are wild beasts, hard winters, and dozens of other dangers. There is a good chance that you will never make it back here. Do you understand what I am saying?"

"Yes, sir," said Jacob in a small but hopeful voice. But Jacob had always wanted to be with his Uncle Zac and be a mountain man. Confused, Jacob asked, "Mr. Weatherbee, are you trying to discourage me? It sounds to me as if you don't want me to do this."

Looking chagrined and somewhat caught off guard, Mr. Weatherbee's face flushed a deep red as he tried to control his anger. "Of course not, Jacob," he sternly said, "I am only here to enforce your late uncle's will, and I am only pointing out the obvious things that could befall anyone as inexperienced as you, before you go into the wilderness. Now, this is the document I have drawn up as required by Zachariah's will." He quickly shoved the paper across the desk at Jacob. "Sign. It is up to you. You are old enough now to make your own decisions. If you would rather not, I have been authorized to give you sufficient funds to book passage back to Boston."

Jacob didn't want to lose the opportunity of his lifetime and he finally realized he had a chance to be a mountain man like his Uncle Zac was.

"I will sign it," Jacob said, and accepted the pen offered by Mr. Weatherbee. He wrote his name with a trembling hand.

If the attorney seemed to notice, he said nothing as he drew the paper back, blew on the fresh, wet ink, and then said, "Before you go with Mr. Hafenbrack, there is something Zachariah left in my care for you. It was to be yours if you accepted his challenge."

"What is it?" Jacob asked eagerly.

"Come with me. It's in the next room," Mr. Weatherbee said, as he struggled to lift his bulky frame from his chair.

He led Jacob to the door where he had earlier heard the murmuring of voices. As Mr. Weatherbee reached to open it, Jacob distinctly heard another door softly close from somewhere beyond. The attorney heard it too, and said, "Be careful, my boy. There are those who care about your uncle's gold. Many men have died in this land over the love of the yellow metal that made your uncle rich."

The room held a chill and Jacob shivered visibly. Was he making a mistake? Was he really man enough to handle the challenges extended to him by his dead uncle? Did his uncle really have that much faith in him?

Then he saw a trunk. It was huge! His heart raced.

Before he could approach it, the door opened across the room, and in walked a man dressed in weathered buckskins. The stranger was taller than Mr. Weatherbee, but half the weight. Wearing his buckskins, Jacob could see that he had a slight frame. He held a brown cap made of an indistinguishable fur in one hand, and his face was deeply tanned and weathered, a thick black beard hiding much of it. He had long dark hair, which, although thin on top, hung down midway to his shoulders. Jacob's eyes fell to the man's feet. He wore leather moccasins that laced up and over the bottom of his pants. Jacob lifted his eyes again, looking for a sign of who the man was.

"This is Zed Hafenbrack, Jacob," Mr. Weatherbee said.

Jacob was stunned. He had expected a big man, not this shriveled up little man who was supposed to teach him how to be a mountain man.

Zed was not to be fooled, it was as if he read Jacob's mind. He said, "Boy, don't let my size fool you. I'm more for my height than you'll ever be—you and that city frame of yourn," the mountain man said.

Caught off guard, Jacob began, "No, I . . . ah . . . didn't think you—"

"Don't lie to me, boy! If you and me are to get along, you better learn one thing right now. Don't ever lie to me or to nobuddy else. You savvy, boy?"

"Yes, sir," Jacob mumbled with a red face.

Mr. Weatherbee cleared his throat and held out a large brass key, "Here's the key to that trunk. The trunk belongs to me, but your Uncle Zac wanted you to have a few of his things if you accepted his challenge. Mr. Hafenbrack and I will leave you to go through the contents of the trunk alone."

With shaking hands, he approached it as the other men left the room and wondered if Uncle Zac's most prized possession was inside.

Chapter 5
Buckskins

The brass key turned easily in the lock, and Jacob, with pounding heart, lifted the lid of the ancient trunk. A woolen Indian blanket covered something near the bottom. He leaned over and lifted the blanket. A grin creased his face as he hurriedly threw the blanket aside and pulled out a set of neatly folded buckskins. He held the leather shirt up and was surprised that it appeared to be very close to his size. Eagerly, he removed his shirt and slipped into the soft buckskin. It fit him almost perfectly.

He feared that the pants would be too short but was pleasantly surprised that they fit him very well. A pair of tall moccasins that had never been worn were also in the trunk. He tried the pair on and laced them up. They fit just right and came up just a few inches below his knees. "How did he know?" Jacob exclaimed. He suddenly felt transformed, as if he were indeed a mountain man. He had to restrain himself from shouting out with excitement.

The next item out of the trunk was a long .50-caliber Tennessee rifle. Jacob tried it for balance, holding it to his cheek and sighting down the barrel. He checked the flint; it was a new piece. The barrel was oiled and the wood polished. It was a beautiful weapon. The rifle was not new, but had obviously been given excellent care. He could hardly wait to get into the hills.

His Uncle Zac had also left him a good supply of ball and powder that was in a leather possibles bag that mountain men used to keep their personal items in.

Jacob carefully examined a long, very sharp Bowie knife that he pulled from a leather sheath. Again, it showed signs of use but also of excellent care. He strapped it to his waist with the leather belt and scabbard he found coiled in the bottom corner of the trunk. A hat, not unlike the one Uncle Zac's friend Zed was wearing, was also in the trunk. Upon close inspection, Jacob was quite sure it was made from the pelt of a badger. With it on his head, Jacob was sure he would pass for a real mountain man wherever he went.

Once more, Jacob leaned over the trunk. Next to where his hat had been was a tomahawk made of steel with a carved wooden handle. As he picked it up and held it in his hand he noticed immediately that it was well balanced. Jacob was stunned by the beautiful gifts he had received.

Leaning over and examining the inside of the trunk once more, he noticed a small bag in the corner next to a bow and a quiver full of arrows. He opened the bag and it contained gold coins. He tucked them in his waistband

Jacob picked up the bow; it was made of white ash and was beautifully polished. Jacob wondered if it had been made by some of his uncle's Indian friends or if his uncle had made it himself.

Just then the door opened, and Zed and Mr. Weatherbee walked back in. "That bow was made by your uncle, Jacob," Mr. Weatherbee said. "It is just like the ones the Indians will use that you'll be living with."

Jacob straightened up and shut the lid to Mr. Weatherbee's trunk securely. He felt self-conscious as Zed looked him over. "Let's see you there, boy. My, but yer old uncle left you some real man clothes," Zed said without a flicker of a smile.

"Yes, you look just like a real mountain man, Jacob," Mr. Weatherbee said with a grin on his wide face.

Zed's brown eyes narrowed. "I'm afraid it'll take a lot more than a set of buckskins to make an eastern city boy into a mountain man," he grumbled.

Jacob shifted uncomfortably. He could see that Zed was not overly fond of him. Unless something changed, the next two years could be long and agonizing. Mr. Weatherbee sensed his discomfort and said, extending a hand to Jacob, "Well, you best take your things and be on your way. Zed tells me you two will be leaving early in the morning, so you both have things to do. I will see you both in a few years, if you make it. Now I have other work to do," and he motioned for them to leave through his side door.

Jacob picked up his personal items and followed Zed out of Mr. Weatherbee's office. When they walked out into the warm California sunshine, a fresh sea breeze rustled the fur on Jacob's new cap, and he heard Zed muttering something about having let old Zachariah really get him into something.

That night at the inn, Jacob wrote a lengthy letter to his parents. In it he tried to explain why he had made his decision, and told them he felt he was going to find himself in the next few years. He explained about his inheritance and what was required of him, and he told them what he had learned about his Uncle Zac and that he was grateful for the opportunity his uncle had given to him to make something of himself. Most of all, he was thankful for the few memories he had of spending time with his uncle.

After finishing the letter, Jacob wrote a detailed journal entry, outlining the events of the last two days and then went to bed, not knowing what tomorrow would bring.

Jacob arose early the next morning, and found Zed waiting impatiently at the livery stable. "Plan to sleep all day, boy?" Zed remarked gruffly. Zed handed Jacob a big leather bag in which he would put all of his personal items. It was Jacob's own possibles bag.

"Sorry, sir. I thought—"

"My name's Zed, boy. Nobody never called me 'sir'!"

"Yes, sir . . . I mean, Zed."

"That's better! Now, let's get yer things loaded.

Zed had picked up supplies for his ranch and there were boxes of different items on the ground that needed to be packed on the mules.

"Lend me a hand," Zed said as he began to pack the things they would take with them on the back of three large brown mules. During the time they were packing, Zed never spoke another word to Jacob. Two horses were soon saddled and tied to the hitching rail. When the mules were finally packed, Zed looked at Jacob and said in a condescending tone, "Can you ride a horse?"

Jacob replied that he had ridden horses before. Zed frowned and pointed to one of the horses and said, "You ride that one."

Both men mounted and Jacob followed on his horse while Zed led the pack mules away from the livery stable. Jacob quickly wheeled his horse around and looked behind him, again feeling the hair on the back of his neck come up. Zed yelled, "Boy, what's the problem? Did ya get cold feet?"

"No!" Jacob said as he quickly turned his horse to follow Zed. He then spurred the animal and caught up to the pack mules, and followed them closely, not daring to look behind.

After crossing the bay on a large wooden ferry, Zed led the way north. They rode the entire day, stopping only occasionally for water and to give the horses a rest.

At sundown they finally made camp and Zed hobbled the stock and let them forage. Jacob was tired and sore after the day-long ride. He tried to help around the camp but felt like he was in the way. He asked Zed a couple of times what he'd like him to do, but was only answered with a mumble. Zed continued setting up camp as if he were by himself.

After eating a meal of beans, biscuits, and dried meat, Zed settled back with a cup of coffee, and Jacob watched the fire. Jacob asked a question, not really expecting an answer after the day's moody silence. "Where are we going?"

To Jacob's surprise, Zed answered, "To my ranch. It used to be your uncle's, but he gave it to me." His voice was sullen and distant. "Now hit the sack." He paused and looked closely at Jacob and said "Yer not sleeping in again. We'll leave at first light."

Jacob was determined that he would learn from Zed, yet he shivered. It was clear that Zed resented him, and after hearing that Uncle Zac had given his ranch to Zed, he wondered if the little man also resented the fact that the gold mine and the ships would one day be Jacob's.

After a few minutes, Zed rolled himself in his bedroll and was soon snoring. Jacob tried to sleep, but found it impossible. Never had he felt so alone. Here he was, out in the middle of nowhere, with a man who did not care for him and perhaps even hated him. He felt homesick and he desperately missed his family.

He thought about Uncle Zac and the loneliness he must have felt over the years, not only because he was by himself in the wilderness, but also because he was without family. Jacob's family didn't approve of Zac's lifestyle and Jacob realized that his family felt the same way about him. Jacob closed his eyes and eventually faded into the security of his dreams.

The next thing he knew, he was being awakened with a kick to his feet. It was still pitch black and the air was chilly. Zed grumbled something about having a long way to go and for Jacob to get the horses and mules ready while he fixed breakfast.

The sky was turning a light gray in the east before Jacob succeeded in bringing in the stock from their feeding and was leading them back to camp. Zed had already finished eating, so Jacob gulped down his breakfast while Zed saddled the horses and prepared to pack the mules.

Zed was still quiet and sullen. Jacob, however, was refreshed and anxious to show him he was a willing pupil. He watched carefully as Zed made sure the packs on the mules were balanced and then covered them with an oil canvas to keep everything dry and clean. By the time the sun peeked over the eastern horizon, they were in the saddle and heading north again.

They rode in silence all day, continuing west. They crossed a small river about noon and climbed large hills covered with long, dried yellow grass. The air was cool and clear and refreshing. The loneliness of the night before was gone, and Jacob was not about to let Zed's sullen attitude ruin a beautiful day.

In the late afternoon, they pulled up to let the animals rest after a long climb. As their horses grazed, Zed got off his animal and stood staring toward the distant mountains. Jacob dismounted and decided to try and break the barrier that seemed to have formed between them. "Zed, what is the problem? Why don't you like me?"

Zed nodded, but said nothing. Jacob pressed on earnestly, "How can I learn from you if you ignore me? I know I'm young and inexperienced in the ways of the mountains, but I really want to learn. I want to be a good pupil because I promised Mr. Weatherbee, and in a way also my Uncle Zac that I would listen and learn from you. How can I do that if you won't speak to me?"

Zed slowly turned around and took a deep breath and said, "I guess yer right, boy. I didn't ask fer this here job, no more than you asked fer me to be yer teacher, but I did give my word to yer uncle before he died. Now I need to keep my promise."

Jacob replied, "Zed, I am sorry to put you through this. It wasn't my idea. I realize that I have a lot to learn but . . ."

Zed waved a skinny arm impatiently and broke in. "It's just that I'm used to being alone or with someone like Zachariah. We knew what was on each other's minds. We didn't need to discuss anything because we both knew what we were thinking and what needed to be done. I ain't nary been stuck with a city boy before." He paused for a moment, and said, "So, like your uncle said in his letter, you gotta listen to me, boy. I don't want to lose my hair on account of no city boy who don't know nothing. If you do what I say, maybe we can both come out of this here dream of yer Uncle Zac's alive."

"We better get moving, boy." Zed said as he got to his feet. We got a far piece to cover before dark."

Once on their way again, Zed let Jacob ride alongside him for a while. "We're gonna push it every day fer the next few weeks," he said without looking at Jacob. "We'll head northwest into the Utah Territory and along the California border where my ranch is. You be alert, boy, 'cause I got a heap of things to show ya, and I don't know if ya can or can't learn them all."

"I'll do my best, sir."

"See there!" Zed exploded. "What did I tell you, boy? My name ain't 'sir'. It's Zed."

Jacob reddened, but he retorted quickly, "And mine ain't 'boy', it's Jacob."

Zed quickly wheeled his horse around and glared at Jacob. "Boy," he growled, "I am the teacher here, and until you can prove to me that yer a man, I'll call you 'boy'."

"Yes . . . Zed," Jacob said, swallowing his pride.

Over the next few days, Zed gradually loosened up. He took time to show Jacob how to improve his aim with the rifle Zac had left him. He even seemed a little surprised when Jacob demonstrated that he already was an excellent shot.

While Isaiah had taught Jacob how to defend himself, he had also taught him how to use a rifle.

Zed occasionally talked about the lay of the land, pointing out prominent places that Jacob should remember and use as landmarks in the future. He taught him to not just look at the lay of the land, but to look at the land and the trees and rocks and vegetation. "If you watch where you are going and where you have been, you'll never get lost. An Indian could be hiding, and if you weren't aware of the signs, it could be the end of yer life. Always watch and listen," cautioned Zed.

Jacob concentrated on making sure that his questions, when he asked them, were good ones. Zed would carefully answer, making sure Jacob understood.

As they spent time on the trail, Jacob was more and more surprised at the breadth of the little mountain man's knowledge and common sense. Perhaps, he thought from time to time, Uncle Zac was right about Zed. If he listened to and learned from him, he might be able to survive the next two years.

At the end of a long and tiring journey of almost two weeks, Zed pointed to some mountains that loomed ahead in the distance. "My ranch is in them hills," he said. "If we ride hard fer the next two days we can sleep in the comfort of a bed in my ranch house."

They rode through scrub oak and buck brush for the next day and a half, and slowly they began to see an occasional pine tree. The air grew cooler as they climbed, and before Jacob knew it, the pines towered overhead and he breathed deeply of their fresh scent. As they traveled through the forest and up the mountainside, Zed appeared to be looking for something.

Finally, he muttered, "Here it is," and he turned onto an old Indian trail. They followed it for the next three hours and finally rode onto the top of the pass. As Jacob stared out over the land, he was stunned at its beauty. Below them stretched a beautiful green valley that appeared to be six or seven miles long east to west and at least two miles wide. Pines stretched down the mountains in front of the two riders. On the far west end of the valley, towering rock cliffs rose steeply up into the blue of the sky. A stream meandered slowly from the east and disappeared in a narrow gorge at the west end of the valley.

Pointing, Zed said almost reverently, "The ranch is down there."

"It's beautiful," Jacob said.

"Yer uncle and me, we spent many a happy day down there."

The trail down the mountain was steep and rugged. It took over an hour to reach the lush grass that touched the horse's bellies at the valley floor. They rode east and Jacob was enthralled. On the far side of the valley were several small canyons that cut through the rocky ledges, leading to the north at the west of the valley. He suddenly ached to explore them.

After riding for three or four miles, they rounded a grassy point, and the ranch yard suddenly appeared magically before them. The log house was large, unlike anything Jacob had ever seen. Heavy logs had been used in the building of the home. There was an open porch that went the full length from one end to the other. At the center of the home, on the east side, a large door was built as the main entrance. A barn, also made of logs, was situated about forty yards north of the house. The back of the barn was surrounded by corrals made of lodge pole pines that covered most of an acre. A fenced pasture enclosed another five or six acres of rich pasture of which a stream flowed through. Jacob counted about thirty head of cattle grazing nearby. At the far end of the enclosed pasture were a dozen horses and mules.

Jacob found himself yearning to stay in this beautiful secluded spot. Zed, as if reading his thoughts, said, "We'll be spending the winter here, boy. If old Zachariah hadn't made me promise to take care of you fer a couple of years, I'd have been retiring here to spend the rest of my life."

Jacob couldn't imagine a more beautiful setting He never imagined such a place as this existed.

Zed smiled one of his rare smiles. "There's a lot of places like this in the West. You'll see more if you stick by me and the Indians. 'Course, this place is more advanced than most," he said, puffing out his skinny chest proudly.

He pointed out to Jacob that the meadows stayed green all summer long and into the fall because Zachariah had learned from the Mexicans how to divert the stream of water at key places and irrigate the grassy valley floor. "It would be yellow and dry like most of the country we come through if it weren't fer that."

Three Mexicans came out of the bunkhouse running and enthusiastically waving their hands and yelling, "Señor Zed, Señor Zed." They spoke to Zed in a language Jacob could not understand. He could see they were happy to see Zed, as they excitedly shook hands and then gave him sound thumps on his back after he dismounted from his horse. Zed handed his reins to one of the dark-skinned men and then said, "They do a good job of keeping this place going when I'm away. I couldn't do it without their help."

Darkness closed in quickly over the valley, delaying Jacob's opportunity to get acquainted with the ranch until morning. He was up early the next morning, and hurried outside where he found Zed already busy cutting and stacking wood.

"When are you gonna learn to get out of bed in the morning?" Zed said, as Jacob strolled out. Jacob glanced at him, and was pleased to see a smile teasing the corners of the little man's mouth.

Grinning Jacob said, "I'm working on it. I used to get up to run every morning at four or earlier back in Boston."

Zed appeared genuinely surprised and pleased. "Is that right?"

"Yup, and I'll get at it again, if it's all right with you."

"It's all right with me, but right now you can take over my wood cutting and start doing yer chores."

Chapter 6
Most Prized Possession

Zed handed Jacob the ax and started to walk toward the house. Before Zed had gone even a few steps, a horse whinnied over by the barn. Jacob glanced up. His eyes widened when he saw the magnificent buckskin stallion that had made the sound. The stallion pranced up to the fence and tossed his head. "Zed, is that your horse?" Jacob had never seen such a beautiful animal.

"Nope," Zed replied. "He's yers. That there horse was the most prized possession yer Uncle Zac had. Why, he meant more to yer Uncle Zac than anything in this world. He raised him from a colt, and the stallion is now five years old. Yer Uncle Zac and that horse were inseparable and they went everywhere together. Zac told me that I was to see that you got him." Sarcastically, he said, "So there he is."

Jacob could only stare for a moment, and then finally said, "I can't wait to ride him."

"Well now," Zed said with a grin, "that just might be a problem. Nobody but yer uncle has ever been able to ride that horse."

Jacob, rather sure of himself, said, "My grandfather was a horse trainer, and I used to help him. I think I can handle that horse all right."

Walking toward the house, Zed said, with a sly smile on his face. "Suit yourself, boy, but I think you might find him a mite bit more horse than you can handle."

"We'll see about that, "Jacob said confidently.

"You sure will," Zed agreed, chuckling to himself, and repeated "You sure enough will."

The following morning, Zed made it clear they would spend the afternoons together. "You got a heap to learn before we go to the mountains, boy. You'll have to work hard every afternoon 'til I feel you learned what you need to know to keep both of us alive."

"So when can I work with the buckskin?" Jacob asked.

"The mornings are yers for the next few weeks. You can do what you want as long as you stay in the valley. You can explore some of the canyons, but stay below the rim. I don't want you gettin' lost. I don't have time to come lookin' fer ya." As an afterthought, Zed added, "Be careful around that horse, boy."

Nodding his head, Jacob confidently said, "I have ridden all my life, Zed. I can handle the horse." Jacob thought maybe Zed didn't remember, but in the cities anyone who owned a home had their horse for transportation; there were nothing but carriages and horses that filled the streets of Boston.

Jacob intended to ride the new horse and explore the side canyons that Zed had mentioned. He was sure he could have the horse gentled in a matter of days.

As soon as breakfast was over, Jacob headed for the corral to work with the stallion and Zed followed behind him to watch.

As Jacob reached the corral, Zed drew a small folding knife from his pocket and reached for a stick on the ground. "Boy," he drawled, without looking at Jacob, "I don't want to have to bury you, so you listen good before you climb in that corral."

Jacob was already straddled on the top rail of the corral. He turned to Zed and said, "You really don't think I can handle the horse, do you?"

Zed opened the blade on the knife and began to whittle, still not looking up at Jacob. "You can ride, boy. I seen that already. This buckskin here, he's different. You might say he's a one-man horse, and yer Uncle Zac was that one man. He don't like nobuddy and never did trust anybody but yer uncle. Zac raised him from a colt after his mama died and even milked a wild cow to keep him alive."

Jacob thought for a moment, and then turned to look at the horse that stood on the far side of the corral, tossing his head proudly. "Why didn't somebody geld him if he was so mean?"

With a shake of his head, Zed said, "Don't make no sense to cut a spirited horse. It would take all the fire out of him. This horse would run for your uncle 'til he dropped. That buckskin is special. If you cut him, he would become nothing but a nag and that would ruin him for sure."

Jacob nodded his head and studied the horse. Zed was right. The stallion was a magnificent animal. It began to run along the fence as Jacob watched in awe. Each movement was graceful and powerful, with his head held high and his long tail flying behind him.

After watching the horse run for a few minutes, Jacob thoughtfully said, "I'll take it slow and easy with this one. He'll be fine."

Zed's eyebrows raised, and he stopped carving the stick. "Boy, before yer uncle died, he told me you'd want to tame him. And I told him it would be useless because you'd have to be a lunatic to even try. I figure now there's not much difference between the two of you when it comes to that horse. I figure yer uncle was a little crazy himself to have that horse. Do me a favor, boy. Go dig a grave before you try to touch that big fella. It'll save me the trouble after he stomps you."

Zed was so serious that it set Jacob back. After listening to Zed talk about the stallion, Jacob thought, *Maybe Zed knew what he was talking about. After all, he was the teacher.* But Jacob had his pride and desperately wanted to ride that horse.

"Zed," he said, "how about if we both work together? I know eastern horses because I have trained them, but with your experiences in the West, you may have a better way, and I'd listen to you."

Zed just laughed. "You ain't listening, boy," he said. "I told you, this here is a one-man horse. And I ain't the one man no more than you are. Nope, he's yer horse, but I suggest you keep him for a stud. He's pretty to look at, but keep yer distance, that's all." Zed threw his stick to the ground in disgust and headed back for the cabin knowing full well that Jacob would not listen to him. Zed muttered, "He's just like his uncle. He won't listen to reason."

"Hey, what did Uncle Zac name him, Zed?" Jacob called after him.

"Buck. What else?" Looking back, Zed growled. "Remember I told you so. Now don't be no fool."

For a long time, Jacob leaned against the fence and watched Buck with mixed emotions. Finally, he muttered, "Can't be that mean. No horse can." Instead of climbing into the corral Jacob stayed on the outside of the rails.

Jacob climbed to the top rail and called out using his most gentle and soothing voice. "Come here, Buck. I just want to be your friend. I won't hurt you, I promise."

At the sound of his name, the big horse threw his head high in the air and whinnied, while stamping his feet and rearing. Jacob laughed. "You're not so bad are you, Buck," he called out. "Doggone if I'm not going to gentle you. Soon we'll be good friends. If you could be gentle with Uncle Zac then you can be gentle with me."

With his misgivings gone and throwing all caution to the wind, Jacob plucked a handful of the greenest and most tender grass he could find and jumped down into the open corral. With his hand outstretched, Jacob started across the corral. Jacob had gone just a few steps when Buck's demeanor changed. The horse's ears laid back and his neck stretched out as he lowered his head. Jacob hesitated and then took a few more steps.

Suddenly, the stallion let out an ear-splitting scream and charged toward Jacob with his head outstretched and his mouth open, showing his teeth. Jacob, seized with panic, dropped the grass, and made a mad dash for the fence with Buck's hot breath blowing at his pants. Jacob cleared the fence and hit the ground on with a resounding crash.

The stallion slid to a stop, crashing into the fence so hard that Jacob thought the stallion was coming through. However, the poles were sturdy and were the only thing that protected him. Buck's teeth were bared and his eyes burned with hate, as he let out a deafening scream while trying to grab Jacob. Jacob got to his feet and backed away from the fence, trembling.

From behind him, he heard a slight chuckle. "Horse trainer!" Zed sputtered. "Maybe that'll learn ya, boy." Zed had snuck back from the house to watch the training.

Jacob didn't turn around. His face was burning too badly. He heard Zed's footsteps retreating, and he sat down on the ground and stayed there until the trembling in his arms and legs had subsided. Stubbornly, he approached the corral again. The stallion was still glaring at him. Jacob said evenly, "Buck, maybe you are as mean as Zed said, but I'm not giving up on you."

Early each morning Jacob got up and took long runs up the valley into each of the different rocky canyons. Upon returning, Jacob would always stop by the corral and talk to Buck. He would lay a handful of tender grass on the top rail for the horse.

At first, Buck refused the grass, but after a few days, he'd cautiously approached the fence after Jacob had backed off a few paces and began eating. Then Jacob would slowly approach the fence, talking softly to Buck.

One day, Zed said, "I admire yer pluck boy, but yer wasting yer time."

"We'll see," Jacob said stubbornly.

In the afternoons, Zed spent hours teaching Jacob survival skills that he would need in order to live in the wild. One afternoon, Zed told Jacob to get his bow and quiver of arrows. When Jacob returned with them, Zed carefully grabbed the bow in his left hand and extended his arm out as far as it would go. With his right hand, he took his first two fingers, interlaced the arrow between them, and then notched the arrow to the sinew string.

Instructing Jacob, he said, "Now look down the arrow with both of yer eyes open and follow the tip of yer arrow to what yer aiming at." There was a stump some distance off and Zed let the arrow fly toward it. The arrow hit just in front of the stump.

With a chuckle Jacob said, "Zed, you are my teacher but you can't even hit what you aim at!"

"That's 'cause I am always shooting at moving varmints," Zed said, somewhat embarrassed.

"Oh, sure you do." Jacob smiled.

Then, as if by providence, a rabbit dashed from the side of the cabin in front of Zed. In a split second, he reached for an arrow and let it fly. The arrow struck the running rabbit.

Zed said, "Clean it and we'll have it fer supper. We don't waste meat."

The following days were spent practicing with the bow until Jacob began to slowly master the art. While still teaching Jacob to use the bow, Zed added more weapons for him to practice with: the tomahawk and bowie knife.

Then, to add to the list, Zed taught Jacob to reload his rifle while running through brush and heavy timber. He lectured Jacob, saying it was not enough just to fire a rifle, but that rifle has to be apart of you.

Zed shouted unmercifully at Jacob whenever he spilled any powder or dropped a ball. After endless hours of practice, Jacob learned the art of loading, firing, and reloading on the run. It became a smooth and fluid motion.

"Yer getting it, boy. Darned if ya ain't."

Zed taught Jacob how to track game, both large and small, using the wind to his advantage. After weeks of practice, Jacob was able to stalk and replenish their meat supply.

To further Jacob's skills at tracking, Zed would lay a difficult trail through the woods, and then spend long afternoons teaching Jacob the signs and how to read and follow the elusive trail he had left.

Jacob gradually began to understand and was able to move through the woods so that he left minimal sign himself. He was also confident in which direction he was going even on the darkest of nights.

In time, the very feeling of the woods and nature became ingrained in Jacob's mind and he felt one with the forest and his surroundings.

Jacob enjoyed what Zed had been teaching him each afternoon; however, he also looked forward to his personal time alone each morning with the stallion. Thinking back to Mr. Weatherbee's office, Jacob smiled and realized that two years would not even come close to qualify him as a mountain man. He could see why Uncle Zac had spent fifteen years working with Zed. Each day was a learning experience.

Jacob enjoyed spending time with the horse each day. After a few weeks of Buck accepting his gifts of grass, Jacob felt he was responding to his voice and friendly overtures. He decided it was time to take the next step and really get down to training.

On an early December morning, a small layer of snow dusted the mountains and valley, turning Zed's ranch into a wonderland of white. For the second time, Jacob entered the corral and advanced toward his horse with an outstretched hand of dried hay, talking softly as he went. A cold north wind scattered some of the hay from his hand. Buck snorted, threw his head, and pranced to the farthest corner of the corral. Looking at Buck's determination, Jacob decided to let well enough alone and backed slowly out of the corral. He repeated his performance the next morning, and the stallion let him come closer before whirling and prancing away.

After four days, Buck let Jacob come within a yard before turning away. Greatly encouraged, Jacob decided to try a bolder move. The following day, Jacob entered the corral with a bunch of hay in one hand and a halter in the other.

"Easy, boy. I won't hurt you, Buck," he murmured as he approached.

Buck's ears pricked forward, and he snorted, but stood his ground, his eyes now on the halter. Jacob was feeling confident and proud that he was making progress. But just then, the stallion began to paw the ground like an angry bull. With a bellow of rage, Buck laid back his ears and charged. Seeing Buck's mouth wide open and teeth bared, Jacob shouted in horror and made for the fence, running for his very life. As Jacob leaped to dive over the fence, he felt the stallion's teeth sink into his buckskin pants.

Like a bird in flight, Jacob sailed over the fence and fell on his belly on the far side. It was several moments before he recovered his breath enough to sit up. He reached and massaged his now very sore bottom. He turned his head around to see the stallion. Buck was now rearing and pawing the air, while striking the top rail with his hooves trying to get at Jacob. The angry horse made Jacob feel lucky that the only wound he carried from the incident were the imprints of teeth on his buckskins and a sore rear end.

"Are you enjoying yerself, boy?" Zed said, leaning against a big tree not too far from the corral. Jacob had not seen him approach.

Jacob pulled himself slowly and painfully to his feet without answering. Zed grinned and tugged at his bushy black beard. Speaking surprisingly softly and with some compassion, he said, "Do you see what I mean, boy? This is a one-man horse."

The blood rushed to Jacob's head and he exploded, "You old goat," he shouted. "I'm not a quitter. This may be a one-man horse, but Uncle Zac is dead, and now I aim to be that one man!" Shaking with anger and massaging his behind, Jacob shouted again, "Do you hear me? I am not a quitter. I will do it, and no one is going to stop me."

"No, I don't suppose I can," Zed said, shaking his head. "Yer more like your Uncle Zac than I would have ever figured."

Jacob faced the corral again and approached with a limp. Buck snorted and laid back his ears from the other side of the corral. "You win today, Buck, but I'm not through with you. You won this battle, but I aim to win this war, so you just as well get used to me."

Later that evening, as Jacob was getting ready for bed, he realized it was just a few weeks before Christmas. The next morning, he reminded Zed who told him that they never celebrated any holidays except maybe the Fourth of July. Jacob insisted they at least celebrate Christmas with a nice dinner. After some coaxing, Zed agreed.

The day before Christmas, Zed had Jose, one of the ranch hands, bag a turkey, and the group met together on Christmas Day for a dinner of turkey, venison, trout, potatoes, onions, beans, and biscuits.

After dinner, Jacob retired to his room, and by lantern light, began writing in his journal like he had faithfully done since he had left Boston. He also wrote a long letter to his parents and felt a little homesick. His letter was long overdue. He admitted to missing his family, but not the lifestyle he had left in Boston. Jacob realized that it was unlikely that his parents had received his first letter because it took eight months by ship to get to Boston. Jacob felt he still needed to write a letter and as he wrote he described his experiences and admitted that he had much more to be taught. But, in time and with Zed's help, he felt he would eventually learn.

The next week passed quickly, and soon it was January 1856. Jacob decided with the cold weather settling in deeper, he would wait until spring to resume his work with the stallion, but he still continued to feed him every day. While feeding Buck one day, Jacob remembered a trick his grandfather had used once on a horse that would bite and strike at everything and everybody. His grandfather cured the horse of the habit. Jacob decided he would try the same approach on Buck when spring came.

Each morning, Jacob ran up the long valley, even in deep snow. He was determined to keep in shape. Zed and Jacob also spent hours tramping up and down the long valley in snowshoes exploring the canyons. In February, they spent several days camping in the mountains around the ranch.

Zed continued to school him in even the smallest details. Jacob was amazed at the extent of Zed's knowledge. He taught Jacob to tan hides and make and repair arrows. He also taught him how to smelt ore for lead balls for their .50-caliber Tennessee rifles. Zed liked to stock up on a large amount of ammunition. "You can never have too much gunpowder and ball," he told Jacob as he taught him how to make his own gunpowder. In Boston, it was easy for Jacob to go to a mercantile and buy supplies. Zed was three weeks from the nearest town.

As spring approached, Zed's beautiful valley began to change. As the mountain snow melted, the entire valley blossomed with new growth. There were young calves and colts running throughout the fields as Mother Nature came alive, flooding the valley with new life.

Chapter 7
The Training

It was last July when Jacob had sailed into San Francisco to meet with Mr. Weatherbee and that was eight months ago. The time had gone by quickly and Zed would soon want to head out to the Dakotas to the Sioux Territory. It was now early March, and Jacob spent less time running and more time at the corral working with Buck. He had the ranch hands help him build another enclosure just outside of the corral to use for training the stallion. It was a long narrow chute: a little wider than the width of a horse, similar to the one his grandfather had used to train horses back in Boston.

At the middle of the corral, Jacob made an opening, which would allow Buck to enter into the chute and eat at a built-in hay feeder at the far end. The chute was made with two sturdy poles set side by side and placed seven feet apart and buried deep into the ground. Long poles were laid between each set of the two poles from one end to the other end where the hay feeder was built. Five rails were placed one foot high between each of the two poles above each other and gradually became the same height as the rails on the corral.

Jacob looked at Buck on the far side of the corral. "When I get you in this chute, you'll be a lot easier to handle," he bragged. "Course, I'm not sure how I'm going to get you in there, but I'll find a way."

That afternoon, after a few strenuous hours of training, Zed said to Jacob, "Yer learning, boy, but we got a lot more to go over. We need to take our trip to the Dakotas. You get Jose to help you pick out a good horse so you can get used to him. I want to leave in two weeks."

Two weeks! He needed more time to train Buck. "Listen Zed, Buck is my horse, and I intend to train and ride him if it's the last thing I do!" he responded to Zed rather hotly.

Zed shook his head sadly and replied, "Well that might be, boy, and it might be the last thing you do." Then he walked away.

More determined than ever, Jacob was at the corral at daybreak the next morning. He took a little grass that the ranch hands had cut in the pasture and placed it inside of the chute opening. Jacob backed away and waited for Buck to eat the grass. Moving slowly and warily, Buck entered the opening and would grab a mouthful of grass and quickly retreat outside of the chute before Jacob could shove a pole behind and lock him in.

The next couple of days Jacob started feeding Buck at night and leaving the hay in the feeder.

After three nights of late feeding, Jacob slipped quietly from the cabin late in the evening. Checking the direction of the wind, Jacob knew that Buck would not get his scent. Stealthily, he crept toward the end of the enclosure where Buck was eating.

Jacob carefully picked up a short pole and slid it across the chute to the other side. Suddenly, the pole scraped the edge, and Buck quickly backed up and found the pole against his legs. Kicking violently, he tried to dislodge the unfamiliar object, but to no avail. Jacob added the extra poles behind his back legs, securing Buck snuggly in the chute. The stallion screamed and reared, but could not get out of the enclosure.

Early the next morning as Jacob prepared to eat his breakfast, Zed approached him. Motioning toward the corral, he said, "Now that you got him in there how you gonna ride him?"

With confidence, Jacob said, "My grandfather had a mean horse and the method he used proved successful, so I am going to do the same with Buck."

Zed chucked, "Well, that we agree on, boy. Buck is one mean horse. Get yer shovel out Jacob, you may just need it today fer yerself."

Jacob didn't reply. He needed all his wits about him, especially today.

After feeding the stallion, Jacob gave him another hour to settle down. Standing in front of Buck and avoiding his snapping teeth, Jacob threw a couple of rawhide ropes around his head and tied him fast to the sides of the chute to keep him from rearing. Buck fought violently, but finally realized it was useless and calmed down.

Jacob reached between the rails and stroked Buck's soft neck, talking to him. Jacob removed the ropes, threw some hay to Buck, and went after a bucket of water.

As Jacob started to ease the bucket beneath the bottom rail, Buck reared up, snorting and tossing his head. Jacob was patient and gave Buck more time to settle down before pushing the bucket back a few more inches. After giving the horse some water, Jacob retired for the night.

Over a hot supper of roast beef and beans, Zed remarked, "Boy I planned fer us to leave in a week or so."

"I sure hope Buck and I'll be ready by then," Jacob said.

Frustrated, Zed said, "One thing's plain as a wart on a cow's nose, boy. Yer no good at all as long as that horse is here. So, if you need another day or two to either tame him or get yerself killed, I guess it really won't matter."

A full moon lit the valley as Jacob left the cabin early the next morning. Slowly the gray light of dawn filtered through the trees as Jacob prepared to spend as much time as it took to settle Buck down. Buck was not happy to see Jacob as he approached the chute. The stallion lowered his head and laid his ears back, pawing the ground.

Jacob spoke softly, stroking him through the rails, and felt the horse tremble at his touch. After an hour, just as the sun was finally casting its golden rays over the valley, Jacob again threw the ropes over Buck's head and tied him down. He then added additional logs behind Buck, so close that the horse couldn't move backward. Jacob finally climbed the rails, preparing to mount the back of the majestic stallion.

Then Jacob carefully eased his left foot over Buck's back, talking softly at the same time. Buck was not dumb. He knew exactly what Jacob was about to do. Buck fidgeted and snorted, and when he attempted to rear up, the ropes held him fast. Jacob finally lowered himself onto Buck's back with a feeling of exhilaration and triumph. He slowly lowered his legs down on Buck's front shoulders and held them in place. His hands were still on the top rails of the chute in case he had to raise himself up in a hurry. After several minutes, Buck seemed to relax, and Jacob actually felt Buck enjoyed having him on his back. "We're getting there, big fella," he said confidently while stroking the side of Buck's neck. Still nervous, but feeling much encouraged, Jacob was content to sit for the moment on the stallion's back, taking in the feeling of this powerful animal.

After a few minutes, Jacob let go of the rail with both hands and again stroked the stallion's neck, talking to him softly while he lowered his legs, gently squeezing Buck's sides with his legs.

Buck suddenly leaned hard to the right, pinning Jacob's right leg between him and the rail. Pain immediately shot through Jacob's leg as Buck leaned harder and began to move back and forth, grinding Jacob's leg into the rail. Jacob frantically tried to shove Buck back away from the rail, even placing his left leg on the opposite rail trying to pull himself up off the stallion's back.

Buck, however, had other ideas and was firmly in control of the moment. Panic started to set in as the pain in Jacob's leg became excruciating. Jacob kicked Buck with his left leg, but the pressure only increased. In desperation, Jacob reached up and solidly cuffed Buck along the side of his right ear. With the force of the impact, Buck jerked his head up and quickly moved while releasing the pressure just long enough for Jacob to jerk his right leg free and clamber over the rail to safety.

Jacob trembled as he put all his weight on his left leg. His right leg was bruised, scraped, and bleeding. The only thing that had kept him from further serious injury was the thick leather of his buckskin pants. Jacob looked at Buck, knowing that this animal was capable of killing him. Buck just stared at him with his dark eyes and snorted while laying his ears back and bobbing his head up and down as far as the leather restraints would hold him.

Now angry, Jacob remembered all of his grandfather's training. How do you cure a mean, leg-crushing horse? Well, he would show him. Limping in pain, Jacob secured a stout six-foot long pole, six inches in diameter. Searching in the shed, Jacob found an ax and split the pole in half creating two long planks. Next he drove a dozen square nails in each plank six inches apart. The nails protruded about an inch or two out from the wood. He then whittled a handle on one end of each pole.

By the time he finished, his leg was hurting worse than ever, but Jacob was determined to get on with his plan to cure Buck of leg crushing. Jacob limped back to the fence carrying the two planks. He placed each plank at the outside of the rails on both sides of the chute and climbed back up to the top rail where he would mount Buck.

Buck snorted and tried to throw his head, but the rawhide ropes held him securely. As Jacob lowered himself down painfully onto Buck's back, he could feel the animal tense. However, this time Jacob did not immediately lower his legs.

The stallion trembled and gave three short bucks, trying to dislodge Jacob. Speaking in soothing tones, Jacob reached for the two planks and lowered each one down on the inside of the chute with the nails turned toward Buck's side. Buck calmed down as though he were waiting for Jacob to put his legs down so he could crush him again.

Jacob did just that, but when Buck leaned to the side in an attempt to pin Jacob's leg again, the nails bit into his tough flesh. Buck screamed in defiance. He swiftly twisted his big body away from the right side and attempted to pin Jacob's left leg with the same painful results. It took three attempts at crushing Jacob's legs before Buck realized that his actions were only hurting himself. Finally, the stallion gave up and stood, not daring to move to either side, fearing that any movement would cause him pain.

After several minutes of sitting on Buck's back, talking softly and stroking him, Jacob triumphantly dismounted painfully and removed the nail-filled planks. He mounted again, but the stallion made no attempt to crush him this time. Jacob stayed on Buck's back until Zed came for him at noon.

Zed did not let up on Jacob's training just because of a scraped and swollen leg. After a long and painful afternoon of lessons, Jacob returned to the stallion. Again, he tied him down and successfully crawled on Buck's back, spending several minutes just sitting. Feeling quite sure of himself and elated over his victory, Jacob finally removed the ropes from Buck's neck and threw some hay in the feeder.

A few minutes later, he shoved a bucket of water under the rails. "We're going to be friends after all," he said with a grin, reaching through the rails to pat Buck on the neck. An instant of carelessness proved an opportunity for Buck. The horse reached down and grabbed Jacob's shoulder with his teeth, lifted him up, and threw him to the side with a toss of his head.

Jacob hit the ground violently and lay there for a moment, stunned. Then painfully he got to his feet, holding onto his shoulder.

Jacob screamed angrily, "I've been nothing but good to you, and this is how I get treated in return? Who feeds you? Who waters you?"

Jacob sunk to his knees in agony, trembling while holding his painful shoulder. Then a realization hit him. Whenever Buck hurt him, he got rewarded in the form of feed and water. Slowly, Jacob rose to his feet and carefully removed the bucket of water and hay from the front of the feeder. Buck was not tamed. Jacob realized that the stallion was just smart and would get his revenge when and where he could. *Well,* Jacob thought, *maybe if he got hungry and thirsty enough, he would change his attitude.*

Zed said nothing about Jacob's new injuries that night. He also mentioned nothing further about their immediate departure on the trip he had planned. Over the next three days, Jacob ignored the horse. If Buck wanted water, he would have to call for it, and it would be on Jacob's time.

Jacob spent most of his time nursing his wounded shoulder. After the second day, he began to work with his bow, bowie knife, and tomahawk. Jacob could use his right arm and shoulder although it was painstakingly slow.

The weather was turning warm, and Buck undoubtedly was getting very thirsty and hungry while standing in the chute still tied down. Jacob strolled over with a bucket of water just before noon on the third day. Buck watched him warily as Jacob set the bucket down and splashed water from the bucket on his own face and over his head, but the horse stood silent.

The next morning, long before sunup, Jacob awoke to the sound of Buck whinnying.

Jacob hurriedly dressed. Taking his time, he purposely walked slowly to the corral as if not interested in Buck at all. The stallion watched him.

"Good morning, Buck," Jacob said, in a serious tone. "Are you ready to eat and have a drink?"

Buck nickered eagerly, and Jacob's heart lifted. He filled a small portion of the bucket with fresh water and approached Buck. The horse shook his head and nickered again, his ears forward. "All right, my friend, if you are ready to mind your manners, you may have some of this."

Jacob slowly slipped his free hand between the rails and scratched the stallion's nose. Jacob held the bucket in his other hand, but didn't immediately offer it to the horse. Instead he continued scratching Buck's nose and then eased his hand along his cheek, and finally patted his neck. Buck made no attempt to bite and his ears remained forward. Jacob then gave him the water and at the same time reached under the horse's chin and scratched him. Buck quickly drank the water and nickered for more. "No, not yet ole boy." Jacob said, "but you can have some feed."

Jacob fed him two small handfuls, and then moved away. Jacob could hear Buck whinnying. Taking his time, Jacob finally returned to Buck's coaxing in the late afternoon and gave him a small amount of water and feed.

That night Jacob released him from the chute into the large corral, but he still withheld the feed and water except for when Buck whinnied for him. An idea occurred to Jacob, and each time Jacob fed and watered Buck, he put his two fingers in his mouth and whistled. This continued for several days as Jacob continued to patiently work with Buck.

Over the next two weeks, Jacob slowly increased the amount of food and water he gave the horse. Whenever Buck ate, it was always from Jacob's hand and on Jacob's time. Finally after the third week, Jacob walked out to the corral late one afternoon. He whistled and called, "Come here, Buck." Then he waited.

To his delight, Buck ran to him, nickering and prancing as he moved. Jacob was ready for the big test. He climbed the fence and entered the corral. Jacob glanced toward the house and saw Zed leaning against the porch railing, watching intently. Jacob had felt that Zed approved of what he was doing. However, Zed had never commented on his progress. Jacob's heart raced as he turned and approached Buck, talking as he walked with his outstretched hand. Buck snorted and ran to the other end of the corral and then turned to face Jacob. As Jacob continued to walk toward the center of the corral, he knew he would be in serious jeopardy if Buck decided to attack him.

Jacob stood his ground, aware of where the fence was, in case he needed to run, but he kept his wits about him. Buck once more faced Jacob, put his head down, and then charged with his ears back. Jacob had no room to run. He was too far from the fence, and there was no chance of reaching it in time. Instead, Jacob raised his fingers to his lips, and taking a quick deep breath blew with all his might. The whistle was shrill and loud. Jacob could see an instant change in Buck's eyes. The stallion slid to a stop, showering Jacob with dust and dirt. Jacob whistled loudly again, and then his next whistle was soft and low.

Buck, as if coming out of a trance, nickered and took a few steps toward Jacob and stopped again. Once more, Jacob whistled softly. Buck snorted, backed away, and threw his head in the air. "Come on, Buck, please." Jacob pleaded.

Buck's eyes seem to clear, and the big horse suddenly neighed and pranced toward Jacob, his tail sticking straight out behind him and his head bobbing up and down. "Easy, boy. That's it. Come on, boy," Jacob called. "You've been a long time without a friend, haven't you? I know you've missed Uncle Zac, but I'll be just as good to you. I promise."

And then it was all over. Buck had surrendered. He nickered and nudged Jacob with his nose and walked forward and put his head over Jacob's shoulder as Jacob scratched his neck and under his chin. Then he put his arms around the magnificent animal's neck.

Jacob looked up and saw Zed standing just outside the corral. Jacob hadn't thought about him since entering the corral. When they made eye contact, Zed shook his head in disbelief. He turned toward the big cabin before wiping a tear from his eye.

After Zed entered the house, Jacob tugged on Buck's mane. The stallion responded and followed him to the barn. He accepted a halter without any resistance, and Jacob led him around the corral for a few minutes, and then he spent the rest of the day until long after dark, brushing and currying Buck until his coat shone.

Chapter 8
Secret Canyon

The next morning, after eating a quick breakfast, Jacob dashed to the barn, haltered Buck, brushed his coat, and led him around for a few minutes. He retrieved a saddle, blanket, bridle, and saddlebags from the tack room. As Jacob approached Buck, the big horse's head bobbed up and down as if anticipating a ride.

Zed ambled over to the corral and leaned against the gatepost, watching silently. Jacob threw the blanket on Buck's back and saddled him without any difficulty. He exchanged the halter for a bridle, and led him out of the corral. All the pain and frustrations of the past weeks were swallowed up in the satisfaction Jacob felt as he put one foot in the stirrup and carefully eased himself into the saddle.

"Looks like you won him over," Zed said in disbelief. "Take the whole day, boy."

"Thanks, Zed."

"And be careful, boy. I'd say don't get lost, but with that there critter beneath you, it ain't likely," Zed said, as he shook his head in amazement.

After pulling his badger skin hat more snugly onto his head, Jacob waved at Zed, gave Buck a little slack with the reins, and squeezed with his knees. The stallion responded like no other horse he had ever ridden. Like a ball coming out of his Tennessee rifle, Buck surged forward, almost unseating Jacob. Pulling gently on the reins, Jacob slowed Buck to an easy lope. They loped for a mile or more up the valley, almost to the extreme east end.

Jacob tugged at the reins and turned Buck to walk him toward the north, across the two-mile wide valley. Jacob felt Buck take the bit in his teeth as if wanting to go someplace special. After a few minutes Jacob gave him his head. Buck veered to the west and raced toward the far end of the valley, leaping over a small stream and through the brush. In a short while, they reached the rocky slopes that bordered the towering cliffs on the west side of Zed's valley.

Following an old Indian trail, Buck picked his way carefully through the rocks, buck brush, and scrub oak. "I don't know where you're going, old boy, but as long as you don't leave the valley, you can have your way," Jacob said with a grin.

Buck then raced passed the openings of several narrow canyons, most of which Jacob had already explored. The stallion increased his pace as he loped steadily toward the west end, passing through the grassy openings of one of the larger side-canyons. Eventually, they reached the very last canyon that supported the towering rock walls of the valley.

Jacob had never been in this canyon. The opening was small and narrow. Buck turned sharply and leaped the small meandering stream that poured into the opening and the gigantic walls towered on both sides and seemed to melt together. As they closed the distance, Jacob figured that it definitely had to a box canyon. Buck slowed down and walked through more sagebrush and sparse trees, and eventually faced the sheer wall ahead.

"Looks like we've hit a dead end, Buck. It's about as far as we can go," Jacob said, but Buck continued, as if he knew something that Jacob didn't. To Jacob's right was a small stream. It looked like the same stream Buck had jumped over when entering the canyon. Jacob figured that it originated from the east end of the valley. The water gathered at the solid wall of rock in a large swirling pool and filtered down into the ground. "Well, guess we better go back," Jacob said as he prepared to turn around.

As Jacob reined him in, Buck tossed his head and snorted. "What's the matter, Buck? This is as far as we can go. Let's head back to the ranch."

However, Jacob quickly realized that Buck had other ideas. The horse grabbed the bit in his teeth and continued forward. Jacob, curious as to what he was up to, slackened the reins and let him have his head. Buck traveled for the next thirty yards to the back wall of the canyon. The stallion then veered around a large boulder and climbed a short ancient path. Jacob figured they were about as far as they could go when

Buck continued on and carried him around a large sugar pine, the only one that could be seen at the end of the canyon.

To Jacob's amazement, an almost unseen opening appeared on the other side of the tree. The opening had blended in with the canyon walls making it almost invisible. It was about five feet wide and cut at a right angle going directly into the towering rock ledge where the swirling pool of water disappeared underground

The entrance was enclosed entirely at the top, giving Jacob the impression of passing through a narrow tunnel. Jacob had to lay forward against Buck's neck because of the low ceiling in the tunnel. Buck followed the tunnel downward for some distance, and then made a sharp turn to the right.

As they came out of the opening, Jacob saw a waterfall flowing into a large basin below. Once again, Buck led him down around a bolder, entering into another passageway carved out by time and soon they emerged into the light.

Buck climbed a steep rocky slope edged by a large vertical rock wall with protruding ledges. A small rock suddenly tumbled onto the trail. Buck gave a shrill whinny, and as Jacob looked up, the hair on his neck suddenly stood up. Buck raised his head and again whinnied.

Reaching down and touching Buck's neck, Jacob said, "Quiet, Buck." He had the feeling he was being watched.

Jacob studied the top of the ledges, expecting to see someone peering down at him. But there was nothing but the blue sky and a few trees along the ridge. Suddenly Jacob realized that he was here without his trusty Tennessee rifle.

Jacob recalled Isaiah telling him to trust his feelings. Dismounting from his horse, Jacob methodically scanned the area and watched for any unseen enemy, not knowing if it were man or beast. In a short time, the feeling abated and Jacob remounted, his senses on full alert. He gave Buck his head, and they continued on.

Jacob remembered the promise he had made to Zed that he would not go beyond the rim of the valley. Well, he hadn't done that, but he was a fair distance from the ranch and in an unfamiliar area. He debated if he should head back, but Buck forged ahead and veered past a large pile of slough rock.

"Wow," Jacob said, as a beautiful valley opened to his view below. "A hidden valley," he breathed in awe. "And I thought Zed's valley was hidden."

Buck nickered and began to pick his way down a narrow trail that twisted between tall pines and fallen boulders, hiding the valley momentarily from his view. Jacob continued to let Buck lead the way. When they finally emerged from the trees, the valley reappeared.

Jacob stopped Buck and studied the valley intently, amazed at the walls of sheer rock that surrounded it. From where he stood, he couldn't see any other way into the canyon. Green grass waved from the valley floor, which opened up for at least three miles to the southwest. A stream meandered through the rocks and trees, watering the rich and fertile valley below. Jacob looked to his right to see where the stream had originated. He followed the stream to the canyon wall, and found a large pool of water bubbling up from under the low rock wall. Dismounting, Jacob studied the water and realized that the water was simply the same stream he had encountered when he entered the canyon, and it originated from Zed's east valley.

Buck nickered as if he were impatient and stretched his neck out, tugging on the reins. Quickly mounting, Jacob said, "Okay, big fella, show me why you are in such a big hurry."

Buck turned and followed the stream. After a quarter of an hour, Buck whinnied loudly, and from far up the canyon and over a rise came an answering call.

"There are horses in here!" Jacob said in amazement.

In a moment, Buck whinnied again and started prancing with excitement. Shortly a chorus of calls answered, followed by the sound of thundering hoof beats. A herd of horses suddenly raced into view. Jacob felt a touch of panic. What if there was a stallion in that herd? Buck would definitely want to fight. Jacob reined him to a stop and realized that if a saddle were on Buck it would be a hindrance if he fought another stallion. So he swiftly tore the saddle and gear off, freeing Buck.

As the herd of horses ran toward him, Jacob quickly realized that there were no mature stallions in the herd and was relieved that there would not be a fight.

The herd that Buck had called to ran at full speed toward them. Buck proudly raced forward to what appeared to be a herd of thirty or more mares, most of them with foals at their sides and some yearlings. Jacob shook his head. Buck had led him here to his own private harem; Jacob surmised with a chuckle.

His chuckle was short lived, as Buck raced to greet his mares through the trees, and into the lush green meadows at the end of the valley. A sickening feeling enveloped Jacob as he suddenly realized what he had just done. He had freed his stallion to be with the mares he had come looking for. Jacob stood dumbfounded. What would he do? How would he get back without a horse?

When Buck reached the other horses, he touched many of the mares' noses and nipped their sides. He strutted and pranced around greeting each of his mares personally. After several minutes, Bucked moved away from the other horses, lay on the ground, and rolled in the grass.

As one mass, Buck and his herd turned back the way the mares had come and disappeared over a small rise in the distance. Jacob realized he was now without his horse, or any horse for that matter. It was a long walk back to the ranch. He berated himself for his foolishness, and after several minutes, he thought of whistling for Buck. Then he realized Buck and his mares were long out of sight and far up the valley.

Jacob thought of the stupidity of what he had just done. Disheartened, he picked up his saddle and gear and walked after them, wondering if Buck would respond to his whistle if he could get within hearing distance. He topped the rise and watched as the horses continued to move further to the southwest. It was about noon, so Jacob started walking and soon entered a small grove of pines and lay down, using his saddle as a pillow. If he waited long enough, maybe Buck would return. Reluctantly Jacob sat down and leaned his back against a tree and contemplated what he would do if he were Buck, and this was his family that he hadn't seen for some time. Would he return? Jacob lay down with his head on his saddle and closed his eyes as sleep tugged at his eyelids.

Jacob was startled from his sleep by a slight sound. There was no sign of anyone. He imagined himself being attacked by a savage Indians or a wild animal.

For an hour or more he worried, but eventually his fears subsided as a gnawing hunger tore at his gut. He had not eaten since leaving the ranch. He had intended to return at noon at the ranch and eat, but took Zed up on his offer to ride the rest of the day.

The sun was sliding slowly behind the towering valley walls to the west when he noticed a cool breeze and realized it would soon be nightfall. Jacob knew he had no choice but to spend the night since Buck hadn't returned. He carried his saddle and gear to the base of the cliffs beyond the grove of pines he had napped in. After gathering several armloads of dry wood and stacking it, he built a small fire.

Jacob hunted and found a straight lean sapling and with his bowie knife, cut it down and fashioned it into a spear at the end. Hiking over to the stream, he found that the stream was loaded with trout, and within a short period of time, he had speared three large ones. After wrapping them in some wet green grass, he placed them on the hot coals.

After eating a solitary meal, Jacob banked his fire and went in search of his stallion and the mares. He was hopeful they were near but the canyon continued on for at least another two miles and they could be anywhere. Several times he whistled, but Buck did not appear. Darkness overcame him before he had wandered too far, so he returned to his little camp, discouraged that he hadn't even sighted the horses. At different times Jacob thought he could smell smoke from a distant campfire. Jacob resigned himself to spend the night alone in the valley.

That night, with the stars overhead, Jacob lay with his back to the rock wall, warming himself from the night chill beside his small fire. He worried about what Zed was thinking, remembering the earlier warning to not get lost.

Watching the fire as it slowly burned down, Jacob reminisced of home and thought about his mother and father. He wondered if his parents had received the letters he had written to them and if they were thinking of him. He eventually drifted into an uneasy sleep beneath his blanket.

In the early morning hours, the sound of a snapping twig woke Jacob. He sat up with a start, pulled his knife and was prepared to use it, because it was his only weapon. He scanned the gray-tinged darkness, but saw nothing. He finally worked up his courage to call for Buck. He shouted his name several times and whistled, but the big buckskin did not respond.

For breakfast, Jacob speared and roasted more trout wrapped in grass with a few wild mushrooms and onions that grew near the stream. He was grateful for the schooling Zed had given him, and as he ate, he made a mental note to carry salt in his saddlebags. After finishing his breakfast and extinguishing his fire, Jacob shouldered his saddle and gear and headed in the direction Buck and the mares had gone the previous evening.

After walking a couple of miles, Jacob approached the upper end of the valley before he spotted the horses in the far distance. Raising his fingers to his lips, he whistled loudly. Several of the mares raised their heads. A couple of them even trotted a few steps in his direction, but Jacob could not see Buck.

All the more disheartened and wondering where Buck could be, he whistled again as loud as he could and waited. Suddenly, he could hear in the distance the pounding of horse hoofs. Then he spotted Buck coming over a small rise, leading a large group of mares.

Whinnying, Buck slid to a stop with his mares behind him and pranced toward Jacob. Approaching Jacob, he nickered and slowly walked forward and put his head over his shoulder. Jacob, with a flood of gratitude and relief, threw his arms around the stallion's neck, talking to him and telling him how much he had missed him. Jacob notice that the mares and yearlings that stood behind him were watching with interest. He reached out to touch them, but they quickly backed away.

Mounting Buck, Jacob rode through the herd of skittish mares and yearlings, looking them over carefully. They were all in excellent condition, and all of them carried traits of their father, Buck. All of the young horses were strong, with straight backs and clear intelligent eyes. There was not a swayback animal in the herd, and there were no roman noses, bowed legs, or any other disfigurement that was common to some horses. In all, they were of excellent quality. Jacob resolved to return someday in the near future and claim his herd, and perhaps even claim this hidden valley as his, if it was not already Zed's.

As Jacob and Buck crossed over the top, Buck whinnied long and loud, and Jacob scanned the skyline. Again, the same old uneasiness began creeping over him. As he expected, he saw no one, and was soon back into the twisting, narrow passages. He arrived at the ranch in the early afternoon.

Zed came into the barn while Jacob was rubbing and combing Buck. "Well, did the two of you have a good trip?" he asked, seemingly unconcerned.

"Sure did. Sorry we didn't get back last night. I—"

Zed smiled and shook his grizzled head. "Wasn't surprised, boy. Whenever Zachariah and that horse took off, they usually was gone overnight, and sometimes longer. That horse took him to some secret place that only the two of them ever knew about. Zac claimed he had some mares, but I never seen them. He sure brought some good colts back from time to time though."

Jacob smiled. "Zed," he said, "You have taught me so much and I owe you everything. I want to show you where Buck has his herd of horses. He took me to a beautiful valley, and I don't know if it is part of your ranch, but if it is, then it's yours."

Looking very much surprised, Zed replied, "Boy, I would like that, and if it's mine, then it's yers. I'm just glad ya offered it to me."

Chapter 9
The Contest

Now that Jacob had tamed Buck, Zed informed Jacob that they would leave in two weeks for their long wilderness retreat in the Dakotas. It was the middle of June, and Zed still needed to teach Jacob additional survival skills.

During the nights beside campfires in the woods, Zed taught Jacob many useful Sioux phrases to use on their trip deep into the Utah and Dakota Territories.

Jose was in charge of the ranch, and the Mexicans were also a source of learning to Jacob over the past winter. He became somewhat conversant in Spanish, a language Zed told him was good to know in the West.

In early July, Zed and Jacob left the comfort of the ranch and headed for the territories. Jacob was excited, but apprehensive. It had been over a year since he had departed from Boston. On several different occasions, when he and Zed were separated for even a short while, he experienced the feeling that he was being watched. He usually shrugged it off, but the feeling left a knot of fear in his gut. When Jacob told Zed his concern one afternoon, Zed just scoffed, "You'll know when yer in real danger, boy."

"I hope so," Jacob replied. "But what would make the hair on the back of my neck stand up at different times? And I feel like I am in danger."

"You're still a greenhorn, boy," Zed said with a chuckle. "But don't ignore them feelings none. Who knows, like Weatherbee said, maybe there is another recipient—oh, just be careful, boy. Yer safe enough. I'll let you know when yer not."

A greenhorn was a word that referred to a person who was not familiar with anything pertaining to the West.

By midsummer, they had traveled further into the wild, untamed country known as the Utah Territory and then into the Dakota Territory. Zed told Jacob more about his Uncle Zac. Jacob already knew a lot of things from stories his mother had told him. When they were young children, their mother and one of her four children had died during a cholera outbreak. Because of his loss, Zac's pa had grieved so much that it killed him at an early age, leaving the three surviving children alone as orphans. Zac was the oldest and had stuck it out with the others for a while with his aunt in Boston, but at the age of fifteen, he had quietly disappeared. He and that uncle had never been able to get along.

Jacob told Zed he had enjoyed three visits with his Uncle Zac when he was younger, but all of a sudden the visits stopped. This dashing mountain man had told Jacob of some of the adventures that had shaped his life over the years before he went to the mountains. Zed helped fill in the pieces for Jacob, giving him a more complete picture of the man whose wealth he was to inherit.

That evening, after making camp and finishing their meal, Jacob checked the horses and sat near the campfire thinking over their previous discussion about his uncle. Zed continued the narrative.

"At the age of fifteen, Zachariah left on a merchant ship from the Boston harbor. He'd signed on as a cabin boy. He spent ten years at sea, visiting some of the most far-off and exciting ports in the world. He had a fair command of several languages, boy. Did you know that?"

Jacob didn't.

"Yep, he could talk with a China man, a Mexican, a Frenchman, and a host of others. He took to those languages like a duck takes to water. And he knew the Indian languages even better'n me, and that's saying something. Yer uncle liked to read, and during the long years at sea, he had plenty of time fer that. He told me once that it was the story of Lewis and Clark and their expeditions that made him leave the sea and strike out fer the frontier. He told me that by the time he had made up his mind to leave the sea, he already owned two cargo ships and some smaller ships in Boston. He had carefully invested his money with bankers and had an agent to take over his shipping line when he set out fer the mountains. Told me he never regretted leaving the sea, even though he loved it. Zac was one that loved to discover, and that he did. He discovered a love fer the mountains that was even greater'n his love fer the sea."

Jacob broke in and said, "He told us he lived with the Indians and took him an Indian wife. That bothered our family and my mother the most. It never bothered me because I never associated falling in love with the color of a person's skin. How did he come to live with them?" asked Jacob.

Zed smiled and leaned back against a pine, his eyes took on a faraway look as he remembered Zachariah's story. "It was quite by accident, really."

"What was?"

"His falling in with the Indians. He rode into an Indian raid after starting across a small valley late one fall. He was heading fer a range of mountains to do some trapping. He would have stayed out of that fight if he could have, but he was still green at the time and stumbled right into the middle of a war before he'd known what was happening. Pure luck was that he ended up on the winning side, but he didn't know that. Why, with all those arrows flying around his head, and Indian's screaming war whoops so loud it nearly scared the life out of him. And me too when he told me about it!"

"What did he do?" Jacob asked, tensing with excitement at the story.

"He rode, boy. The only sensible thing to do. He rode fer his life."

"Oh, was that all?" Jacob asked disappointed.

"No, that wasn't all, boy. Not by a long shot. A brave on horseback cut him off. Zac threw his knife just as the Indian was lifting his tomahawk. He was so scared; he told me that he threw that knife harder'n he ever had before. It buried itself right in that brave's chest. Killed him deader'n ever."

"What did he do then?" Jacob asked, leaning forward in anticipation.

"Leaned down from his horse and pulled his knife out, of course. Couldn't leave that, you know. Before he knew it, another Indian was there, knocking him off his horse. That was when he was in a fight fer his life. He didn't know it at the time, but he had just killed the chief's brother. It was the chief that jumped on him.

"I suppose that the chief figured he'd have an easy scalp from him being a white man and all. 'Course, he didn't know ole Zac. He'd learned to fight years before when he spent some time in China. I mean, really fight, boy. Some of what I been teaching you I learned from yer Uncle Zac. Anyway, that poor Indian never had a chance, even with him being almost twice the size of yer uncle. They wrestled for several minutes, and then the chief broke loose and tried to run. Guess he didn't know he had picked a fight with a mean ole mountain lion, 'cause like I said, he got up and lit out fer his life. As he run past Zac, he just did that Chinese stuff and kicked his legs in the air and brought that Indian down hard. Broke the chief's neck. He could kick higher'n his own head, old Zac could.

"What Zac didn't know right then was that he had an audience. Those warriors from both tribes seen him kill the chief. Anyway, Zac jumped on that horse of his and lit out fer the hills."

"Did he make it?" Jacob asked his eyes wide and heart racing.

Zac looked at his pupil and was pleased that he could still spin a yarn that would keep him spellbound. "Course not, boy. He'd never come to live with the Indians if he had. No, they took after him. Somebody put an arrow in his back. Last thing he remembered was falling off his horse," Zed said. "He was lucky, though. When he finally woke up, he was in some tepee. A couple of Indian maidens were tending to him. Yer Uncle Zac said one of them was young and pretty as a spring flower. Those maidens, with the help of some old squaws and their medicine man saved his life and healed him up good as new."

"Why did they save him after he'd killed their chief?" Jacob asked.

"Oh, he didn't kill their chief. It was the other tribe's chief he killed. It was one of the other warriors that shot him too! He eventually learned, after he got to where he could communicate with them, that the chief he killed was Running Elk. He'd been a terrible enemy fer years. Made Zac a hero, killing him. 'Cause of his courage, Zac was invited to stay with the Sioux tribe, and the chief even offered him a daughter fer a wife."

"Didn't he get to choose his own wife?" Jacob asked with a frown.

"That chief wasn't dumb, boy. He could see the way yer Uncle Zac looked at his daughter, 'cause she was the one he thought was pretty from the moment he woke up and laid his eyes on her. Yer Uncle Zac said that when he first looked into her eyes, he felt like he'd been kicked by a mule in his heart. That was the one he married. What pleased yer uncle was she felt the same way 'bout him."

"How did he marry her?" Jacob asked. "Did they let him take her to find a preacher?"

Zed laughed, "No, boy. I guess you could say the medicine man done it. Indians marry different than us white folks do. When you live with Indians, you marry like them. That's what Zac did. Usually, it was customary to offer a horse or two fer a wife. Fer a real good wife, a brave might give three horses. 'Course the chief said that Zac didn't need to do that 'cause he had killed their worst enemy, Running Elk."

"That's good," Jacob replied. "Uncle Zac wouldn't have had any horses to give, would he?"

"Not at first, but he told the chief he loved his daughter and wanted to pay for her. So, in time, when he come to know the area and learned to know the Indian ways, he soon became great friends with the tribe. Then early one day, he took off by himself and headed fer Running Elk's tribal hunting grounds. He took his time and eventually located their village. Said he felt like a thief in the night, yup, because of his love fer his wife he would do anything fer her. One thing Indians respected was a great warrior and yer Uncle Zac was that. So he moved like a silent breeze—that's what yer Uncle Zac told me—took out two of their watchers and stole five horses in the night."

"Five?"

"Yup. That was unheard of. Made his new squaw feel mighty important fer a man giving that many horses fer her. She loved yer Uncle Zac and was as good a wife as a man could have. She became known as a five-horse wife."

"What happened to her?" Jacob asked. "I know he was only with the Indians for five years."

"Yup, he was. Zac said they were riding their ponies, and she was expecting their first child. Her pony stumbled in a prairie dog hole and went down, crushing her and the kid, killing them both. Nearly broke Zachariah's heart. He couldn't bear to be with the Indians after that.

Oh, they offered him another bride, but he said it just wouldn't be the same, 'cause he never could love another woman like he loved his squaw, so he left.

"He wandered fer a few years after that. He visited the tribe often and he felt they were the only family he had. Then I met up with him, and we was partners ever since. One time he took me back to visit the tribe. They sure loved yer Uncle Zac. He was a hero to them. He never got over that Indian gal. Fact is, one day when he was moaning about her, he told me about his family in Boston. I told him maybe it was 'bout time he went back to where his roots were, there in Boston." Zed reached over and stirred the fire, and continued.

"Wasn't long after that he headed fer Boston," he continued. "You was just a little pup then, youngest of yer mother's litter. You made a hit with him, boy. He told me once that you was the only reason he returned a few years later. He felt drawn to you like you was his, and he just had to see you. Yer mother ferbid him from seeing you. Said it put ideas in yer head. Yup, ole Zac he sure took a fancy to you, boy. He talked about you almost as much as that squaw and kid he lost."

Zed reached over and put two larger logs in the center of the fire and prepared to continue his yarn. Jacob found himself feeling sorry that he had never really gotten to know his Uncle Zac. When Jacob told Zed his regrets, Zed just said, with a kind of strange look in his eyes, "Zac would have liked to been where I am right now, boy. He sure would. 'Course, he always knew his sister would never let you go to see him. He said that you had to cut them apron's strings somehow and not just stretch them.

"Was in 1854 when I received a letter from yer Uncle Zac telling me that he was real sick in Yreka, California, where his gold mines were. He had grubstaked two men, which means he gave them money for mining equipment and food to sustain them while they worked their mining claim, and each man struck it rich. He said he had consumption and didn't have long to live. Yer Uncle Zac said he didn't trust anyone but me and asked me to teach you the ways of the mountains and have you live with the Sioux tribe. He wrote, 'Don't bother coming 'cause I will be dead when you get here.' I went anyway, and I was too late 'cause he was dead. I visited his grave where they said he was buried. Real bad yer uncle had to die to bring this all about. So, yer stuck with me, boy. I know I ain't much of a substitute, but—"

"Don't say that, Zed," Jacob broke in with a rush of emotion. "I appreciate all you have done for me. Why, I've learned more in the past few months since we've been together than I did in all the years of schooling I had in Boston."

A feeling of peace seemed to settle over Zed. He nodded and turned his head away from Jacob, concealing the mist in his eyes.

Early the next morning as they traveled east, Zed kept them out of the open and under cover most of the time. They never skylined themselves on a ridge, but rode the wooded valleys whenever possible.

"Can't be too careful, boy. There's Indian signs around, and some of them would love to hang my greasy scalp and yourn on their belts," he said. "And I don't reckon I go much fer that!"

Jacob learned to keep his rifle ready and his powder dry. They never knew from which direction danger would come from. Late one afternoon, Jacob began feeling uneasy again. This was the second time he'd had that feeling since they had been on the trail. The feeling was stronger than ever before, but he hesitated to say anything to Zed about it.

Zed looked back more often than usual, but said nothing. Jacob rode closer to Zed, watching the ears of their horses. They were perked up, attentive. Jacob shivered, even though it was a warm afternoon.

Finally, after several minutes, Zed leaned toward him and asked, "Yer rifle loaded, boy?"

Then, for the first time since he had left the ship in San Francisco, Jacob really knew that danger was near, and he shuddered. Zed appeared calm as a summer breeze, but he was more wary than Jacob had ever seen him. Buck snorted and became skittish, and Jacob reached down and stroked his neck.

That night, shortly before dark, they made camp the same as usual, except that Zed kept the horses and their two pack mules packed. The animals were kept close to camp. Zed wanted to stop and rest for a while. Shortly after dark, he whispered to Jacob, "Stay here, I'll be right back." Then he disappeared into the darkness.

Jacob was tense. He knew something was wrong. His teacher was gone for only a few minutes, but when he finally materialized out of the darkness, it made Jacob jump.

"Well, boy, if you can help me fer a moment, we'll get some jerky cause we ain't stopping and we'll eat on the way." Zed again faded into the darkness toward their horses and pack mules and Jacob followed, with his Tennessee rifle gripped tightly in his hand. Zed reached up under the canvas of one of the mules and grabbed a handful of jerky, and gave some to Jacob. Then Zed quickly mounted his horse without a sound and took the two mule's lead-ropes in his hand. Jacob was not as quiet, but very quickly scrambled onto Buck's back.

Zed whispered, "Boy, there's trouble behind us," and he spurred his horse and they rode in darkness for several hours before Zed even uttered a word. Finally he said very softly, "I think we shook 'em, boy."

"Shook who?" Jacob asked in a tense voice.

"I don't know. That's why we shook 'em."

"So we will never know? Do you think it was Indians, Zed?"

"No. Felt different to me, but I had a feeling that we were being followed and I don't know by who, but I aim to find out who or what it was. They followed us most of the day, and they wasn't far from our camp when we left."

"Why do we need to find out?" Jacob asked. "Why don't we just keep going?"

Zed replied impatiently, "If we got something they want or someone they are hunting fer, they'll find us again, more'n likely. No, we'll circle back and catch them before they catch us. Boy, you learn it's best to know yer enemy and always be prepared."

Two days later, after continuing on toward the Dakotas, just a few minutes shy of sundown, Zed signaled Jacob to stop and dismount. In a whisper, the two communicated in as few words as possible. Zed thought he'd caught a whiff of smoke in the air. Jacob had not smelled a thing, but he did not doubt Zed's word for a minute. They tied their horses and mules and crept almost soundlessly through the brush and trees along the bank of a small stream.

Jacob soon caught the smell of smoke, his muscles tensed and stomach knotted. Zed motioned for him to stay put, and the mountain man moved silently ahead by himself. Jacob waited for a few minutes, but was jumpy and couldn't stay put, and if he admitted it, he was afraid.

After several more restless minutes without hearing Zed, he crawled through the brush in the direction he had gone.

Like a snake, Jacob moved quickly on his belly, confident that he was not making a sound. Suddenly, Zed appeared at his side, frowning. Whispering very low, he said, "I heard you coming! I told you to stay put."

"I thought you might need help," Jacob said sheepishly, also trying to whisper quietly.

Zed sighed. "All right, but be quiet and keep yer head down."

They moved a little further before Zed touched his arm. Jacob turned his head to see Zed holding his finger to his lips. Then he pointed ahead. Whispering so softly that Jacob could scarcely hear him, he said, "Up there next to the side of that large rock is a camp."

Jacob strained to see, and then raised his head just a few inches. Right where Zed had indicated were a couple of men in dirty buckskins. They were huddled near a small fire and appeared to be making their supper. Three horses and five mules were tied nearby. Movement in the trees caught Jacob's attention, and he finally spotted a third man. He had a rifle in his hands and was peering intently into the darkness in their direction. It appeared he was standing guard.

"They know we're here," Zed whispered.

The breeze was blowing toward Zed and Jacob. The man on guard seemed to sense that someone was near.

"I know those three," Zed growled quietly.

"Friends?" Jacob whispered.

"Not so you'd notice. They're no good. Probably them was following us the other day."

"Maybe that's them who's been following me ever since I left the ship," Jacob said.

Zed just looked at him with a frown. Then he said, "The big one standing guard they call Graff. Zac and I seen him whip a man near to death about four years ago at a trading post. The one leaning over the fire is a Swede named Johnson. The other'n is Irish, called McGreggor."

In a whisper Zed said, "These are dangerous men, and they would take yer life in the blink of an eye.

He said no more, as they watched the men intently for several minutes. The one named Graff kept looking in their direction as darkness closed about them. Then Graff said something and the other two picked up their rifles. "Let's go," Zed whispered, and moved back in the dark to their horses.

When they were a safe distance Zed said, "See what I mean, boy. An experienced mountain man can always feel when someone is watching him."

Jacob shivered. That was a feeling he understood all too well.

In a warning voice, Zed said, "Boy, Graff is a bad one. He's mean and strong as a bull and loves to fight. And he will try to pick a fight with ya. The others are mean, but Graff is the worst, so you stick close to me and mind yer manners."

"Are we going to ride all night again?" Jacob asked. "Now that you know who has been following us?"

"Nope, boy. We're gonna join 'em."

Jacob's mouth gaped open. "What? I thought they weren't your friends."

"They're not, but we're in Indian country, and them three is the best of Indian fighters. If we stay with them we'll all be safer together for awhile."

"Oh," Jacob muttered, not at all sold on the idea.

"Let's get our horses and ride into their camp before they come looking fer us. It's safer that way, boy."

Zed and Jacob paused and looked the camp over before entering. It was dark, and the light of the fire reflected from the large rock on the backs of the three alert mountain men. They had spread out in the trees and were watching carefully into the darkness, their rifles cradled in their arms. Jacob's chest constricted and he felt a shiver of fear creep up his spine. To approach the three men any closer than they were now without being seen would be impossible, so Zed called out, "Hello, the camp!"

"Ride in, but keep yer hands in sight," Graff called out gruffly.

"Come on, boy, let's go," Zed said as he started his horse forward.

Graff cursed lightly and said, "Well, will you look there, boys. It's old Zed himself." He chuckled and then added amiably, "Come on in fer a set."

Zed and Jacob dismounted, and as they did so, the man called Johnson drifted out of the trees, with his eyes on Jacob's horse. The unkempt man then reached to pat Buck's neck. Jacob bristled but wisely kept his lips together. He didn't want to bring attention to himself and Zed had told him not to speak.

Buck would have none of the business. Like a striking rattler, he grabbed at Johnson's arm. He caught a piece of Johnson's buckskin sleeve. However, the man jerked his arm back with surprising speed. He swore, and without looking at Jacob, he stepped back.

"Tie the horses, boy, while I jaw with my old pals," Zed said easily, handing the reins of his horse and lead ropes to Jacob.

As he led them away, he heard Graff say, "Glory be, it's been nary three years since I laid eyes on yer ugly frame, Zed."

"Longer'n that," Zed responded, sounding like an old long lost friend, even though Jacob knew better. "Four years, I'd say. Last time was when you nearly killed that Englishman at some trading post. Don't remember rightly where that was."

"The fool. He sure had it coming," Graff said with a cruel laugh.

When Jacob returned a few minutes later, Graff eyed him with menacing eyes. "Where'd you pick up this one, Zed? Smells like a city boy to me. Why, those buckskins he's wearing look so new I can smell the deer they come off." He turned to his two pals and added, "Still shaves . . . or maybe he ain't man enough to grow a whisker yet." He and the others laughed heartily, including Zed, but Jacob found it hard to even smile.

A dark feeling came over Jacob as the three continued to look him over and make rude comments. He felt nothing but revulsion for the three uncouth mountain men.

"Can't you laugh with the rest of us, city boy?" Graff demanded.

Jacob choked back an angry response as Zed poked him with an elbow.

"Was you gonna say something?" Graff demanded with a fierceness that shook Jacob to the core.

"Got nothing to say," Jacob mumbled.

Zed quickly interrupted and said, "You boys got any grub? I'm so hungry my stomach thinks my throat been cut. Ain't had nothing in my belly but stale jerky all day."

That caught Graff off balance, and the big man said, "Sure, Zed. We was about to set fer a bite. Help yerselves."

The five of them sat on rocks and logs around the fire. As they ate, they swapped stories, Zed doing much of the talking. Jacob was silent.

After a few minutes, Graff, still surly, asked, "So you and the city boy was spying on us, huh?"

Jacob spoke up, "Nope, not us. We just happened—"

Graff's glare, coupled with Zed's warning look made Jacob snap his mouth shut. Graff swore and said, "Don't take us fer fools, boy. We knew you was there. Just look at the front of yer buckskins. If that ain't dirt from crawling, then I ain't the meanest man you'll ever meet."

"Sure thing, boy," the one called Johnson added. "Ya ain't so smare cause any man worth his salt would have smelled our fire and checked us out afore riding into camp."

Jacob nodded, red-faced. Graff turned to Zed and asked with a snarl on his lips, "Where'd you get this greenhorn from, Zed? He's ain't too smart. Won't last long in these mountains."

Jacob clenched his fists, but another warning look from Zed prompted him to keep his mouth shut. Zed then explained how Jacob had come west following the death of his Uncle Zac Sherwood. That name brought a subtle change over the three, and Graff, in a lighter tone said, "Shucks, Zed, we could sure help out in training this young one. Glad to give a hand in old Zac's memory."

Johnson and McGreggor both grinned, making Jacob feel more nervous than ever. Johnson was missing two of his front teeth, and Jacob had to listen carefully when he spoke because his words sort of whistled. His hair was long, black, and greasy and he wore a scraggly beard that looked more like a bird nest.

McGreggor was as unkempt as the other two, but was almost as bald as an eagle. What hair he did have was red and hung like an old mop on his shoulders. His beard was redder than his hair, and he was a little shorter than Jacob. His eyes were icy blue and they made Jacob feel cold whenever he looked across the fire at him.

Graff stood at least two inches taller than Jacob and outweighed him by a good seventy-five pounds. It didn't take a second look to realize he was all muscle and bone. There was not an ounce of fat on Graff. His beard was thick, with a reddish tint to it, and his dark brown hair was shoulder length.

Jacob had never laid eyes on filthier, tougher looking men in his life. And he didn't think they had bathed since the last time Zed had seen them. He suspected that if they jumped in a stream, they'd lose thirty pounds just getting rid of the dirt and stink from their bodies, and most likely pollute everything down stream for man or beast. As they ate, it reminded Jacob of a pack of stray dogs in the back alleys of Boston.

Jacob listened to their rank stories and watched their crude behavior as long as he could stand it. Then he mumbled, "Zed, I'm about done in." He left the group and went in search of his bedroll.

It was clear that the three men were also headed for the Dakotas, and the next morning, they invited Zed to join them. "The kid, too," McGreggor added. "Maybe we can learn him a thing or two."

Zed thanked them and said, "He's willing to learn." Then he turned to Jacob and added, "These three are the best I know when it comes to fighting Indians. Hope we don't have to, but if we do, you could learn a lot from them."

Hearing their names praised, the three assured Jacob that Zed was right. Jacob could clearly see one thing they didn't lack was confidence. Jacob wondered how long he and Zed were going to have to abide their company.

As the days wore on, Jacob's resentment for the men increased. They openly gave him all the dirty little jobs none of them wanted to do. Zed had always split the work evenly, but such was not the case with their new companions. After the third day, Jacob commented on his mistreatment, but Zed shut him up before he did more than make the three of them frown. He whispered to Jacob a little later to take it in stride. "You just be patient, boy," he cautioned. "We need them a lot more'n they need us, remember them's the best Indian fighters I ever done seen."

Another sore spot with Jacob was the way Johnson talked about Buck and the way he constantly eyed the big stallion. One day, as they were riding through light timber, Johnson rode alongside Jacob and asked, "Boy, how'd you get that harse to let you ride him? He seems like a mean one to me."

"He's a one-man harse," Jacob said, mimicking Johnson's pronunciation. Jacob knew he was getting into deep water but her couldn't help himself. He continued, "I'm the only one he'll let ride. Ain't another man alive he'll let on him."

Johnson snorted at that. "Ain't a piece of horseflesh walking that I can't ride, boy."

Jacob smelled the chance for a little revenge. Despite a warning glance from Zed, he said, "Maybe ya can, Johnson, but not this har horse. Ain't a man alive can sit a saddle on old Buck for more than a count of twenty," he bragged.

Johnson swore and said, "I can ride anything that has hair and four legs. That includes that critter yer riding."

Just then they broke out of the timber, and the jawing stopped as they scanned the hills ahead. When they were satisfied there was no danger, they started again. Zed fell in beside Jacob and spoke quietly, "Better be careful, boy," he warned. "You keep goading Johnson about not being able to ride yer horse and you just might find yourself with a peck of problems."

"Shucks, Zed, he can't ride Buck, and you know it. Why should I lie?"

"I didn't say you should lie, but the way yer going about it is like putting honey on an ant hill. Yer making him want to try awful bad. Keep it up, and you'll have to let him have a go at it, and when that happens, he'll get dumped."

Jacob grinned. "I know. And what could that hurt?"

"He'd get madder'n an old coyote with a sore tooth, boy, and that could be dangerous."

"Okay, so what do I say the next time he brings it up?"

Zed shrugged his shoulders. "Search me, boy. You saddled this bronc, and now you got to ride'm or get off. It's yer problem, but you best be careful."

Jacob could soon see he was in a fix, because Johnson kept eying his horse and grinning. Every time they stopped, he would approach Buck, but he did not reach out to him. Each time Johnson approached, Buck would bare his teeth and lay his ears back, daring Johnson to touch him. In a way, that made the situation worse, making it a game with Johnson. He constantly egged on the big stallion, staying just out of reach of his snapping jaws.

It irritated Jacob more than he could say, so one afternoon he intentionally tied Buck with a little slack in the reins. Johnson, as usual, sauntered over and began pestering the horse. When he got close, Buck laid back his ears as usual. Johnson laughed. "You think yer something, don't you, harse?" he taunted, reaching his hand within inches of Buck's nose.

Buck lunged, taking up the slack in the reins, and clamped his teeth on Johnson's arm. He bit hard enough to draw blood and rip a hole in the sleeve of his buckskin shirt. Johnson shrieked and cursed and turned to Jacob, who was grinning and doing his best to hide it. Johnson said, "You gotta do something about that harse, boy. Can't let a mean one like that think he's boss. Ya better let me trade you fer a spell, and I'll learn him some manners."

Jacob was delighted, despite Zed's warning. This was exactly what Jacob had hoped would happen. Wiping away his smile, Jacob said seriously, "I don't know, Johnson. I've never let anyone mess with my harse. He's kind of special to me, and like I told ya before, he's a one-man harse."

Johnson snorted, edged closer to Jacob, and said, "I'll tell you, boy; that harse needs taught some manners, and I'm the one can do it."

"Well," Jacob said, acting uncertain, "I don't know. Are you sure you want to try him? He can buck something awful fierce."

Johnson guffawed, "I'll show you a thing or two, boy. You just let me take that harse for a while."

"Well, maybe on one condition," Jacob said slyly, setting the bait and intentionally not looking toward Zed, because he knew the mountain man would be trying to warn him not to do what he was about to do but he was tired of this filthy, foul, and dirty man.

"What condition is that fer?" Johnson said, now grinning widely as if he smelled victory.

"Well, I'm tired of being the gopher in this company."

"What you mean gopher, boy?" Johnson asked with his mouth wide enough to catch flies.

"You know. For the past week every time you, Graff, or McGreggor want something, you make me gopher this or gopher that," Jacob explained, and it went over Johnson's head and he never got the meaning of Jacob's little remark.

"Sure enough, but what'll that got to do with yer harse?" Johnson asked, walking neatly into the trap Jacob was laying.

"Well, I was just thinking," Jacob said, rubbing his sparse whiskers, for he had quit shaving since joining up with the three men.

"Thinking what?" Johnson pressed eagerly toward him, showing Jacob his missing front teeth and laughing. Jacob backed away due to the foul odor that emanated from Johnson's mouth.

"Well, I might let you ride Buck."

"Course you will, boy."

"On one condition, like I said. If you can't stay on him for the count of twenty, you have to do all the chores until we get to the Dakotas."

Graff who had been standing on the side laughed and said, "There's a deal for you, Johnson. Better take the kid up on it and show him what a real horseman can do."

Zed cleared his throat and said, "Johnson, I've seen that horse buck and he's—"

Johnson cut him off. "Don't ya worry none, Zed. The boy'll be doing all the work he has and then some."

"Johnson," Zed said, "Then you mind yer manners and take off yer spurs, it'll go easier fer you with the stallion."

Johnson laughed and reached down and removed his crudely made steel spurs.

Instead of Zed giving a warning eye to Jacob, there was a touch of mirth. He turned back to Johnson, "If yer sure, Johnson, a deal's a deal. If you get throwed, you do the dirty work around camp."

McGreggor cut in, "Course he will. I'd stake my right arm on Johnson's keeping his ward. Thar ain't a harse alive that can pitch him."

The three dirty men huddled together in a circle, putting each of their arms across the other's shoulders. They talked quietly with some laughing and then stood up. Graff said, "It's a deal, boy. And there ain't no time better'n right now to get on with it. But here's what we want. First, ya gotta help Johnson get on, just to keep yer harse from biting. Next, Zed does the counting, 'cause none of us'n can count too good. Then, when Johnson makes his ride, you do all the work we ask ya to, and . . ." he paused and grinned. Then he added, "And then Johnson gets to use yer horse for a few days."

Jacob replaced the bridle with a halter so the stallion could buck without hurting his mouth, then he led Buck into a clearing and tightened the cinch. He whispered to him, "Now, old boy, there's going to be a varmint on your back in a minute that you're not going to like. I want you to shed him like winter hair, but please, be quick about it, Buck. If you take more than the count of twenty, we'll both be in misery."

Johnson sauntered over, and Buck threw his head and snorted. Jacob looked up at Johnson and asked, "Are you sure?"

"You just hold him, boy, and I'll get on and show you how a mountain man rides" Johnson was grinning like he was about to take candy from a baby.

Jacob had to admit there was not a grain of fear in the man, and it worried him; he hoped he wasn't that good to ride Buck. Jacob, took a hold of the leather lead rope in his hand and gripped the halter tightly. "Get on," he said.

The buckskin's muscles tensed and his eyes rolled back as Johnson swung aboard. Jacob handed Johnson the lead rope. Patting Buck's neck, Jacob leaned over and whispered, "Shuck this varmint and I'll give you the sweetest mountain grass we can find."

Jacob released the halter and stepped back. Buck looked at him as if to ask what was going on, if his master put someone on him he didn't know what to do. Jacob waited tensely for him to explode.

Zed started counting loudly, "One . . . two . . . three . . ."

Buck trotted in a circle not knowing what Jacob wanted, and then the men laughed, yelling loudly. Graff hooted, "My, what a wild pony you got thar, boy."

"Looks like yer about to be our servant," McGreggor agreed.

"Zed, you keep counting!" Graff shouted.

Zed had never quit. "Six . . . seven . . ."

Jacob's heart was sinking. He had to do something. "Buck," he shouted, as if to remind him what was on his back. "Dump him, Buck." Then he whistled loudly. At the sound of Jacob's whistle, Buck stopped trotting, tucked his head between his legs and left the ground like a jack rabbit being chased by a coyote.

"Eight . . . nine . . ." Jacob heard.

"Shuck that varmint, Buck," Jacob yelled.

Again at the sound of Jacob's urgent voice, the big stallion went up, twisting violently in mid-air, fish tailing at the same time. Jacob caught a glimpse of Johnson's face. He was not grinning anymore. His face was tight and his eyes were bulging—hanging on for dear life. Buck went up again and came down with a jar that shook the ground. Johnson's head snapped, but he stayed in the saddle.

"Eleven . . . twelve . . ."

When Buck threw himself into the air again, his head came around, and with his mouth open, he reached for Johnson's hand as he was propelled forward. The rider saw it coming and jerked his hand back in time to avoid being bitten, but in doing so he lost a little of the grip he had. Jacob's hope soared.

"Thirteen . . . fourteen . . ."

The stallion twisted and bucked, then rose on his hind legs and fell down backward. Johnson was an expert, Jacob had to admit, and he leaped away from the saddle, but as soon as Buck rolled to his side and started to get up, he was back in the saddle again. Zed kept counting.

Buck lunged to his feet, kicking, twisting, and throwing his body high into the air. Johnson still rode. But he was loose in the saddle, one foot out of the stirrup. Jacob's heart ached at the abuse he was putting Buck through as the stallion put his muscular body into every position possible, and it was for Jacob.

"Sixteen . . . seventeen . . ."

With all the energy he could muster, the gallant buckskin exploded into the air, gyrating violently. When he came down, Johnson fell forward across the saddle horn. Graff and McGreggor were yelling for him to stay on. Jacob shouted for Buck to fight harder. Zed counted, "Eighteen . . . nineteen . . ."

With a final thrust of power, Buck sent the rider over his head. Johnson landed in a heap, cursing at the top of his lungs.

"Twenty!" Zed yelled.

"You did it, Buck!" Jacob shouted as he ran to his horse, throwing his arms around his neck.

Buck stood trembling and sweating profusely. Zed shouted, "The boy won!"

Jacob spoke to the stallion, "I'm sorry, Buck. You did something I will never forget. And I'll never put you through it again."

Meanwhile, Graff, and McGreggor helped Johnson to his feet. He looked around, dazed and badly shaken. Graff was the first of the three to speak. "Well, seems to me he made the twenty," he drawled.

"Yup," McGreggor agreed. "Johnson wins."

Zed stepped toward. "You boys wasn't listening too good. Johnson was eating dirt by the time I said twenty, and I'm the judge."

The men glared at Jacob, who had his arms around Buck's neck. Without another word, they helped the limping Johnson back to a log where he sat down, and held his head in his hands. Jacob staked Buck out in some rich mountain grass before joining the others.

"How you feeling?" Jacob asked Johnson.

Johnson lifted his head. "I ain't gonna fergit what ya done," he snarled. "Ya, and that harse of yers played a mean trick on me."

"That was fair and square, Johnson," Jacob defended hotly. "You are a good rider. I'll hand you that. But I told you, no one can ride Buck but me."

"Too bad we didn't shake on it," Johnson said, rubbing his eyes with the back of his dirt-streaked hand.

Jacob bristled, "I thought you were a man of your word. Zed always told me mountain men were men of honor."

Zed stepped in. "That's right, and Johnson intends to keep his word, don't you Johnson?" he said firmly.

Johnson carefully pulled himself to his feet. "That's right," he said. "I'm a man of my word." There was more contempt than promise in his voice, and Zed cast Jacob a worried glance.

The three men huddled together, talking softly. Zed said to Jacob in a whisper, "Boy, I think we better light a shuck in the morning. I thought these men might at least keep their word, but I don't think so. I think we'll be safer on our own."

They made camp right where they had stopped, even though it was still early in the afternoon. Johnson spent the rest of the day on his bedroll. Jacob spent time with Buck, washing him in a nearby stream and rubbing and brushing him down.

That evening, he waited for Johnson to get some wood, but when he did not, and darkness started to settle in, Jacob approached him. "I'll get the wood tonight, Johnson, because I can see you're hurting. But after this, you'll have to do it," he said, knowing that he and Zed would probably be gone before the sun was up.

Johnson got up from his greasy bedroll and shook a finger at Jacob. "Boy, me and the others talked it over. We figure we been cheated with that thar harse of yars. You lose, and you will either do the work or wish you had."

Graff and McGreggor joined him. Graff shoved his way past Johnson and glared with open contempt at Jacob. "I ain't liked you since I laid my eyes on you the first time. You don't belong here."

Like a bolt of lightning, Graff's arms shot out and grabbed hold of Jacob, spinning him around. Johnson and McGreggor leaped to his aid, pinning Jacob's arms. Graff grinned and drew back a fist the size of a small boulder. Jacob leaned back into the two that held him and swung both feet as hard as he could at Graff. One heel caught the big man on the chin, knocking him to the ground. Graff reached up, touched his mouth, and pulled his hand away with blood on it.

In a slow and deliberate tone, he said, "Boy, you won't live through the night to regret what you done." He shoved himself to his feet and once again drew back a gigantic fist.

Jacob braced himself and prepared to kick again. McGreggor and Johnson gripped him more tightly. Then a voice rang out from behind them. "Hold it, boys. Don't move."

"Drop that rifle, Zed," Graff demanded, still holding his fist cocked. "You ain't gonna interfere. This here is just punishment fer a cheater."

Zed never missed a beat. He said, "Back off, Graff. I mean it, or I'll put a hole in ya bigger than yer fist."

"You put that gun down or you are my enemy, Zed," Graff hissed.

"I never was yer friend," Zed countered. "Now, you boys, let loose of him."

Johnson and McGreggor apparently heard something in the tone of Zed's voice because they did as he ordered. Then Jacob backed toward Zed. Graff lowered his arm, but his eyes followed Jacob with hatred that made him shudder. "Saddle the horses and pack the mules, boy," Zed ordered. "We're leaving."

It took Jacob several minutes as he gathered up the stock, saddled the horses, and packed both of the mules. The whole time, Zed stood with his rifle holding the three mountain men at bay. When Jacob finished, he mounted Buck and led the mules and Zed's horse to where Zed was standing. Zed slipped easily into the saddle, still holding his rifle and not taking his eyes off the men.

Graff, who had murdered men in the past, said in a loud voice, "Jacob, no matter where you go, I'll be after you. No matter what tree you ride by, approach it with caution, 'cause I'll be hiding behind it. The time will come, boy—you can count on this—I will find you. Before you die, I will show you what pain is. And the same goes fer you, Zed. You both are riding out of here with one foot in the grave."

Without a word of response, Zed and Jacob backed their horses out, watching the three men closely and then turned and rode out into the gathering darkness.

Chapter 10
Life & Death

Zed employed every trick he knew to throw Graff and his partners off their trail if they came after them. They rode all night, picking rocky areas, small streams, and heavy timber, stopping only occasionally to rest their animals. With only starlight to guide them, Zed and Jacob traveled painstakingly slow, but they both knew that their lives might depend on their willingness to separate themselves from their enemies, so neither of them complained.

Dawn revealed a remote range of mountains nearby. "Right where I hoped we'd be," Zed remarked with a tired smile, and he was grateful to be in the Sioux Indian Territory. "There's game aplenty in them hills," he said. "We'll push on fer a few more hours, and then we'll take a rest and replenish our meat supply."

It was past noon before they climbed into the foothills. Finally, Zed called for a stop. They rubbed their horses down and staked them in some deep grass. Then they fixed a quick meal, ate, and slept.

In the late afternoon when both were refreshed from their short sleep, Zed said, "Boy, it's time to do some hunting. It'll be up to you, 'cause I figure on staying behind to watch fer Graff and his friends. I think we are a safe distance ahead of them boys, but I can't be too sure."

Jacob readily agreed to hunt by himself. "I'll head north," he said. "When I get something, I'll hang it in a tree and come back for you."

"Just don't get lost, boy," Zed warned. "And don't waste any powder! The less noise we make, the less chance there'll be of trouble with Indians. There could be some around, you just never know. We are mighty close now to the hunting grounds of the Sioux. They get real mean if anybuddy hunts on their ground without permission, so don't go too far."

"Will they give us permission when we get into their lands?" Jacob asked, as he lifted his rife and grabbed his possibles.

"No, I don't reckon so, but we need meat. A man can't go hungry when there's game about," Zed said dryly.

Jacob was confident he could bag a deer with one shot. It just had to be the right shot. He left their camp on foot and hiked for close to an hour before he came to a small tributary off the main river. No sooner had he crossed the river, when he spotted a large buck and two does feeding a short distance from the riverbank.

They were upstream and upwind, so Jacob decided on the closest doe, because the doe meat would be tenderer than that of the buck. He sat with his back to a tree and took aim, but one of the does suddenly for no explainable reason, bounded into the trees, with the other one following. The buck lifted his head when the does ran, but apparently he found no reason for alarm. He dropped his head and went back to eating.

Jacob shifted his position, dropped to one knee, and carefully took aim at the buck. He wasn't that far away, so Jacob decided on a head-shot, not wanting to spoil any meat. He slowly applied pressure to the trigger. There was an explosion as the powder ignited, firing the rifle. A cloud of smoke obscured his vision. As it cleared, Jacob could see the buck was down.

Leaping to his feet, Jacob ran into the clearing. The buck was lying on its right side with its head toward Jacob. He walked straight to it, eager to dress his deer and show Zed how much his green pupil had learned. He laid his rifle across the tufts of grass and grasped the large antlers with his left hand while withdrawing his knife with his right. He extended the knife to the buck's throat to cut his bleeder, but as he touched its neck with the blade, the buck blinked.

Before Jacob could draw the knife across the deer's throat, it threw its head and attempted to rise. Horrified, Jacob dropped his knife and caught the other antlers with his right hand. He realized he must have only grazed the buck's head, knocking him out for a few moments. The startled animal tossed its head again in an attempt to dislodge Jacob, but Jacob firmly gripped the antlers, knowing that if he let go he would be gored to death.

The deer snorted and gathered its feet beneath itself. Jacob was a substantial weight on its huge rack, and the large buck began pushing against Jacob. Jacob's one hundred and eighty pounds wasn't much against the buck's two hundred and fifty or more.

The big buck was terrorized. It would have likely preferred to flee from this strange creature, but Jacob was holding onto his antlers, so fight was its only option.

The buck started to whip Jacob about like a dog with a rat in its mouth. Jacob thought about turning the animal's head away and then run, but no matter what he did, the buck countered his efforts and tried to gore him. The buck struck out with its forefeet and tore Jacob's buckskins over his left leg. He struck again, this time connecting with Jacob's right hip. Jacob could feel blood oozing down his leg as he continued to grapple with the antlers.

Jacob's heart was pounding and sweat poured off his forehead and into his eyes.

He couldn't let go without being severely injured, but if he continued to hang on, he would soon be cut to shreds by the buck's feet, and the buck could more than out last him. Jacob was close to hysteria.

Through the haze of fear and pain, Jacob could almost hear Zed's voice telling him to never approach a deer and attempt to bleed it until he was sure it was dead. Also when he did approach, it should never be directly from the front, but rather from the side or behind. "Put your knee on its neck so he can't move, then cut fast and deep," Zed had told him plainly. And he had demonstrated it time after time—lot of good that did him now.

Everything Jacob had done from the moment he had fired his Tennessee rifle had been wrong. He swore that if he somehow miraculously lived through this, he would never forget the lesson he hadn't learned.

Men draw on things they have learned throughout their lives when death is staring them in the face.

As Jacob began to reach desperation, he suddenly recalled his brother's neighbor in Massachusetts. This man had a small farm outside of Boston and had literally taken a bull by the horns one day. Then he twisted its head until the animal had fallen on its side. Jacob decided to try the same type of maneuver with the buck.

Jacob's hands ached and were slippery with sweat. He strained, pushing upward, raising the buck's head, which gave him a chance to plant his own feet firmly under him. With his feet in place, Jacob used his weight to twist the animal's head to the side.

The buck again struck out, barely cutting Jacob's front thigh. But Jacob kept his grip and gradually, the deer's head began to turn and as the head went, the body slowly followed.

Jacob's eyes stung with sweat and dirt. His legs shook and his arms trembled, but he continued to apply pressure on the buck's neck. In one final attempt, Jacob put every ounce of strength into the effort and snapped the buck's head to the side. With a thud, the large buck fell to the grass.

Grateful that he was still alive, Jacob twisted the buck's head even further holding him down. With the buck's head in a grotesque position, Jacob constantly applied pressure while the deer thrashed, kicking dangerously, trying to get up. Jacob looked for his knife.

Jacob's strength was fading fast. Suddenly, he became aware of a painful lump under his left side. It was his knife! His hopes soared as he continued to shift and pull the buck forward until his knife was in front of his left shoulder. He knew he had but one chance to use his knife because he was losing his strength. Shaking with exhaustion, Jacob in one quick movement, picked up the knife, thrust it deep into the buck's neck, and ripped. The buck made one final attempt to get up, and then lay still.

Jacob let go and lay back on the grass, totally exhausted and winded. As he regained some strength, he began to shake. Reflecting on what just had happened, Jacob realized that his own carelessness had nearly lost him his life. Then his inheritance would go to another worthy recipient, as Mr. Weatherbee had constantly emphasized. Alone in the wilderness, he could not afford to make any mistakes.

Lying on his back, Jacob gulped for air and slowly tried to calm his mind as he watched the clouds in the sky and the slowly sinking sun. He was just grateful to be alive.

Behind him, he heard a sound. "Well now," a voice said. "Ain't you the lucky one?"

Startled, Jacob sat up and looked while rubbing the sweat and grime mixed with deer blood from his eyes. There stood Zed standing a few feet away watching him.

"How long have you been there?" Jacob demanded, dragging his exhausted body up.

"Well," Zed drawled slowly, "let's see now. I saw you shoot the buck. I'm afraid it was my scent that made those does run. I saw you take a bead on them, and you were right. They would have been the best meat, but this will do."

Jacob's trembling now included rage. "Why didn't you shoot him?" he shouted.

Zed shrugged his thin shoulders. "Why? You were holding yer own, boy. It would have been a waste of good ball and powder. Besides, boy, I told you never approach a deer from the front. When a man makes a mistake, he should learn from it."

"But you were right there, Zed! You saw it all. You could have helped me."

Zed spoke softer, shaking his head slightly. "Boy, I could have lent you a helping hand, but I must say, you done just fine by yerself. That was one plumb smart way you twisted that critter's neck and brought him down. I never would have figured that myself."

Jacob lay on the ground trying to calm his mind and thinking of what Zed had said. He went over his total ordeal and thought as usual, Zed was right. If Zed had killed the deer, the lesson would not have sunk deeply into Jacob's mind. He remembered how his father would give him a job to do and then would say, "Son, figure it out for yourself if you can. That's why the good Lord gave you a brain. I'll help you after you've given it your best effort, but not until you've done your part."

Jacob's anger subsided. He dropped his gaze and said, "Sorry, Zed. And thanks, too."

Zed said, "I want you to know one thing boy, and that is that I wouldn't have let that critter kill you. I had a bead draw on him the whole time."

"Thanks," Jacob repeated. Then he gazed at Zed, puzzled. "I thought you were going to stay in camp. Why did you follow me?"

Zed grinned. "Ain't easy teaching no city boy. This was a test, that's all. I just wanted to see how you done on yer own."

"Not too well," Jacob said sadly. "I've got a lot to learn."

"But yer learning, boy. Yer learning," Zed said.

Jacob went to the stream and washed the dirt out of his eyes and face, then washed his wounds. He reached into his small possibles bag he had strapped around his waist and took out herbs and quickly made poultices, wrapping them in cloth and putting them over his cuts to stop the bleeding. Once his wounds were cared for, he went back to help Zed gut and clean the deer.

As they worked in silence, Jacob had the opportunity to think about the mistakes he had made. There was no doubt that he had learned more from his errors he had made than any single thing Zed had attempted to teach him over the past few months. It was a hard lesson to learn.

Zed cut a small lodgepole pine while Jacob tied the buck's front feet together and then his back feet. They slipped the pole between the animal's front and back legs and then hoisted the pole onto their shoulders and started back toward camp with their rifles in hand.

Just before entering their camp, they put the deer down to catch their breath. When they picked it up, Jacob caught a brief glimpse of someone on horseback through the trees.

"Zed, there's someone over there," he said softly.

Zed turned his head and saw who it was. "There's a lot more'n one, boy. Let it back down." Zed began to lower his end of the deer.

Jacob started to shoulder his rifle. "Is it Graff and the other two?"

"Put down the rifle boy. Them's Indians out there."

"But maybe it's Graff—" he began.

"No, it's Indians. They must have been watching ever since ya shot that deer."

Slowly, watching every move Zed and Jacob made, seven nearly naked Indians approached them on horseback through the trees.

Chapter 11
White Fawn

The Indians spread out on both sides, surrounding Jacob and Zed. One Indian, who appeared to be the leader, rode up to Zed. He was trying to communicate using sign language. Zed answered in Sioux. All the Indians seemed surprised that he could speak their language. The leader of the braves then spoke rapidly to Zed, his voice deep with guttural sounds. They conversed for a minute or two, both of their faces serious, unsmiling.

Jacob began to sweat as he stood nervously, shifting his weight from one foot to the other. Zed turned toward him. "They want us to follow them to their camp, but they'll take our rifles and let us keep our horses and mules."

"But . . . what . . . will we do without our rifles?" Jacob stammered.

"Never mind now, boy. We'll just do as they say."

Two of the braves picked up the deer and loaded it across a pony. Two other Indians grabbed their rifles, then all the Indians followed as Jacob and Zed led the way to their camp.

Gathering their possibles, they saddled their horses and packed their mules. The group then headed north, presumably to the Sioux's camp. The braves surrounded Zed and Jacob as they rode, keeping the two men in the middle of their formation, with one Indian riding lead.

Zed spoke again after a few minutes. "Well, boy, looks like we're in a mess of trouble. Seems they claim this area is their huntin' grounds. I guess they're huntin' in a bigger area than I thought."

"What are they going to do to us?" Jacob asked nervously.

"Don't know yet. However this is Sioux Territory and they remembered Zachariah from years ago, at least the older ones do. It warn't looking good until I mentioned his name. They're taking us to their council to let them decide what to do with us," Zed explained calmly.

Jacob felt anything but calm. However, he was a little reassured by the way Zed was acting because he certainly didn't appear to be frightened.

"How far is their camp?" Jacob asked.

"I don't know, boy. We may have to spend the night somewhere before we get to where their main camp is located. Seems they had a battle with another tribe back somewhere. They raided it but didn't get much fer their trouble. They lost a brave or two in the effort. They heard yer rifle and come this way to investigate. We're really lucky they didn't scalp us right off, 'cause after losing their warriors they ain't in much good humor about now."

Jacob considered what Zed had said for a moment, and then he suggested, "Let's make a break for it. We have better horses than they do!"

"Don't talk nonsense, boy," Zed said angrily. "I know yer scared, but where'd we go? They know this land better'n I ever will. No, we're caught. We just got to see what they plan to do with us and go from there."

After a few hours they were joined by another twenty braves, and they all made camp a couple hours later. Zed and Jacob spent the night with rawhide strips binding their hands and feet, listening to the chatter and laughter of the band of warriors. By the time the braves cut them loose early the next morning, Zed and Jacob's wrists and ankles were chafed and swollen.

They rode again for about ten hours before the small group reached the banks of a large river, which Zed said was the Missouri. They crossed it and turned west. The Sioux camp was located further downstream, situated in a large, grassy valley with mountains on both sides.

As they approached the Sioux camp, Jacob quickly counted well over two hundred tepees spread over the large valley floor.

Forests bordered the valley on both sides, but heavier forests were further to the north. "Should be plenty of game nearby," Zed drawled as they rode into the center of the large village.

Jacob was sure Zed was right because they had seen both deer and moose earlier in the day. The Indians need a lot of game to sustain them and the area was plentiful. However, that was the least of his concerns now. He was growing more worried by the minute about his scalp. He repeatedly ran his hand under his badger-skin cap to reassure himself he still had hair. But looking at Zed, he seemed composed and calm as a summer's day.

The number of men in the village frightened Jacob even worse. Jacob had never been around Indians and Zed said from the number of tepees in the distance there had to be at least seven hundred or more. Most of the men wore little more than a loincloth, although some wore buckskin breeches, not unlike his own. Women and children gathered around Zed and Jacob like a flock of birds. Children in large groups ran up to the two of them and touched their skin and then ran squealing back into the crowd. It was almost like a game of tag.

"Why are they doing that, Zed?" Jacob asked.

"Don't guess they never seen a white man a'fore, boy, least not as prisoners. If yer Uncle Zac lived with them some years ago they little ones would not have been born. We're kinda something new here 'cause there are very few white men in the area except trappers and very few of them live with the Indians," Zed said, seemingly undisturbed by the games of the Indian children. "Boy, right now we're neither their friends nor their enemies. I got some tall talking to do when the chief appears. So it's best we quit our yapping. It's considered rude to speak before spoken to when yer a prisoner of the Sioux."

The braves who were escorting them rode directly up to a large tepee and stopped. A tall, muscular man with dark brown skin came out, squinted for a moment in the sunlight, and then frowned at the two white men. He was older than any of the braves in the raiding party.

When he spoke, the noise of the crowd died out, and all eyes turned to him. He clapped his hands together, and the women, children, and younger braves all turned away. In the next minute there were only a few male Indians standing close by, while the main war party that had captured them dismounted. Zed made no move to do the same, so Jacob sat still and waited in fearful anticipation.

The stately Indian spoke rapidly with the leader of the raiding party, pointing occasionally at the two white captives. After a few minutes, the chief—for it was obvious even to Jacob that the stately one was the chief—spoke to Zed. Zed answered calmly. Then he got off his horse, signaling for Jacob to do the same. Zed and the chief conversed for several minutes. Jacob had learned enough of the language of the Sioux when Zed had taught him different words and phrases over the many evenings they spent together. Now he understood that Zed was pleading their cause.

Eventually, a couple of men attempted to take their horses and mules. When one Indian reached for Buck's reins, the big buckskin reacted swiftly, biting so deeply he drew blood. That brought a round of laughter from the other braves. The injured brave, now holding his bleeding arm, glared at Buck. Zed said something in Sioux to the chief, who nodded his head and responded. Then Zed turned to Jacob and said, "They want you to tie him up. I told him how he won't let nobuddy touch him but you."

Tying Buck took only a minute, and then Jacob was escorted back to where Zed stood waiting. Four braves escorted them in front of a large tepee.

"They want us to wait here," Zed said. "So we might as well make ourselves comfortable. The Indians have some other matters to take care of before they get around to deciding what to do with us, so don't do anything stupid boy, 'cause we're their prisoners."

The leather flap of the tepee was pulled back, and upon entering the tepee, Jacob turned, sat down, and watched out the opening as groups of women scurried around the village. Some were carrying baskets of food, others were carrying firewood, and still more carried carved wooden bowls.

From where he was kneeling, Jacob could see the disorder that had erupted when he and Zed were brought into camp was gone. Everyone was busy. Even the children had gone back to their chores and games.

As the afternoon wore on, many of the women busied themselves over fires. Some seemed to be cooking from large iron kettles. Zed explained that the kettles were the result of trading with trappers and other white men over the years. Before that time they had used clay pots of their own making. Jacob could see some of the braves sitting in the shade of their tepees working on arrows and arrowheads or braiding leather.

Zed soon stretched out on some thick buffalo robes and tried to sleep. Jacob lay on his back, with his hands behind his head looking out through the opening. Zed was already asleep, but Jacob couldn't relax. He thought about home and had to brush away a tear as he considered how unhappy his mother would be if she could see him now—especially if he didn't have any hair. Looking at his surroundings, he regretted ever leaving his home in Boston, berating himself for chasing after adventures and riches dreamed up by his Uncle Zac.

The sunlight of the door was suddenly blocked, and Jacob turned his head to see who had entered the tepee. For a moment, he thought he was dreaming. A beautiful Indian maiden, probably the prettiest girl Jacob had ever laid eyes on, was standing in the opening. She appeared to be about Jacob's age, seventeen or so. Her dark brown eyes were wide with wonder as she looked at Jacob. As their eyes met, both were drawn to each other, neither of them looking away. Entranced by her beauty, Jacob turned on his side, propped himself on one elbow, and grinned at her. He just couldn't help himself. She was so beautiful.

She appeared to be surprised, and when he grinned, she lowered her eyes, fluttering her long black eyelashes. Her hair was long and shiny, hanging in loose braids about her shoulders. She was taller than most of the other women in the camp than Jacob had seen, and he could not take his eyes off her.

After a moment, she looked up again, and Jacob grinned. A shy smile touched the corners of her small mouth, and her eyes glowed with pleasure; at least, that's how Jacob interpreted the look she gave him in response. As she walked closer, Jacob wanted to touch her, but from what Zed had told him, since they were prisoners he knew it was forbidden.

Next to him on the floor of the tepee was a piece of long dried grass. Jacob picked up the piece, and extended the grass until it touched the top of her foot above her moccasin. She quickly pulled her foot back, and then slowly put it where the grass was extended. Jacob wondered if she felt what he was feeling. Just then a second maiden, shorter and much heavier, entered the tepee and stood next to the pretty maiden. She glared at Jacob, jabbed the first maiden, and pushed her forward.

With a start, the pretty Indian maiden's brief smile faded and she began gesturing with her hands, repeatedly putting her hand to her mouth. It was obvious that she was trying to ask Jacob if he and Zed were hungry. He said the word food in Sioux. Her eyes lit up, and she smiled. Jacob nodded his head vigorously because he was famished.

The two maidens turned and left the tepee. "I think we'll have some vittles here soon, boy," Zed drawled.

Jacob hadn't realized that Zed was awake. He turned to him and said, "Yeah, not too bad, huh?"

"What? The food or that gal there?"

Jacob grinned. All of a sudden the world was looking a whole lot better.

Zed said, "If you plan on making eyes at the gal like she was dessert or try to tickle her fancy with that grass trick of yers, you better get ready to lose that thick head of brown hair you got, boy. When them two come back again, you just be neighborly like, but don't go making eyes at the pretty one. Somebuddy might just take offense to that."

"Sorry, Zed, but she sure is—"

"Never mind what she is or ain't, boy," Zed cut him off. "We got to think about saving our hides and that's all!"

Jacob said nothing more. He just lay back down and thought about the beautiful Indian maiden. She made little Lucy Johnson back in Boston look downright faded and—well—ugly, he thought.

In a few minutes, the maidens returned. They carried large gourds filled with some sort of stew. Jacob again couldn't help looking at the tall girl, but he didn't allow himself to smile. The short, stocky girl scowled while Zed and Jacob were eating. But the tall one, although not smiling, certainly didn't look like she hated being there.

Whenever Jacob looked up from his stew, she was watching him with her warm brown eyes. They reminded him of a fawn's eyes. When Jacob had cleaned up the last bit of stew, the tall maiden abruptly turned and left. She went back to a nearby fire, dipped a ladle into one of the large iron kettles, and returned with it dripping.

She pointed to Jacob's empty gourd and poured the contents of the ladle into it. Then she held the ladle over his wrist and let some of the hot juice drip on him, but it didn't hurt. Jacob quickly jerked his hand away, looking up at her in surprise. She was flirting with him and she fluttered her long eyelashes and smiled a smug, teasing smile. Jacob's heart soared. Zed cleared his throat and mumbled something in Sioux. The girl's eyes widened with surprise as he spoke. She quickly gave the rest of the stew to him.

The other girl grunted and glared at the one with the ladle. Both maidens abruptly sat down and waited until Zed and Jacob finished eating. Then they took the empty gourds and left. Jacob watched as they walked away. He was smitten, and he knew it.

So did Zed. "You about gave me an apoplectic fit, boy! The way you and that maiden was carrying on. What's the matter with you? Don't you got no sense at all? I'm only going to say this once, so you best listen good. If the wrong brave sees you eye-balling that gal, we'll both be dead fer sure. You got that?"

Before Jacob could indicate whether he did or didn't, an old Indian stuck his head into the opening and motioned for Zed and Jacob to follow. Zed led the way, and followed the old man to a larger tepee. As they entered the tepee, Jacob saw half a dozen men sitting in a circle. In the center of their circle was a small fire. Each brave had feathers in his hair, denoting authority. Some wore headbands to hold their long hair out of their faces while others had their hair in two long braids.

They all looked very serious and sat stiffly, almost stately. The chief sat directly opposite of the opening, and he spoke after Zed and Jacob had sat down as directed. He addressed Zed in Sioux. Zed listened attentively and spoke a few words from time to time. After a while, others spoke, and Zed, looking each in the eye, spoke quietly to them. Their hard faces seemed to soften, and some even smiled. Jacob just watched and listened.

Finally, all talked ceased. It was all Jacob could do to keep from asking Zed what was going on, but he knew if Zed wanted him to know, he would have said something.

The chief picked up a long smoking pipe and packed something into the bowl, then lit it with an ember from the fire. The chief drew deeply on the pipe then blew the smoke into the air. He handed the pipe to the man next to him who repeated the act. When it reached Zed, he puffed on it and handed it to Jacob.

Jacob was about to wipe off the end before putting the pipe to his lips, but a stern glance from Zed changed his mind. He gingerly pressed the pipe to his mouth and sucked. He was careful not to let the smoke get in his lungs and managed to blow it out without coughing. Then, feeling a certain amount of pride, he passed the pipe on.

When they had all taken a turn with what Jacob assumed was a peace pipe, the chief spoke again to Zed. They conversed for what must have been at least an hour. At times other members of the council would make remarks and smile as if they approved of their conversation. All the while, Jacob's legs were hurting from sitting cross-legged for such a long time. He painfully fought the urge to wiggle or stretch his legs out.

As the chief and Zed talked, a big Indian with a cruel, homely face seemed to have more to say than the others. It was all very mysterious to Jacob, but seeing the relaxed look on Zed's face and the fact that they had smoked the famous peace pipe eased Jacob's fears. His mind kept wandering back to the pretty Indian maiden. He wondered if one of these stern braves was her father. That thought made him shudder.

When the conversation was near an end, the chief pointed at Jacob. Zed nodded in approval and said something in Sioux before turning to Jacob. "Boy," he said slowly, "it seems that the big ugly one don't like us. He just as soon have our scalps hanging from his belt!"

"Why does he feel that way if the others don't?" Jacob asked, somewhat alarmed.

"He ain't got no good reason 'cept he just don't want no white men around here. He seems to think that if we was allowed to stick around here fer awhile that others like us might come, and then he figures our kind would take over."

Jacob didn't want to lose his life so he said, "We won't invite anyone."

"You don't need to tell me that, boy. It's Lone Wolf, the ugly one that needs convincing. I told 'em about the agreement with your Uncle Zac. The chief remembers yer uncle well and was proud that Zac would want you to be taught by him and his people. All the others agree, 'cept Lone Wolf."

"So can Long Wolf have his way if—"

"Quit worrying, boy. If the rest of the council decides to let us stay, Lone Wolf has to go along with it. 'Course, that don't mean he'll like it. And me and you, especially you, could have a little trouble with him, I reckon."

"You mean I might have to fight him sometime?" Jacob asked uncertainly.

"Maybe. But ain't it wonderful, boy? That's just what yer old Uncle Zac would of liked. Makes a good challenge fer you and some excitement fer the rest of us," Zed said with a chuckle.

"Yeah, a good challenge for me while Uncle Zac is looking down from the other side and laughing his fool head off!"

"Now, boy," exclaimed Zed in a quiet manner, stroking his bushy black beard. "Don't be getting mad at yer uncle fer wanting to see a good contest between you and an Indian."

"So when do the others decide?" Jacob asked, not at all happy with the way things were shaping up.

"Soon as we've paid the price fer trespassing on their huntin' grounds."

"Just how do we pay the price? What do we have to do?"

"Not we. Just you, boy."

"Me? Why just me?"

"'Cause you was the one who shot the deer."

"Me?" Jacob repeated. He braced himself for the worst when he asked the next question, "What will they do to me?"

"They want ya to be in a contest. We can save face that way."

"Contest!" Jacob said. "I don't know hardly anything about the Indian ways, only what you've taught me. I don't think—"

"Hush, boy! Yer poor manners will get us both in a heap of trouble."

"But what do they want me to do? What kind of a contest is it?" Jacob asked, becoming more panicked.

"Hush, I says. Don't ask no more questions fer now. Just smile and look like you have a lot of guts, boy. They admire men with courage, not snivelers." Zed turned to the chief.

"Yeah, their guts and my blood," Jacob mumbled under his breath.

As Zed and Jacob were ushered back to their tepee, they could see a dozen braves watching them. Lone Wolf strolled over and began talking to the other braves. He pointed his finger in the direction of Zed and Jacob, and they all laughed at whatever he had said. Jacob felt as if the whole world were collapsing in on him. Things had gone from good to bad, and he again thought about never seeing the beautiful maiden.

"I don't want to die," he said quietly to Zed. He could just see himself in a fight with someone like Lone Wolf, trying to wield a knife, or worse yet, a tomahawk. He wouldn't stand a chance.

Zed hadn't heard Jacob. "Quit fussing, boy. Yer as strong as any of 'em," Zed said almost gleefully.

Jacob's face burned. What was Zed trying to do to him? He looked toward Lone Wolf and his friends again. They were standing in front of a large tepee. The pretty Indian maiden suddenly appeared from behind the tepee. Jacob's heart leaped.

"Where do you suppose that maiden lives?" he asked, trying to sound unconcerned.

"Probably in that tepee she is walking past. So does Lone Wolf, I reckon."

"What do you mean?" Jacob demanded.

"I think Lone Wolf is her pa," Zed said mischievously.

Jacob's heart sank. That topped it all. He gazed at the tall, slender girl, and he thought his heart would break. What a mess he was in.

"Boy, you are not listening to me," Zed growled.

They had reached their tepee. Jacob took one last look at the beautiful Indian maiden and stepped inside. "I was just thinking about the battle I'm going to have to fight," he said.

"What battle, boy? Who said anything about a battle? Surely you don't think you would be expected to have a fight to the death!" Zed said.

Relief flooded over Jacob. That was exactly what he had thought. "Then what kind of contest did you mean?"

"That will be up to you, boy. You get to choose, but I would suggest that you don't use yer horse," Zed said. "He could easily outrun anything the Sioux have, and then you would lose face 'cause it was yer horse that won and not you. Anything else goes, so you be thinking about it!"

Jacob didn't have to think. He already knew.

Chapter 12
The Race

Besides the upcoming contest, Jacob thought of only one other thing that night and that was the Indian maiden. He didn't even know her name, but he knew he liked her. He also knew that if she were Lone Wolf's daughter, then her father hated him.

The following morning, the same two maidens brought them their breakfast. It was the same thing they had eaten the night before, but it was delicious. He especially enjoyed the present company, or least half of it, anyway. The short maiden did nothing but scowl; however, the tall, slender one watched Jacob constantly. The way she looked at him made him all the more determined to win the contest, which, Zed had told him, might be held that very morning.

"So, have you decided what the contest will be, boy?" Zed asked after the maidens had gone.

"Sure have," Jacob replied confidently.

"What'll it be?"

"I aim to have a long-distance race."

"Race? Are you crazy, boy? These Indians love to run. Didn't you know that? Things will be a lot better fer the both of us if you at least make a good showing, but a foot race won't do it. Why, you wouldn't stand the chance of a mouse in a den of rattlers. Think some more, boy, and this time use yer head," Zed growled.

"I can run," Jacob said. "What do you think I did all those mornings before I gentled Buck?"

"Boy, all yer running wouldn't be enough to make a difference 'cause these Indians run every day. You ain't got a chance, I tell you. Hurry and think of something else."

Jacob almost said something about all the long hours of training he had done in Boston, but he didn't. It wouldn't have mattered anyway because Zed had already made up his mind.

Exasperated, Jacob said, "You told me to choose the thing I can do best, and I can run. It's the only thing I can do. If I lose, at least I'll lose trying, and they'll know I gave it my best."

Zed shook his head, mumbled something about an unwise city boy who had no brains, and walked out of the tepee.

Jacob looked around the area and spotted Buck. He was still tethered a short distance away. Jacob whistled and Buck raised his head and nickered. He needed water and grass. If he didn't take care of him, then no one would, because Buck wouldn't allow anyone else to touch him. So he unsaddled Buck and unpacked the mule and put their belongings in their tepee.

As he led him to the river, Lone Wolf followed him at a distance, as if he were afraid Jacob was going to make a break for it and try to avoid the contest. Jacob was sure that was what Lone Wolf wanted, but he would be disappointed. After letting Buck drink his fill, Jacob led him back to their tepee and spent several hours rubbing him down.

Several times throughout the day he spotted the pretty maiden watching him with her big brown eyes. Whenever he turned around, he would always see Lone Wolf glaring at him.

Noon came and the maidens brought food again. Jacob smiled at the pretty one. He ate light, not wanting a full stomach in case they had the race today. The pretty maiden encouraged him to eat more, but Jacob patted his stomach and said, "You're a good cook."

She nodded as if she understood and took his bowl. "Thanks," he said in Sioux, his voice soft. He hoped it would convey his meaning.

Apparently it did, for she finally smiled, briefly nodding her head. She held his gaze a moment longer, and then walked away. After the maiden departed, Jacob started to stretch his legs. He squatted down and then stood up and ran in place. When his muscles were warm, Jacob returned to spending time with Buck, giving him something to do to take his mind off the contest.

The afternoon wore on. Zed was quiet, almost sullen, and totally ignored Jacob. Finally, as evening approached, Jacob watered Buck and released him with the Sioux herd and returned to the tepee. He knew Buck would not wander off.

As Jacob entered the tepee, he saw Zed sitting on a buffalo hide, with a frown stretched over his face, pouting like a child.

Jacob had had enough. "Zed, I know you are mad at me because you think I should choose something else," he said. "But running is what I do best. I wish you had a little more faith in me."

Zed still said nothing.

"When is the race? I thought it was today."

"You got lots to learn about Indians, boy. They'll have it when they get around to it."

"Tomorrow?" Jacob asked anxiously.

"Maybe. Just have to wait and see."

The next morning, two different maidens brought Zed and Jacob their meal. After eating a little, Jacob walked around the camp. He had been up in the early hours exercising his leg muscles in case the race was scheduled for today.

As usual, Lone Wolf was nearby watching him with a suspicious eye, just as he had done the previous day. As Jacob returned to his tepee, Zed announced gravely, "I think it'll be this morning, boy."

"What makes you think that?"

Zed pointed to a young brave who was approaching their tepee. He was of medium height and was built long and lean. He motioned for Jacob to follow him. Zed trailed behind as the three walked to the west end of the camp where a large crowd was gathering. Jacob estimated there were at least five hundred tribal members present and more were coming. *Apparently this is a big occasion for the Sioux,* Jacob thought glumly. He felt so alone and he was the only young white man in the tribe and no one believed in him but himself.

The chief, wearing his large feather headdress, took charge. He spoke to Zed as he pointed to Jacob. Zed must have told the chief what Jacob had decided to do for their contest. A slow smile crossed the stately chief's face, which didn't make Jacob feel too confident.

Zed told Jacob that the chief's name was Two Clouds who now spoke to the tribe, and soon everyone was laughing and poking each other in the ribs. It must have been very funny to all of them, except one young maiden. Her large eyes were filled with concern, which made Jacob all the more determined to make this race one that his opponent would never forget.

Zed called to him, and Jacob pulled his eyes away from the sad face of the beautiful maiden. He stepped closer to Zed. "They have agreed to have a race, boy. And as you can see, they think it's real funny. You better run like you never run before, because the last thing I want is to be made the laughing stock of this whole tribe!" scowled Zed.

Jacob nodded and asked, "When will we race?"

"Right now, boy!"

"But I need a little time to warm up!" Jacob protested.

"Warm up? Boy, yer either ready or you ain't," Zed growled, running his hands over his dark beard. "And you better be ready. The way I sees it, boy, you better just run as fast as you can at first. Maybe fer awhile you can keep up, but when you fall behind, you remember you need to keep going no matter how tired you be. There is honor in finishing the race even if yer last."

Zed's obvious lack of confidence in Jacob was making him lose confidence in himself. Jacob looked around and spotted Lone Wolf standing by himself some distance away. Seeing him standing there gave Jacob an uneasy feeling. As Lone Wolf stood glaring at him, Jacob sensed that he was up to no good, and it only increased his nervousness.

Something his brother Isaiah had said suddenly came into his mind. "Jacob, my little brother," he had said, "sometimes you have to use the fierceness of the badger, and other times you need to be as sly as a fox. If you can combine both of these animal traits in your actions, you will always do well."

With that advice in mind, Jacob began to plan his strategy. These Indians might be fine runners, but maybe, just maybe, he had a chance.

"What are you smiling about, boy?" Zed asked. "Don't you believe me? I tell you, there ain't no city boy that can dust one of these braves!"

Jacob ignored him. The chief signaled for one of his braves to step forward. It was the one who had first come for Jacob. *So he is to be my opponent,* Jacob thought with humor. He didn't look that great. His physique was below average at best. He was thin and didn't even look like he was in the best of health.

As the chief stood in front of Jacob, he put forth his hand and gestured as he introduced his opponent. Then from behind the first brave, whom Jacob thought was his opponent, stepped forward a perfect specimen of an athlete. He looked to be about twenty years old, and from his build, Jacob knew he could run. His muscles were toned and he wore nothing but a breechcloth. He looked at Jacob with an air of superiority and arrogance.

"This is Running Bear," Zed announced.

Jacob gulped, the brave certainly looked like he could live up to his name. The athlete caught Jacob's eyes and glared. Jacob lowered his head, hoping to make his opponent think he was already defeated. The brave puffed out his chest and said something that made the others laugh. *That's okay*, Jacob thought. He wanted Running Bear to think he was superior.

Out of the corner of his right eye, Jacob saw Lone Wolf suddenly leave the gathering and head down into the far ravine that led up toward the mountain where they were to run their race. Jacob made a mental note to keep a watchful eye out for his new enemy. From the first time both he and Zed entered the Sioux camp, Lone Wolf had wanted him dead.

The chief spoke to Zed, pointing far to the west, parallel with the river. Zed translated for Jacob. "See that bluff away off there?" he said, pointing his finger toward the mountain. "There's a huge rock sitting right on the top of that point."

Jacob squinted. He could see ravines and a few low hills and then there was a gradual incline to the top. He thought he could see the rock. "Yeah, I can see it. Must be five or six miles up there," he said.

"That's it. You're to run there and back. Don't be surprised if you see an Indian waiting fer you because he will make sure you make it. You will run around the brave and back down the mountain. The first one back here wins. Do you understand?"

"Yes," Jacob said confidently, and without asking any further questions he began to run in a small circle.

Zed stared at him. So did the Indians. After a couple minutes of running, Jacob stopped and began to do squats, stretching his legs and loosening up his muscles to avoid cramping. After remembering what Isaiah said about being as sly as a fox, Jacob now had a plan and was beginning to work it. He kicked his feet high into the air and jumped around like a rabbit.

He noticed the tall maiden, her eyes wide as she stared at him. Jacob had the feeling she was a little embarrassed. He just grinned and winked at her, and kept up the antics of hopping around. He soon had the whole crowd laughing. The brave whom he was to race was doubled over laughing so hard that tears streamed down his face. Then he began to copy Jacob's antics.

Zed was not laughing when Jacob glanced at him. He rolled his eyes in disgust. Jacob, while still warming up dramatically, looked up the mountain for Lone Wolf. He could see him going into a copse of trees on the south side of the trail. He was just a speck in the distance. Jacob made a mental note of exactly where he felt Lone Wolf would be waiting. He knew Lone Wolf wouldn't bother him going up because Running Bear might seem him, but he could try to keep Jacob from completing the race coming back down. Common sense told him he would lose face with the tribe.

In a few minutes Jacob's muscles were loosened up. He felt good. His exercising in the early hours had paid off, and he was ready. As a final move, he leaped high into the air. When he came down, he groaned and grabbed at his right thigh. He limped around for a second. Zed hurried over to him. "What'd you do, boy, go and hurt yerself with all yer fooling around?"

"I think I pulled a muscle," Jacob lied with a straight face.

Zed cursed and turned to the chief. They conversed for a moment, and then Zed said to Jacob, "The chief says you can race tomorrow. He don't want you to run while yer hurt."

"No!" Jacob protested. "The race is today, and I intend to run it."

Zed scowled and spoke to the chief again. The chief nodded solemnly, but he smiled at Jacob. "He likes yer spirit, boy. I just hope you ain't hurt as badly as it looks."

"Tell him to start the race," Jacob said, anxious to get started.

The chief raised his arm. Jacob glanced at the beautiful maiden. She looked solemn and worried. Jacob smiled at her and again winked. But it didn't cheer her up.

The chief dropped his arm, and Jacob started limping dramatically toward the distance bluff. Running Bear was not beside him, so he looked back over his shoulder. The young brave was laughing and pointing at Jacob. Then he began mimicking Jacob's warm up exercises again. Everyone laughed.

Jacob limped away from the tribe and saw that Running Bear had not yet started, but was pointing at him and making fun by copying his antics. Then Jacob dropped down into a small gully unseen from the tribe and he grinned in satisfaction, grateful for the early lead he was getting through his deception.

As Jacob came out from the gully and entered a copse of trees, still unseen, he took one last look at Running Bear before dropping out of sight as he ran into a ravine that ran in the direction of the bluff. The young brave had finally started, but he was limping badly and turned back to the crowd, making the other Indians roar with laughter.

At bottom of the ravine, Jacob dropped his deception and began to run. His strides were long and strong. He began to feel a slight stress in his breathing, but after laboring a few minutes, he began to breathe deeply and felt new energy. He felt strong. He could run.

After a few minutes had passed, Jacob was getting curious as to where Running Bear was now. The ravine led to the base of one of the hills he had seen earlier. It was one of several that led constantly upward to the big bluff, which was the turning point of the race. After running for some time, Jacob saw an area ahead where he would have a good view of the trail below.

Jacob stopped at least halfway from the top of the bluff and saw Running Bear still taking his time a great distance away. Jacob grinned; since he was an experienced runner, he now wanted the young brave to run with his heart and not with his head. His goal was to get Running Bear mad so he would use up his energy.

Running Bear had not yet spotted Jacob, so Jacob climbed up on a large outcropping of rocks where there was a flat stone. He lay down and propped himself up on one elbow. He then put his two fingers to his lips and whistled as loudly as he could. His whistle carried down to Running Bear who looked up and saw Jacob lying on a rock in the distance and waving to him. That did it! He knew he had been had, and in a fury he came running up the mountain.

Jacob watched him for a second and then again whistled and waved at him again to further taunt him. Running Bear ran swiftly up toward the steep bluff. Jacob knew that as hard as Running Bear was running, it would soon tire him out on the upward climb that faced both of them. That would be to Jacob's advantage.

Now running toward the top, Jacob noticed the shadow of a man ahead of him to his left pulling back into the trees. It was Lone Wolf. Now Jacob knew where his enemy would be waiting for him. When Jacob first caught a glimpse of Lone Wolf up the mountain, he was just a small speck in the distance, now he knew exactly where he was.

Jacob lengthened his stride and was breathing hard by the time he reached the top of the huge rock. As Jacob rounded the large rock that marked the turnaround point, there was the Indian Zed told him about who he should run around.

The brave simply pointed back toward the camp, appearing more than a little surprised to see Jacob in the lead. Jacob grinned at him, waved, and started down the long slope. He didn't want to be seen by Running Bear after the trick he had pulled on him, so he swung a little wider to his right, keeping out of Running Bear's sight.

His strategy was to run easy the first two or three miles on his return because it was mostly downhill. As he looked over his shoulder, he saw Running Bear running up the hill, still about a half-mile back. His late start had him expending much needed energy.

As Jacob ran swiftly down the mountain, he caught a brief glimpse of Running Bear further down the trail on the other side running toward the top, but this time he was straining with all his might. Jacob was confident that he could win this race. His only concern now was Lone Wolf and what would happen if he met Jacob on his return. On sudden impulse, Jacob changed his route and veered further to his right. Jacob hoped that by taking a slightly different direction he could bypass him. He didn't think the Indian would dare kill him, but if Jacob got hurt, he could say Jacob stumbled and fell. It would be Jacob's word against the Indians.

A few miles down the mountain, Jacob neared the place where he had last seen Lone Wolf. He scanned the area, looking for signs and noticed a shadow deep in the woods off to his left. It was Lone Wolf and he was watching the trail where Jacob had passed earlier and was waiting for his return.

Just seeing him there made Jacob mad. The trail he now ran on was parallel to the one he had come upon, which was where Lone Wolf was now watching. Jacob began running faster and almost soundlessly, every step taking him closer to his enemy.

Lone Wolf was so engrossed in watching for Jacob that he had allowed himself to be careless.

When Jacob was almost there, he let out a bloodcurdling scream. Lone Wolf spun around, his eyes wide with fear. Jacob charged right at him, wanting to take advantage of both his speed and weight.

In a split second, he threw a wicked left punch without losing a stride. It landed perfectly right on Lone Wolf's chin, propelling the brave backward and out of sight. Isaiah would have been proud.

Jacob ran on, now following the original trail. He ran hard and steady. He was getting tired, but he had enough energy in his legs to finish, so he gave it all he had as he approached the crowd.

Glancing over his shoulder, he spotted Running Bear in the distance. The young brave was coming on hard, but he was still at least half a mile behind. Jacob raced toward Chief Two Clouds, who marked the finish line of the race. As he ran, he could see Zed jumping up and down like a crazy man. Jacob ran past the chief to win the race.

Jacob stopped right in front of the pretty Indian maiden. His chest was heaving and his legs suddenly began to shake. Jacob reached out to touch her arm when Zed suddenly spun him around. "There'll be plenty of time fer that later, boy," he said gleefully, as he slapped Jacob on the back. "You sure surprised me, boy! Yessirree, you sure did! We can come and go in peace now. You just won us the respect of this whole durn tribe, boy. You sure can run. Why, that brave was their finest runner. Nobuddy—and I mean nobuddy—never beat him before!"

All of Indians now were excitedly yelling and jumping up and down. Two Clouds walked up, reached over, and gripped Jacob's forearm tightly, smiling as he did. He said something to Zed and then turned to watch for Running Bear who sprinted up a few moments later. All eyes were on him as he ran into the crowd and stopped, gasping for air. He looked at Jacob, slowly approached, and stopped in front of him.

Zed stood beside Jacob and asked, "Is there anything you'd like me to tell Running Bear fer you?"

Jacob knew he had won only because of his deception. Oh, he could have made a fair race of it, but he felt he would have lost. He didn't want to make an enemy of Running Bear now that the race was over. He thought for a moment, gasping before he replied, "Tell him that he is the greatest runner I have ever met. And tell him that if he had not been so generous and given me a head start that I would certainly have lost."

Zed interpreted for Running Bear. The crowd, including the pretty maiden, listened carefully. The brave smiled and said something to Zed. Zed translated. "Running Bear says that not only are yer feet fast, but yer as cunning as a coyote." Then he added, with a puzzled look on his face, "And he says that if yer quiet enough to approach yer enemy from the rear and count coup without killing him, yer indeed a great warrior."

The crowd broke out in celebration because the contest was over, and they honored the runners. The young Indian maiden watched Jacob, smiling from a distance as the other members of the tribe congratulated him by slapping his back and pumping his arms.

A few minutes later, while walking back to their tepee, Zed was still chuckling. "Boy, you sure did make yerself famous with beating Running Bear. I sure am proud of you. Never thought you could do it."

Just then, Running Bear approached. He did not smile, but he looked at Jacob for a long moment. Jacob slowly reached out his hand in a gesture of peace. Running Bear forcefully grabbed his forearm, his face breaking into a big grin. Jacob knew he had made a friend, one that he could always count on.

Festivities were held that evening, and Jacob was the center of attention, yet he was quiet and subdued as the evening wore on. Running Bear sat next to him as they ate. He watched Jacob closely and appeared concerned. Finally, he said something to Zed.

Zed listened, and then turned to Jacob. "Running Bear wonders what ails you? He says yer acting like you don't feel good. He wonders if yer feeling badly because you tricked him like a fox."

"Yeah, I sure do," Jacob said.

Zed spoke to Running Bear and then said, "Boy, he says to tell you that the sign of a great warrior is one who can win a battle by strategy. He said you both planned well and fought well. Today you were like the fox!"

Jacob smiled and said, "Tell Running Bear it is the sign of true friendship when one can tell what his friend is thinking."

Zed interpreted Jacob's words, and the young brave laughed and nodded with approval. Slapping Jacob on the back, Zed said, "Boy, you sure know the right words when you needs them. You know you might just become one of them thar congressmen someday the way ya honey up yer words when you needs 'em."

As the sun went down, the squaws cleaned up the food, and a large fire was built in the center of the camp. Soon drums were heard and the Indians began to sing. It seemed really more like a chant to Jacob, but he felt peaceful. Jacob moved away from the fire as the braves began to dance around it in rhythm to the beating of the drums. Running Bear tapped him on the shoulder and motioned for him to dance. Jacob was embarrassed and shook his head with a grin.

Zed yelled above the beating of the drums and pointed to Jacob's left. There stood the beautiful maiden. She nodded her head toward Jacob, indicating that she approved of his winning. Zed yelled, "Her name is White Fawn. She wants you to dance."

Jacob mouthed her name, White Fawn. The name was as beautiful as she was, and it fit her perfectly. He nodded his head and stepped toward the fire. He joined the circle of dancing braves, feeling awkward but very much alive. Soon he was one of them, as he danced in rhythm to the drums.

Zed shouted at him, "Great job, boy! Jest don't get no crazy ideas. We have a long time to go befer we get back to San Francisco!"

Jacob no longer cared about San Francisco or his inheritance or anything else. All he could see was White Fawn. As he glanced toward her, he was startled to see the swollen and bruised face of Lone Wolf standing next to her. He scowled fiercely at Jacob. The look reminded him of the hatred he had seen on Graff's face. Jacob shivered. He had made new friends, but he had also gained another bitter enemy.

Chapter 13
White Man's Customs

Jacob was relieved the next morning when he learned that Lone Wolf was not White Fawn's father like Zed had led him to believe. "Lone Wolf is White Fawn's uncle. He's the father of the short, squat girl that hangs around with White Fawn," Zed explained. "I asked Running Bear last night," Zed continued. "Running Bear laughed when I asked him. He said, 'How could one so pretty be the daughter of the ugly one? No, she is the daughter of Two Clouds, the chief.'"

"I agree with Running Bear," Jacob said. "She is so . . . well . . . nice, I guess. And besides that Lone Wolf is just plain mean and ugly. I am glad she is nice . . . like her father, Chief Two Clouds." Jacob tried not to show the extent of his relief to Zed, but the crusty old mountain man was not an easy one to fool.

Zed smiled and said, "Yes, she is nice, and as you have noticed, she is very pretty, so be careful, boy. Even if she isn't the daughter of Lone Wolf, ya still need to watch yer step."

Jacob nodded and changed the subject. "I must work hard to learn the language of the Sioux."

"I agree, boy. And I know just the way to help you."

"You do?"

"Yep, sure enough. I'll just quit speaking English. Then you'll have to learn Sioux. After all, how can you expect to learn their language if all you do is speaking English?"

That set Jacob back a notch, as he tried to accept Zed's plan. "We could try that, I guess," he said.

They had now been living with the Sioux tribe for almost a month. Jacob considered he would learn the language and then in just under a year, they would return back to California and collect his inheritance.

Zed responded in Sioux, grinning broadly. From that moment on, Zed spoke only Sioux. The following days Jacob had to rely on sign language when he was around Running Bear or any of the other tribal members.

Two Clouds had taken a personal interest in Jacob since he had won the race. Seeing Jacob struggling with the language, Chief Two Clouds suggested to Zed that Jacob be taught by the tribe's medicine man known as One Who Walks Tall. Zed willingly agreed to this plan.

So for the next four months, Jacob spent most of his day with One Who Walks Tall. During that time, Jacob became adept at both the language of the Sioux and the sign language of the region.

After four months with One Who Walks Tall, Jacob had learned a lot about Sioux customs, but he was becoming restless. He had seen little of Running Bear and even less of White Fawn. He had not even been allowed to hunt. Chief Two Clouds had specified that Jacob was to be tutored every day. Then he spent the evenings with Zed, practicing the language.

One cool morning in the late fall, Jacob was sitting with One Who Walks Tall and wondering why the old medicine man was so silent. He was staring at Jacob with unblinking eyes. "Are you not pleased with my learning, One Who Walks Tall?" Jacob asked in the native tongue of the Sioux.

The wise old man slowly nodded his head and replied, "My son, you have proven that you have a keen mind. You have mastered the language in a short time and for that I am pleased. But I am even more pleased that you remember the stories I have told you and the lessons they teach. It has been four moons since our great chief commanded me to teach you our language and customs. Yes, I am very well pleased. You are an honorable white man."

"Thank you, One Who Walks Tall," Jacob said humbly.

The medicine man nodded again and said, "I wish only that all white men were as kind and fair to the Sioux as you are. You are talked about around our fires at night, my son."

"I had no idea," Jacob answered in surprise.

"Yes, we have noticed that you help our old women in their work. You shame us. It has been our ways that no man does the work of women, but then you say it is a sign of love in the white man's custom to lighten the load of others, especially the women. Some of our men now help their women."

Jacob had noticed that, but did not take credit. He listened as the medicine man continued, "The Great Spirit is pleased with you and will bless our people for teaching you and for the wisdom you give to us." He was silent for a moment, and then continued, "It has been many moons since you have been on a hunt. I can see it in your eyes. Is that not so?"

"It is true, One Who Walks Tall," Jacob said softly.

"Then you may hunt. You have seven suns in which to hunt and enjoy the forest. Go, my son, and be one with the land."

Jacob was both surprised and elated at the opportunity to get away from camp and do something different. He had to restrain himself to keep from bounding to his feet and hurrying away. Out of respect for the medicine man, he simply said, "I thank you. But before I go, is there something else you wish for me to know or do?"

One Who Walks Tall shook his head. "No, you may go now, my son."

Jacob rose slowly and left the tepee of the medicine man. He went in search of Running Bear and Zed. It was still early in the morning, but he soon discovered both already were on a hunt. Disappointed, Jacob decided to go by himself. Looking at the meadow, he saw Buck grazing with several of the Indian ponies. He started toward him, but stopped. He needed the exercise, so he decided he would walk. After retrieving his Tennessee long rifle from his tepee, he was recognized by a Sioux sentinel and was given the signal to continue into the forest. He left at a brisk trot, keeping a watchful eye on his surroundings. The forest stretched almost endlessly to the north with its vast mountains and valleys as far as the eye could see.

Having been mostly confined to a tepee for the past four months, Jacob thought how wonderful it was to be in the forest again, breathing in the clean mountain air. He thought of the stagnant air of Boston he had breathed on his early morning runs. The mountain air made him feel free and exhilarated. He laughed silently to himself and lengthened his stride. The mornings became cooler and there was a hint of fall in the air.

Before Jacob had gone too far, he spotted a lone figure slipping through the trees and underbrush. He had no idea who it was, but they were using the forest for cover just as he was. He had caught only a fleeting glimpse before the figure melted into the trees. It could be an enemy from another tribe or simply someone who did not want to be seen. Jacob expected the worst, and to be on the safe side, took greater care to blend into the cover of the shadowy forest. He moved silently toward the area where he had last sighted the lone figure.

With his rifle ready, Jacob waited. Several minutes passed without anyone coming into view. Then a soft voice came from behind him, saying, "If you keep trying, you will one day be as one of us, Jacob Morgan."

He spun around and there stood White Fawn. She continued, "An Indian maiden must have the ears of the deer and the eyes of the hawk."

"Your father taught you well," Jacob said with a big smile. She opened her mouth to speak, but before she could, he asked, "Where are the army of warriors that accompany you?"

The beautiful maiden's eyes sparkled with mischief. "Why would many braves be needed to protect me?" she asked. "I have no valuables that anyone would desire."

Jacob became very serious and said, "Because of your great beauty, White Fawn."

She dropped her eyes and turned away in embarrassment.

"White Fawn, did I offend you? Is it wrong to speak the truth?"

She turned back to Jacob and lifted her soft doe eyes to meet his. "I am aware of some of the white man's customs, but your words are sweet like the honey of the bee."

For a moment, he studied her eyes, fascinated by her beauty and innocence. Finally, he said, "My people have many customs that are different from yours. My words are meant to gladden the heart and soothe the mind."

"Your words, in the language of the Sioux, are soft to my ears," she said timidly.

"Thank you, White Fawn." He recalled the past four months of studying her language. Now he was grateful he had spent hours learning, studying, and practicing the language by repeating it to Zed.

Now he wanted to be the teacher, and he was looking at the most beautiful pupil he had ever encountered. Jacob softly said, "I was hoping that I could teach you some of the customs of my people so you might understand how the white man thinks and lives."

"I would like that," White Fawn eagerly responded, and then she shyly asked, "Does the white man take more than one squaw as is the custom of the Sioux?"

"No," Jacob replied with a chuckle. "We believe that one squaw is all that a man can handle. We choose a squaw for life."

Chapter Fourteen

Lone Wolf

Running Bear finally returned from his own hunting trip, and Jacob greeted him.

"My brother," Running Bear said with his familiar grin. "It's good to see that you are allowed to come among the living again. You study too much and grow weak and fat like an old woman."

It was true, Jacob had seen very little of Running Bear while undergoing his training. "It is good to be living," Jacob returned in good humor.

Running Bear said, "My brother, let us go and do something together."

"I'd like that," Jacob said. "One Who Walks Tall has given me seven suns to hunt and do as I wish."

"Then let us go and get our horses," he said. "We will ride until the sun drops over the hills."

As they walked toward the large herd of Indian ponies, Running Bear said, "Let us ride tomorrow, and let me show you how to use the war lance today."

A broad grin spread across Jacob's face. "So you want to teach me? Why would you want to do that?" Jacob asked suspiciously. He remembered that during the race with Running Bear, he was the one who was sly as a fox and he didn't know if it was now Running Bears turn. They walked beneath a grove of towering pines, and Running Bear stopped and looked at Jacob with a big grin. "My brother, I will teach you how to use a war lance, and then I will have a chance to beat you. I will not let the sly fox trick the fierceness of the badger."

"I will not trick you, Running Bear," Jacob promised. "I am here to learn and not to win."

Running Bear spent the next hour showing Jacob the stances he should use when using a lance and what moves to make when going against a warrior in battle. Running Bear explained, "You must always watch your opponent and be alert."

Jacob practiced his new skill with the war lance until Running Bear was satisfied that Jacob understood. Running Bear said, "Now let me show you how to use a knife." Running Bear reached down into his leggings and pulled out a knife. He then circled around Jacob in a half-crouched position, while switching the knife smoothly from one hand to the other.

From the corner of his eye, Jacob saw Lone Wolf and his three surly companions approaching. They were laughing and pointing at Jacob. They were the same Indians who had stood in front of Lone Wolf's teepee when Jacob first arrived in the Sioux camp. Jacob was positive Running Bear was aware of their presence, but he gave no sign of acknowledging them.

Jacob refocused on his lesson. Running Bear grabbed his lance and said. "I will show you how we throw a lance and how we use it in close battle." He held the lance with both hands, one at each end and stretched it out in front of him. "My brother," he said with a grin, "Try and take it from me."

Running Bear was standing in the cool sand along the riverbank, slowly moving in a circle and shifting his feet. Jacob approached him warily, alert for any trick his friend may play on him. Their eyes locked, but Jacob could see no sign of trickery in Running Bear's face.

Jacob slowly reached with both hands and grabbed the lance just inside of Running Bear's hands. The young brave swiftly jerked the lance in a backward, twisting motion, and Jacob lost his grip before it was firmly set and almost fell to his knees.

"My brother, you must trust no one," Running Bear said. "Once you get a firm hold, make sure you do not let loose."

Again he offered the lance to Jacob. By then, a dozen or more Indians had gathered to see the fun. They were grinning, obviously expecting Running Bear to do something to Jacob to repay him for winning the race so many weeks ago.

As the sun reflected off the river Jacob began to sweat so he removed his leather shirt. He slowly moved in a circle, facing Running Bear, who held the lance. Jacob placed his hands in front of him while he watched the lance with a steady gaze. Then, without warning, his hands shot out with lightening speed, and he tore the lance from Running Bear's hands.

The young brave stared at him with a gaping mouth and said, "My brother, you are very quick with your hands."

Jacob grinned and responded, mocking in a deep guttural sound, "My brother, you must trust no one."

Running Bear began to laugh, and several of those that had come to watch joined in. After a moment, Running Bear's face grew serious again, and he asked, "Must you always win?"

Jacob smiled and shrugged his shoulders and said, "No, but now you and I are even. That is one for you and one for me."

Before Running Bear could respond, a harsh voice from behind Jacob called out, "White Dog, catch this!"

Jacob turned just as a lance came flying at him sideways. He snatched it from the air and glared at Lone Wolf, who said in a taunting voice, "Is it the white man's custom to play games only with one brother and not with his other brothers?"

Running Bear stepped past Jacob and said in a sneering voice, "Since when are you a brother to Jacob Morgan? This is our time. You were not invited. Your kind of play causes hate and perhaps even death."

Jacob spoke up, "Running Bear, I am not afraid of Lone Wolf, and I would not be ashamed if he beat me. Maybe it is best that he and I get this over with right now."

"Jacob, you don't have—" Running Bear began.

"It is all right, my brother," Jacob said softly. Then he faced Lone Wolf. Looking around him, Jacob could see there was a large crowd gathered. "Come, Lone Wolf, now you will be my teacher."

Jacob threw the lance at Lone Wolf and he caught it. Lone Wolf held the spear in front of him with both hands as Running Bear had done and approached Jacob in the soft sand. Jacob grabbed the spear firmly, and without warning, he jerked it violently toward himself. Lone Wolf fell forward onto his knees, but he held onto the lance. Jacob held it tightly to keep Lone Wolf from plunging face first into the sand. Then he pulled slowly up, helping his enemy to his feet.

"Lone Wolf," Jacob said, "Running Bear told me to trust no one. His advice is good, and I especially do not trust you."

With that remark, Lone Wolf let out a bloodcurdling scream and pulled the lance toward him, lifting his right foot at he did so. The foot caught Jacob in the stomach. The next thing Jacob knew, he was flying over Lone Wolf's head.

Both men were now on their backs and they quickly rolled over and stood up. Lone Wolf still held the lance in his hands. Jacob reached forward and quickly placed his hands on the lance and repeated Lone Wolf's own move by planting his feet on Lone Wolf's stomach, propelling the warrior over his head. The movement caused Lone Wolf to come down hard on his back, and Jacob quickly jerked the lance away and bounded to his feet.

Slowly getting to his feet, Lone Wolf now with deep anger in his voice said, "So you think you can make a fool of me, do you? I will have your heart!"

He motioned to one of his sullen friends. The brave pulled a knife and threw it to Lone Wolf, who began circling Jacob, as Running Bear had demonstrated. He crouched low and deftly shifted the knife from hand to hand.

Running Bear jumped between Lone Wolf and Jacob, shouting, "Enough, Lone Wolf!"

Lone Wolf continued to crouch, but he shifted his glare to Running Bear. "If you try to interfere, I will also have your heart!"

"Running Bear!" Jacob yelled.

The young warrior stepped beside Jacob, never taking his eyes off the face of Lone Wolf. Jacob whispered, "This has gone too far, my brother. He was beaten at his own game. He will never be able to save face now, unless he fights me."

"No, Jacob, he—" Running Bear began.

"Running Bear," Jacob interrupted firmly, "Let me handle this my way."

"Are you sure?"

"I am sure."

Running Bear stepped back, and Jacob said, "Lone Wolf, are you such a mighty warrior that you need a knife to fight me, while I only have my bare hands? You are older and wiser than me, and it would not be a fair match this way."

The crowd laughed, siding with Jacob.

Lone Wolf said, "You are afraid?"

Jacob looked directly into Lone Wolf's eyes and said, "I am not afraid. Let me choose the weapons, and we will fight until one is down and can fight no more. Let us fight with our hands."

Pleasure washed over Lone Wolf, and he grinned. The warrior nodded his head in agreement and tossed his knife back to his friend. "Let it be with the hands," he agreed.

Running Bear walked over to Jacob and whispered, "My brother, be careful. He is very powerful. He will try to break your legs or arms before he puts you down." Jacob nodded in understanding.

Jacob shivered, but there was no turning back. He was committed. He knew he was no match for Lone Wolf if he wrestled Indian style. Lone Wolf may be strong, but he did not know of Jacob's skill with English boxing.

A large crowd had now gathered and more were running from the village. In a few moments, the crowd had formed a large circle around the two adversaries. Jacob felt like he was in an arena in Rome, and it was the lions versus the Christians.

Crouching low like a cat stalking its prey, Lone Wolf closed in on Jacob. Jacob's feet began to move, dancing smoothly and rapidly. His hands were held out in front of him, his elbows bent in the traditional English boxing pose.

Instead of charging in and wrestling like most Indians did, Jacob warily circled Lone Wolf twice trying to find the best way to fight him before the surly brave asked, "What is this, White Dog? Do you think you can trick me like you did Running Bear?"

Without reply, Jacob suddenly danced forward and threw a blinding punch, striking Lone Wolf squarely on his squat nose. Lone Wolf's head snapped back like a branch in the wind. Before Lone Wolf could recover from the sudden punch, Jacob threw a flurry of blows to his midsection. Lone Wolf let out a gasp of air and leaned forward to catch his breath. Jacob then threw a powerful uppercut with his right hand that caught Lone Wolf directly on the chin. The burly warrior flew backward landing in the sand on his back.

Taking advantage of the situation, Jacob stood over Lone Wolf and took several deep breaths. The warrior did not move, so Jacob stepped back, wondering if he had really won so easily.

Lone Wolf suddenly sprang to his feet like a raging bear. He dove for Jacob, trying to ram his head into his stomach. Jacob deftly stepped aside, and as Lone Wolf passed by, Jacob caught him with a striking blow to the side of his head that sent the warrior sprawling.

More enraged than ever, Lone Wolf regained his footing and again circled, watching Jacob's slowly moving fists. Suddenly, Lone Wolf leaned over, grabbed a handful of dirt, and flung it into Jacob's face. Jacob saw Lone Wolf grab the sand and he closed his eyes to keep the sand from blinding him. With his eyes closed, Jacob reached up with to wipe away the sand.

Taking advantage of Jacob's momentary blindness, Lone Wolf grabbed a large stone and threw it, striking Jacob in the stomach. As Jacob fell forward to the ground Lone Wolf jumped on him, screaming and striking Jacob's head with violent blows.

Jacob fought to keep his senses and managed to roll over on his back. He pushed Lone Wolf away and kicked the warrior with his feet, sending him sprawling. Jacob wiped the sand from his eyes in time to see Lone Wolf's foot coming down in an attempt to break his leg. Jacob eluded the blow by rolling away and coming to his feet in one swift movement. As Lone Wolf lunged, Jacob moved to the side, and his right fist caught Lone Wolf on his left temple.

Lone Wolf quickly spun toward Jacob to meet him head on. Jacob stepped in with a hard blow to the stomach, and then kicked Lone Wolf's feet out from under him. While going down, Lone Wolf managed to grab Jacob's arm and pull him down as he fell. Jacob landed on top of Lone Wolf and he reached for Jacob's head, trying to gouge his eyes. Realizing this, Jacob kicked, and pounded with his one free hand and managed to push Lone Wolf away. In one fluid move, Jacob stood up and regained his fighting stance.

As Jacob circled, Long Wolf bounded to his feet and faced him, slowly crouching and looking for an opening. The burly Indian had met someone who did not fight like him, and now realized he had to do something to save face. Jacob knew that Lone Wolf would rather die than to be beaten by a "white dog."

Jacob motioned with his right hand for Lone Wolf to come closer. He would rather be on the defensive rather than the offensive. He had the advantage and wanted to get in a few more punches before Lone Wolf figured out a way to defend himself against the quick, short jabs of English boxing. Lone Wolf advanced slowly, but Jacob darted in quickly and threw a hard right to Lone Wolf's stomach. He followed swiftly with a left fist to Lone Wolf's already mangled face.

The warrior reached up to wipe away the blood on his lip and, seeing the amount of blood on his hand, looked up in disbelief. Jacob moved in and threw his hardest punch of the fight. There was a crunch as Lone Wolf's squat nose flattened under the force of the blow. Blood flowed down his face, and he grabbed for his nose and staggered back. Jacob followed, hitting him in the stomach with his left fist and then with his right and again with his left in rapid succession.

Then, like a whip, Jacob's right fist connected with Lone Wolf's chin, snapping his head backward. Lone Wolf staggered a step, but Jacob moved with him. Lone Wolf screamed in rage, and shouted obscenities. In frustration his hands groped blindly for any body part to grab onto, but Jacob's lightning moves avoided Lone Wolf's violent thrusts. Jacob hit him three more times, a left, a right, and then another left. Then he pivoted to the left and threw one powerful punch with his right fist to the left side of Lone Wolf's jaw.

Lone Wolf staggered like a wounded buffalo, trying to keep his knees from buckling. His hands flailed at his sides as he fought for balance. There was deathly silence. Every eye was on Lone Wolf as he fought to keep from falling. Jacob actually felt sorry for his enemy, but he knew he did not start this war. Lone Wolf was the one who had brought this fight about, and Jacob knew he should close in once more and put him down and out, that had been the rule.

Jacob had been lucky. He had fought smart, but as he watched Lone Wolf struggling, he could not bring himself to hit him again. He knew Lone Wolf would not answer him so he turned to Running Bear and said, breathlessly, "Ask Lone Wolf if he has had enough."

Running Bear stepped over to the staggering brave and spoke to him. Lone Wolf screamed and shouted more obscenities. He ignored Running Bear and shouted, "White Dog, I would rather die than surrender to you!"

Jacob shook his head sadly. "You are beaten, Lone Wolf. I do not wish to hurt you anymore. This was a game, not a coup of one's enemy." Jacob turned and walked away as the sinking sun slowly cast dark shadows on his tired face.

Lone Wolf continued to shout and scream, and everyone in the crowd except for Lone Wolf's three friends followed Jacob. To Running Bear, he said, "Lone Wolf and I could have been friends if he hadn't hated Zed and I so much when we first came, but he would not have it."

Zed, who had been in the circle of spectators, shouldered his way through the Indians to Jacob's side. "You fought well, but you now have a very dangerous enemy in Lone Wolf. Like Graff, both of these men are evil and no matter what you do to become friends with them, neither of them will rest until you are dead. Boy, you must be on the lookout fer trouble, and watch yer back at all times."

"I will be careful," Jacob said. And at that moment, he made up his mind that he would learn any and all types of self-defense. He must excel in all styles of fighting if he were to live in this rough western frontier where fate and his Uncle Zac had brought him.

Chapter 15
A Buffalo Ride

A cold wind blew as Zed and Jacob exited their tepee. Jacob took a deep breath and said to Zed, "I like the smell of the winds off those peaks. It reminds me of a new birth from one season into the next."

Zed rolled his eyes and said, "All I need now is fer some city boy to use big words and talk about something that just means winter will soon be here." Then sniffing the air, Zed said, "The Indians think we will have an early winter, and I believe them. It feels like it's coming soon."

Every area of Jacob's body ached from the fight with Lone Wolf the day before. He rubbed his aching legs and sore bottom, trying to take some of the pain away.

He looked up at the snow-covered peaks in the distance. It was late fall in the month of October and winter was approaching. The trees and shrubs on the hills had changed to deep red and gold, as if painted on a beautiful canvas.

Each day was growing colder and brought increasing puddles of ice. The frost lay like a thin, white veil over the grass.

One Who Walks Tall had given Jacob seven suns off for hunting and gathering with his friends. It was now the third sun.

Jacob needed this time off to replenish the much needed food supply that would be used during the winter. Above him a flock of geese flew, calling loudly to the earthbound creatures as they started their migration south.

On this cool autumn morning, the women of the tribe were bustling before dawn. The men left in the early morning hours on another hunt for buffalo. The squaws spent the days drying the meat from previous hunts in preparation for the cold nights and shorter days. Starvation was a real threat in this region, and if one didn't work to provide for his family, they would all perish. Women were constantly foraging for onions, berries, and roots used for food and medicine. They would then preserve them for the winter to supplement their diet.

Running Bear was not married, and he, like Zed and Jacob, had no one to provide for except himself. The three men had previously decided to share their large catches of meat with the less fortunate and other members of the tribe. By doing so, they would receive food for themselves in the winter from those they had helped.

It was the custom of the Sioux to weed out the older generation. When an older squaw's husband died, she was left to her own plight. Unless she had children, she had no one to care for her, and she would eventually starve or freeze to death in the ensuing winter months. Seeing the plight of some of these unfortunate widows, Zed and Jacob became mindful of their needs. The traditions of the tribe were not the teachings Zed and Jacob had received during their younger years. They had been taught to provide food for the destitute, and if they could, they would prolong the life of a grandmother who had given so many of her past years in service to her family.

In the early morning, Jacob, Zed, and Running Bear left the village and traveled south of the river to hunt game. They brought two mules for packing the meat they would kill. A few hours later, Zed cut buffalo tracks. There were a dozen or more in a small herd moving south, and the three men began to feel the excitement of a hunt.

Jacob had never killed a buffalo, and he was excited to do so. The tracks led them through a marshy meadow next to the river and up a gentle slope. Silently crawling to the top of the rise, the three spotted a dozen of the creatures that had sustained the Indians for generations.

Returning to their horses, the men mounted and slowly circled the herd, keeping a good distance away so the buffalo wouldn't catch their scent. Then one old bull raised his head and stamped his feet. It was clear that he had smelled the hunters approaching.

At the bull's signal, the herd thundered off, splitting into two groups. Running Bear followed one group at a hard, thundering run over a small hill. One cow from the other group ran alongside the river and Jacob cut her off. She swerved to her right and jumped into the surging water, attempting to cross. Jacob raced to the river's edge and plunged Buck into the water alongside of the thundering beast and Jacob leaped on the cow's back. Aware of the unwanted burden, the cow swam toward shore, bellowing with fear. Jacob retrieved his long Bowie knife, and leaning to his left, quickly thrust his blade deep behind the front left shoulder. Jacob repeated the action another two times. As the buffalo reached the shore and ascended up the small hill, it struggled for breath and collapsed.

About that time, Zed's horse came charging out of the water with the two mules in tow. His face was red with anger, and he shouted as he dismounted, "Why did you do such a fool thing as that, boy?"

Indians would never jump on a buffalo; it was a good way to get killed. Since the beast was in the water Jacob knew there really was no danger. All the animal could do is swim to shore.

Jacob grinned sheepishly and replied, "I wanted clean meat, and I don't have powder to waste."

The anger drained from Zed's face as he smiled and realized that Jacob had it under control all the time. He said, "Well, you was needing a bath fer sure."

Jacob whistled for Buck. The big stallion lifted his proud head high and with his reins dragging, leaped into the water and swam across. As soon as he reached the shore, Jacob patted his neck and then focused his attention on the buffalo.

Turning the big cow onto her stomach, the men pulled the legs out to each side, preparing to skin her. Jacob smiled. It reminded him of a stuffed pig without the apple, and he chuckled as he pulled out his knife. He tested the knife's edge for cutting and said, "It's sharp as a mad squaw's tongue," he said to Zed, as the blade glistened in the early morning sun.

"Well, then use it boy," Zed said.

Jacob grinned. He was happier that he had ever been in his life.

Standing over the cow, Jacob smiled and looked at Zed. "Well," he said, "I've had the best teacher in these hills, so here goes."

Zed rolled his eyes. "We can do without yer sweet talk, boy. Just get going with that mad squaw you have in yer hand, or we may have problems. In case you ain't noticed, the wolves are already here waiting fer their share."

Jacob looked up in surprise. There hiding behind a group of small shrubs were five wolves eagerly waiting for their portion of the kill.

"They got a sixth sense, boy," Zed said. "They know when a buffalo's about to git killed, I swear. They'll hang real close and wait fer whatever we don't pack off on our horses."

Zed was right. And in addition to the wolves, a flock of noisy magpies chattered from the scrub oaks nearby, eagerly awaiting their turn at the buffalo. Soon a half dozen buzzards appeared, circling in the clear blue sky overhead.

Running Bear had followed the other herd of buffalo after a cow and calf and hadn't returned, so Jacob and Zed assumed he had been successful. As they both gutted and cleaned the cow, they paused several times to throw some of the entrails toward the waiting wolves. The wolves gulped the offerings down in less time than it took Zed and Jacob to toss it.

"There won't be nothin' left here in a few hours but shiny white bones." Zed said. "Ain't nothin' wasted in this country. Now let's see what you remember, boy. Skin the old gal."

Using his knife, Jacob sliced across the wide part of the buffalo's neck toward the back of its head. With his left hand, he grabbed the heavy hair of its neck, cutting the skin away from the neck first and then the shoulders. From there he cut the hide from the mid-back to the tail. Zed helped him peel the hide down on the sides.

"This is harder than a deer," Jacob said as the sweat poured down his face. He was thinking about when Zed had taught him how to remove a deer hide. If they had a horse available, they would tie the deer to a tree by its neck. Next they would cut the hide free around the neck and pull it down a ways over the shoulders. Then taking a rope, they would tie it to the end of the hide, wrap the rope around the saddle horn, and let the horse pull the hide off in a matter of seconds.

The large buffalo was more difficult, but Jacob finally completed the task at hand. Both men began to cut large chunks of meat from the bone and packed it on the mules wrapped in the hide.

Zed remarked, "Since we don't have wives, we have to do this ourselves." Jacob reminisced about when White Fawn had helped him clean a deer earlier that week. He would have enjoyed having her with him now.

As if reading his mind, Zed said, "Boy, don't you get any of those yearnings. Remember you still have to go back to San Francisco to get yer inheritance. And then I can go to my ranch and retire."

Then looking around at the wolves eagerly waiting for what they left, Zed said, "We got most of the meat loaded, so you gather up the tongue, liver, and as much of the fat as you can, and we'll be gone."

They had no sooner led their mules and horses away than the wolves, buzzards, and magpies rushed in and began to clean up what was left behind.

A while later, they joined Running Bear, who had killed a large calf. His heavy-laden horse was carrying the meat. Together they returned to the village bearing gifts of meat that would be much needed for the winter. Running Bear laughed as Zed told him how Jacob had killed the cow. "You are a brave hunter, my brother," Running Bear said with a chuckle, and then he gave a long and hearty laugh.

"Foolhardy and crazy is more like it," Zed added. However, he could not hide the twinkle in his eyes as he repeated what Jacob had said, "Wanted to get clean meat," and he chuckled.

Chapter 16
Food for Thought

On the fourth evening of the seven suns Jacob had been given off, Jacob prepared to go to the lodge of Chief Two Clouds, the father of White Fawn, for an evening meal. Chief Two Clouds was a tall, well-built Indian of about fifty. Besides White Fawn, he also had one son and two other daughters, but all were married and had their own tepees. Jacob had met the daughters before, but none of them could compare to White Fawn. She was the youngest and still lived with her parents, Two Clouds and Dancing Light.

Jacob combed his hair and fussed with his thin growth of beard. He did not like the beard. He longed to cut it off because it itched fiercely. He envied the Indian men who did not have to worry about beards. They had it made, in his opinion, while he had to contend with his fuzzy face.

Zed entered the tepee just before he was ready to leave. "I hate this beard," Jacob said in frustration.

Zed just stroked his own, which was much thicker and a lot longer than Jacob's. "Don't curse what the good Lord gave you, boy," he said sternly in English. It was the first time Zed had spoken English to Jacob in over four months and Jacob wondered what was coming. He soon found out, for Zed added, a little testily, "So, yer seeing White Fawn tonight?"

"Sort of," Jacob answered with a foolish grin. "Two Clouds invited me for a meal is all. I suppose White Fawn will be there."

"Boy," Zed said, with a growl that would have frightened a bear, "if you ain't careful, yer gonna be in a fix you can't get out of."

"What do you mean, Zed?" Jacob asked in surprise.

"If you don't know what's going on here, boy, you better open up them there big blue eyes of yers and pay attention. The ole chief, he's checking you over to see if yer good enough fer his daughter. This is no game, boy. White Fawn is marrying age, and Chief Two Clouds is looking at you as a potential husband. There are plenty of braves in this village that would give all their ponies fer her, that is if she wanted them, but from what I can see she only has eyes for you. You have proven yerself a formidable warrior, and White Fawn does like the color of yer skin."

"Ah, go away!" Jacob said embarrassed. "Sure I like her, but I ain't thinking about marrying her—least not yet."

"Listen, boy, and you listen good now," Zed groaned. "Yer like a son to me, and I gotta take care of you like I promised yer Uncle Zac. We have at least another two years before we head back to see ole Weatherbee. Then you can claim yer inheritance, and I can retire to my ranch. Yer my responsibility now and what you do is my problem."

Jacob bit his tongue, angry words in his head just waiting to be spewed out. Zed went on. "You gotta sit this thing out fer a few years, boy. At least 'til yer two years is over with. Then I suppose you can do whatever you want."

Jacobs's patience would stand for no more. "That's two more years!" he thundered. "By then I'll be an old man like you!"

Zed rolled his eyes until all Jacob could see was the white. Then he looked directly at Jacob with a look that would strike fear into a grizzly's heart and said, "She's an Indian, boy! I gotta get you back to some place where you can see some white women. You're fergettin' what they looks like."

After Zed's fiery speech, Jacob said, "I'm a mountain man, and I don't want a white woman because none of them could live the way I would. Only an Indian woman would," he finished.

"I suppose yer right," he said wearily. "If you want to be a mountain man, that's up to you. But remember, boy, you gave yer word to Mr. Weatherbee. You also shook hands that you would follow through on yer uncle's wishes to the very end."

Leaning toward the crusty old mountain man, Jacob said, "You didn't really mean that, did you? I know you didn't."

Zed leaned forward, until their noses were almost touching. Jacob about choked on the rank odor from his breath. "Absolutely, boy," Zed said quietly.

"Aaaah! How low can a man get?" Jacob said. "Why, yer stooping so low you'll have to reach up to touch the underside of a buffalo chip!"

Zed took a deep breath of the heated air in the lodge and cleaned his teeth with his tongue. Then letting the air slowly out, he said, "Boy, you just go tonight, and when Two Clouds talks to you about yer future plans, you just tell the chief that you have a couple more years to learn to be a man. If you don't have the nerve in yer city boy frame to tell him that you will be gone in two springs, then at least tell the girl. You owe her the truth."

"But, how—"

"Just listen, boy. If you have any real feelings for that girl and her fer you, then, you can still have her sometime in the future."

"But—"

Zed interrupted again, "I remember back when I was a strutting bull myself, boy. I had me a woman."

"You did?" Jacob asked.

"Course I did! I was in love with her, and she was in love with me. She was the finest filly a man ever laid eyes on. Well, she wanted to marry me awful bad, she did. And her ma and pa, they liked me, awful good."

"So what did you do?" Jacob asked.

"Well, I asked her to wait fer me," Zed said, stroking his beard with a faraway look in his eyes.

"Why did you do that?"

"I can't rightly remember now. But I was real stupid and I gave her some darn excuse. I kick myself everyday fer not marring her. But I can still see her face in my mind, boy. She was a beauty."

"Did she wait for you?" Jacob asked anxiously.

"I don't rightly know," he said softly. "I was in the mountains with yer Uncle Zac and never had the chance to go back and find out. Jacob looked over at Zed and realized that Zed had loved and lost. And Jacob wanted to find out where his relationship was going. He had to go back and collect his inheritance but he also realized it was no place to take White Fawn. Jacob had some decisions to make.

Jacob walked out of the tepee and he heard Zed's voice ringing out after him: "You just wait 'til he starts asking you about yer intentions, boy. He'll roast you like a chunk of buffalo meat!"

Jacob walked on in the dusk. The sun was sinking, preparing to light up some distant land, while a cool breeze blew across the river and chilled his face and hands. It smelled of water, pines, and autumn.

Jacob paused to collect his thoughts before entering the large tepee of Chief Two Clouds. As he entered, he saw the chief sitting along the edge with a stoic look on his dark, weathered face. He reminded Jacob of a wooden Indian he used to admire outside a mercantile store in Boston when he was a young boy.

Chief Two Clouds greeted Jacob and invited him to sit across the fire from him. Dancing Light, his wife, sat behind him with White Fawn at her side. As soon as Jacob saw White Fawn, he noticed her eyes lifting shyly to meet his. Then, like a whisper in his ear, he could hear Zed's words again, *Tell her you'll be gone in two springs.*

"Jacob Morgan, are you listening to me?" Two Clouds asked, and Jacob realized he had not heard a word White Fawn's father had said.

"Oh . . . ah . . . please excuse my bad manners. I had other things on my mind."

Dancing Light seemed to take that as a hint of some sort, and she looked at White Fawn whose eyes met Jacob's. Jacob quickly tore his eyes away from her and concentrated on Two Clouds, who glanced back at his daughter and then motioned for her and his wife to bring the food.

The two women scurried out and were soon back with a tantalizing meal. They had prepared a pot of stew from buffalo meat. A separate pot contained an array of vegetables, consisting mainly of mushrooms, wild onions, watercress, and several bulbs that Jacob could not identify. The food was served in gourds and was delicious. Jacob savored every morsel and even had seconds. When the men had eaten their fill of the meat and vegetables, the women served dried wild berries with honey drizzled over the top.

Jacob enjoyed the meal, and as he sat back and rubbed his stomach, he could again hear Zed's words. "Boy, the way a woman reaches a man's heart is through his stomach." That was not so far-fetched, Jacob concluded.

After sitting a few minutes in the silence, Jacob cleared his throat and said, "In my custom it is very important to thank those who prepared the food. The food was excellent. This is the best meal I have eaten in many moons."

White Fawn's mother beamed. "My daughter went out and gathered the vegetables and prepared the berries herself. She hoped it would please you, Jacob Morgan. Are you pleased?"

Jacob glanced at White Fawn who quickly lowered her eyes. "Yes, I am most pleased. I will savor this meal for many suns," he said.

Two Clouds stirred. Jacob looked nervously at him. The proud Indian Chief said, "Did you enjoy the buffalo hunt? The stew was made from the meat of the cow you killed with your knife. We thank you for your generous portions given not only to us but also to many others of our tribe. Are all white men as kind and generous as you are, Jacob Morgan?"

Jacob blushed and didn't know what to say to Chief Two Clouds. "I know that there are many white men who are concerned only for themselves. I have been taught by good parents to give and to share with those around me and to those who are less fortunate."

Two Clouds answered, "I have known some white men, and many are as you say. They only think of themselves and what we can give to them. I thank your parents for teaching you good things. The Great Spirit is well pleased with you, Jacob Morgan."

"I owe my thanks to the whole tribe," Jacob said quickly. "They all have taught me much. One Who Walks Tall has been especially patient with me as he has taught me the ways of your ancestors and of your tongue."

"You have learned our tongue well, Jacob Morgan," Two Clouds said. He looked deeply into Jacob's eyes. Jacob squirmed under the intense scrutiny of the chief. Two Clouds asked, "What is your purpose in learning of our people? Do you wish to become one of us?"

Zed's words came back to Jacob like a thunderclap, ringing in his ears and jolting his mind. Jacob chose his words carefully. "I desire to know the ways of your people, and I am listening for the prompting of the Great Spirit to tell me what he wants me to do." Jacob was referring to God, but since Chief Two Clouds didn't know about God, Jacob continued using words that Two Clouds would understand.

Jacob continued, "I know the ways of my people. There are ways of the white man I like but others ways I do not like."

"What are some of the things that you do not like of the white man?" Two Clouds asked.

"Well . . . white men take things too much for granted. If you give them a little space of the earth, they think they should have the whole valley," Jacob said. He watched Two Cloud's face for any reaction as he spoke, but his face was impassive. Jacob continued, "Many white men are not content with just one buffalo. They want to kill the whole herd for the hides to sell for profit and do not use the meat. They are greedy and wasteful."

Finally, Chief Two Clouds nodded in agreement. Then he asked, "What ways do you like of my people?"

Jacob had the uneasy feeling that Two Clouds was searching for more than he wanted to reveal. However, he answered truthfully, carefully weighing each of his words, "What I admire most is the respect your people have for your leaders. When the chief speaks the final word, there is unity. Some may not like it, but they will abide by his decision. Also, a child is the child of the whole tribe. Each family helps in raising the children of other families. In this, there seems to be unity and respect for each other."

The chief frowned at what Jacob had first said. "It is not always as it seems, Jacob Morgan. We have our problems also. Lone Wolf is the husband of the sister of my squaw, and he is one of those problems. You must be aware of him at all times."

Jacob solemnly nodded he head in understanding, and the discussion turned to other things. After about two hours, Jacob prepared to leave. He thanked them for their hospitality and kindness and stood up. The family seemed touched by what he said, and Two Clouds got up and grasped Jacob's forearm. He said, "Jacob Morgan, you are always welcome in my tepee."

Jacob felt as though the chief wanted to say more, but Two Clouds released his grip on his arm, and Jacob turned and stepped out into the cool night. He had enjoyed himself, but he was pleased that Two Clouds did not do as Zed predicted. A peace came over Jacob, and he felt that things would eventually work out for him, but he didn't know exactly when.

Jacob walked slowly toward his tepee. The stars were dim because of the brightness of the moon that had topped the mountains to the east, casting its brightness throughout the valley. Casting his eyes around, Jacob saw Indians gathered around their campfires with their families and friends. The village was at peace.

Jacob decided he was not ready to retire for the evening, so he wandered toward the meadow where he had left Buck earlier. He whistled when he approached the large herd of horses. In a large mass of at least three hundred horses, Buck nickered and trotted briskly, shoving his way through the Indian ponies toward Jacob.

When the stallion reached Jacob, he gently put his head over Jacob's shoulder. Jacob rubbed Buck's neck and scratched his ears. He spoke softly to the big buckskin. After a moment, Jacob sat down with his back against a lone pine and Buck hung his head down and nuzzled Jacob's shoulder.

Reaching up and scratching the stallion's ears, Jacob said, "Buck, ole boy, a man sure has to make some tough decisions in this life. Why can't a man just do something for the pure enjoyment of doing it instead of having to please everyone else."

Suddenly Buck snorted and raised his head. A shadow moved some distance away, and Jacob reached for his knife, fearing it was Lone Wolf sneaking up on him. He was relieved when he heard a soft voice calling him. It was the voice of White Fawn.

Sheepishly, he returned his knife to its sheath and stood up. Then he spotted her and walked to meet her. When they were just few feet apart, she suddenly rushed forward and threw her arms around him, kissing him soundly on his lips. He eagerly responded to her warm embrace, not wanting to spoil the magic of the moment. When she finally pulled back, she said, "Jacob Morgan, I do like your customs, and I will only use this custom with you."

He took her soft brown hands in his and replied, "White Fawn, I like sharing my customs with you and only with you, but we need to talk."

She stood like an innocent child in the soft light of the moon. Jacob let go of her hand and dropped his hands to his side. "What do you want to talk about?" she asked apprehensively.

"You might not like it," he warned, not wanting to say what he was about to say. He felt her body tense.

"I like whatever you say," she responded stiffly.

"I must go away in two springs, because I gave my word. When a warrior gives his word, it is sacred. I have two springs to live here, and then I must go to make changes in my life."

She interrupted, "Jacob Morgan, I understand. You are wise and you will make decisions that will be right for you. I can't make your choices. You must make your own. You are the warrior, and it is your life."

Jacob quickly inhaled his breath and realized that was the answer. It was not Zed's decision, but it was his decision. His Uncle Zac had an Indian wife and he loved her. It was his decision then just like it was Jacob's decision now.

White Fawn lifted a small hand over her heart and said, "I have strong feelings here for you, Jacob Morgan. I have never felt this way for any of my people, not for anyone but you. And you are white."

"Yes, I'm white," said Jacob. "But what is color? I feel it, too, White Fawn. If what we feel it is right, then no matter what happens, it will work out for the best. If we are for each other, then no power—Indian or white—can stop us." Jacob fought to keep his voice from breaking.

White Fawn reached up and put her arms around his neck. Jacob drew her close and kissed her gently for a long, lingering moment. He felt her heart pounding madly and he released her, longing for more. She whispered, "Jacob Morgan, your words are from one who is wise."

Jacob could almost hear Zed's throaty chuckle at that remark.

"You are beautiful, White Fawn. Will you wait while I make plans for our future?"

"I will wait, Jacob Morgan. There is no room in here," she said, pulling away and touching her heart again, "for anyone else."

She leaned forward and gently placed her lips on his. Then suddenly she fled into the darkness of the night, while Jacob was left to ponder his future.

Jacob thought of the times he and his family had surrounded their family table after meals and talked about religion. Professor Morgan had read the Bible to the family each night for years. Jacob had a belief in God, but had not considered its necessity. He always felt his own strength was sufficient. He relied on his own wisdom and judgment.

Jacob was now in a dilemma with no answer and had no one to turn to and suddenly he fell a need to pray.

Glancing around in the moonlit forest, Jacob found a secluded spot where he would be hidden. Finding himself alone, he sunk to his knees and pondered what he needed to say in his prayer. His father had always mentioned to the family that God would always hear their prayers. And Jacob believed him.

Jacob had never prayed out loud before, let alone on his knees, so he was a little nervous as he started. "God," he said, "it has been some time since I have talked to you." Jacob paused for a moment before continuing. "God, I need your help. I need to know if I should marry White Fawn. I love her and I don't know what to do. I know I have to see Mr. Weatherbee and collect my inheritance, but what should I do right now? Uncle Zac was happy with his Indian wife, and all I want is to be happy and do what you want me to do. God, I have no one to talk to about this but you. Amen."

Jacob paused and looked up into the immense space of uncountable stars. There were as many stars as the grains of sands on the seashore, and he knew there was a God who resided there. Suddenly, a peace came over Jacob that engulfed his entire body. It was a warm feeling that spread from the top of his head to the tips of his toes. He had never experienced such a feeling in his life. Jacob knew that his prayer had been heard. There was a God. Jacob knew it, and he knew that God would answer his prayer. When the answer would come didn't matter. It was enough to know that his prayer had been heard. He didn't care what Zed would say. What mattered most was what God would say.

Chapter 17
The Vision

Struggling to sleep, Jacob tossed and turned late into the night. All he could think about was the wonderful experience he had. He did love White Fawn, but he had to wait for God to tell him what to do. Since he had come west, Jacob realized he now was happier and more content than he had ever been in his short life. And to add to that, he had found love. White Fawn was not of his race, but what difference did that make?

In confusion, Jacob whispered to himself, "Just what should I do?" Struggling to control his emotions, Jacob closed his eyes and slowly drifted into a deep sleep.

In the early morning hours Jacob was awakened and he heard a voice calling him by name.

"Jacob, are you listening to me, son?" Jacob looked up and there stood a smiling personage in front of him and then he realized it was his mother.

She said, "Jacob I have been given permission to visit you. Son, we have been watching you and what a kind and thoughtful thing you did when you and Zed gave food to those who were so destitute in the village. I was so proud of the way you treated those helpless old grandmothers."

His mother was enveloped in a soft white glow and she looked so much younger. "Mother, you look so beautiful and young," was the only thing that escaped Jacob's lips.

His mother said, "Jacob I know you have been struggling with the decision to marry White Fawn. You wonder if we will approve of her.

Son, I want you to be happy, and be sure you do what your heart tells you. And yes, son I do approve of her."

As she finished speaking, she faded away into an unknown realm.

Jacob immediately sat up and realized that his mother had died some time after he had left Boston, and she was given permission to visit him from the other side.

Jacob had sat up with a sudden start. His movement was enough to awaken Zed. "Boy, are you okay? Are you sick? What's wrong?" Zed asked in a concerned tone.

Shaking his head and trying to understand what he had just experienced, Jacob replied, "Nothing, I just had a good dream."

Zed moaned and was soon sound asleep, making a raspy sound with every intake of breath.

Jacob slowly turned onto his back, and looked up through the small opening of the tepee where he could see the stars in the heaven. It was impossible for Jacob to sleep after having that sacred vision. In the distance, a coyote howled. All else was quiet in the Teton Sioux camp in those early-morning hours.

Jacob quickly dressed and exited the tepee. The morning air was crisp and clean. His first thought was to see Buck, but he needed to think and visiting Buck wouldn't help that. The best way he knew how to clear his head was to run.

With ground-eating strides, Jacob headed west, racing downstream along the banks of the Missouri. He filled his lungs with clean morning air. As he entered the deep forest, his senses were on alert but his body was relaxed. Running always awakened him and cleared his mind. As Jacob ran, he began forming a plan that would ensure that White Fawn would be his wife.

Suddenly, Jacob heard the approaching of a running horse. His first thought was of Lone Wolf. He reached down for his knife inside the upper legging of his moccasins. It was his only means of defense. Running around trees and jumping over rocks, Jacob found seclusion in a small grove of trees.

The sound of hoofbeats stopped, and slowly a horse walked to where Jacob was hiding. Sweat poured off Jacob's head and his heart was racing as he gripped his knife more tightly. In the still of the night came a soft nicker and Jacob breathed a sigh of relief.

"Buck, what are you doing here? Did you follow me?" Jacob asked in a relieved tone. With the moonlight filtering through the trees, there stood his stallion. Buck nickered again and quickly walked up to Jacob putting his head over his shoulder. Jacob put his arms around the stallion's neck and held on while speaking to him in gentle tones.

Jacob returned to camp riding Buck. He turned Buck lose in the large feeding area for the tribal horses. In the early hours before dawn, the women were busy preparing morning meals. Smoke was already hovering above the encampment like a dense cloud.

Upon entering the tepee, Jacob saw Zed putting a piece of meat in his mouth. "Good to see you, boy. I was gettin' a mite worried. I 'member yer having a terrible time in the early morning. I thought maybe you was sick." Then chuckling he said, "Thought maybe you got sick from the food you ate at Two Cloud's lodge—or maybe love sick."

Jacob replied with a serious tone, "Not sick from food, but sick in love with a woman I plan on marrying."

Zed nearly choked on the piece of meat in his mouth. "Now, boy, I meant it last night when I said you were my responsibility and I didn't want you to git yer heart all set on that maiden."

With a defiant look, Jacob replied, "Zed, this is not your decision to make. It's mine. I am old enough to make up my own mind. You said Uncle Zac was happiest when he was married to his squaw. And if I want happiness, I will be the one to choose and not you. A lot can happen before our time is up, and I would appreciate it if you would support my decision. If not, then you can go back to your ranch and retire, but I am staying here."

Jacob did not want to tell Zed about his experience of praying in the forest or the vision of his mother. Suddenly Jacob grinned. Since he had gotten his answer, he knew what to do.

Zed snorted and fussed, but said nothing. He got up and walked out of the tepee without finishing his meal.

It was at least two hours before Zed reentered the tepee. Jacob sat mending a hole on his torn buckskins. Outside, the sky was clear and cold. Winter would soon be upon them; however, that wasn't the only thing that was cold. Zed sat directly in front of him and said, "Boy, I've thought it over, and I made a promise to yer Uncle Zac. I will follow through on my promise and stay with for three years then I'll head back to my ranch and retire. I don't agree with ya, but I'll be hanged if ya ain't just like yer uncle. He was just as stubborn as you when it came to changing his mind. I'll do it fer ya, and I'll stick by my promise to you. So if you want my help, I'll do my best."

"Thank you," Jacob said as he reached over and gently squeezed Zed's shoulder.

For the rest of the morning, Jacob asked Zed how to go about getting White Fawn to marry him. "Boy, you will not have any problems of her accepting yer offer. I can see it by the way she looks at you." Thoughtfully, Jacob said, "I know there is the Indian way to do things, but I would like to go about it my way."

Zed rolled his eyes and said, "Here we go again."

Jacob quickly stopped him and, raising his hand, said, "Zed, I know I am different, but I think that Two Clouds will respect me after I speak with him." Then Jacob explained his idea.

Zed looked thoughtfully at Jacob as he spoke and then chuckled. "I think you should do what yer heart tells you. I'll just stand back in the forest and watch ya. If you need any help, I'll be there to lend a hand, or, if needs be, my foot."

Jacob waited until the evening meal to say something. When White Fawn brought their food, she entered carrying two large gourds full of stew. After placing the food in front of Zed, she moved over to where Jacob was sitting. As White Fawn stooped down and placed the meal in front of him, he whispered in her ear, "Meet me by my horse this evening." She looked confused, and then seeing his serious demeanor, nodded her head in approval and went about her tasks.

After finishing their supper, Zed turned slowly toward Jacob and spoke. "Well, that was a mite sneaky, boy." With a hint of sarcasm in his voice, he added, "Are you sure yer doing it yer way, ain't you supposed to first ask her pa fer permission to marry her?"

Zed rolled his eyes and lay on his back and pretended to take a nap. It was obvious that he didn't want to talk about it anymore.

Jacob looked at Zed and exited the tepee. Jacob felt the cold air hit his face. The wind was blowing with no clouds in the sky, and it still felt like it was going to storm.

The half-moon had crossed over the eastern ridge, showering the forest with a faint, white light. Jacob walked over to the horses and waited for White Fawn. He was more nervous than a squirrel waiting for a badger. He reached over and stroked Buck's thickening coat, due to the approaching cold weather. The Indians had predicted that it would snow within the month.

Buck's ears pricked forward, and in the lengthening shadows, a lone figure approached. Jacob could see the soft moonlight caress White Fawn as she slowly approached. He didn't need any light because he could feel her presence. Just looking at her, his whole body became warm, and he suddenly didn't feel the cold. She had a blanket wrapped around her shoulders. When she saw Jacob, she ran to him, throwing her arms around his neck. As they embraced, their lips met. He felt the heat of her body and a wonderful feeling of love overpowered him. It was right. He felt it. Never had he felt this way about any woman. Had Uncle Zac been this happy? Was this the way he felt about his Indian squaw?

Whispering in his ear, White Fawn's soothing words poured out, "Oh, Jacob, I have missed you so much. All I ever do is think of you. My mother scolds me because I always have this faraway look in my eyes. She often has to repeat what she wants me to do. My heart is only for you."

"White Fawn, we must talk," Jacob said in a serious tone. "I want to know if you believe in my wisdom?"

A look of seriousness passed over her face and she said innocently, "Oh yes, Jacob. You are such a wise man. I have tried to be a good pupil and learn your customs."

Eager to please him, she asked, "Am I a good pupil, Jacob Morgan?"

Jacob's face reddened, and he smiled as he thought of his mother's remark about his teaching White Fawn his customs.

"White Fawn, in my wisdom, I do not want you to be my pupil any longer."

White Fawn immediately looked downcast and frightened. "Do I not please you, Jacob Morgan?"

Jacob could see the fear in White Fawn's eyes and understood that to dismiss her as a pupil meant he didn't want to share his customs with her any more. He gently placed his hands on her shoulders and drew her close and gently kissed her. "White Fawn, I love you and only you. I do not want you to be my pupil and teach you my customs." Jacob smiled and continued, "I want to have you as my squaw and share my customs with you for the rest of our lives."

White Fawn paused as if she didn't hear him. She said, "Jacob Morgan, what words did you say to me?"

Jacob repeated that he loved her and wanted to marry her. She stood still and didn't say anything. Jacob's heart raced, and he wondered if he had hurt her. Is she not sure? he thought. Didn't she want me as her husband and, her protector? Then, looking intently into her eyes, Jacob saw them start to mist. Then she reached up and put her hand over her mouth and began to cry. The cry quickly turned into an uncontrollable sob. Jacob embraced her and said, "White Fawn, did I offend you?"

Slowly White Fawn pulled from his embrace, still crying and said, "Ja . . . Jac . . . Jacob Morgan, is it true? Do you want me always?"

He nodded his head and softly said, "Yes."

Taking a shaky breath, White Fawn said, "I cry with joy and happiness. I have always wanted to be yours ever since I first saw you when I entered the tepee. There you were sitting, and you gave me a big smile. I have loved you since then."

They talked for the next hour and Jacob explained to her that he wanted to approach her father and ask him if she could ask for her hand, as was his custom. White Fawn explained that the tribe's way was different. Nevertheless, she agreed that he should do it his way.

The following evening, Jacob sat in front of the stoic chief of the Sioux tribe, White Fawn's father. They were the only two in the tepee. A brave had been asked to stand guard in front of the chief's tepee to see they were not disturbed.

"Now, Jacob Morgan, what is this important thing you have to speak with me about?"

Jacob nervously cleared his throat. "Ah . . . ah . . . Chief Two Clouds, the white man's ways are different from the Indian's. Some are good and some are bad." Jacob swallowed and took a deep breath, "I have come to discuss one of my customs that will join myself and Two Clouds together as friends." The proud Sioux chief sat confused, looking deeply into Jacob's eyes, not knowing what to expect, he nodded for Jacob to continue.

Taking courage, Jacob slowly spoke, "In my custom, if a man loves a woman and wants to take her for his wife, he will go to her father. As a sign of respect for him, he will ask for permission to take his daughter as wife. I know this is not your—"

Two Clouds put up his hand stopping Jacob. "Jacob Morgan, you are different than any white man I know. Most white men will gamble to win a father's daughter or trade goods. You have come offering me nothing for the value of my daughter?"

Jacob quickly interrupted the chief. "Oh, Great One, I have come out of respect for you as the father of your daughter. In my custom, a young man goes to the daughter's father and asks for her hand. I do not expect to receive her without placing a value on her. I have come to ask for her as my wife. If you give your permission, then I will comply with the Indian tradition and pay something of value for her."

Two Clouds looked at him and said, "Jacob Morgan, there are many braves in our tribe that want my daughter as their squaw, but I can see her heart is only for you. I know you will make my daughter happy, so I give my permission for you to have White Fawn as your squaw, and you can determine her value.

Two Clouds then stood up. Jacob followed, smiling as he did so. Two Clouds extended his arm and gripped Jacob's forearm tightly as a sign of completion. Then Two Clouds looked into his eyes and, with a kind smile, said, "It will be well for my daughter to have you. You are a good warrior."

When Jacob returned to his tepee, Zed looked up said, "Well, boy, did you get permission fer yer woman?"

Nodding, Jacob solemnly said, "All I have to do is to pay for her with gifts. I don't own anything, and I won't give up Buck. The chief couldn't ride him anyway. I don't know what to give."

Zed drawled, "Ya got yer brain, don't ya? Boy, if ya really love that gal and I can't change yer mind, then use yer brain and come up with some gift that'll please her pa."

Chapter 18
Gifts

Jacob knew Zed was right about the gifts. In the custom of the Sioux, horses were given as the main gift for a daughter. Most braves Jacob had known had given two, three, or even four horses for a squaw. What bothered Jacob was that many squaws felt like their value was based on horses—usually one or two horses only. The main thing that Jacob wanted was for White Fawn to know that he loved her more than three or four horses.

Turning to Zed, Jacob stood up, smiled, and said, "I know just what to do, but I'll need your help."

Zed wasn't exactly pleased with Jacob's plan, but he could see that it would be enough to show the chief how much Jacob valued White Fawn.

"Boy," Zed said seriously, "The only reason I am going along with this is that I ain't lettin' you go and git yerself kilt without me being with you. Do you realize how long yer idea will take? It will be at least a month or more, depending on how well yer plan goes. Where we are going, we might just have our scalps hanging from some brave's lance before then."

Jacob paused and replied, "Yes, but it would be worth the try. I just need to speak to one more person for some additional help."

Jacob explained to Running Bear about his meeting with Chief Two Clouds, and his desire to take White Fawn for his squaw. He then unraveled his plan on how to get gifts for the chief so he could ask for

White Fawn. "No one can know about this. I will not tell White Fawn. I do not want to risk Lone Wolf finding out and interfering with my plan."

A look of amusement spread over Running Bear's face. He chuckled and said, "Jacob, my brother, I will go with you. This is a warrior's work, and you will need me."

Jacob said, "I must speak with One Who Walks Tall. He'll advise me. We will leave in four suns."

One Who Walks Tall approved of Jacob's plan and dismissed him from his studies. He suggested an older brave in the village who could help implement his plan. His name was Horse Tracker, and he was familiar with the territory they were planning on traveling through. He would lead the way and guide them through the valleys and rugged mountain passes.

Jacob's plan involved a long journey to the northwest. With winter quickly approaching, it was essential that the group start as soon as possible in order to cover the distance they needed to travel while the weather was still good. Jacob had Running Bear spread the word around camp that they were going on a long hunt and would be back in a few weeks.

Jacob traded for the items needed for their journey. From their winter supply of food, he packed a small amount of their preserved meat, berries, and other dried food. He placed all of their supplies on the first of the three pack mules they would take with them. The second mule carried a large amount of rawhide rope, and the last mule was loaded with parched corn.

Early the next morning, Horse Tracker dressed in heavy buckskins, led the way out of camp on his horse as the three horsemen followed behind leading the pack mules. It was cold and patches of ice gathered in small puddles. The high mountains were already covered with snow.

A cold wind was blowing with the promise of snow in the air as they followed their guide into the northern country. The first day, the travelers camped about thirty miles from the Sioux encampment. The following days took them deeper into the forest, avoiding any man-made trails.

When the trees became sparse, they traveled in low-lying ravines, which kept them from being skylined. Their mission was what Jacob needed rather than what he wanted, and if they were not careful, they would be hunted. As they drew closer to their destination, they camped by day, hiding in secluded areas, and then traveled by night to avoid detection by those whose land they were trespassing. Horse Tracker took them in a northwesterly direction. They needed to ride for at least another week until they would reach their destination. Not wanting to carry a lot of meat, they killed a buffalo calf with a bow and arrow on their journey. The meat was well preserved due to the cold weather, and one of their pack mules was now loaded with fresh meat. They dare not use their rifles, as the sound of a rifle shot would carry throughout the mountains and surrounding valleys.

In the far northwest mountains, the Nez Perce tribe had established their camp. This tribe was renowned for having beautiful horses. They were the only tribe of Indians that had their own breed of horses. These horses were known for their beauty and stamina and were called Appaloosas. They had taken the Appaloosa horses from the Spanish and over the years had developed their own breeding methods. There were hundreds of horses in the Nez Perce camps.

But Jacob and his companions were not heading for the Nez Perce camp. They were heading for the Crow camp. The journey to the Nez Perce camp was too long and dangerous and they would have to cross a mountain range. It was well-known that the Crows had stolen Appaloosas from other tribes who had stolen them from the Nez Perce. These were the prized horses Jacob was after; they were the finest in the territory

The main tribes Jacob and his group had to avoid were the Blackfoot and Flathead. They now proceeded cautiously at night, walking and leading their stock in the forest to avoid being seen. As they neared their destination, they made their camps in ravines or in unseen areas during the day, making smokeless fires by banking their fire and using small amounts of dry wood to cook with.

There was great anticipation as Jacob and his companions talked about their upcoming raid. In an attempt to conceal their voices from unseen ears, they spoke in hushed tones. Early one morning, the four companions were within four miles of the Crow camp. It was located near a small river that ran through a valley. The valley was about two miles wide and five miles long. It had small ravines on both sides and towering mountains to the north. Tepees were scattered throughout the length of the entire valley.

Before leaving their secluded camp, Jacob explained his plan to everyone. They had counted at least seven hundred and fifty horses spread throughout the valley. To the north was a small ravine cutting into the side of the mountain where a small herd of horses had gathered together for protection against the cold wind. Jacob's plan was to enter the ravine and slowly approach the horses without spooking them. They would give the corn to the horses to quiet them.

Leaving their stock hidden in a secluded area four miles back from the Crow village, Jacob, Zed, and the two warriors stealthily approached the herd in the middle of the night. They quickly identified where each of the sentries were located.

There was less than a quarter-moon and clouds were gathering, indicating an approaching storm. This was a perfect time for Jacob to steal the horses. The clouds would hide the moon and when it snowed it would cover their tracks. Besides, what tribal sentry meant to guard the horses would go out on a night like this? It was perfect.

Jacob didn't want to hurt anyone. His intention was to get the horses, move out as quickly as possible, and return back to the safety of the Sioux tribe. Three weeks had already passed since their departure and winter was upon them.

Stealing horses was a way of life with the Indians. Every tribe stole from another tribe. The Indians first stole horses from the Spaniards. That is where the American mustang and other horses came from. The Appaloosa horses were most prized for their different color and size.

Jacob now wanted these prized horses so he could offer a wedding gift to Chief Two Clouds for his daughter.

About seventy-five horses had gathered in the canyon for protection from the cold wind. The four companions spread out and slowly approached the herd. Each of the men were to take seven horses. The wind was blowing against them, so the horses had not caught their scent. As they approached the herd, it started to rain. The rain quickly turned to sleet and then snow. *What a wonderful time to gather a wedding present,* Jacob thought.

It was in the early hours of the morning and with the cloud cover and snow, the four men were able to approach the canyon unseen. The wind was howling and blowing snow and sleet. Horse Tracker was sure the sentries were huddled in a warm buffalo robe, content to not have to check on their animals. After all, who would be crazy enough to steal horses in this type of weather?

The horses were eager to taste the corn and the four men each quickly attached the rawhide ropes around the horses' necks and led them slowly away. Some of the horses left behind continued to follow the group wanting more corn.

When they were some distance from their camp, each man mounted a horse and led the other six horses to their main camp. With their horses and pack mules waiting, the four quickly took the rawhide ropes and tied the head of each horse to the tail of the horse in front of it. Since they were Indian horses, they all were well trained to lead in this manner since most horses were not only used for riding, but were also used for packing. They now had four strings of seven horses, three pack mules, and their own riding horses. Within a half hour they were heading out, moving fast. They wanted to distance themselves as much as possible from the Crow camp.

It would be at least another four weeks, depending on the weather, until they would reach the safety of Sioux territory. Horse Tracker kept to the open prairie moving at a fast pace. The further they traveled, the safer they would be, but they still had to travel on other tribal lands.

With the approaching of dawn, the storm continued to rage, covering their tracks with snow. All throughout the day they traveled and as the darkening shadows of evening approached, the small group made their camp in a secluded grove of trees. The area was a perfect place to hide with good feed for the horses and an excellent windbreaker for the exhausted travelers.

Jacob examined all of the stock. The horses they had taken were all Appaloosas with an assortment of colors. The men separated the horses into different groups from the best to the worst based on their muscle build, height, and size. Both mares and stallions were put in individual groups, with the mares being chosen for breeding. The corn was handy in managing the horses—all the horses eagerly stayed with the group, anticipating more of the special treat.

Throughout the night, the snow fell followed by a fierce north wind. The four men and thirty-five animals were a long way from their morning camp before the light penetrated the darkness that morning. Each rider was covered with a warm buffalo hide as they struggled forward, fighting the bitter cold wind. Zed suggested that rather than exhausting their own riding horses, every four hours they should stop and switch to one of the Crows' horses, and that included relieving the pack mules.

Jacob was miserable, and he knew Buck was exhausted. He spoke gently as he reached down and stroked Buck's soft wet winter coat. He had ridden three other horses to spell Buck. Grass to feed thirty-five animals had been difficult to find, and Jacob was grateful that Horse Tracker was familiar with the country. Each night he guided them to different hidden coves with sufficient feed to sustain their stock.

Late one afternoon they approached a small grove of trees and prepared to make camp. A doe was startled by the visitors and soon became a delicious meal for the hungry travelers.

Throughout the night, the wind howled constantly and by morning, large snowdrifts lay ahead of them, making it difficult to travel.

"Boy," Zed yelled to Jacob, "you couldn't have asked fer better weather than this. You sure are lucky." Zed had lived in the mountains and wilderness and he knew that bad weather could sometimes be a blessing.

Jacob thought that it really was a perfect time to go home to White Fawn and to his new family. Jacob felt he was now a member of the tribe. He was following their custom to obtain his wife. Just knowing White Fawn was waiting for him made it easier to travel in their difficult situation.

On the sixth day on the trail, now that they were far enough from the Crow camp, the group split. Horse Tracker's plan was to divide into three groups. Running Bear went north and Zed went southwest, to act as decoys in case they were being followed. Horse Tracker and Jacob continued southeast toward the Sioux camp.

Running Bear and Zed were to each take seven horses. Four good ones and three of the lesser quality. They would go deep into the woods to their assigned areas and release the three of their worst horses still tied together. This would make it difficult for any search party to follow their tracks. They all would meet up again in three days at a predetermined rendezvous. When a horse was tied to another horse's tail by rawhide after about three days, the rawhide would come loose due to the wet snow that would make them loosen and fall off

In the early afternoon on the third day after their separation, Jacob was relieved when he saw Zed and Running Bear come into camp with eight horses in tow. The group continued on together and was lucky to have four days of good weather. As they traveled, the sun glistened like diamonds from one continuous valley to the next as far as the eye could see.

It was now going on three weeks; the snowstorm had slowed them down. With the extra horses to ride, they had almost made up their lost time. Horse Tracker said they possibly could be back at the Sioux camp in another two weeks. He led them to an area he was familiar with and they made camp early to give their stock a chance to forage for the dried grass beneath the fallen snow. Jacob continued to feed the horses small amounts of corn, trying to make it last because Horse Tracker said they were now close to Sioux Territory.

Another storm gathered and lasted two days and it was just what they needed. All their tracks would once again be covered. Jacob felt their trip had been a success. After an eight-week absence from the Sioux camp and long days of hard riding, the small group was finally back in the safety of the Sioux encampment.

As the four weary travelers approached the camp in the late afternoon, scouts were dispatched to greet them. A crowd of over three hundred tribal members gathered and cheered their approval of their successful raid.

Running at the head of the group was White Fawn. When she reached the travelers, she ran alongside Buck and reached up and grabbed a hold of Jacob's hand. "Oh, Jacob, I have missed you so much. Did you not go hunting?" she asked.

Jacob replied with a wide grin, "Yes, White Fawn, we went hunting, and we got what we were hunting for." Her face showed a lack of understanding, and Jacob spoke softly. "And I have come back and found you."

As the four entered the Sioux encampment, word had spread of their successful raid against the Crow. Some members of the tribe gathered around the prized horses, admiring and touching them. At a distance, Jacob saw Lone Wolf. He skulked around the perimeter, keeping his distance but staying close enough that Jacob could see the hatred in his eyes. He held his glance toward Jacob for a long moment and then with an angry scowl, turned and stormed away.

The four men gathered their horses at the tepee of Chief Two Clouds. The Chief exited his warm comfortable lodge and welcomed the four successful warriors back. He paused to look at the many horses and commented on their beauty. "One would be proud to have horses such as these," he said, as he touched different horses, stroking their necks. Then he dismissed the group.

Jacob had promised each of the three men who had accompanied him three horses as a thank-you for making the raid possible. As they left the chief's tepee, Running Bear and Horse Tracker turned their prized horses in with the other Sioux horses. Jacob and Zed rode to their tepee and unpacked their mules. Then Jacob unsaddled Buck and rubbed him down before giving him the last remnants of the corn, while Zed unsaddled his horse.

The new owners would put a colored dye somewhere on their horse's body indicating ownership. The four of them then turned their new horses and stock lose with the other tribal horses.

Zed and Jacob walked wearily toward their cold tepee, carrying their supplies inside. When entering, they found that a fire had been started for them, warming the inside and taking the cold bite away. Jacob was relieved to finally be home.

White Fawn soon entered and started toward Jacob expecting a kiss. Jacob tilted his head toward Zed, and White Fawn reluctantly held off. Jacob wanted desperately to take her into his arms and show her how much he had missed her.

White Fawn said, "I didn't want you to come back to a cold tepee, so I built a fire." She left the tepee and soon returned with warm food for their supper and then reluctantly left again.

As they ate, Zed said nothing, and when he finished, he went about putting his personals away without even looking at Jacob.

Not knowing what to say, Jacob began, "Zed, I want to thank you for your help in getting those horses. I couldn't have done it without your approval or your help. I'm so grateful for all you have done for me."

Leaning toward Jacob, Zed replied in a choked whisper, "Boy, I am so proud of ya, and I know yer Uncle Zac would have been too. I can't believe it ya're just like yer uncle. Ya both think and act alike. You could easily have been his son."

Jacob reflected on what Zed had just said. Zed didn't hand out compliments very often, but this time he had said he was proud of him. This was the same Zed who was always berating Jacob for not doing what he wanted him to do.

Now it was Jacob's turn to choke up. "Zed, I can't tell you how much I have enjoyed working with you," Jacob said. "Everything I know about this wilderness is because of you.

Chapter 19
War Party

Jacob heard approaching footsteps outside his tepee just before a young brave entered and announced that Chief Two Clouds had asked that both white men meet with him. Within the hour, Zed, Jacob, Running Bear, and Horse Tracker were seated in front of Chief Two Clouds.

The chief sat motionless for one minute, staring at the men as if not knowing what to say, he asked, "Where have you been, and what have you done? It has been many suns since you departed."

Together the four men explained where they had gone and what they had done. It was late in the evening when they finished.

Two Clouds sat mesmerized by their adventure. Finally he raised his hand to interrupt and asked, "And this was planned by you, Jacob Morgan?"

Jacob's face flushed. Again he did not want praise. He had not done it to gain praise or wealth among the Sioux nation, but only for the purpose of winning White Fawn. He lowered his head and said, "We all worked together. Our raid was very successful."

Two Clouds looked at Zed and then to Jacob. "The Crow are a powerful nation," he said. "To steal their horses is a great thing. They are our enemy and by what you have done, you bring honor to the Sioux nation. Do you think they will follow?"

Jacob and Zed knew the concerns of the chief. If they were followed, the Sioux could stand a good chance of losing more than just their horses if they were not prepared. It was to be expected. It was the Indian way of life. Each young boy was taught as he grew up that his main purpose in life was to be a warrior.

Zed spoke up. "Chief Two Clouds, Jacob and I have talked. We had storms to cover our tracks. The Crow are warriors. They know how to track and what to watch for. They also know about the powerful Sioux nation. If they found our trail, they would not lose the chance to make a raid on our horses."

Zed stopped for a moment. Jacob tried to analyze the look on the chief's face. "May I speak freely?" The Chief nodded his approval and Zed continued. "The Crow will want revenge. Jacob and I would ask that scouts be sent three suns out to see if the Crow are seeking your village. If so, that would give us time to prepare to meet them a good distance outside the village to keep them from stealing any women or children."

The Chief sat concentrating on what he had heard. He then looked first at Zed and then at Jacob for a long time without speaking. He nodded his head in approval and said, "What you have said is wise. If the Crow come, our people will gladly meet them in battle. I will send out scouts to search for any Crow warriors. We will wait."

Jacob nodded to Two Clouds and then asked, "May I speak?" He then presented a plan that he had been thinking about. When he finished, they all retired to their own tepees for the night.

The cold evening was interrupted by large gusts of wind that beat mercilessly against the tepees of the village. Jacob and Zed had gathered firewood and piled it as high as possible around the sleeping area inside their tepee. Zed and Jacob had taken turns adding wood to the fire in an effort to temper the cold throughout the night. Then, they would quickly crawl back under their warm buffalo robes. By early morning the wind had abated and a gray haze of smoke hung in the air over the entire Sioux encampment from over three hundred tepees.

In the early dawn hours of the sixth day, there were shouts of riders racing into the encampment. Dressing hurriedly, Jacob and Zed proceeded to the large council tepee where Chief Two Clouds waited to address the higher ranking chiefs and other warriors who had gathered.

Two Clouds began to speak, "A scout has reported that a war party of forty-five Crow warriors was seen three suns from our encampment."

A chorus of war cries and screams echoed from the young warriors and older men as they eagerly awaited the new challenge. Two Clouds raised his staff and all was quiet.

"Our white brothers talked to me six suns ago," the chief continued. "They asked that I send scouts to seek out the Crow. I thank them for their wisdom. If the Crow attack our village, they will not only try to take our ponies, but will also try to steal our women and children. We will go as one and together we will defeat our enemy in battle to protect our wives, our children, and our winter provisions." There was a deafening sound as the packed mass of tribal leaders shouted their approval.

Two Clouds slowly paced back and forth in the crowded tepee and thoughtfully said, "I will choose who will stay and who will go. We must not underestimate the wisdom of the Crow warriors. If we all go as one group to meet the enemy, more enemies could come from another direction and attack the village. We must not leave our families unprotected. One group will go and battle with them one sun distance from our village. Another group of warriors will wait in our village and surprise them if they come. I thank Jacob Morgan for his wisdom."

Jacob thought it didn't take wisdom, but was common sense. Many times the Indians would make war on another tribe and would not leave sufficient men to guard their camp for another warring tribe, and while away, another tribe would come in and steal their wives and children and horses.

Zed whispered to Jacob, "Now, boy, that really makes sense. Good idea. Glad you mentioned it to Two Clouds."

As Two Clouds called off the names of those who would go with the main group, Jacob heard both Zed and his name along with Running Bear. He did not hear Lone Wolf's name mentioned.

"I demand to go with the main group," a brave shouted from the front. Jacob looked and saw Lone Wolf, his face twisted in anger. "I am one of the leaders, and I have the right to choose which group I will fight with." He was right; his position allowed him to choose where and with whom he would travel.

Zed nudged Jacob. "I think we need to keep an eye on him. He might want to fight, but with whom?"

By afternoon, sixty braves were painted with the traditional Sioux war markings on their faces and their buckskins. They had marked their horses with signs and symbols of their family and their skills. One hundred and twenty braves were divided into eight groups consisting of fifteen braves each. Each group was positioned in different areas throughout the village, hidden in tepees where they could stop any approaching enemy should they decide to attack their encampment.

The main group of sixty warriors set out to meet the Crow away from the village with Chief Two Clouds leading them. Throughout the day, they silently plodded through the cold snow at sundown, as they prepared for their evening camp when four braves rushed into camp. They were returning from spying on the Crow.

The four stood in front of Two Clouds to report what they had found. The Crow were not aware of their approach and were one-half sun from them. Chief Two Clouds assembled the chiefs, telling them of his plan of attack and asked for their approval. After the tribal chiefs went over Two Cloud's plan, all chiefs unanimously agreed to proceed.

Everyone prepared and then waited. Jacob couldn't sleep, nor could many of the other warriors. It was not because of the bitter cold, but because of the excitement and anticipation of battle. For some of the younger warriors, it would be their first encounter with the enemy, and they needed to prove themselves. Others were more experienced, yet they did not take the Crow for granted. The Crow were great warriors and they knew that they would need more than skill to beat them. They would need surprise, and Two Clouds had devised a great plan for that.

Jacob sat next to Zed and listened to him snore. He was frustrated and not experienced like Zed was. He muttered to himself, "How could he sleep at a time like this?" He nudged Zed and said, "How can you sleep at a time like this? Tomorrow you could be dead!"

Zed grumpily replied, "If I am going to die in the morning, then I want to make sure I get a good night's sleep."

Exasperated, it was Jacob's turn to roll his eyes. Zed didn't notice the sarcastic look Jacob gave him; he was content to sleep, so he just rolled over and settled back into a deep, sound sleep.

As dawn broke, it was very cold and there were no fires. The smoke could drift for miles and the Crow might happen to smell it and the Sioux would lose their advantage. The warriors were divided into four groups of fifteen. Two of the four groups would be hidden on each side of the trail that the Crow party would pass through. The third party would hide further up the trail and wait for the Crow to pass, allowing them to close in behind them.

The fourth group was to be led by Chief Two Clouds. They were to act as bait and lead the Crow into the middle of the concealed Sioux warriors. On Two Clouds signal, all four groups were to converge on the Crow all at once, having them completely surrounded.

About mid-morning, Two Clouds led his group of fifteen warriors toward the Crow. Jacob, Zed, and Running Bear rode behind him, along with eleven other warriors. Taking their time, Two Clouds moved his warriors past the secreted Sioux warriors on both sides of the trail and continued up a gentle slope. Upon reaching the top, Jacob saw the approaching Crow war party a short distance ahead of them.

With an earsplitting scream, Two Clouds raised his lance, whirled around on his horse, and made a hasty retreat to the front of his small party of warriors, preparing to spring the trap. Seeing this, the Crow warriors charged the fleeing fifteen Sioux warriors, knowing their forty-five warriors would have no problem defeating them. They shrieked and shouted with excitement as they followed the retreating Sioux warriors, who were running like a bunch of scared squaws. As the Crow raced forward, they passed the Sioux warriors secreted behind the long hill without noticing them. The trap was ready to be sprung.

The Sioux warriors came out from their hiding places unnoticed and fell in behind the Crow. The other two groups of Sioux warriors waited until Two Clouds and his warriors passed.

Raising his lance as a signal to all his warriors, Two Clouds signaled his group to wheel around and charge the approaching warriors. In perfect unison, the warriors on both sides of the trail charged the oncoming enemy, surrounding them on all sides. The Crow never knew their fate until it was too late. They were attacked from all sides.

One should never underestimate his enemy, and that was the Crow's mistake. The Crow thought it would be an easy victory.

As the attack commenced, the warriors from both sides met in a clash of spears, clubs, and knives. The Sioux leaped from their horses onto the Crow warriors, pulling them off their mounts, and thus began the fierce hand-to-hand battle. To Jacob's left, a large Crow warrior was trying to escape from the main group, racing his pony toward the forest for protection. Needing no coaxing, Buck raced toward the fleeing Indian and hit the Crow's pony with his right shoulder, unseating the brave. Jacob leaped from his saddle with his knife in his hand.

As he was about to bring his knife down on the warrior's chest, he heard the pounding of horse hooves behind him. Suddenly, he was hit violently from behind by a horse's shoulder. Jacob was thrown into the snow as the animal and rider rushed past him. Gathering his bearings as quickly as possible, Jacob resumed his fight with the Crow warrior.

The Crow warrior, who had also fallen from his horse, was quick not to lose the afforded opportunity. The large warrior leaped onto Jacob, wrapping his hand around his neck to choke him. As he held onto Jacob's neck with one hand, he grabbed a knife with the other and thrust it toward Jacob's chest. Jacob deflected it with his arm and the knife went deep into his shoulder. Screaming in pain, Jacob looked at the Crow warrior and saw him smile, the victory of Jacob's death reflecting in his eyes.

The warrior raised his arm to strike the fatal blow to Jacob's chest, but stopped short when a shot rang out. The Crow warrior pulled back and tried to run, but fell at Jacob's feet. Within moments Zed was at Jacob's side, talking to him, and reaching for something to stop the bleeding. "Boy, don't you leave me. You understand me, boy? Don't you die on me."

Jacob slowly sank into a deep, cold blackness and desperately called out, "Mother, are you there? Mother, where are you?" No one heard his voice from either side of the abyss. Jacob tossed and turned, moaning in pain and calling out for White Fawn. First, he was burning and on fire as the fever consumed him, and then he was icy cold, unable to get warm. It continued over and over until everything went black and numb.

"Jacob, Jacob, can you hear me?" A voice called. Jacob tried to respond, but he couldn't will his eyes to open. Stiffness and pain had spread throughout his whole body. His shoulder ached, and he was having difficulty breathing. The voice repeated his name but Jacob was unable to answer.

It was five days before Jacob finally opened his eyes, and there in front of him was White Fawn. In relief and excitement, she cried out, "Oh, Jacob! We were so worried. We thought the Great Spirit would take you home."

In a brief moment, Zed was at his side. "Boy, you sure had us worried. We thought you was a goner. I had the durndest time trying to stop yer bleedin' to death. If it weren't fer One Who Walks Tall, you would have been a goner. He sure got powerful medicine."

Jacob's right shoulder throbbed with excruciating pain while his arm and hand were numb and unable to move.

"Boy, just take yer time. You'll do good, but it'll just take some time." Zed encouraged.

"What happened to me?" Jacob asked. "I saw everything," Zed quickly replied. "Chief Two Clouds has asked fer a special tribal meeting this evening and wanted to know if you would be well enough to attend. I told him we'd make a bed fer ya and carry ya over to the meeting."

"Is it really necessary?" Jacob asked weakly.

"In yer predicament, boy, I think it's best that ya hear what I gotta say," said Zed softly. Jacob was puzzled and in a great deal of pain. However, he agreed and didn't complain as Zed and Running Bear picked him up and carried him to the special council on a crudely made litter.

The council meeting was packed with tribal leaders and warriors. Two Clouds stood and, raising his ceremonial lance, addressed the group.

"I have been asked to make judgment at this council on a member of our tribe who has endangered another warrior in battle."

Murmurs rose up throughout the group, everyone wondered who would do such a dishonorable thing. Two Clouds continued, "In our victory over the Crow tribe—" This brought cheers and whoops from among the warriors.

Raising his lance, the chief quieted the group and continued, "Our warriors fought well, and we won the battle. It was well that we had our warriors hidden in tepees surrounding the village. When we departed from the encampment, the village was attacked by a large band of Crow warriors. Our warriors hiding in the tepees killed most of them. A few escaped. I thank Jacob Morgan for his warning." Again there was cheering and yelling.

For the third time, Two Clouds raised his staff to quiet the enthusiastic warriors.

"Our friend, Zed, has told me that one of our braves purposely ran into Jacob with his horse while he was fighting a Crow warrior." This time there was a hush. For a warrior of the Sioux tribe to do this to one of his own tribe was unforgivable.

Shouts of "Who was it?" and "Who is the guilty one?" sounded throughout the tepee.

Two Clouds turned and pointed to Lone Wolf and said, "The white man, Zed, said it was Lone Wolf."

In a rage, Lone Wolf leaped to his feet and shouted, "This is a lie. I was busy fighting other Crow warriors. I was not even near the white dog." Pointing to Zed he continued, "This white man lies for the boy, Jacob Morgan. He could not win a fight with a Crow squaw."

Jacob watched and listened as Zed stood up and faced Lone Wolf. Zed angrily said, "I saw you ride your horse into Jacob and then continue riding on. You watched from a distance when I shot the warrior before he could kill Jacob."

Lone Wolf looked at all of the gathered warriors and said, "Would you take the word of a white dog over a great warrior such as I? This white man is a dog; he is a coward. Will you believe him when there is none else to accuse me?"

From the back of the crowd, a voice spoke out, "I accuse you, Lone Wolf." All turned to face the accuser as he pushed through the mass of tribal warriors. There stood Running Bear. He raised his arm and pointed toward Lone Wolf. "After you left your group, you hunted for Jacob. When you saw him in battle, you ran your horse into him to let the Crow warrior kill him. I saw it because I followed behind the white man, Zed."

Lone Wolf screamed. Grabbing his knife, he rushed toward Jacob. In an instant, a half dozen braves jumped on top of him, violently wrestling him to the ground. They held Lone Wolf down and disarmed him as he struggled and screamed.

Chief Two Clouds nodded, and the warriors forcefully jerked Lone Wolf to his feet. The chief faced him, raised his ceremonial staff, and said, "Because of your deceit and hatred, you are banished from this tribe for the remaining days of your life. Your wife and children may stay, but you will gather your things and leave. If we see you in our encampment ever again, you will die. I have spoken."

Chapter 20
Bargaining

Jacob was beside himself as he lay on his bed of buffalo hides. He was miserable and had no patience with being an invalid, but he knew that he had to stay down if he wanted his shoulder to heal. Every time he moved, the throbbing in his shoulder and numbness in his hand and arm returned. He couldn't grip anything and was forced to feed himself with his left hand. Food spilled down the front of him as he attempted to spoon it into his mouth. White Fawn entered the tepee, with the flap closing softly behind her. There was little light in the tepee except for the slow burning fire in the center, creating dark shadows that danced along the walls. Smoke slowly curled up and gathered like a great mist before slowly rising out the top of the tepee.

White Fawn looked at Jacob, and she could see he was miserable. Then with the understanding and compassion that only a woman would have, she knelt next to him and gently picked up the gourd with the wooden spoon and proceeded to feed him.

Jacob was exasperated to say the least. Here he was the great, proclaimed white warrior of the Sioux tribe, and he couldn't even feed himself, let alone stand up. He scowled and turned his head away as she started to bring the spoon to his lips. She abruptly reached over and lightly slapped the back of his head.

Startled, he turned to her and asked, "Why did you do that?"

With a stern look, she replied, "Zed said you were feeling sorry for yourself. I do not want to treat you like a small child, but if you want to get well, you must eat. I am here to help you get well fast."

Many members of the tribe had come to visit him, bringing food and small gifts for his part in protecting their village. Nevertheless, he still felt like an invalid. He just lay there, trying to look cheerful as he thanked others for their kindness.

Looking up, he asked White Fawn, "Why would you want me to get well fast?"

A mischievous look came into her eyes. She grinned and gently squeezed his good shoulder and asked, "Did you not bring ponies back from your successful raid from the Crow village?"

Puzzled, Jacob eyed her with suspicion, and then he understood. She continued, "Jacob Morgan, if you decide to use your horses, my answer will be yes. I have come to help you get strong so you can talk with my father."

Jacob chuckled.

"What did I say wrong?" she asked.

Jacob reached up to tuck a strand of hair behind her ear that had come loose from her braid. Touching her cheek with the fingers on his good hand, he said, "You said nothing wrong, my love. You have just reminded me of what was most important. I must get well so I can talk to your father. I will need your help every day to gain much needed strength for this great task."

Devilishly, he went on. "I know it will be difficult for you, but giving me a kiss will make me stronger." Then hopeful he said, "I think we need to practice each day." Making his voice sound much weaker, Jacob said, "Do . . . you . . . think we could practice now?"

Exasperated, White Fawn punched Jacob in his good shoulder and raised her voice, saying, "Jacob Morgan, you're impossible. I come to help you get well fast, to feed you, and to apply medicine to your shoulder, and all you can think of is practicing your customs!"

"Ow! Ow! That hurt," Jacob said, faking pain in his good shoulder where she had punched him. "Why do you have to be so mean?" he tried to sound hurt and serious.

White Fawn looked contrite and immediately replied, "I am sorry, Jacob Morgan. I just want you to get strong."

Jacob reached up, and touched the left side of his mouth, and said, "It hurts right here."

White Fawn slowly reached her head down and gently kissed him.

She got up and started to leave, when Jacob reached out and gently grabbed her hand. Playfully grinning, Jacob asked, "Can you come back tomorrow and help me get better?" He pointed to his lips again.

The corner of her mouth came up in a small grin, and she said, "We will see."

During the next few weeks, Jacob had many visitors, including Two Clouds, who seemed very concerned over his progress. As Two Clouds visited, Jacob felt that the chief wanted to talk seriously about more than just his health. But he only asked general questions, as if wanting Jacob to bring up something. Jacob inquired about his horses, and Two Clouds informed him that he had made sure Jacob's horses were well cared for.

Jacob added up the number of horses he now owned in his head. The total the men had stolen, or gathered, was twenty-eight Appaloosa horses. Zed and Running Bear had released six of them to throw off any pursuers from the Crow tribe. That left twenty-two. Subtracting the three horses that each of the other men had taken, Jacob quickly calculated that he was now the proud owner of thirteen heads of excellent horses, plus three pack mules and Buck. That was a total of seventeen animals. He owned more horses than most members of the Sioux tribe.

Two weeks later, Two Clouds sat facing Jacob in the empty tepee. He was finally in a position to ask for White Fawn. He knew Two Clouds liked him, but Jacob wondered just how much.

Throughout the months that Jacob had lived with the Sioux, white trappers had visited the village to trade for valuable beaver and buffalo hides. Jacob had taken note of their bargaining skills. He had also read about the travels of Lewis and Clark and their experience in trading with the Indians, as they tried to find a route to the Pacific Ocean.

In both of these examples, Jacob noticed that when it came to trading with the Indians, the white men were the shrewd ones. They would bring small trinkets worth absolutely nothing, such as a few fishhooks or beads, and trade the Indians for valuable animal hides and fur. The Indians loved the beads, especially the blue ones, and would trade a lot for them, receiving only a little in return. However, the white man's items such as steel pots, tomahawks, and knives had a much higher bargaining power.

During the past year while Zed and Jacob had lived with the Sioux, many trappers had come to trade their trinkets and were surprised to find other white men living among them. Each time the trappers would ask Jacob and Zed if this was their village for trading and bargaining for pelts and hides. When Jacob and Zed told them it wasn't, the trappers were relieved—that is until they brought out their cheap trinkets for trade.

Zed and Jacob had talked to Chief Two Clouds about the white man's trading schemes and told him the white men wanted their hides far more than the Indian needed their small trinkets. If they understood the white man's greed, they could bargain for much better items. With this information, the Sioux tribe became very shrewd bargainers when it came to trading for white trappers' goods.

Now before Jacob sat the most powerful man of the Sioux tribe, Two Clouds, its chief. Jacob was about to participate in the most important bargaining of his entire life. The wise old chief had something that Jacob wanted, and Jacob believed it was more valuable than anything in the land.

Still weak from his wound, Jacob struggled to sit upright. He pushed himself against a pole and sat at an angle to keep from putting pressure on his injured shoulder. Looking at Two Clouds, he weakly said, "Two Clouds, since we are alone, I must speak to you of important things. Will you give me your time?" Two Clouds nodded in approval.

Taking a deep breath, Jacob began slowly. "Chief Two Clouds, I think you know of my respect for you as the chief of this Sioux tribe. You have been kind and generous to Zed and me by giving us permission to live among you. You knew my Uncle Zac. He was a great and respected white man and warrior. As a member of his family, I have sought to follow in his footsteps."

The chief nodded his head in approval.

Moving again to get more comfortable, Jacob continued. "Many moons ago when we sat to eat, you asked me what my purpose was in learning of your people. You asked if I wished to become one of you. As you remember, I said, 'I desired to know the ways of the Sioux. I am listening for the prompting of the Great Spirit on what he wants me to do.'"

Two Clouds raised his hand to cut Jacob off. "Has the Great Spirit given you a vision?" the chief asked.

Jacob, surprised at his question, looked directly into his eyes and said, "Yes."

Two Clouds now was the one who was taken aback by Jacob's answer. He replied sternly, "Only One Who Walks Tall can receive visions for the tribe."

Jacob replied quickly now, raising his hand and saying, "I have not received a vision for the tribe. I am not the great medicine man One Who Walks Tall. I have received a vision for myself."

Again, Two Clouds was taken back and puzzled. He asked, "And what question did Jacob Morgan ask the Great Spirit?"

Jacob decided the best thing he could do was to be honest with Two Clouds. So, he briefly related his prayer when he had asked about White Fawn and the vision he had received two moons before, but did not explain it in detail.

Two Clouds paused and looked at Jacob for the longest time without speaking. Jacob wanted to ask him if anything was wrong, but decided to wait, as this was the custom.

The turmoil on the chief's face made Jacob nervous. Jacob knew that White Fawn was his most prized daughter. She was beautiful and well loved by the entire tribe. There wasn't a brave in the tribe that wouldn't give up to three, four, or five horses for his beautiful daughter.

"Jacob Morgan," he said, "you are a white man. Would you take my daughter away from her people to live with your people?"

"Honorable chief—father of the woman I love—I will not take your daughter from her family. I want to live among the Sioux perhaps until the end of my days."

Relief swept over Two Cloud's face, and taking a deep breath, he said, "Then, Jacob Morgan, I will consent to this joining. My daughter, White Fawn has said that she would be honored if only one horse was offered from Jacob Morgan. Never have I seen any of my people love as my daughter loves you. Even at her young age, her love is strong and deep. I can see it in her eyes and in all her actions. Yes, I am honored, Jacob Morgan, to give my approval."

Two Clouds was about to stand, when Jacob motioned him to sit down again, and said, "I have one more thing I must speak with you about."

The chief looked puzzled and resumed sitting. Jacob continued, "We have talked in the past about the value of White Fawn," Jacob said. "I know it is the Indian tradition and I want to offer something of value."

Two Clouds quickly interrupted and said, "Jacob Morgan, you are a white man, and I do not expect this from you. This is the Indian way and not the white man's way. We have talked about the value for my daughter in past suns, but the value you already gave was when you saved our village and that is enough."

Struggling to raise both hands due to the pain in his right shoulder, Jacob said, "Did I not tell you that I wanted to live with the Sioux perhaps to the end of my days? I am one of your people, and I will follow the Indian way. Because of my love for White Fawn, I do not have enough horses of value that would pay for her bride price. She is not a three- or five-horse woman. I don't have much, but I wish to give ten horses to you as my gift for your daughter."

Two Clouds was too stunned to say anything. Instead he sat staring dumbfounded at Jacob. No one had ever given a gift of over six horses plus buffalo hides for any maiden.

Jacob continued, "Chief Two Clouds, if I were to follow the Indian way, I would have a friend place three horses in front of your tepee to start out with and perhaps you would receive them. However," Jacob went on, "I value White Fawn's love, and to me she is worth far more that all the horses I could ever give for her, but ten horses is what I have."

Two Clouds slowly open his mouth and said, "It has not been heard of, Jacob Morgan. Never has anyone given such a great offer for any Indian maiden, especially the great horses that you wish to give."

Jacob quickly retorted, "Great Chief—father of White Fawn—never has there been such a beautiful and favored daughter as White Fawn among the Sioux nation. I am the one who gets the greater prize."

The chief was silent. Jacob quickly reached his left arm forward to seal their agreement before the chief could argue anymore. Still silent, the chief grasped Jacob's left forearm and nodded approval. Then, smiling broadly, Chief Two Clouds stood and left the tepee.

The news spread quickly among the tribe. Everyone was interested and eager to talk about the price Jacob had agreed to pay for White Fawn.

That evening as the sun was settling over the western ridge of the valley, two different maidens brought Zed and Jacob's meal. One stayed and helped feed Jacob. After completing their meal, Zed sat relaxing with his back against the side of the tepee.

Looking at Jacob for a long moment, he said sarcastically, "Well, boy, I guess the cat is out of the bag, and you have made yer bargain. Your great offer has really shocked the tribe. I hope you know what you've done. It ain't going to go too well fer some of them young bucks when they start bargaining fer some maiden. The parents of the daughters will now want more ponies. You surely done set a high mark and opened a can of worms."

Pausing, Zed looked at Jacob and then slowly continued, "Now, I wonder just what you had in mind. Did you want the others to look up to you as some kind of a special warrior who paid ten horses fer the chief's daughters?"

Jacob quickly responded and quietly said, "Oh, Zed, that is not the reason."

Again, Zed retorted sarcastically, "Then what could be the reason?"

Jacob stared ahead and silently whispered, "I love her, Zed. I've listened to the squaws in the village talking about the price that was paid for them. One squaw would brag that she was better than another squaw, because her husband gave three ponies for her. How would the squaw feel when her bride price was only two ponies? I wondered just how that two-horse squaw felt. I didn't give ten horses to outdo anyone. I gave ten horses because I never want White Fawn to wonder if I loved her. I wanted the other squaws to know that I valued my White Fawn more than any other woman in this tribe. I already told White Fawn that if I had one hundred horses, it would not be enough because of my love for her."

Zed slowly leaned forward, a little misty-eyed, and whispered, "Boy, I misjudged you. I apologize. I thought you were trying to be known as the great white man who gave ten horses for a squaw."

Each day Jacob got stronger and by late spring, he was mostly healed. After talking with Chief Two Clouds, they decided Jacob would be strong enough for the wedding in another fourteen suns. Since Jacob had no family to make a tepee, tribal members took it upon themselves to make him one. Soon a tepee was assembled for Jacob and White

Fawn and gifts of all types were presented before the end of the first week—buffalo hides, deer hides, food of all types, a steel cooking kettle, pairs of moccasins, and clothing were all placed inside their tepee.

One day when Jacob and White Fawn were out walking, they passed their new tepee. "That will soon be our home," Jacob said, smiling at White Fawn.

White Fawn reached over and lifted the flap, and they both peered inside.

Glancing quickly around to see if anyone was watching, White Fawn quickly pulled him into the tepee and kissed him soundly, and then she fled.

Arrangements were made for a Sioux marriage festival, which consisted of feasting and dancing, including a dance that only the women and children participated in.

In this dance, the women and children formed a large circle in the center where four drummers beat drums. The bride or groom did not attend. The women who were not dancing cooked soup and meat and then served it to those on the outside of the circle. Then they would get food for themselves before rejoining the dancers in the inner circle. When a dancer got too weary to continue, they would go to the outside and sit and eat before returning to the center.

This dance continued throughout the day of Jacob and White Fawn's wedding. Meanwhile, Dancing Light and other women put the bride and groom's tepee in order, arranging buffalo hides, clothing, and cooking utensils in anticipation for the arrival of the newlyweds.

Friends of Jacob and White Fawn took them over to inspect their new home. Her mother and friends had already made the tepee up for their arrival. After the tepee had been arranged and Jacob and White Fawn entered their tepee, according to Sioux custom, they became engaged. The master of ceremonies, One Who Walks Tall, arrived with the friends of the bride and groom and told them the hour of proclaiming their marriage had arrived. Four warriors appeared and spread a large blanket over Jacob's and White Fawn's heads, each warrior taking one corner of the blanket. The four warriors then escorted the couple through the village while White Fawn and Jacob walked under the blanket. Their friends followed behind, and soon a long procession of people followed them.

One Who Walks Tall held a green ash wand that he used as a baton and walked ahead of the procession and loudly proclaimed the wedding ceremony and sounded praises for the happy pair throughout the village. When this pageant had ended, Jacob was taken to his new tepee by his close friends and White Fawn was taken to her father's tepee.

Jacob made a fire and Zed, Running Bear, and Two Clouds waited with him. Soon Jacob heard women singing outside his tepee. When he looked out, he saw White Fawn being carried on a blanket. When they came to the flap of the tepee, they entered and deposited White Fawn, according to custom, at the feet of Jacob. They were officially married. The tepee filled with their close friends and White Fawn's family. White Fawn prepared a meal for everyone and they all sat down together and ate. After the meal, Jacob stood, holding White Fawn's hand.

"It is the tradition of the white man to thank those who attend his wedding. My squaw and I thank you for your friendship and gifts."

Slowly people started filing out of the tepee. As Zed ducked through the flap of the tepee, he turned and smiled at Jacob, nodding his approval. Running Bear smiled and mouthed, "My good brother, Jacob Morgan."

As Two Clouds and Dancing Light stood to leave, Two Clouds said, "You are not only a member of our tribal family now, but I welcome you into my family." He reached his right hand forward. Jacob weakly raised his right hand and gripped the chief's forearm as tightly as he could.

As Two Clouds prepared to step out of their tepee, he turned and swept his hand in front of him, indicating this tepee was now their home. There they would consummate their love and join together as one. White Fawn's parents were the last two guests to leave the tepee, and as the flap fell closed, Jacob heard hoops, shrieks, and yells ringing through the air as the tribal members celebrated one last time.

Inside, there was a warm fire and many buffalo robes spread on the ground. Jacob stood in front of his new bride and just looked at her. He could not believe this was really his wife. Here he was, a continent away from his family, living with the great Sioux Indians. Who would ever have imagined that his great adventure would lead to this wonderful event? The beautiful woman that stood looking up into his eyes was his. This moment and time was theirs.

Slowly he gathered her into his arms and pressed his lips to hers. She needed no coaxing and soon they were both snuggled beneath a warm buffalo robe.

Chapter 21
Broken Heart

The first two months after the wedding passed quickly. Jacob was happier than he had ever been in his life. He loved White Fawn more than life itself.

Two years had passed since Jacob had left Boston. He had arrived in San Francisco in July of 1855 and it was now June of 1857, and he had reached the ripe old age of nineteen years old. Zed was forty-four and Jacob felt he was ancient.

It was around this same time that they discovered White Fawn was with child. Jacob rejoiced when White Fawn told him and he looked forward to being a father.

As changes continued daily, Jacob grew concerned and confided in Zed. "I didn't know it would be like this. My poor wife is suffering so much, and I can't do anything about it. I feel so helpless."

Zed grinned, as if to say, "I told you so." He then patiently touched Jacob's arm. "Boy, yer Uncle Zac went through the same thing. He told me his beautiful squaw had the same problems. It goes on everywhere with all women when they are having their young'uns. The main thing is to just give her space and don't try to take away her sickness. She knows it is her lot and will bear it. I think she is doing a great job."

Still concerned, Jacob said, "I'm just glad I'm not a woman!"

Zed chuckled, "Yer right, boy. But the reason yer so worried is because ya love her."

"Wow, how about that," Jacob retorted teasingly. "Here you have never been married and already you are full of information on babies and women."

Zed's face flushed with embarrassment.

"Oh, Zed, I'm just joshing you, my friend. You have great wisdom."

With that, Zed punched Jacob in the arm and said, "Thank you, Professor Morgan."

When Zed called Jacob Professor Morgan, it brought a feeling of nostalgia to him. Because of his spiritual experience he had he knew his mother was dead and he wondered how his father and two brothers were faring. When he thought of his family, it stirred fond feelings in his heart. There was no way he could have written a letter to them since the nearest postal service was at least two months away or further. It could take up to a year before his father would even hear from him.

Spring was in full bloom. Rain showers blanketed the area, and new life was everywhere. Jacob saw many beautiful buckskin colts running throughout the herd. Jacob patted Buck on the neck and said, "Ole boy, you are not the only one who's been busy. I am positive many of those young ones are your sons and daughters."

During the summer, the Sioux tribe made their encampment near the banks of the Missouri river. Buffalo, elk, and deer were in great supply in the mountains and valleys along the Missouri. There were also more plants for gathering and drying.

Jacob had become very adept at hunting the rabbit, squirrel, and marmot that lived in the neighboring valleys. His skills at using a bow and arrow had improved, and after much practicing, Jacob prided himself in being able to hit a waterfowl in mid-flight, but he was not as good as Zed or Running Bear.

Running Bear had taught Jacob how to fish using a spear or weirs that trapped the fish. They fished for salmon, trout, suckers, and sturgeon to eat. Additionally, Zed continued to teach Jacob basic survival skills, such as how to make harpoons and dip nets from bone, wood, antlers, and sinew.

While Jacob hunted, White Fawn was busy gathering berries, roots, and nuts for their family. Jacob wanted to know for himself what they needed for survival. At first, White Fawn was hesitant to teach Jacob the art of gathering roots and berries because she felt it was the responsibility of the squaw. However, with Jacob's persistent asking, White Fawn finally gave in and taught Jacob how to identify and gather roots, including camas, wild carrots, onions, and bitterroot. They worked together, with White Fawn teaching Jacob as they went along. Many of the other braves teased Jacob for helping White Fawn, but Jacob didn't pay any attention. He was just happy to be with her.

In the late summer, White Fawn led Jacob to a small tributary of the river. Within a short distance, they found gooseberries, currants, and chokecherries, along with blackberries, Jacob's personal favorite.

"Jacob Morgan, you are a strange white man," White Fawn teased. "You'd rather spend your time doing woman's work than spending time with the other warriors."

Jacob was ready with a reply. "The first time we met in the woods, I told you that you needed someone to guard you at all times because of your beauty, didn't I?" He paused and popped a blackberry he had just picked into his mouth. "Well, here I am to protect you!"

Laughing and looking around to see if they were alone, White Fawn reached up and kissed him. "Jacob Morgan, I am yours and yours only. Now get back to work!"

After they finished picking the berries, White Fawn explained how to dry them in the sun and then store them in earthen vessels. The food would be used during the cold winter months.

At certain times of the year, other tribes would meet with the Sioux and participate in ceremonies, such as marriages and contests which consisted of horse racing and hunting, wrestling, spear and tomahawk throwing, and gambling. Trading between friendly tribes was common, and everyone participated. Jacob was accepted as a Sioux warrior from other tribal members and participated in most hunts. He learned new techniques used by the Indians in hunting buffalo. In some areas, fires were lit, which encircled the animals, keeping them at bay while they were killed. Most of the hunts were Sioux tribal activities, where the braves would travel as a group and all received equal portions of the meat for their participation and preparation for winter.

As summer faded into fall, forage for the horses to eat was running out and game was becoming scarcer, so the whole tribe migrated to a new valley. Jacob had never seen a more efficient group of people working together. They could pack up and move everything in a short period of time, and it was all done in perfect harmony. Their tepees were made of long sturdy poles in the center with buffalo hides sewn together and wrapped around the poles. When the tribe moved, the leather hides and poles were very portable. Different travois, which consisted of two poles connected together at the middle, were made of different sizes depending on what needed to be pulled. One end was fastened over a horse's or dog's back, depending on the weight and size of item that needed moving. The horse or dog would drag each travois. Every adult and child had a specific task when they broke camp and moved to a new encampment, that could be days or weeks away.

Winter quickly approached, bringing with it the time for White Fawn to deliver her baby. On the day White Fawn started feeling pains, Jacob was sent out of the tepee and asked to wait outside. Two tribal midwives came to sit with her and make sure she was comfortable. Jacob was not allowed to enter the tepee while White Fawn was in labor.

At one point, he quickly poked his head in when he heard White Fawn crying out with pain. She had been with the midwives for over a day and a half. The second time he checked on his precious wife, her skin had a gray cast and she looked exhausted. Jacob couldn't help but worry. Finally, in the early morning of the third day she gave birth.

More squaws came in and out, each carrying hot water and making poultices. Jacob was told that Indian woman usually would squat down to deliver their child. In most cases, while in this squatting position, she would catch her own baby as it came forth from her body. This was not so for White Fawn. She was unable to squat due to the exhaustion from being in labor so long. She had torn badly when the baby finally came, causing her to lose a lot of blood. The poultices were used to try and stop the intense bleeding.

Finally, one of the midwives beckoned Jacob to enter the tepee. Another midwife held his baby in her arms. It was a boy, and he was beautiful with brown hair like Jacob's. The midwife handed the baby to Jacob. As he took his child, Jacob glanced at the midwife and saw concern on her face. At that moment, Jacob knew something was wrong. He saw sorrow in her eyes as she lowered her head, and averted his gaze.

Worried, Jacob touched the midwife's shoulder and said, "Tell me. I need to know the truth."

The midwife's eyes misted; she took a small breath and reverently said, "She dies, your beautiful one. She has not long to live. Take your son and be with her. Your son will soon follow."

Jacob's world was falling apart. How could such complete and endless joy end with such total devastation? Jacob felt like he was being pulled down into a dark suffocating corridor. His stomach twisted into a knot, and hot bile rose in his throat. He gagged. Then, putting his head into his right hand while holding his son in the crook of his left arm, he wept. With the innocence of a young child, Jacob sobbed. He felt a hand on his shoulder and looked up to see Zed standing there, his face also flooded with grief. Tears streamed down Zed's face as he unashamedly wept and mourned with Jacob.

Jacob knelt next to White Fawn, placing their son next to her. He then gently picked up her head and cradled it in his left arm. She looked up into his eyes, and with a love only two people have shared, she smiled. With difficulty, she said in a soft weak tone, "J-Jacob Morgan, never could I love anyone as much as I have loved you. I know the Great Spirit will call me home soon."

"Shhh. Don't speak, my love. You need all your strength to get well," Jacob said through his tears, although he didn't believe it.

Quietly and tenderly she whispered, "Is not our son beautiful? He looks like you, my Jacob Morgan. He has your strong face and eyes of wisdom."

With that the child let out a weak cry. White Fawn tried to reach for him, but she was too weak to even lift her hand. Jacob tenderly picked up their son and placed him gently on her. She smiled weakly, and again looking at their child with satisfaction said, "Is not this our own son, Jacob Morgan? Is he not ours?" She then looked up at him and whispered, "My only sadness is that . . . I . . . will not be able to bear you more sons and daughters. We will not be able to grow old together."

She struggled, wincing in pain as she tried to speak. She looked deeply into his eyes and said, "Jacob, do . . . do you think we will ever see each other again? I cannot bear to think that I will not be with you on the other side." Jacob didn't know what to say. Was there an answer to her question? Did anyone have an answer?

Jacob was unable to control his emotions. He kissed her forehead and cheeks. His tears spilled onto her face as he wept uncontrollably.

She reached up with her small trembling hand and gently touched his face, slowly running her fingers through his tears and over his nose and chin. She rested her hand on his chest, and then placed it over her heart. "Jacob Morgan, you have the best customs. They were only for me. I . . . love you . . . Jacob Morgan." She gently touched her hand to his chest, and it slowly fell as she gave one last sigh and slipped from this life.

A bloodcurdling cry ripped from Jacob's throat. He felt as if his heart would burst and he could not endure the pain. He reached for his son, and as he touched him, there was no life. She had taken him with her.

Jacob tried to stand, but couldn't. Sobbing uncontrollably and gasping for breath, he fell helplessly to the ground. Zed was immediately at his side, accompanied by Running Bear. They put their arms around his shoulders and helped him back to Zed's tepee.

Chapter 22
The Abyss

Jacob lay on the soft buffalo hides in Zed's tepee. The soft glow of the fire's embers was slowly dying away. Jacob felt like the fire. There was no warmth in him. Everything was dying, leaving behind nothing but coldness in his mind and body. He was numb inside, and it took every effort to breathe and think. The last moments of White Fawn's life played over and over again in his mind, as he saw her hand slowly slipping from his chest and falling limply to her side—a sharp reminder that she was really gone. He had lost his White Fawn; she had departed this life and taken their son with her.

Jacob remembered the first time he had seen her and it was still clear in his mind. His tears flowed uncontrollably with wracking sobs. He was in an endless abyss, not wanting to live. There was no purpose in life without his beloved White Fawn.

Jacob knew that he had loved her from the first moment he saw her. And now his beloved wife was gone. His whole world was turned upside down.

Jacob felt a hand gently placed on his shoulder and looked up to see Zed. "Boy, are you okay?" Zed said, his voice softer than Jacob had ever heard before. "I am so sorry fer yer loss. We all loved her. She was something special. Come, boy. You have to get up. It's been over a day since she passed away, and she needs to be placed on the brier for burial. The chief is waiting for you with his family."

Zed patiently helped Jacob to stand. In a daze, Jacob put on his buckskins, leaning on Zed for support. Zed helped him walk through the flap of the tepee. Running Bear was waiting for him just outside, ready to give whatever support was needed to his friend.

Slowly, they walked out of the village and over a hill from the encampment to the burial site. The entire tribe had gathered there in the cold. They all stood reverently watching the three men approach. Jacob's eyes slowly looked from one face to another; they had all come to pay their last respects to his beloved White Fawn. Finally he looked at Chief Two Clouds. Standing next to him was his wife, their son, and two remaining daughters. The death of his daughter had aged the chief, and it looked as if the world were on his shoulders. White Fawn had been his favorite child. Jacob knew that he had been looking forward to having a new grandchild. Jacob could see Dancing Light had been crying, and she looked exhausted. Her eyes met Jacob's, and then slowly she nodded her head in understanding.

One Who Walks Tall stood in front of the crowd. He solemnly greeted Jacob with a sorrowful nod of his head and then proceeded with the burial ceremonies. Jacob didn't hear a word; he couldn't take his eyes off White Fawn, lying there wrapped in a beautiful white buckskin robe with a buffalo hide neatly tucked around her. She looked so peaceful,

As Jacob stared at his beloved, he noticed a bump on the left side of her breast. It was their son, Zac. The baby was to be buried with his mother. The child's small head protruded just above the top of the hide, his beautiful brown hair barely showing. They both looked so peaceful, resting in eternal sleep, mother and son.

One Who Walks Tall chanted the burial ceremony. When he finished, he turned toward Jacob and gently touched his arm. He sadly said, "Jacob, my friend, not only do I grieve for you, but all our people grieve for the loss of your squaw, White Fawn, and your son." One Who Walks Tall then turned and nodded to Chief Two Clouds.

Zed, Running Bear, Two Clouds, and White Fawn's brother walked solemnly over to where she and her son lay. They carefully lifted the brier up and placed her gently up on top of four notched polls that had been placed in the ground. Here she would be protected from the wolves, but not from the ravages of time.

Jacob stood without weeping or moving. As he looked up and saw White Fawn upon the brier, he recalled her dying words: "Jacob, do you think we will ever see each again? I cannot bear to think that I will not be with you on the other side." Jacob was frightened. There lay his White Fawn, the only woman he had ever loved. As if on cue, the entire tribe began weeping and wailing, both men and women grieving for the loss of the dead. During the time Jacob had lived among the Sioux, he had learned to love the people and their culture. Because of this, he had gained many friends. Yes, he had helped save the tribe from a disastrous loss of their women and children from the Crow raid. But he was loved by the people because he was a part of them. They were his family.

Weeks passed and Jacob still didn't respond to Zed and Running Bear's encouragement to come back to the land of the living. He didn't eat enough to keep a small animal alive. His eyes had lost their zest for life. His whole countenance was void of hope.

One day, as Zed sat across from Jacob, he said, "Boy, it has been weeks since you lost yer wife. I know it's tough, but what can I do to help you? If White Fawn were here, she would want you to continue to live."

In anguish, Jacob replied, "Zed, how . . . how can I go on? I feel as though my heart has been torn from my chest. I feel as if I died with her. I feel dead." Zed leaned over and touched Jacob's shoulder and tenderly said, "Boy, I never lost a woman. My ma and pa died when I was just a young'un and there was the loss of yer Uncle Zac. Other than that I don't know what it is to really grieve."

Pausing for a moment, Zed slowly swallowed and looked at Jacob as if not knowing what else to say. Then he continued, "I don't know how you feel, so I can't put myself in yer place. The only thing I know is that White Fawn loved you very much. She would have wanted you to go on with yer life. I can't say if we'll ever see our loved ones again, but I've always had a feeling there's more to life than just the here and now."

Zed stood up and looked sympathetically at Jacob and added, "Boy, I just hope that what I said will help you. Now, please get up and at least try to eat something. Buck has been nickering fer you for the past week. Please don't neglect him, 'cause he don't understand." Zed gently patted Jacob's shoulder and then left him alone with his thoughts.

Jacob realized Zed was right, he couldn't go on feeling sorry for himself. He knew he had slipped into a deep hole. He asked himself, *Will there ever be an end to this night of blackness? How long will it take before I can shake off this despair?*

Jacob sat down and ate a few morsels of food. The food was dry and tasteless in his mouth. He drank some water from his leather canteen and it had a brackish taste. He spit it out. Miserably, Jacob stood and left the tepee, walking slowly toward the large meadow where the Sioux horses were grazing.

The bleak winter was past, and signs of spring were everywhere. The cool winds were blowing off the mountains as Jacob walked through the village to take care of Buck. As he passed tepees of the other villagers, people called out to him and greeted him with a gentle touch to his arm or shoulder, saying encouraging words of compassion. He kindly acknowledged their presence and thanked them for their thoughtfulness.

Before reaching the mass of grazing horses, Jacob could hear a loud whinny. He looked up and saw Buck. As he got closer, Jacob could see the stallion running with his head held high and his tail flying straight out behind him. Buck came to a sliding halt just in front of Jacob, showering him with dirt. Nickering and bobbing his head up and down, Buck slowly laid his head over Jacob's shoulder.

Jacob reached up and put his arms around Buck and began to weep with deep, gulping sobs. With all his grieving over the past weeks, Jacob thought he had no more tears to shed, but they continued to fall, wetting Buck's neck. Jacob stood there for over an hour weeping and holding onto Buck.

Jacob couldn't communicate with anyone, not even Zed. Buck was the only one he could really talk to. Buck couldn't say anything in return, but it seemed as if this magnificent stallion understood all his pain.

Jacob slowly walked back into the tepee and sat down in front of Zed. In a whisper, he said, "Zed, I need to leave. I need to be by myself. I want to go where nobody knows me and nobody cares."

Zed looked up dumbfounded at Jacob. How was he supposed to watch over Jacob if he was gone and nowhere in sight? Knowing Jacob, Zed knew it would be fruitless to argue, or to try and persuade him to stay. Slowly nodding his head, he said, "Boy, I understand," even though he didn't.

All Jacob wanted to do was to get away and find a place to hibernate and heal. Early the next morning, Zed and Running Bear loaded a packhorse with Jacob's personals and a supply of food. They loaded hides for warmth and other necessities to keep him alive until he found himself.

Zed handed Jacob his Tennessee rifle and asked, "Got your powder and lead?"

Nodding his head, Jacob thanked him. Then with a forced smile, he embraced his two friends and told them not to worry and that he would be fine. Jacob mounted Buck, turned, and didn't tell anyone he was leaving or where he was going. Jacob didn't know, so what could he tell them?

Buck led out followed by the packhorse, and Jacob never glanced back as he disappeared from their sight.

Buck walked slowly alongside the Missouri for several miles and then turned north into the deep mountain forest. To the Sioux, these mountains were known as the Black Sacred Mountains. It was early spring, and there was no trail to follow, so he let Buck have his head and let him make his own trail. By early afternoon, Jacob was among the tall and stately pines and aspens. The sound of wind rushing through the trees reminded him of the sea back in Boston. It was then that he thought of his family. He wondered how they were doing and if everything was well with them.

Buck slowly picked his way up the steep incline, maneuvering around fallen trees and boulders for the better part of an hour. Jacob pulled up and let Buck and the packhorse rest. Breathing in the cool mountain air, his mind began to clear. It reminded him of when Zed and he were riding high in the mountains of California, heading toward Zed's ranch. It was the same smell—cool and crisp—and Jacob felt as if he were coming out of a fog. Topping the rise, there in the distance stood tall pinnacles of rock reaching upward into the sky like sentinels. Jacob felt something reaching deep inside him, and he felt pulled toward them by an unseen power and Jacob felt it was God.

Was this what he needed to heal his broken heart? As he forged onward from one ridge to another, he followed no trail. Jacob gave Buck his head again, letting him make a trail where perhaps his destiny lay ahead. It was late in the day when Buck finally reached the majestic overhang of rock that stood like a lone sentinel in the sky.

All around him, aspens and pines seemed eagerly awaiting his arrival. In the distance, barely visible behind a large pine, there appeared to be a cave cut back into the side of the mountain. Jacob turned in his saddle, trying to get a better look. It was difficult to see, but through the trees he could see the very top of the cave. He pointed Buck in that direction.

Slowly, Buck continued his way up a steeper incline, carefully stepping around trees and boulders, making a new trail until he stopped a short distance below the opening of the cave. Dismounting, Jacob tied Buck and the packhorse to a tree. He then worked his way up to the mouth of the cave where large clumps of brush blocked the opening.

With some effort, he pulled away enough brush to allow himself an entrance. Cautiously entering the cave, Jacob looked around. The top of the cave reminded him of a small cathedral, which opened and pointed toward the heavens. From the outside, one would never suspect it was so immense inside. At the entrance of the cave, the opening was just wide enough to ride a horse through.

Jacob walked further back into the darkened interior. The cave became smaller in the back with just enough room to comfortably stable his horses at night. He could hear water falling into a stone basin in the blackness, off to his left.

Further exploring, Jacob found ashes from a fire built long ago from some ancient visitor. Leaning against the wall next to the remains of a fire were two primitive stone knives, different than any he had ever seen. Picking up the knife, it was made handcrafted and made of solid stone. A knife was not something one left behind unless he had been taken either by man or animal. The thought brought a shiver up his spine, and Jacob vowed to be watchful. Glancing around at his new surroundings, he didn't know long he would be here, but he made up his mind that this would be his new home.

Jacob walked back to the opening of the cave and pulled away all of the brush that blocked his view. He wanted an open view to see out in case someone, or something, tried to come upon him unseen.

Untying Buck and the packhorse, Jacob mounted and slowly began exploring his new surroundings. Within a short distance from the cave, there was an opening to a ravine. It gradually opened into a small box canyon, hidden from view by the rocky ledge overhead. There was sufficient forage in the hidden enclosure that would feed the horses for some time.

Retracing his steps back toward the cave, Jacob heard water running and went to inspect. Following the sound, he found the source of the water. It was bubbling up from an underground spring next to the side of the rock wall. Jacob surmised it must have been the same water he had heard inside the cave.

Jacob unpacked the horse and stored his supplies in the cave. He unsaddled Buck, and then rubbed Buck and the packhorse down. As he was going through his supplies, he found an ax. He had not thought of bringing one and realized gratefully that Zed must have put it with his supplies. This was a much-needed item, and soon he started cutting wood for his fire.

Working kept Jacob's mind off his sorrows, so he worked hard for the remainder of the day. He found branches and leaves to make a soft sleeping area. Then he placed one of the buffalo robes over them for comfort. It had been warm outside, but the coolness of the cave made Jacob feel refreshed.

When darkness approached, Jacob gathered both horses and brought them into the cave for safety. He would need to keep a close lookout to avoid bears or mountain lions that made these mountains their home —and an even closer lookout for man.

Searching in the forested area earlier, Jacob found dry wood for a clean fire. Green wood created a lot of smoke, and he didn't want it coming out his cave where it could be seen from below. The rising smoke from his small fire thinned out as it filtered to the top of the ceiling and then escaped out into the night. Jacob felt secure. He was hidden and didn't want to be found.

Jacob tossed and turned during the night, dreaming of White Fawn. He saw images of her lifeless body lying on the ground. In his dreams he begged for her to awaken, to speak to him. Frantically he yelled, "White Fawn, I can't find you. Please come to me." He awoke gasping for breath, his heart racing. He was wringing wet with sweat. After calming down, he fell back into a fitful sleep.

In the early morning hours, Jacob awoke, sat up, and tried to rub the sleep from his eyes. He moved over to where he had stored his things and searched through one of his saddlebags.

Before leaving his tepee, Jacob had retrieved one of White Fawn's buckskin garments. He had packed it in his saddlebag with his personal belongings because he wanted something of hers to remember her by and keep her close.

He now fumbled, searching for the garment and found it tucked away securely in the bottom of his saddlebag. Slowly, he pulled it out and held it close, smelling the fragrance of her body. He touched it softly, reverently, and gently caressed it, wanting the warm vibrant body of White Fawn to appear. Then he was again gasping for breath with loud wracking sobs, wailing and crying like a child. This went on until the morning. Jacob wondered if it ever would be over with. How could he forget his beloved White Fawn?

The early light of morning filtered through the trees, illuminating the opening of the cave. The horses stamped their feet, and Jacob suddenly awakened with a start. He was drained and exhausted. This was the worst night he had experienced since White Fawn's death, and there seemed to be no end to his pain.

As Buck continually nickered, Jacob felt guilty and realized the animals were still under his care and he was neglecting them. He dressed slowly and led both horses to the small ravine, and turned them loose to graze. He knew Buck would not wander off and that the packhorse would stay with him.

Jacob was weak from lack of food and still numb with grief. Taking his time, he made a small fire and realized he needed nourishment, not only for his body but also for his soul. He filled his leather canteen with water from the small collecting basin in back of the cave. The water was so cold that it made his teeth ache when he drank it. He immediately plunged his head into the cold water and gasped as if the water brought him back to life.

He made Indian tea. He needed something that was strong enough to keep him awake. He laid back on his soft buffalo robe and closed his eyes to think. Before he realized it, he had drifted off into a restless sleep.

Jacob awoke suddenly. A menacing feeling came over him, and he was on full alert. He could see the shadows of late afternoon on the cave's entrance. The hair on the back of his neck stood up. It was that same feeling he had off and on since he had gotten off the ship in San Francisco.

Quickly grabbing his Tennessee rifle, he moved to the cave opening. Scanning the area, he crept to front of the cave. Up on a ledge, he saw a score of dark figures moving cautiously along the skyline. They were Indians!

He didn't know if they were a raiding or a hunting party. However, he was well concealed, and it would be nigh impossible for them to see the cave or find him or his horses, especially by the wide overhanging ledge that was above the canyon where his horses were pastured. Even though Jacob was well hidden, he was not without doubt that in time, someone or something could eventually find him, and this made him uneasy.

Jacob drifted with difficulty from one day into the next. He spent every waking moment remembering his White Fawn. It had been three weeks since Jacob had found his new home. Each day he tried to keep alert, but with little sleep and constant nightmares, Jacob became more exhausted. He wasn't eating and his grief was literally consuming his life.

As Jacob prepared to retire late one evening, a storm approached. The wind blew with lightning accompanied by the crack of thunder. Jacob felt different as he lay down and tried and sleep. Slowly, he drifted, falling into a deep, overpowering sleep. As Jacob lay on his back he was enveloped in this abyss. He felt a peace settle over him, unlike anything he had ever experienced before. It was much like the same feeling he had experienced when he prayed to God. Slowly, an unexplainable feeling of peace enveloped his entire body.

Totally immersed and hypnotized by this powerful feeling, Jacob suddenly felt a soft cheek touching the side of his face. He sat up and opened his eyes, and there in a brilliant light stood White Fawn. Stunned, he watched her. Was she real? Jacob slowly stood up and reached out to touch her. He felt her, and his heart raced. It was his White Fawn!

When Jacob reached to embrace her, she smiled and stepped back shaking her head indicating for him not to touch her. There was someone else standing next to her. Jacob looked into the face of the other person he loved and recognized—it was his mother. They both looked at Jacob and smiled.

That same brilliant white light that Jacob had experienced with his last visit from his mother now encircled them both. White Fawn spoke first, "Jacob, please do not grieve. I have been taken home for a special purpose." In her arms she held a beautiful baby, their son.

Jacob's heart raced. "Is it really you, White Fawn, and our son? Is that really you, Mother?"

His mother and White Fawn nodded their heads. Smiling, his mother said, "Yes, Jacob we are real. We have been allowed to visit you due to your grieving. We came to tell you to live—"

White Fawn interrupted, "Jacob, my love, you must go on with your life. This is just the beginning for you. I will always be with you, and yes, Jacob, we will see each other in the next life."

"I want to come with you," Jacob frantically replied, realizing that she may leave him again.

White Fawn slowly shook her head.

Now his mother spoke. "My son, remember when I told you that I approved of your marriage to White Fawn? She has now completed her work, but you must live to complete your work. There is much for you to do in this life, and there is also someone special waiting for you. We will be waiting and when it is your time to come home, we will be there to meet you."

As she said those last words, Jacob felt a greatest feeling of love that totally engulfed him. White Fawn stepped forward and placed her hand against his cheek just like she had always done. Then she gently said, "I love you, Jacob Morgan." She looked at his mother, and she nodded her head. White Fawn continued, "We must go now, please, Jacob, don't waste this chance to heal, not only your heart, but also your body. We will always be with you." Slowly the light gathered around them, and they departed into an unseen realm.

Jacob wept for joy. She was well. His White Fawn, his son, and his mother were real. They had actually spoken to him. They were all in a place that was real. He had now lost the two women whom he most dearly loved. Who else had he lost since he'd left? Was his father well? Was he alive? He must be or he would have come with his mother.

Jacob inhaled deeply, contemplating what had just happened. In his heart, a great healing had taken place. The feeling of peace that had come over him, stayed with him. He felt as if his burdens had been lifted and his soul had been filled with joy. Jacob promised himself that he would get well, and he would live for both White Fawn and his mother. But, most of all, he must live for himself.

The days now drifted easily into one another as Jacob concentrated on getting well. He spent more time with Buck and began to eat more food and slowly began putting weight back on. Within a few weeks the old Jacob was left behind him and a new Jacob was emerging.

Early one morning after three months had passed, Jacob looked at his surroundings and said out loud, "It's time to leave."

As the shadows darkened that evening, Jacob gathered his scanty belongings and prepared to leave the following morning. He was now at peace with himself and knew that an unknown mission lay ahead of him. Jacob stabled Buck and the packhorse at the back of the cave and ate his meal and prepared to retire for the evening.

Just before drifting off to sleep, Jacob lay on his back contemplating his new life and eagerly anticipating the new experiences that awaited him on the horizon. As he lay there thinking and listening to the peaceful sounds of the night outside the cave, he heard a sudden rustling of leaves. Jacob's hair stood up on the back of his neck. Then he heard the faintest sounds of footsteps, as one foot was slowly placed in front of the other outside the opening of his cave. Grabbing his rifle, Jacob pulled back the hammer. In the stillness of the cave, it made a loud click. The footsteps stopped and then quickly retreated.

Moving quickly and crouching at the entrance of the cave, Jacob carefully stepped out, listening for anything abnormal. He didn't hear anything except the quiet sounds of the night. Scanning the area, the only light Jacob could see was the brilliance of the stars in the blackness of the heavens. All was quiet, yet he was still uneasy. Something had been there, and it was not an animal.

Long before the sun had crested over the mountains, Jacob was up. He grazed his horses while he prepared and ate his last breakfast in his fortress of solitude. He carried his rifle, as he quickly gathered the horses and with last night's experience still fresh in his mind, he was now all the more alert. He packed the last of his belongings, and bid his healing home good-bye.

It had been an experience Jacob would never forget. He now felt alive again and knew it was time to head back to California.

Chapter 23
Leaving

The following afternoon, a short distance from the Sioux camp, Zed and Running Bear met Jacob on their horses.

"Well, if you ain't a sight fer sore eyes." Zed said.

The three men dismounted their horses and walked toward each other. Zed grabbed Jacob and pulled him in to a huge bear hug. Jacob was taken aback by the crusty old mountain man's reception because Zed just wasn't the hugging type. He pulled back and looked gratefully at Jacob.

Running Bear yelled, "My brother!" He extended his arm, and grasped Jacob's forearm with powerful strength, and then pulled him in for a hug.

With a look of concern, Zed asked, "Did you find yerself, boy?"

A broad smile covered his face, and Jacob said, "Zed, not only did I find myself, but we are going back to California."

"Yahoo!" yelled Zed. "Boy that is the best news I've heard all year."

Running Bear, who had been listening, asked, "Jacob, what is California?"

Jacob now needed to tell his good friend that he would be leaving the Sioux camp and going away. Jacob replied, "I will explain later today." That satisfied Running Bear, and both he and Zed proceeded to ask Jacob all sorts of questions about his last few months of solitude. Jacob promised he would tell them everything that had happened— that is everything except his visit from White Fawn and his mother. He would keep that experience locked up and treasured in his heart. It was too sacred. The only person he would share it with would be his father and his brother Isaiah if he ever saw them again.

His return to the camp was announced before he could even approach his tepee. Many friends gathered around him, slapping him on the back and excitedly asking him endless questions. He was glad to be back and he felt safe among his friends.

Jacob, with the help of Zed and Running Bear, unpacked the horses and his belongings. Jacob removed Buck's saddle, rubbed him down, and turned him out to the Sioux grazing area.

Upon returning to his tepee, Jacob found Chief Two Clouds and his wife, Dancing Light, waiting there. She moved to Jacob and placed her hands on his shoulders. Placing her cheek to his, she whispered, "Jacob, our son, we have worried for you. It is good to see you are well."

Jacob choked back his emotions and realized this was his family. Nodding, he replied in a voice barely above a whisper, "I am well. It is good to be back with my family."

Two Clouds gently touched Jacob's shoulder. He looked at Jacob with pain-filled eyes and asked, "Jacob, is your heart now healed?" He then extended his arm for Jacob to grasp. Jacob didn't grasp his arm but reached up and gave him a firm embrace, and Two Clouds returned his embrace. "We must talk," Jacob said.

Later that day, Two Clouds, Dancing Light, Zed, Running Bear, and Jacob all sat in a circle in Chief Two Cloud's tepee. All eyes were on Jacob, when Two Clouds nodded for him to begin.

Jacob, cleared his throat with emotion and said, "I didn't want to hurt anyone when I left. My heart was greatly wounded and needed to heal. I have spent many suns weeping and searching for understanding. I did not find any."

There was a pause, and everyone looked at Jacob in surprise. He put up his hand and continued. "I did not find any understanding on my own, but it was given to me by the Great Spirit."

Thoughtfully, Jacob continued. "I left my friends behind and traveled to the Sacred Mountains." Jacob then asked. "Do you know of the tall rocks that stand above the clouds where they who are warriors silently watch over the Sioux nation?" Jacob directed his question to Two Clouds, who immediately nodded, signifying that he knew the sacred place Jacob was referring to.

Jacob continued. "As I looked at those Sacred Mountains, I felt drawn by the Great Spirit and compelled to go, so I obeyed. I, Jacob Morgan, who was lost, needed to be found."

Jacob shifted his body and said, "I found a cave that had been used long ago by ancient ones as a resting place. I, as they long ago, needed rest, not only for my heart, but also for my body. There I spent many suns. I had much time to think. I mourned much because of my love for your daughter." Looking at Dancing Light, he went on, saying, "While I slept one afternoon, the hair on the back of my neck stood up. I have found this to be a gift given to me by the Great Spirit. It tells me when danger is near. I left my place of mourning, and saw above me ten dark figures crossing the ridge heading toward the village—"

Two Clouds raised his hand to interrupt. "Yes, our scouts saw ten Crow warriors. They were coming to steal our horses. They were all captured."

"Did you kill them?" Jacob asked concerned.

Two Clouds shook his head and said, "We let them live and made a treaty with them. They are now our friends and they left in peace."

Zed motioned for Jacob to continue. Jacob took his time. He now had everyone's attention. "One night I fell into a deep sleep, and I had a vision. I cannot tell you what I saw because of the sacredness of the vision, but I know it was given to me by the Great Spirit. I will tell you this one thing: White Fawn and my son are safe and well. I have seen them."

Incrediuslously, Zed looked at Jacob and his jaw dropped. Running Bear's emotions showed on his face, and Jacob knew he believed him. It was Dancing Light who put her hand to her mouth, turned her head, and sobbed softly. She started to leave and Jacob said, "Please stay, I have more to tell." She slowly sat down, while continuing to cry softly.

Two Clouds' eyes were now misty with this new revelation. Nodding his approval, he said, "Please, Jacob Morgan, speak more."

For a long moment, Jacob remained still as he reminisced over the wonderful spiritual experience he had been privilege to receive. Reverently, Jacob continued, "I can tell you that this life is the time of preparation for each of us to come to know the Great Spirit." With that said, a feeling of peace suddenly came over all of them.

Zed looked at Jacob and knew he was talking about God. "We are not alone," Jacob continued. "I have learned that there are those of our loved ones who have passed on that are given permission to watch over us and help us while we are here."

Two Clouds nodded his head in agreement, and everyone was mesmerized and silently processing what Jacob had just told them.

Jacob chose his next words carefully, not wanting to offend them. "There is more. In order for me to obey the Great Spirit, I must leave the Sioux nation and go back to where I came from. My work is not completed there, and I must return." Jacob ended his speaking and lowered his head.

There was a gasp and a groan from Running Bear. "No, my brother," There was anger and frustration in his voice, as he struggled to control his emotions. He said, "Jacob, my brother, I have just found you, and now I lose you?" He immediately stood up and hurried out of the tepee.

Jacob saw a change in Two Clouds's and Dancing Light's countenances. It was difficult for them to accept this new information, but they both nodded their heads in agreement, believing in the truth of Jacob's vision.

There was a feeling of sadness, and Two Clouds looked at Jacob and asked, "When do you leave?"

Looking at Zed, Jacob said, "We will go in four suns."

The news of their leaving spread like a wildfire throughout the camp. The story told was that the Great Spirit had commanded Jacob to leave. Jacob was grateful that he had not told them all that had happened to him in the cave. He wanted to keep the sacred vision locked away in his heart. If he had told them all of what really happened, others would tell his story differently and soon all the sacredness of his experience would be lost.

The day before Jacob and Zed were to depart, they visited many friends in the tribe and attended two tribal councils in their honor. The tribe members asked many questions about the white man. Other tribes had told them that the white man would come into their land and steal it. They wanted to know if this was true. Jacob and Zed's opinions were not encouraging. These people were family and they wanted to be honest and tell them what they knew. Zed told them it was their thought that eventually the white man would trespass the Indians' hunting grounds and steal their land.

Zed explained that there were as many white men as there were stars in the sky. This created a somber mood among the tribe as the tribal elders contemplated this new information.

A voice was heard in the back of the gathering, "We will die fighting for our wives and our children!"

Zed looked at Jacob and nodded his head in agreement, and said in poetic prophesy, "I'm sure this is true," Zed said quietly to Jacob, "In not many years, the ways of the Sioux nation will be no more."

On the morning of the fourth day, Jacob and Zed prepared to depart on their journey. They had said their good-byes and they now stood next to their horses with their animals packed, ready to leave. A young brave approached, leading five horses: two stallions and three mares. Jacob had given ten horses to Two Clouds as a gift for White Fawn. Two Clouds now took the leather lead ropes to the five horses and handed them to Jacob.

"Since you gave many horses for my daughter," he paused with emotion and said, "because of your love for her, I now give you these horses back to you as a token of that love. Go in peace, my son, and may the Great Spirit watch over and protect you."

Jacob's eyes were misty, and he said, "I accept these horses and will always remember the friendship and I will honor my Sioux family." Turning slowly, Jacob cast his eyes over the faces of his family and friends. No people had ever touched him more, and he would never forget who they were and who he was.

As Zed and Jacob mounted, they raised their hand in farewell, and rode slowly away, the Sioux tribe fading into their past.

After an hour on the trail, Zed turned to Jacob and said, "I didn't see Running Bear."

"I looked for him but couldn't find him either," Jacob replied. "I was wondering what had happened to him."

Just as he finished speaking, Jacob looked to his right, and there riding down a small incline was Running Bear. He stopped in front of them and slid off his pony. Jacob dismounted, grateful to see his friend. As they approached, each embraced in a brotherly hug. After embracing Jacob, Running Bear stepped back and looked into Jacob's eyes, and with emotion said. "My brother, I could not let you depart without you knowing of my feelings." He looked at Zed and then to Jacob and continued, "Never have I had a brother with whom I have felt at one with. When you came to our encampment, I knew you were a great warrior. You have proven it by the way you have lived." With a sense of sadness he went on, "My heart aches for your loss of White Fawn and your son. I know the Great Spirit has many things planned for your life. Because of you, my brother, I am a better warrior and I have found a true friend."

Then, without waiting for Jacob to reply, he turned, mounted his pony, and raised his hand in farewell. Then, as an afterthought, he paused and said, "Jacob, my brother, there is danger near; I feel it. You must ride very carefully." He then turned and was gone.

Jacob looked at Zed and said, "He didn't even give me a chance to reply."

Nodding, Zed said, "Boy, there was no need to. He knew how ya felt. I think we need to give heed to his words and watch fer danger."

Throughout the day, Zed and Jacob followed an ancient trail leading through the mountains, constantly on alert, as they led their eleven horses and three mules along the steep mountain trail. They carefully made their way across the switchbacks and continued their climb over the mountain passes. They were now high in the mountains among the timber and Jacob once again enjoyed the fragrance of the pines. His mind was clear and his heart was at peace.

Zed rode point and Jacob rode drag, which was the last rider, and he kept a watchful eye out for trouble in all directions. Reaching the top of the last mountain pass and preparing to descend, a vast prairie opened to their view as far as their eyes could see.

Zed turned in his saddle and cautiously said, "We'll be out in the open by tomorrow. It's best we keep ourselves alert and hidden; this still Indian country."

Zed then slowed his horse and motioned for Jacob to come alongside. When Jacob was next to him, Zed turned and thoughtfully said,

"Jacob I'm sorry to say, but we had ta tell our Indian friends the truth. The white man will come here by the thousands and destroy all the Indians' way of life—and I don't think it's that many years away."

Both men paused to scan the area of any Indian sign and then Zed continued. "These mountains and wide prairies are the Indians' sacred hunting grounds, and there will be much bloodshed. The Indians will not let the white man trespass without a fight. This will mean war, and the white man will eventually destroy the Indians. The way of the Indian will be lost forever." Zed paused for a moment, again his eyes scanning the area both close and far around him, and he continued. "Boy, we were lucky to have lived with the Sioux and known their way of life. Things will change for the worse, and we will either have to change with it or go against it. I think it's best we be prepared."

The two men sat on their horses and looked out over the vast prairie below them. Jacob felt a strange sadness stir his soul. He knew Zed was right, but he had become a part of this land with its strange canyons and unending forests. The thought of losing it filled him with great sadness. He wanted to explore and see everything before it was gone.

As Jacob led out, suddenly the hair on the back of Jacob's neck stood straight up. Without warning, Buck spooked, and turning around he raced back toward the safety of the pack animals that were behind him with Zed. Jacob pulled him up and reached down stroking his neck to calm him. He could feel Buck's fear as he snorted and bobbed his head up and down. "Buck, what's wrong?" asked Jacob as he pulled his rifle out of its scabbard. Zed, not seeing what had happened, immediately rode from behind and asked what happened. Jacob quickly explained what Buck had done and, without saying a word, Zed was off his horse and running. Jacob quickly slid off Buck and followed.

Zed said, "That horse of yers don't act like that unless something's wrong, and from what I see, this here is a perfect place for an ambush." Ahead were large rocks with hidden openings where one could wait unseen. Zed looked around and then said, "You go to the right, and I'll circle round to the left. Jest keep yer rifle ready and yer wits about ya, boy."

Jacob was off and running to his right, circling the large rock formation in front of him. He needed to get ahead of Zed in order to protect him if need be.

Jacob slowly eased around a large boulder. Ahead of him, he saw an Indian hunched over a rock leaning in the direction they would have passed. To his left, Zed was making his way slowly around the other side the boulder. Jacob raised his hand and motioned for Zed to stop. Lifting his rifle, Jacob pulled back the hammer. It made a loud click, but the Indian didn't move.

Taking aim, Jacob yelled in Sioux, "Stand up."

Still, the Indian didn't move. Zed was now walking cautiously toward the Indian. Moving closer, Jacob recognized the figure and mouthed to Zed, "It's Lone Wolf."

Zed approached Lone Wolf from behind and nudged him with the barrel of his rifle. He didn't move. Zed, not trusting him, kicked him in his side. This still brought no response. As Jacob took aim, Zed carefully advanced and reached out to touch Lone Wolf.

"He's dead," he said, after checking his pulse.

Zed examined Lone Wolf's body and said, "His neck has been broken. From what I can see, he was waiting fer ya." He scanned the ground, and looking carefully around he said, "Someone or something got to him before he could get to you." Zed carefully crouched down and checked for footprints. From what he could see there were neither man nor animal tracks and the grass had not been disturbed.

Jacob said, "Zed, I don't know what's going on. While in the cave, twice the hair on the back of my neck came up, just like it did moments ago. It warns me of danger. I told you about it before when we were first on the trail after we left the ranch. It also happened before in San Francisco after I got off the ship. I felt it when I walked into Weatherbee's office. It's the same feeling I just encountered with Lone Wolf."

Zed looked at him apologetically and replied, "Yer right, boy. I remember ya tellin' me about it before, but I didn't pay it no mind."

After a few minutes, Zed replied, "Boy, there is somebuddy out there that's trying to kill ya. I'm beginning to think there's someone else who wants to be the recipient of yer Uncle's will, and I don't know who it is. I don't think it's Graff and his partners 'cause we would be fightin' them by now. Whoever it is their mighty good at coming and going without being seen. It's best we be on the lookout, fer yer life may depend on it."

Chapter 24
New Beginnings

The lonely travelers slowly made their way down the sacred Sioux mountains and on to the vast, unending prairies. After weeks of traveling, they finally arrived at Fort Hall where Zed purchased needed supplies from the trading post. It was their intention to follow the Oregon Trail and cross the Utah Territory to California and find a trail to Sacramento. Once in Sacramento, they would cut across to San Francisco Bay and meet with Weatherbee.

The late summer evenings were cool. Time was on their side as they slowly meandered through the wild and unexplored country. Jacob wanted to remember everything about the area because once he got his inheritance, he didn't know if he would go back to Boston or what he would do.

In the distance, clouds of dust rose up as hundreds of white covered wagons slowly made their way along the trail, with pioneer families seeking a new way of life.

Jacob and Zed kept to themselves as their small caravan slowly crossed the vast miles of wasteland, keeping a watchful eye for trouble—either white man or Indian.

Zed decided that he wanted to try a shortcut to the Nevada Mountains. Within six weeks, the large mountain range came into view. They were called the Sierra Nevada and in Spanish, it meant "snowy mountain range." It looked formidable in the distance with its snow-covered peaks as it stretched for miles from east to west.

Forging their own trail, they made their way toward a distant mountain pass. The following day they found themselves on the top of a long flat mesa. After following it all day, it came to an abrupt end.

Looking down over the mesa edge, they saw that they could either go down the steep incline or turn around and go back and find another way down. If they took another way, it would take them at least another half a day's travel. After discussing their options, Zed and Jacob decided to take the shorter, straight route that went over and down the side of the mesa.

As they urged their horses off the top of the mesa, they started sliding down the long incline in the soft sand and shale. The horses sank up to their knees in some places, and sat back on their haunches for balance as they swiftly slid down the long sandy slopes to the bottom.

For the next two days, they traveled cautiously, keeping to the less traveled country. They were careful not to skyline themselves. If a man rode along a ridge or crested a hill, his enemies could see him from miles away. When he stayed hidden in the shadows below, he avoided unseen eyes and enemies.

Zed and Jacob wanted to avoid being seen by either white or Indian, especially traveling with their quantity of horses.

Early one morning, Jacob spotted a settlement in the distance. By midmorning they had entered the town. Their little caravan raised small puffs of dust as they meandered slowly down the main street. It wasn't a large town, and the people seemed friendly and waved at them as they passed by in their buckboards.

A buckboard was a wooden box wagon with four wheels. It had two seats, one in front and one in the back, and was pulled by a team of horses. Jacob took in his surroundings. Directly ahead of him was a saloon situated in the middle of town with a few horses tied to the hitching rail in front. To its right was the mercantile store. Across the street from the saloon was the barbershop with bathhouse and next door was a gunsmith.

There was a church at the far end of town, and in the distance was a building that resembled a schoolhouse. On a side street off from the saloon was a two-story building with a sign that read, "Landes Hotel," and at the rear was a livery stable and blacksmith shop. Homes were scattered around the town in the outlying areas.

Jacob liked the looks of the town; it seemed friendly and safe. This was the kind of town he wouldn't mind settling down in one day. But right now the only thing Jacob was interested in was a bath, a shave, and a table to put his feet under with a good home-cooked meal.

As they passed the saloon, the doors suddenly flew open as a young man was bodily thrown out into the dusty street. Two rough-looking men followed and proceeded to kick him. Then the smaller of the two men picked up the lad and held him while his partner continued to beat the young man senseless.

Jacob spurred Buck forward and Buck's right shoulder struck the man that had been hitting the boy, sending him sprawling. Jacob came out of his saddle, and before the other man knew what was happening, Jacob had knocked him down.

Bellowing with rage, the man that Buck had knocked down got up and yelled a string of curses, asking Jacob what he thought he was doing. Then he got up and started swinging at Jacob.

Jacob took a blow to his shoulder and then blocked a punch with his left arm. Then, quickly pivoting to his right side, he hit the man on the side of his head and the man went down. From the corner of his eye, Jacob saw the other man staggering to get up while swearing profusely. As he rushed forward, Jacob drop-kicked him in the chest with such force that he knocked him backward into a watering trough.

The first man, now screaming obscenities, was on his feet and charging like a raging bull. Just by the way the man moved, Jacob could see he had been drinking. As he lunged forward with both fists swinging wildly, Jacob ducked, and his right fist landed in the man's midsection. The man buckled with a whoosh and he fell to the ground. As he struggled to get up, Jacob hit him in the face with his left fist, creating a large gash on his right cheekbone, and then with a right upper cut, sprawled the man on his back, unconscious.

Jacob walked over to the man lying in the water trough and pulled him out since he didn't want him to drown. Dragging him up by his collar, Jacob laid him in front of the boy he had beaten. The man spit and sputtered as he tried to regain consciousness. Bending over and speaking in the man's ear, Jacob said, "Tell the boy you're sorry."

Jacob looked and there stood Zed to his side nodding his head in agreement.

By then, at least a dozen townspeople gathered around to watch the excitement. Some whispered, "Strangers were in town cleaning up some of the riffraff."

The man, now fully awake, looked incredulously at Jacob and swearing said, "You just keep yer—" Jacob reached back and hit the man directly in his nose and he fell on his back, with blood spurting out of his mouth and nose.

The man screamed, "You broke my nose! You broke my nose!" Jacob grabbed him by the front of his shirt and loudly said, "Now where were we? You were just about say you were sorry to this young man you just beat."

With hatred, the man glared at Jacob and said, "Just who do you think you are?"

Jacob swung twice and knocked the man on his back, splitting his lips and causing a large cut over his right eye.

Jacob was not one to lose his temper, but he was furious. There lay the young boy on the ground bleeding and there was no need for two grown men to beat a boy senseless. He grabbed the man by his shirt and again said, "For the last time, you will apologize to this boy, or I promise you will not walk away from here. Now, let me hear your apology."

Fear and contempt was on the man's face, but he knew the man in buckskins was not one to disobey. He looked at Jacob with hate-filled eyes and said to the boy, "Billy, I'm sorry that I hurt you." He now glared at Jacob.

Jacob added, "And I promise it won't happen again."

In defiance the man said nothing. Now seething with anger, Jacob shouted, "Say it!"

The man hung his head and meekly said, "It won't happen again."

Jacob reached down and took a hold of the boy's arm and asked, "Are you okay?"

The boy was shaking was holding his ribs, while bleeding from his mouth. He nodded weakly and said, "I'm okay."

Jacob led the boy over to the water trough, scooped water into his hand, and started washing the boy's face. A woman suddenly appeared at his side and using her hankie, she wiped the blood off the young man's face. The boy winced in pain, but said nothing.

A man wearing a store apron walked up. He had been standing among the large gathering of town folks. He asked, "Billy, are you okay? Can you make it home?"

Billy struggled to walk and weakly said, "I can make it." Then he took a step and fell down.

Jacob asked, "Where does he live?"

The man in the apron said, "That's the Windslow boy. He lives about fifteen miles out of town." He then pointed toward the northwest. "Just follow the road."

In those early pioneer days, fifteen miles was considered a short distance. Some settlers lived a half-day or a full-day's ride or further from a town. This was virgin territory and men were trying settle it and develop a ranch in the endless mountain ranges that lay around them.

Jacob looked at Zed and said, "Let's take him home."

Zed rolled his eyes and frowned. He said, "But I ain't had a chance to visit the saloon yet."

"Well, you go visit the saloon and get your fill. When you're finished, you can catch up. We'll be expecting you," grinned Jacob.

A broad smile covered Zed's face, and he replied, "I believe I can do that. You take the boy on home and when I'm finished I'll follow ya."

Jacob helped the boy mount his horse and headed out of town leading the string of horses and pack mules.

It was a beautiful area: the mountain valleys were to the south and the rolling hills went on for miles around them. Twice, Jacob had to stop to let Billy rest. About two hours out of town, Jacob could see longhorn cattle grazing in the distance. As they crossed the vast meadows, the grass was as high as their horses' bellies. Jacob looked over at Billy and he was wincing in pain so he stopped to give the boy a rest. After resting, they continued on and Billy said, "We've been on our ranch for the past hour."

Off to their right, a group of men on horseback had gathered a small herd of cattle for branding. One cowhand had a calf down on its side, with his knee on the calf's neck. Another cowboy had the calf's hind legs held fast with a rope tied around the saddle horn of his horse. A third man held a hot branding iron he had just retrieved from a small fire, and was placing the hot iron on the left hindquarter of the calf. The smell of burning flesh and hair filled the air.

One of the riders holding the herd saw the approaching riders, recognized Billy's horse, and came immediately to investigate. As the rider approached at a run, Jacob and Billy pulled up.

"Billy, are you hurt? What happened to you?" The rider asked.

Billy explained what had happened and that this man, pointing to Jacob, was taking him home.

The rider looked at Jacob and said, "Many thanks, we'll take it from here." He moved his horse toward Billy, but Jacob nudged Buck in front of the rider, quickly blocking his way.

"No," Jacob said, "I will take him home; I've got a partner who will follow!"

The cowboy glowered at Jacob and said in an authoritative tone, "I said we will take it from here!"

Jacob leaned a little forward in his saddle and said, "I am not going to say it again. I will be taking him home."

The man started to move, when Billy spoke up, "Hank, I don't think you want to cross this man. It ain't healthy. You should see the two Brawn brothers who beat me. They won't be working for quite a spell."

Hank cautiously backed his horse up, gave a curt nod, and went back to holding the herd.

After traveling for another hour, Jacob could see a large ranch house with outbuildings, corrals, and pastures filled with stock. The place reminded him of Zed's ranch in California. The home was a long log home that was twice the size of Zed's. He noticed there were two chimneys and a porch that wrapped around two sides. As they got closer, it was evident that the windows all opened from the inside, and each window opening was notched for shooting out. Surprised, Jacob said, "That's not a home—it's a fort. Looks like you could hold off an Indian attack."

Billy grinned, "That's what my pa said. We also have a deep cellar in case the roof takes fire; we can go escape underground."

Jacob was amazed by the watering system around the ranch. There were small canals from a nearby stream that were diverted to different areas of the pasture and one small canal went directly to a large family garden.

As they approached, the front door of the house swung opened and a woman came running down the wooden steps. She was followed by a man and two girls.

"Billy, are you alright? What happened to you?" the woman asked.

Billy slowly got off his horse, and his mother gathered him into her arms. Jacob dismounted and stood mutely with his reins in his hands.

Billy winced in pain from his mother's affectionate hug. He raised his right arm and pointed to Jacob. "If it weren't for this man, I would have been a goner. They really would have hurt me bad." Pausing, Billy turned to Jacob and said, "You know, mister, you never told me your name."

Jacob, somewhat embarrassed, said, "I am Jacob Morgan. My partner and I were passing through town when we saw two men beating up your son. I just couldn't let them pick on someone who was smaller than they were."

The man extended his right hand and said, "I am William Windslow, Billy's father, and this is my wife, Julie, and our two daughters, Emily and Mary."

Jacob took his hand and shook it firmly, nodded toward the three women, and said, "My pleasure, sir. Ladies, it's my pleasure to make your acquaintance." Jacob could see they were somewhat taken back by the formal way he had greeted them. He thought that maybe he should have just said, "Howdy."

William Windslow, now serious said, "Billy, who did this to you?"

"It was the Brawn boys, Pa. I just went in to deliver yer message to the foreman because they said he was in the saloon, but he wasn't there. When I went in, the Brawn brothers saw me and started teasing me and then hitting me. They had just thrown me out into the street when Mr. Morgan came to my rescue."

Just then, a ranch hand came out from the barn. William said to him, "Get the boys together, we've got a visit to make to the Brawn boys."

Reaching up and touching his pa's shoulder, Billy said, "It won't do you any good, pa. They're hurt real bad. It will be a quite a spell before they can even get around."

"What do you mean, son?" his father asked, confused.

"He beat 'em real good, Pa," he said, again pointing toward Jacob. "He made ole Ollie apologize to me for his bad manners with the whole town watching."

"But what about Ed? Didn't he fight? Those two are a couple of the meanest men in this country, and they have hurt many a man. What did Ed say?" his father asked, incredulous.

"He didn't say anything. Pa, he was still out cold when we left town."

William Windslow let out a low whistle and shook his head, as if not believing what he had just heard. He smiled and said, "Jacob, would you like to have dinner with us tonight?"

The offer was too good to refuse. It had been long time since Jacob had enjoyed a good home-cooked meal in an actual house. Smiling, he said, "It will be my pleasure to accept your invitation. I also have my partner, who will be here shortly. Would that invitation also include him?"

Now they all laughed, and Julie said, "Of course. Any friend of yours is welcome at our table." She then reached over and touched Jacob's arm and said, "Thank you, for saving my son, Jacob Morgan."

Mr. Windslow looked at Jacob's string of horses and said, "Are these Appaloosa horses from the Nez Perce tribe?"

Jacob reached over, and stroked one of the horse's necks, and said, "They were a gift to me from the chief of the Teton Sioux tribe."

"Wow," exclaimed Mr. Windslow. "What a wonderful gift. These are some of the most beautiful horses I've ever seen."

"Thank you. Is there any place I can put my stock out to feed?" Jacob asked.

Mr. Windslow motioned to his hired hand and said, "Ren, take these horses and put them in the small south pasture. There's excellent feed in that area."

The cowboy reached for Buck's reins, but Jacob stopped him. "He's a one-man horse and won't let anyone handle him but me." The cowboy nodded and took the string of horses to the pasture, with Jacob and Buck following behind, leading the pack mules.

Two hours later, Zed arrived. Jacob was real proud of Zed. He was standing on his own two feet and not walking crooked.

"Are you okay?" Jacob asked.

Usually when a man went into a saloon to drink they would overindulge themselves and have difficulty walking.

Zed smiled and said, "Don't you never worry, about me boy. I can hold my own when it comes to drinkin'."

Mr. Windslow came from the house and greeted Zed.

Jacob said, "We apologize for the way we look, but we have been on the trail for six weeks and haven't had a chance to clean up."

William smiled and said, "I'll take you to the bunkhouse and you can clean up there."

After Jacob and Zed had taken a bath and cleaned up, they sat down with the family at a long kitchen table. It was the nicest home Jacob had been in since leaving Boston. In the corner of the kitchen was a pantry and a cook stove. Jacob marveled that they even had a dry sink and a well pump in the house. Mr. Windslow watched as Jacob looked around the home and said, "If we were trapped in this home by an Indian raid, we could survive because our home is built so well."

Mrs. Windslow watched Jacob as he carefully looked around the room as if he had never seen the inside of a home. She asked, "Does this seem strange to you?" Jacob smiled and said, "I lived with my parents in Boston at one time, but after being with the Indians for the past two years and living in a tepee, it seems strange to be inside a home and sitting at a table using real dishes, cups, and utensils."

Jacob reflected as he looked around; this home was a lot like his home in Boston. A sudden nostalgia came over Jacob as he thought about home and his parents. With his mother dead, his father and two brothers were all the real blood family he had left.

Mrs. Windslow, watching Jacob, softly asked, "Do you miss your home?"

Nodding his head in the affirmative, Jacob said, "Yes, ma'am, I do. You are very keen in your observation."

Then he thought of his Sioux family, and he didn't really know if he would ever see them again.

Mary, the oldest daughter, sat across from Jacob, and for the first time he took notice of her. Her long, golden hair flowed over her shoulders. She had high cheekbones and beautiful blue eyes. She smiled when she saw Jacob looking at her and shyly turned her head away.

Mary passed the gravy bowl to Jacob and bumped it against his hand, spilling gravy on his wrist. "Oh, I'm so sorry," she said quickly. "I didn't mean to spill it on you."

Jacob had an instant flashback. He remembered over two years ago when White Fawn, with a mischievous gleam in her eye, had spilled hot soup over his hand and flirted with him.

Jacob looked at Mary and smiled. He realized it was an accident. He said, "I'm fine. It just brought back some pleasant memories."

Jacob had loved and lost White Fawn but because of his spiritual experience he had with her and his mother, he was now at peace. His memories of her were now pleasant and not disturbing.

Jacob again looked at Mary. She blushed and lowered her head. He smiled and thought, She is innocent, just like White Fawn.

For the rest of the evening, Jacob and Zed talked about their experiences. Jacob talked about his living in Boston, when he received his letter, his voyage to San Francisco, and his meeting Zed. They talked about Zed's beautiful ranch and his tutoring Jacob. Zed went on to tell them about living with the Sioux Indians, but not knowing the family's feelings about Indians, he omitted Jacob's marriage to White Fawn, and that was also Jacob's personal business. The family was mesmerized by their stories, and Jacob was getting a little embarrassed by all the conversation. Zed was telling it with all his gusto and adding a little extra here and there, embellishing the events to make them all the more exciting.

After supper, Jacob and Zed were shown to a large room at the back end of the house where they would sleep. That night as they lay in their comfortable beds, Zed sighed, "Boy, anytime you want to break up a fight in the future, you just go ahead and help yourself, 'cause you sure are lucky." It was wonderful to sleep in a bed and soon both weary travelers were sound asleep.

Jacob was exhausted when he retired that evening and immediately fell asleep. It was in the early morning hours when he awoke. He remembered his sacred visit where his mother said, "There is much for you to do in this life, and there is also someone special waiting for you"

He lay on his bed wondering if his visit to this family was part of the "someone special waiting for him," or was it just a coincidence they happened to come into town at the time when Billy was being beaten? He asked himself, *Was a coincidence where God remained anonymous?*

Slipping on his buckskins, Jacob quietly left his room and went to the front of the house. As he stepped outside onto the porch, a cool summer breeze blew across his face, and the moon slipped momentarily behind clouds. Outside, the soft silvery rays lit the porch and the surrounding area.

Earlier that day, Jacob had seen a wooden porch swing at the other end of the house. It reminded him of home, and he wanted to sit, swing, and think. He walked softly to the end of the porch, and there sitting on the swing was Mary. She was gazing off into the distance, looking so peaceful. Not wanting to disturb her, Jacob took a breath and started to return to his room. Mary was startled by the noise Jacob made, and immediately stood up.

"No, please, I didn't mean to disturb you, Mary," Jacob said apologetically. "There are times when I can't sleep, so I do a lot of thinking, especially at night. My parents had a swing just like this one at our home in Boston, and I wanted to just sit and think. But I can do it some other time and not disturb you."

The moon's soft rays illuminated her presence. She was beautiful, sitting there wrapped in a soft warm nightgown that covered up to her chin. Pulling her gown tighter around her neck, she took one long look at him and smiled. "This is a small bench, and if you are not afraid of me, I will invite you to sit next to me," she said, patting the swing next to her.

"Yes, ma'am, that would be right neighborly of you," he teased. She laughed softly, and he started to sit down. The bench was small and narrow and there wasn't much room. As Jacob sat next to her, their shoulders touched and it sent a warm sensation rushing through his entire body. Jacob looked at Mary and he could see that she had experienced the same sensation. She was somewhat stunned and turned toward Jacob for an explanation. He asked, "Did you feel that, Mary?" It needed no explanation, because she knew just what he was referring to. She had felt the same thing. He gently placed his left hand on her right hand and they again both felt an undeniable connection.

Jacob, not sure what else to say, said, "Tell me about yourself, Mary.

Turning her head toward Jacob and taking a soft breath, she smiled and replied, "Jacob Morgan, I would like that, and would you please tell me about yourself?"

They talked about anything and everything into the early hours of the morning. Jacob felt as if he had known Mary for years. He told her about his meeting White Fawn and was honest in his feelings about his marriage to her. As he told her of her death, he saw tears in Mary's eyes. She put her hand on the side of his arm and said, "Jacob, I am so sorry. I know you must have loved her very much, and because of that, I know she was a wonderful person. I share your grief."

Zed awoke and heard them talking and listened closely to their conversation. They were sitting directly under his window. Later, Zed said nothing about Jacob's leaving the room.

As they all sat around the breakfast table, William said, "Julie and I have been talking, and we would like to propose that both of you spend a few weeks here to rest up before you go back to California. It has been a long journey from the Dakotas, and it's still a long way to California. This is a good place for you to stay, if you're not in a hurry. It's the least we can do to thank you for saving our son."

Zed looked at Jacob and said, "Boy, it's up to you. We're on yer time, and we ain't in no hurry."

Jacob smiled and replied to their new friends, "I think a rest would be good for both mind and body." Zed turned and noticed there was a change in Jacob's demeanor. His face glowed, and he had an air of confidence since arriving.

Twelve-year-old Billy was drawn to Jacob like a fish to a worm and he wanted Jacob to teach him how to speak Sioux and how to use the bow and arrow. He also wanted to know how to throw a tomahawk and train his horse.

Meanwhile, Zed just relaxed. The Windslow home had a Mexican cook named Rosa, and Zed was always speaking with her, telling her about his ranch in California. They would laugh and carry on in Spanish.

William approached Jacob and said, "I hope there are not three riders leaving this ranch when you depart." Jacob didn't know just who the third rider might be.

Jacob spent the next few days riding and exploring the mountains.

Mary approached him late one evening and asked if he would like company on his morning ride. Smiling, he looked at her and said, "I thought you'd never ask."

She reached over and hit him in the shoulder. He feigned pain and said, "I deserved that. But, since we just met, I didn't want to be too forward."

Teasingly, she said, "Jacob, you only have two weeks before you leave, and I want to know you better."

The early morning was beautiful as they rode south of the ranch and followed the forest deep into the mountains. Mary showed Jacob their ranch boundaries and where some small lakes were located. She explained that when her father and mother had moved here, her father had gotten some of the land for free. Later, he had filed on forty sections from the territory, which was 25,600 acres. It was some of the choicest land in the territory for ranching. She explained how over the years her father had slowly developed it into a successful cattle ranch.

Ahead was a small grove of trees, so they stopped to give their horses a breather.

Mary wanted to ask a question, but hesitated, and didn't know if it would be inappropriate. However, after taking a small breath, she asked. "Jacob, what do you think of our area?"

Jacob looked around, as he took in the immense beauty of the land and said, "I think this is some of the most beautiful country I have ever seen."

And she continued, "Would you ever consider living in this part of the country?"

Jacob paused and chose his answer carefully, "I think I could live anywhere and be happy." He saw her countenance fall and remembering their spiritual experience on the porch swing, he quickly added, "However, I think I could be happier living in this area if I had someone to share that happiness with."

A smile came to her lips, and she asked, "Do you have anyone—" she stopped abruptly and looked over Jacob's shoulder. He saw fear in her eyes.

Jacob slowly turned Buck around, and there sat seven Indian braves on their ponies. They were not painted for war, but Jacob was still very cautious. He wasted no time and raised his hand in peace. He then spoke in Sioux. He knew it was not their language, but many of the Indian tribes had words that had similar meaning.

Their leader's face took on a look of surprise and the Indian quickly communicated with Jacob using sign language and his native tongue. As Jacob spoke with him, he felt calm and in control of the situation. Soon all seven Indians moved their horses in a half circle in front of Jacob. When no one moved behind him, Jacob knew they were safe.

Jacob continued speaking with them for at least a half hour. Their leader spoke with the other braves, and they all laughed and asked questions. Jacob answered and laughed with them, appearing to enjoy himself. Before leaving, each of the braves rode up to Jacob and grasped his forearm with his right hand. He did the same. Some of the Indians spoke to him and reached over and gave him a good-natured slap on his back.

Mary sat silently on her horse watching what was taking place and wondered what type of man was she with. How did his presence command their respect? They not only liked him, but they respected him, and treated him like an old friend.

One by one, each of the Indians raised his hand in peace and then turned their horses and left.

Jacob turned toward Mary and said, "Shall we continue?"

Mary pulled her horse up and said, "Jacob Morgan, what was that all about? It looked like they were your long lost friends, the way they treated you. I have never seen a friendly Indian. They are always so standoffish. So, what were you talking about?"

Jacob, not wanting to draw attention to himself said, "It was nothing, Mary. As I talked to them, they said they had heard about me."

Frustrated, she asked, "Jacob Morgan, what do you mean they had heard about you? I could see they were not a war party, but that still didn't mean they wouldn't have tried something.

Jacob was now embarrassed, and he could tell that Mary sensed it. She said, "Just please tell me what went on."

Jacob replied sheepishly, "I guess stories get passed around from tribe to tribe." Then he went on to explain about his Crow horse raid and when he had helped protect the Sioux tribe from a Crow raiding party. Not wanting to brag, he said, "They heard the language I spoke and put two and two together and they guessed it was me. I wanted to protect you, so I let them know that I was Jacob Morgan." Jacob paused and said, "Mary, when an Indian respects another warrior, as they respect me, they will not harm me or my friends. I told them about your ranch and that you are my woman."

Mary's head jerked up and she said, "Your woman?"

Jacob continued quickly and said, "If they think you are my wife they will never harm you or your family, and they gave their word to me, and Mary, when an Indian gives his word to another warrior, it is a scared bond"

Mary sat for a long moment, looking at Jacob. She was astonished to say the least. She edged her horse next to Buck, and reached over and gently kissed Jacob's cheek. "Thank you, Jacob."

When they arrived back at the ranch, Mary told her father about their incident and, thanks to Jacob, he had made friends with some of the Indians. She then went on to explain the peace treaty he had made in behalf of the ranch.

That evening at dinner, Jacob was all the more embarrassed as Mary related their experience. He wanted to leave the table, but good manners forbade him, so he toughed it out. Both Julie and William brought up their glasses and said, "We want to propose a toast to Jacob and Zed."

Zed immediately held his hand up and said, "Sorry, but I think yer wrong. All the credit goes to Jacob, and Jacob only."

Everyone at the table raised their glasses and William and looked around at his family and said, "Jacob, Mary and I feel it is not a coincidence that you both came here. For that, we are grateful." A warm feeling settled over Jacob. He also knew it was not a coincidence.

Chapter 25
Box Social

By the end of the first week, while sitting at the supper table, Julie announced that the area was going to have a box lunch social to raise money for their new schoolhouse. Both Jacob and Zed were invited.

Jacob asked, "What is a box lunch social?" He jokingly added, "Do you eat a box for lunch at a social gathering?"

Mary chortled at his cute remark and explained. "All of the women in the area make a special lunch and put it in a box and decorate it. Then the men bid on their lunches and the highest bidder wins the lunch and gets to eat with the woman who prepared it."

Zed smiled and mused, "Now that can be a problem, especially if a man bids on another man's wife's lunch."

William, who was listening, laughed and said, "Oh, we respect the other men's wives, and we know which box lunch our own wives made. It's a win-win situation for the husbands."

Jacob chuckled, "Or it can be misery for the husband if he doesn't buy his wife's lunch." They all laughed.

Julie spoke up and said, "It's fun to see the single men and women get together. Everyone will watch and see who is interested in who, and how much the men are willing to pay to eat lunch with a particular young lady."

Thoughtfully, Jacob asked, "What is the most a man has ever paid for a box lunch?"

Smiling, as if remembering her own box lunch, Julie said, "There are two types of prices. One for a husband paying for his wife's box lunch. The highest ever paid was ten dollars." Julie reached over, gave her husband's hand a squeeze, and continued. "For a single woman's box lunch, I think the highest has been three dollars."

"Sounds interesting," Jacob remarked.

Jacob wasn't popular with the cowboys on the ranch because he was always in the house with the boss and his family. They had heard the story of Jacob's run in with the two Brawn brothers and they knew how stories could be over exaggerated. The townspeople were making the city boy look too good to be true. All the cowboys on the ranch thought Jacob was just a city boy who had lived in Boston and dressed in buckskins. They worked hard every day, and he did nothing but ride his horse and spend time with the boss's daughter, which made all the cowboys jealous. They were all waiting for their chance to give Jacob a taste of their country hospitality.

Later that week, Jacob told Zed and the Windslows that he had some business to take care of in Landes and would be back before dark. At the end of the day, as the sun slowly slipped behind the western mountains Jacob arrived back at the ranch. Strapped on the back of Buck were a half dozen packages, making Buck look more like a supply horse. With all of his packages, what Jacob really needed was a buckboard.

In their room, Jacob handed Zed a large package and said, "You're welcome."

Zed looked up in surprise and slowly tore away the brown paper and opened the package. Jacob watched as Zed's jaw dropped. He sat there dumfounded. Inside the package were a new shirt, pants, and a pair of shiny black boots he had bought from the Landes mercantile.

Smiling, Jacob said, "Yes, Zed, you need to change out of your smelly old buckskins." For once, there was no sarcastic reply or eyes rolling back, but only a genuine smile that lit Zed's face.

"Boy, I really do thank ya fer these fine duds. I wanted to take Rosa, the cook, to the box social, and I didn't have nothin' to wear. I saw she was making a box lunch, and I wanted to buy it." Zed paused and then said, "She sure is a special woman."

Jacob raised an eyebrow at Zed's remark. The two had been spending time together, and maybe there might just be another person going back with them to California.

The following afternoon, after bathing in a big tub in the bunkhouse, Jacob and Zed walked back to their room and Jacob unwrapped his packages. On his bed, Jacob laid out a new shirt, pants, short coat, and underclothing for himself. From another package, he took out a new pair of black boots, socks, and a new black felt hat.

Jacob had used some of the gold coins he had found in the trunk in Weatherbee's office.

Zed looked up and said, "Boy, oh boy, you are gonna look like the Boston Baron." Then slapping Jacob on the back, teasingly added, "Yessiree, we are gonna have some fun tonight."

Jacob dressed and then walked out on the porch in all his finery. He stood on the porch with his hat in hand, waiting for the others to be ready. Jacob was not self-conscious about his clothing—he was from Boston and was accustomed to the trappings of a gentleman. He knew who he was and he knew where he was going in life.

Jacob was to inherit more money than anyone had in the whole territory, but not a person would ever know it. Jacob possessed that rare quality known as presence. He was not one to brag or place himself above another. His parents had raised him well, and he was a true gentleman.

When Mary walked out on the porch and saw Jacob standing there, she just stared at him. He had cut off his beard and was now clean-shaven. To her eyes, he was the most handsome man she had ever seen. Zed came out from the house in his new shirt, pants, and boots, and was also clean-shaven. Jacob was very surprised. The family had one carriage and one buckboard. Each rig was pulled by a team of horses and could carry four people.

Jacob was told there would be at least sixty people at the social. People from all over the territory would be in attendance. A box social was usually held once a year in the spring and on special occasions, maybe twice a year. Tonight was the chance for all the single women and men to meet each other. It was also one of the only chances for neighbors to renew their friendships after the long winter. After the box lunch social, there would be a special dance, so all the cowboys were slicked out in their finest.

Julie Windslow wore a beautiful blue dress with white lace on the collar. Both Mary and Emily had new dresses that they had made especially for the occasion. Conditions on the western frontier made it impossible for any women to buy a dress. Every woman had to know how to sew and they made their own clothing for themselves and for their family. William and Julie were the most prosperous family in the area and did not place themselves above any other family. They gave generously to all those who were in need of help.

William drove the carriage with Julie next to him, while Jacob and Mary sat in the back. Zed drove the buckboard, with Rosa at his side, while Billy and Emily rode in back. The other ranch hands followed behind on their horses.

Outside of the schoolhouse were dozens of carriages, buckboards, and horses that were tied to every available tree or hitching rail that could be found.

The schoolhouse was a large one-room building. Students in grades one through six attended, and were taught by a female teacher. When Jacob saw her, he noticed that she was a real beauty. Jacob looked at her and thought glumly, "Too bad Uncle Zac isn't alive." He would have liked to introduce his uncle to her. Jacob had learned that she was a widow and that her husband had died two years ago in an outbreak of cholera in Ohio. One of her relatives had helped her get this job teaching, so she moved west to start over. She was now boarding with an older couple in the area. Mary later told Jacob the schoolteacher was the object of desire of every single man who was hunting for a wife, but she wasn't interested in anyone and intended to keep it that way.

Jacob offered his arm to Mary as they followed William and Julie into the room. Inside the schoolhouse, the students' desks had been pushed up along the walls to accommodate couples eating their lunches. The room was crowded and smelled of people.

Zed, Rosa, Emily, and Billy followed behind, with the other ranch cowboys bringing up the rear. Not only were there single cowboys looking for women, but there were also single women standing around talking to each other, and eying all the available single men. Jacob saw the decorated box Mary had brought with her. As Mary saw him looking at it, she whispered, "I made it myself. Maybe it won't be as good as mother's or Rosa's but—"

Cutting her off, Jacob said, "If you made it, then it has to taste wonderful,"

An old geezer walked to the front and shouting in a loud high-pitched voice for the men to gather in the back of the room. He then asked the women to place their boxes on a large desk in front and stay up front until their box lunch was bought. Soon, the desk was piled high with boxes, and the men eagerly watched to see which woman was bringing which box.

Jacob saw three of the cowboys and two older men watching as Mary took her box up front and placed it on the pile. The cowboys from the ranch all reached in their pockets and counted their money. Some were lucky if they made twenty dollars a month as a ranch hand. For some cowboys, buying a box lunch could be a sacrifice depending on the cost because of the low wages they made each month. The auctioneer stood up and made a remark that the school needed the money, and that no one has ever died from food poisoning at the box socials in the past. Everyone laughed.

He held up the first box high in his right hand and said, "Now let's be generous. This is for a good cause. What do you bid for this delicious smelling box? Now, some of you gents who are big eaters, don't you go buying three or four boxes. That don't hold too good around here," he continued. "You gents also remember you have to share the lunch with the woman who made it." Again there was laughter.

A lone cowboy standing in the back raised his hand and he bid twenty-five cents, then it went to thirty-five, then to forty, and then fifty cents. It was sold for fifty cents. The single cowboy who had made the first bid, walked forward to claim his box. A young unmarried girl giggled as she met him in front. Both looked embarrassed as he paid his money and gathered her box. He then offered his arm to her, and off they went to eat.

Jacob had to wait until the eighteenth box to start bidding. That was when Mary's box came up for auction. He glanced over at the cowboys from the ranch, and they looked at him, their faces set with determination. From what he could see, they had pooled their money and were all set to outbid him.

The auctioneer lifted up Mary's beautifully wrapped box. He asked, "Is there a gun in the box? It's so heavy there either has to be a gun or a lot of good food for some lucky man." Mary blushed as the crowd laughed.

"Do I have a bid?" he asked. Jacob stood back and watched. A cowboy from the ranch raised his hand and said, "Fifty cents."

Another nice looking gentleman raised his hand and said, "One dollar." Still Jacob made no offer to bid.

The hand from the first cowboy went up and he said, "One dollar and fifty cents."

"Oh, this is getting interesting, folks," the auctioneer said. "Do I hear one dollar and seventy-five?"

A man standing in the corner in a nice suit said, "Two dollars." There was a hush from the crowd. Jacob saw Mary look over at the man in the suit and then over at her mother who shrugged her shoulders, indicating that she didn't know who he was. Mary looked at Jacob and gave him a bewildered look. The four cowboys looked at Jacob and one said, "He ain't got no money; he's just a mountain man dressed in city clothes." They quickly pooled their money and said, "Three dollars." Now it was competition with a reputation at stake.

The man in the suit raised his hand and said, "Four dollars." There was a gasp in the crowd. Where was this going?

The auctioneer laughingly smiled and said, "My, oh my, what do we have here, a range war?" This remark brought a great laugh from the settlers, but it was not far from the truth. Jacob could see the dejected looks from the four cowboys. They were bewildered; who was this man in the suit? There the man stood with a big smile on his face.

Jacob thought, *Pride goeth before the fall.* Then he stepped to the side and raised his hand.

The auctioneer, now smiling said, "Yes, sir, do you want to bid?"

Jacob, again grateful for the money Uncle Zac had left him in the trunk, said loud and clear, "I bid ten dollars for that lovely box." No one made a sound. Mary put her hand up to her mouth to stop a gasp. No one had ever paid ten dollars for a single woman's box lunch. Jacob thought, *Mary, I don't want you to be known as a woman who got so much money for her box lunch. I want you to know that I was willing to pay ten dollars for your box lunch.*

Jacob looked at the man in the suit. The smile had vanished from his face and was replaced with a glare of hatred directed at Jacob. The man had been sure he would win, but one look at Jacob's determination, and he knew Jacob would pay far more than ten dollars for that box lunch. He turned and stormed outside.

"Going once, going twice, going three times. Sold to the gentleman in the black hat for ten dollars."

A corridor of people opened up as Jacob slowly walked to the front of the room to collect his prize. He paid his money and reached for the box. Then he extended his arm to Mary, and she gently placed her arm on his. As they walked to the side of the room and sat in two desks, all eyes were on them. It took a few minutes for the auctioneer to get things started again, but soon the bidding was as lively as it had been.

A few minutes later, Zed walked up to them. He bent over and whispered something to Jacob. A broad grin spread across Jacob's face. He replied, "With pleasure, my friend," and reached into his pocket and handed Zed some money as he shook his hand.

In a few minutes later, Zed and Rosa sat next to them. Rosa seemed to glow as she looked at Zed. Jacob watched in amusement, as Zed looked at her like a lovesick puppy and then eagerly dug in to her delicious meal. Once he had tasted the food, Zed complimented her in Spanish and Rosa beamed.

Mary smiled and said, "We may be losing a cook."

Jacob looked at her and replied, "You never know who could be leaving from this ranch. It could be more than one." At that, Mary lowered her head and smiled.

Mary was an excellent cook, and Jacob raved about her meal. He said, "Why does the ranch need a cook when they have you?"

Thanking him, Mary explained. "I want to be more than a cook. I want to be part of the ranch. I do all of Father's books and I arrange for the fall roundups and for driving the stock to California or Nevada. Father says the railroad should be here sometime in the future, which means we could ship our cattle back east and get a better price."

Jacob was incredulous—she was not only beautiful, but she had a good head on her shoulders and could run any ranch or business.

They talked for a long time, enjoying each other's company. As Jacob looked at Mary, he knew he now had a life to live and he knew that White Fawn would want that for him.

There was a commotion at the front of the room. The auctioneer now stood and raised his hands to quiet the crowd and shouted, "If everyone is finished eating, we will now have our dance."

The crowd roared their approval.

Now, yelling above the noise he said, "Grab your partner."

Jacob took Mary by the hand and said, "May I have the pleasure of this dance?"

Curtseying, Mary bowed and teasingly said, "Of course, my prince."

A fiddler started playing in the front and was quickly joined by a guitar player and a banjo picker. Jacob placed his hand at Mary's waist and started dancing to the lively tune. A wonderful warm feeling came over them as they danced around the floor and enjoyed each other's company.

When the music ended, Jacob felt a tap on his shoulder. Turning to see who had interrupted him, Jacob saw the man in the suit whom he had outbid. Smiling, but not with his eyes, the man said in a silky smooth voice, "May I cut in?"

Looking into the man's eyes, Jacob saw disdain and hatred. Who was he? The hair was now standing up on the back of his neck warning him like it had done so many other times. Jacob glanced down at Mary's face and saw her confusion. It was the custom to let another man cut in on a dance, and Jacob didn't want to make a scene, so he released Mary and said, "Certainly."

Jacob stepped aside and watched them dance. The stranger was asking her questions, and she was speaking to him, but not smiling. The dance ended, and the man in the suit started to guide Mary to the other end of the room. Jacob stepped in and tapped him on the shoulder and said, "Excuse me. Mary is my date for the evening. I paid for her box lunch, which includes the woman who cooked it." He took Mary's hand and walked off, leaving the stranger standing in the middle of the dance floor.

"Who is he?" asked Jacob.

Mary nervously replied, "His name is Samuel Benson, from California. He is a cattle buyer and asked me a lot of questions about the ranch. Jacob, I don't like him. He scares me."

Just then the music started again, and Jacob again felt a tap on his shoulder. It was the stranger. He repeated his first request. "May I cut in?"

Jacob extended his hand to the stranger and said, "I don't believe we've met. My name is Jacob Morgan, and you are?"

Curtly, he replied, "I am Samuel Benson, a cattle buyer from California. I am sure Miss Windslow already told you, so why ask me again?"

Jacob retorted, "Mr. Benson, out here we have manners, and it is customary to ask another man his name, rather than having to ask a woman."

Mr. Benson coldly replied, "Well, now that you know who I am, we will have our dance." He took hold of Mary's elbow and started for the dance floor.

Jacob stopped him and, taking a hold of his elbow, replied, "You assume that Miss Windslow wants to dance with you. She does not. And if you have any questions concerning the Windslow ranch, you may take it up with her father."

Benson glared at Jacob, then turned and walked away. Jacob watched him retreat, when suddenly the man spun on his heel, and swung his fist toward Jacob's head. Jacob, not liking the man, had already anticipated his move and blocked the punch, catching Benson on his right shoulder with a glancing blow and knocked him to the floor.

"Fight! Fight!" someone yelled. Benson got up slowly, measuring Jacob's ability to fight. Jacob put his hands up, and replied in a loud voice, over the commotion. "I don't want any trouble. This is a social function, so let's keep it that way!"

Benson shouted, "I have heard about the great Jacob Morgan—a Boston city boy who dresses in buckskins and doesn't know the real rules of the West. I challenge him to a fight here and now, where all of you can witness that he is nothing but a braggart and coward."

William Windslow walked up to Jacob and said, "If you want, we can go home now." Julie, his wife agreed with him as she nodded her head.

Mary walked up to Jacob and put her hand in the crook of his arm, "We can go home now."

Jacob turned and looked at Zed, and he mouthed the words, "No, fight him!"

Jacob was not concerned about his reputation; he knew who he was and what he could do. He would do it for the Windslow family's reputation. They were solid people and if they had a guest visiting their home who was known as a coward, the people of the community would look down on their choice of friends, and Jacob would not allow that. Jacob nodded his head in acceptance to the challenge.

Samuel Benson immediately left the room. A moment later he returned with a long black case that he set it in the center of the floor. The crowd moved back to the sides of the room, creating a large circle. Some men stood on the desks for a better view. Benson walked to the center of the crowd, taking command, as if he were now the auctioneer. He raised both hands, quieting the settlers and said, "I am new in the area. I am originally from Boston where Mr. Morgan comes from. I have heard of his family, and I have met them. I now reside in San Francisco, California, and I am a cattle buyer. I am here to purchase cattle, but this evening, I would like for all of you to have some entertainment." He was smiling as he spoke. "Some of you may not know this, but Mr. Morgan is an experienced swordsman. We call this a rapier. It is used in fencing, or in the past it was used for dueling. I am also experienced in using the rapier. Mr. Morgan does not know it, but my instructor, Mr. Jacques Montclair from France, was also Mr. Morgan's instructor. Since the rapier is a gentleman's weapon, I would like to first demonstrate a duel with Mr. Morgan."

Jacob was disbelieving. This man was from Boston and now resided in San Francisco. Was he the other recipient for Uncle Zac's estate?

Zed now stood next to Jacob and asked, "Boy, are you sure you know how to use that skinny piece of steel?"

Jacob nodded and said, "Yes, when I was younger, my brother, Isaiah, insisted I learn."

Zed shook his head in amazement and replied, "There sure are a lot of things you know that I never heard of." Zed went on, "Jacob, remember he's challenging you, and you can choose the weapon of yer choice."

Jacob leaned over toward Zed and said, "I have a feeling if I choose fists, he will still want to do a demonstration with the rapiers to please the crowd."

William leaned over and whispered, "Jacob, I don't trust this man. He has some sort of vendetta against you. Are you sure you don't know him?"

With frustration, Jacob said, "I've never seen him before in my life."

Walking up to Benson in the center of the human arena, Jacob now raised his hands in the air. Speaking loudly, he said, "Since Mr. Benson is happy to put on a circus for everyone, I choose fighting with bare fists. However, if he wants to amuse you with the rapier, I will be happy to comply."

The settlers roared their approval and smiled with delight. Jacob guessed most of them had never seen a rapier or even heard of one. Benson opened up the case and inside were two beautiful dueling rapiers. He motioned for Jacob to choose one. Jacob reached for one and held it in his hand for balance. He moved the long steel blade back and forth in fluid motion as if he were carving a piece of meat.

Benson went on to say, "On the end of the point is a wooded protector, to keep the point of the blade from entering the body. I have added this to protect Mr. Morgan." There was a low chuckle from the crowd.

Zed moved next to Jacob and asked, "Do you remember what you did to Running Bear? I think you need to do a warm-up and amuse the crowd."

Jacob nodded his approval and started stretching and squatting down. Jacob knew he was making a scene, which was exactly what he wanted to do. Benson pointed toward Jacob and laughed, encouraging the crowd to participate, but Jacob continued his warm-up routine.

Sly like the fox, Jacob thought. Jacob looked over at Mary and, just as he had with White Fawn, he winked at her. The only thing different was, White Fawn was fearful for him. Mary just smiled and nodded her approval. She knew what he was doing, and she also knew what he was capable of doing because he had already shared with her some of his escapades.

Mary sashayed over to Jacob's side. She leaned over and said, "You need not kill him, Jacob, but I would like to see him lose some of his arrogance." She turned to go and leaned over again and said, "All of his arrogance!" Then she reached up and kissed him on the cheek.

Benson saw the kiss and it inflamed him all the more. He immediately went to the center of the circle, where Jacob continued to jump and then squat down. Benson loudly said, "If you are finished dancing, may we proceed?" Again there was laughter from the settlers.

Jacob and Benson met in the circle and slowly advanced, facing each other with their arms extended. As the ends of their rapiers touched, Jacob spun his rapier in a circle and flipped his wrist. The rapier left Benson's hand, and landed on the floor next to Jacob. The crowd roared their approval.

The rapier was a long, slender, sharply pointed sword. It was used for thrusting and not for cutting or slashing.

Benson advanced to pick up his weapon, and Jacob smiled and said, "No, no, no," and blocked him with the point of the blade. With his right foot placed near the hilt of the rapier, he flipped it up to Benson. Benson caught the rapier and lunged toward Jacob. Jacob quickly parried it off to his right. Benson took his rapier, flexed it, and deftly ran his hand toward the end.

"He took off the tip!" Zed shouted.

Jacob could see the protective wooden piece was missing. Benson was moving slowly in a circle around Jacob. Jacob then removed his protective end and said, "It's my turn now!"

Benson lunged, and Jacob parried to the left. Then Jacob lunged forward at Benson, keeping both of his feet on the floor gliding back and forth. Jacob then moved in a circle. He blocked every attempt Benson made to pierce his body. Jacob smiled and then quickly flipped his wrist again. He cut off the button on Benson's vest. He did this twice more, and each time a button was neatly removed, the crowd roared their approval.

In a rage, Benson lunged, and with the hilt of his rapier, he struck Jacob's face. Jacob saw the hilt coming up and turned his head to the right, to lessen the blow, but it drew blood on his left cheek. Benson was furious as he lunged over and over, trying to run Jacob through, but Jacob thwarted his every effort.

Jacob wisely backed to the outside of the circle, brought his rapier up, and saluted Benson. Benson had no choice but to comply. He likewise went to his end of the circle and saluted. The settlers were clapping and yelling their approval.

Jacob put down his rapier and took off his coat, and rolled up his sleeves. Benson followed suit.

They both went to the center and faced off. "No holds barred," Jacob said. "We may fight in anyway, except gouging the eyes out. Is that agreed?"

Laughing, Benson said, "Mr. Morgan, I never have been beaten in any fight. I will make sure you do not walk out of here!"

Jacob seriously asked, "Do you have any friends here with you?"

Benson sneered and answered, "No. Why do you ask?"

"I was just wondering who was going to carry you back to your hotel!"

With that said, Benson delivered a punch to Jacob's jaw that sent him reeling back. Catching himself, Jacob saw Benson rushing at him in a rage. Jacob struck forward with his right foot and connected with Benson's chest and down on his back he went. Astounded by Jacob's kick, Benson slowly got up and circled.

I must not overestimate him, thought Jacob. Sly like a fox and wise as a badger, Jacob purposely backed away. When Benson came on in a rush, Jacob leaped in the air, and with his feet, he connected with Benson's upper left shoulder, sending Benson flying backward again on his back.

Jacob stood waiting for Benson's next move. Lowering his head, Benson rammed it into Jacob's stomach. With one swift motion, Jacob came down hard with his elbow on Benson's upper back and neck. Then, taking a hold of Benson's collar with both hands, Jacob continued falling backward on his back, pulling Benson with him. As Benson was being pulled backward, Jacob planted his feet in Benson's lower abdomen and flipped him over his head. Benson landed with a crash while the spectators jumped to the side for safety.

Jacob was quickly on his feet. Benson was now like a raging bull. He was swearing and shouting obscenities as he struggled to his feet. Jacob changed his tactics and went to English boxing, holding his fists out in front of him. This caught Benson off guard. Jacob struck him in the face, snapping his head backward. Down he went on his back, dazed. He lay there, struggling to get up.

Suddenly two cowboys grabbed Jacob and tried to pull him down. William started to stop them, but Zed pulled him back and said, "There's only two of 'em. Jacob can handle both of them real easy."

The two cowboys were from the Windslow ranch, and it was payback time. This was their chance at revenge for the city kid. One cowboy held Jacob from behind, and the other one's fist came directly at Jacob's face. In a split second, Jacob turned and tilted his head to his left side, and the fist connected with the cowboy holding Jacob from behind. The man holding Jacob folded, and Jacob grabbed the cowboy in front by the arm and flipped him over his head. He landed hard, but quickly got back to his feet.

Now Jacob was mad. He moved in with his right fist to the side of the cowboy's head, and then with his left fist, he connected with an uppercut. Jacob felt a presence behind him, and he kicked back. His foot caught the other cowboy who was trying to take him from behind. There was a scream as Jacob's foot connected with the man's leg. The other cowboy was staggering, so he let him fall to the floor.

He turned and the cowboy he had kicked had started toward him again, and Jacob hit him with an uppercut that sent him flying across the room on his back. Jacob turned in time to see Benson getting up and going for his rapier. Jacob rushed forward and put his foot on the weapon before Benson could raise it. As Benson pulled up, the rapier broke in half.

Jacob grabbed Benson by his shirt and brought his own head forward, striking Benson's nose with his forehead. It broke, and blood gushed from Benson's nose and mouth. He struck Benson's midsection once, then twice, and then hit him two more times in the face. Benson was trying to stand up, but his knees buckled. Jacob stood and watched Benson as he struggled. Jacob thought it best not to hurt him anymore, so he stepped back. He had not started the war, but he had finished it.

With only a slight cut on his left cheek and a few facial bruises, Jacob was unscathed. He picked up his coat and hat and looked at Zed, who nodded his approval. Looking at William and Julie Windslow and then at Mary, Jacob said, "May we go home now?" He took Mary's arm and escorted her out of the schoolhouse followed by the family.

Chapter 26
The Proposal

A cool wind rustled the leaves and stirred up dust clouds along the trail as the horses slowly plodded toward the ranch. William and Julie sat in front of the carriage, while Mary sat next to Jacob as they rode home.

Zed followed behind, driving the buckboard with his passengers. Jacob noticed that Rosa sat closer to Zed than usual, and he seemed to enjoy it very much.

Mary took hold of Jacob's arm and whispered, "I'm so proud of you."

Jacob reached over and touched her hand and squeezed it lightly. He then brought her hand up to his lips and kissed it gently. Jacob thought, *In another five days Zed and I will be going back to California to meet with Mr. Weatherbee. Oh, how I am going to miss her.*

As if reading his thoughts, Mary whispered in his ear, "I will miss you, Jacob."

Jacob never thought he would find happiness so soon after the loss of White Fawn. Without that sacred experience in the cave, he would have mourned for years.

He again gently squeezed and kissed her hand. With William and Julie sitting directly in front of them and not wanting to be heard, Jacob said in a hushed tone, said, "Mary, we need to talk."

She reached up and placed a kiss on his cheek and let go of his hand. She then put her arm through the crook of his elbow and pulled him closer to her. All was well.

The following morning, Jacob prepared for his morning ride. One of the cowboys who had fought with him last night walked up to him. He had a bruise over his right eye and one on his lower jaw where Jacob had hit him. Jacob didn't know if there would be any further trouble with him, so he took a defensive stance, his feet set apart for balance.

The cowboy walked slowly, and extended his right hand. Jacob warily reached out and took the cowboy's hand, not knowing what to expect. The ranch hand lowered his head, looked up, and said, "We were all wrong about you, Jacob. We thought you were just a city boy dressed in buckskins. I want to apologize to you. You beat us fair and square. As a matter of fact, it was more than fair. It was three against one, and you thumped us all but good." Then more serious, he said, "I'm just here to say that it is my pleasure knowin' you, and I'm sorry for my actions."

Jacob looked at the cowboy. He knew it took a great deal of courage to admit he was wrong and apologize. Jacob admired that. "It was Hank, wasn't it?" Jacob asked.

The cowboy nodded his head, also not knowing what to expect.

"Well, Hank, it wasn't my pleasure to thump you because I am actually a peaceful man. But I do admire your courage in asking to shake my hand. It would be my pleasure to have you as a friend."

A broad grin spread across Hank's face and he extended his hand and replied, "Jacob, you have yourself a friend."

As Hank walked away, Jacob heard a door closing from the house. Mary came out smiling and wearing her riding clothes.

"Did you have to teach Hank some more manners?" she asked.

He smiled and replied, "No. I just made myself a new friend."

A few moments later, Hank came back leading Mary's horse over to be saddled. "Morning, Miss Mary," Hank said. "Fine morning for a ride." He handed the lead rope over to Jacob and then walked away, leaving Jacob and Mary to themselves.

Jacob saddled Mary's horse and within the hour they were riding to the upper ranch. As they rode, the crisp autumn air blew gently across the open range. Jacob rode ahead and led them to a small knoll that overlooked the rolling hills and grasslands.

Jacob dismounted and helped Mary off her horse. She stood in front of him. He put his hands on her hips and gently pulled her to him. He said, "I have wanted to do this ever since I first saw how beautiful you were at the supper table." He pulled her close and gently put his lips on hers. Jacob said, "Mary, I love you," He paused and continued, "I never thought I could say those words to anyone again, but I do love you." Jacob could see this beautiful woman was one who would stand beside him during the good and the bad days. He would work, plan, and share all he had with her, and they would make their life together.

Mary put her arms around his waist and said, "Jacob, I love you. Ever since we had that spiritual experience on the porch swing, I knew God had let me know that I found a man I could love. "

She continued. "A year ago, my mother and father wanted me to marry. I liked the man, but I didn't love him. I prayed about it and I never could get an answer." She stopped talking and pulled him in an embrace. "Oh, Jacob. What are we going to do?"

Jacob chuckled and said, "What else is there to do but get married?"

Her hand came up to her mouth and tears came to her eyes. "Do you really mean it, Jacob?"

Jacob leaned down and gently pressed his lips to her and said, "Mary, we'll have to wait a little while. As you know I have some things I need to clear up in California first. It may take a year, but I promise when I have finished I will come back for you and court you properly. Will you wait for me?"

She launched herself into his arms and gently kissed him and asked, "Is that enough to convince you, sir?"

They stayed up on the hill talking for a long while, enjoying the closeness of each other before they headed back to the ranch.

As they neared the ranch, Jacob reached over and took Mary's hand. "Let me ask permission from your father before we announce anything," he said. "How do you feel about that?"

Laughing, Mary replied, "Jacob Morgan, a man out here always tells his woman what needs to be done, and here you ask for my opinion? I feel wonderful about you wanting to ask my father."

As Jacob unsaddled their horses, Mary went into the house. Zed stepped out of the shadows. He reached up and put his hand on Jacob's shoulder, and said, "Boy, I need to talk with you. Can you give me yer time fer a bit?"

Jacob looked at Zed, seeing the concern on his face, and replied, "Certainly Zed, all the time you need."

"Can we sit fer a spell?" Zed asked as he motioned to a bench near the tack shed. As they sat down, Zed sat at the end of the bench facing Jacob. He was looking down and fidgeting with his fingers. Slowly, he looked up and said, "That man Benson that you whipped has gone back to San Francisco, I've been told. Since I first saw him the man has bothered me, and I have some thoughts, but I want to ruminate on it some more and I'll let you know what I come up with." Then the solemn look on his face vanished into a smile, and he announced, "I want to marry Rosa Gonzales."

Jacob knew that Zed lost the opportunity years ago to marry, and now that he had found love again, Jacob was happy for him. Jacob stood up, extended his hand, and said, "Zed, congratulations! It's about time you settled down, you old bugger." And then he pulled him into a bear hug and thumped him on the back.

Embarrassed, Zed sheepishly said, "I didn't know who to talk to but you. I came out here to teach you the ways of the mountain man and the Sioux Indians. I know we have to go back and meet with Weatherbee to fulfill your promise, but here's my predicament. I wanna marry Rosa and take her back to my ranch, but I have obligations to you, and I don't know what to do. I need yer thoughts on this."

Jacob was somewhat taken back. Here was the strong and fearless Zed who always made the decisions and now he was asking him for his thoughts.

Jacob paused and considered Zeds predicament. Jacob placed his hand on Zed's shoulder, and said, "I have just the answer for you. You marry Rosa and bring her with us. When we get to California, you cut off the trail and head for your ranch. I'll continue on to San Francisco, and when I am finished with Weatherbee, I'll go to Yreka and then catch up with you."

Zed shook his head and said, "Boy, I can't do that. I promised yer Uncle Zac that I would stand by you and help you. I need to follow through on my promise."

Jacob tilted his head and rubbed his chin thoughtfully. He asked, "Zed, do you think I am capable enough to go back to San Francisco and meet with Weatherbee?"

"Of course I do," Zed quickly replied. "You are just about as savvy as any man I have ever met, and that includes yer Uncle Zac."

"Well, that settles it. I'll go to San Francisco, and you can take your new bride to your ranch."

"But—"

"No buts about it," Jacob replied, as he slapped Zed on the back. "You just go on back to your ranch with your Rosa. Zed, you will be missed, but I am a man now, and I think I can handle it on my own," teased Jacob.

Zed smiled and solemnly said, "I may never have this chance again. I missed it long ago, and I don't want to miss it again. I thank you, Jacob."

Jacob's eyes misted and he reached over and hugged his good friend again. Since his confrontation with Zed on the way to his ranch three years ago, Jacob wanted to be called by his name. Zed had said, "When I think yer a man, I will call you by yer first name." This was the first time since then that Zed had ever called him Jacob.

Two days later, Zed and Rosa were married by the circuit preacher. They both beamed like little children. Jacob knew that Zed and Rosa deserved each other and would make each other very happy.

Mary edged closer to Jacob after the wedding and whispered, "Have you talked to my father yet?"

"Oh, so you are getting a little anxious, huh?" Jacob teased. Then smiling, he reached for her hand, squeezed it, and whispered, "I plan on talking with him tonight."

After dinner that evening, Jacob approached William Windslow and asked if he could have a few minutes of his time. William motioned for Jacob to follow him to his office. Once they were inside, he reached over and lit a kerosene lamp. Then he motioned for Jacob to sit down.

"What can I do for you, Jacob?" asked Mr. Windslow.

Jacob was not nervous, but was determined to come to the point. He was no longer a young kid sitting in front of the chief of the Sioux tribe. This man was a white man, who observed tradition and appreciated respect.

"Mr. Windslow," started Jacob.

William raised his hand and said, "No formalities, Jacob. Call me William."

"Thank you, William," replied Jacob. "William, I want to talk to you about my life when I lived with the Indians." He went on. "I fell in love with an Indian maiden and her name was White Fawn, and we were married."

William's eyebrows lifted in disbelief, but Jacob went on to tell him of his marriage and then the death of his wife.

Jacob said, "I never thought I would get over my grief, but I did. I had a spiritual experience where my mother and my wife appeared to me and told me to get on with my life. My mother told me there was someone special waiting for me." William listened intently, suddenly wondering where this was going. He must not have thought Jacob's relationship with Mary was that serious. Jacob continued, "I believe it was no coincidence that we came to this area. I believe it was no coincidence when we came upon Billy being beaten by those two brothers in town. I don't believe it is a coincidence that I have met your daughter, Mary. Mary and I had a special spiritual experience and we know we are to be married."

William suddenly sat forward on his chair and started to ask a question, but Jacob raised his hand and said, "Please hear me out, and let me continue."

William nodded with some apprehension and weakly said, "All right, please continue."

Jacob then told him of his inheritance and that he needed to go back to San Francisco to meet with his attorney. When he was finished with his business in San Francisco, he would go to Yreka, California, to meet with the owners of the gold mines his uncle had left him and then on to Zed's ranch for the winter and then he would come back to Mary.

Jacob saw the look of surprise on William's face with this new revelation, but went on. "It will take me at least a year to complete all of my business before I can come back to claim your daughter's hand in marriage. When I come back I want to court her properly. I know you are concerned that we have just met. As for myself, I already have received confirmation that this is what I should do. As a matter of fact, before you give your approval, you need to talk to Mary and see how she feels."

William took in a deep breath, slowly blew it out, and said, "As you know, Jacob, Mary is our oldest daughter. I need to discuss this with Julie, and we'll talk with Mary."

Jacob agreed and started to stand. William stopped him by putting his hand up. "Please don't get up and leave yet. Let me just say one thing, Jacob. I can say with all honesty that you are the finest young man that I have ever met. I have no doubt you can do anything that you set your mind to. And if you are supposed to be my son-in-law, I couldn't ask for a finer husband for my daughter."

In the early morning hours, Jacob headed to his favorite place to sit and think. He was not surprised when he saw Mary already sitting on the swing.

She looked up and smiled. "I was wondering when you would show up. Did my father give you the once over when you asked for my hand in marriage?"

Jacob softly laughed. "No, I'm the one who gave him the twice over."

She laughed and went on to explain, "Mother and Father talked with me for about two hours last night, asking me all these questions about you and your experiences with the Indians. They especially asked me if it bothered me that you had married an Indian squaw. I told them it did not bother me because I felt she was a good person and God had called her home. I then told them of our spiritual experience and that I knew undeniably it was from God. Both of my parents were skeptical, and neither of them have ever heard of anyone having this type of an experience."

Jacob looked concerned but didn't know what to say.

Mary paused and looked deeply into Jacob's eyes before continuing. "Jacob, you need not worry. Last night Father and Mother both gave their approval for us to be married. They liked the idea of us being apart for at least a year. Mother said that our being apart would actually bring us closer."

Jacob reached over, gently kissed her, and said, "Mary, I'm already missing you."

The next morning there was no one to prepare breakfast, so Julie, Mary, and Emily prepared the morning meal. Rosa and Zed were honeymooning in a separate bunkhouse, and would join them when they were ready. After breakfast, William and Julie talked with Mary and Jacob about their future plans. They gave their consent and blessings for their engagement.

The morning was spent packing their horses with the necessary supplies for their journey back to California. Mary spent as much time as she could talking to Jacob, not wanting him to leave. "Oh, Jacob, a whole year is so long. What will I do while you are gone?"

Jacob smiled, "You can just go on doing what you have been doing. We will need a good bookkeeper for our ranch, and I promise you that I will be back as soon as possible."

She pulled him into the tack shed and said, "Let's say our private good-byes now."

Before noon, Jacob, Zed, and Rosa had their horses all packed and ready to go. Rosa said her good-byes to the family and beamed as she sat astride on one of Zed's horses that he had acquired from the raid on the Crow tribe. The entire entourage consisted of three adults, fourteen horses, and two mules. They used the mules for carrying their extra supplies. Zed wanted to use the Appaloosa mares and two stallions to build up their own horse herd at his California ranch.

Before Jacob mounted Buck, he walked up to Julie and William. As he extended his hand to Julie, she said, "Posh, Jacob, give me a hug!" She then reached up and hugged him and kissed him on the cheek. "Come back safely to us, Jacob."

William stood and extended his hand to Jacob. Jacob reached out and firmly shook his hand and then William pulled him in for a fatherly hug. "Yes, Jacob, come back safely, and we will love having you as a member of our family."

Jacob then hugged Billy and Emily. "Emily," Jacob said, "We haven't had much opportunity to get to know each other. But I promise, when

I come back, we will really get to know each other better." She nodded her head timidly and returned his embrace.

Jacob looked for Mary, but she was nowhere to be found. Disappointed, he said to the family, "Mary and I said our good-byes earlier this morning." With that, he mounted Buck, and the small caravan started their journey toward the Sierra Nevada Mountains. As they rode, the ranch slowly faded behind them.

Once they were on the trail, Jacob mentioned that he would like to pass through Landes because he had some unfinished business to attend to. As they entered the town, Jacob dismounted in front of the gunsmith's.

"Can you wait a few minutes?" he asked. "I have to pick up a purchase I made on my last visit to town."

Zed and Rosa patiently waited on their horses in the shade of a large tree. Soon Jacob emerged from the building with two packages in his hand, and strapped around his waist was a gun in a holster.

Zed raised an eyebrow and asked, "Are you expecting trouble?"

Jacob smiled and said, "If you are not going to be with me, I need more than one shot. My rifle has only one ball, and this revolver has five shots." Jacob removed the gun from his holster and handed it to Zed by the barrel, and said, "It's a Colt Dragoon revolver .36-caliber, and I have a feeling that I just might need it."

Zed examined the gun and then handed it back to Jacob. Jacob then handed the other package to Zed. "Now that you have a wife to protect, and with the two of you traveling alone, I think you could use one of these revolvers as well."

Taking the package, Zed said, "Jacob, thank you for your concern."

Chapter 27
Kung Fu

Over the next few weeks, Jacob felt like the proverbial third thumb. It seemed he was always in the way. Zed and Rosa were like teenagers in love. Jacob had never seen Zed look happier. Zed always had his arms around Rosa when they were in camp, treating her with the greatest respect and always trying to meet her needs.

Jacob smiled and thought, *It's Zed's turn for happiness. He deserved it.*

Slowly, the homeward bound caravan followed the California Trail toward the Sierra Nevadas. They stayed on that trail until they reached the Humboldt River, where Zed and Rosa would cross and go on to Zed's ranch.

They made camp that evening and ate their last meal together. Rosa's excellent cooking skills were not lost at the campfire. She was always in high spirits and was forever thanking Jacob for his kindness in letting Zed take her back to his ranch. She never had been married and this was her time to find happiness.

After their meal, Zed was the first to speak up. "Jacob, I have some concerns before I leave in the morning we need to talk."

The remark caught Jacob off guard. He was instantly listening. "All right, Zed, what's on your mind? I've never known you to be concerned unless there was danger," said Jacob.

Zed, nodding his head, said, "Yer Uncle Zac used Weatherbee as his attorney, but he told me more that once that he didn't completely trust him. I've seen him only a few times and the last time I saw him was when we met in his office."

Zed continued, "When you get back to San Francisco, I suggest you check out another attorney to do business with. With California being a new state, I figure there are more than likely a lot of new attorneys in town. Fer a few dollars, anyone of them would check into yer inheritance and see that ya get everything ya got coming."

Jacob looked gratefully at his friend and said, "Zed, that's good advice." Jacob started to get up.

"There's more," said Zed, as he put his hand on Jacob's arm. "Remember that Benson varmint you whipped? I've been thinkin' about him. He said he was from Boston, and he said he knew yer family, so he also must have known about yer inheritance. He made it a point to let every buddy know that he knew all about you, like you both havin' the same fencing teacher."

Jacob asked, "But who would have told him we had the same fencing instructor?"

Zed shrugged his shoulders and said, "That's it. I don't rightly know, but he could have spent some time with yer brother Isaiah, or he could have been sent." Zed went on, "I've been ruminatin' and I have a question. Since when are there cattle buyers from San Francisco? All cattle buyers are from Kansas or Nebraska." Zed sat shaking his head, not knowing what to say. He then cautiously said, "Jacob, ya gotta be careful. I think ole Weatherbee has been up to a lot of no good, and he's behind this whole mess of someone trying to get yer inheritance."

Zed paused in deep thought and continued, "Jacob, 'member how ole Weatherbee tried to talk ya out of goin' with me? He kept mentioning about another worthy recipient. And think about it, Jacob, keep in mind that yer Mr. Weatherbee is holding the purse strings, and you have more money than most people will ever see in a lifetime. He won't want to lose control of that much money."

Jacob sat with his back against a tree and took a long time digesting what Zed had said. Finally, he slowly stood up and said, "You're right, Zed. Weatherbee kept trying to discourage me. I can see him being concerned about me, but when I mentioned it to him, he really became upset as if I caught him doing something wrong."

Zed whispered as if someone were listening, "Jacob, there's one thing I think ya need to do before ya see ole Weatherbee. Take yer time and check out his office and see who comes and goes. Just be patient and stay out of sight, because if ole Weatherbee and Benson are in cahoots, ya best be on yer guard. I think they would try and do ya away fer yer inheritance."

Zed went over and talked with Rosa, giving Jacob time to think about this new possibility. As Jacob was laying out his bedroll, both Zed and Rosa approached him.

Zed said, "Rosa and I've been talking. Since we have no children, we want ta make the most of our days together. We have talked it over and we want ya to have the ranch when we're gone." Zed paused and looked at Rosa, and she nodded her approval. Zed went on, "What we are trying to say, Jacob, is that if we ever had a son, we would want him to be like you."

Tears filled Jacob's eyes as he felt the love they both had for him. Jacob sat and looked at these wonderful friends and said, "Thank you, Zed and Rosa, I couldn't ask for better second parents. I promise I'll take care of both of you for the rest of your lives."

In the early morning, after having explored the Humboldt River for the best place to cross, Jacob finally found a shallow area and Zed led out leading the stock across with Rosa following. Soon they reached the other side to river bank and disappeared. Jacob sat in his saddle and watched them leave. All of a sudden he felt very much alone.

Zed had been his constant companion and friend for the past three years. Behind him at the ranch, Jacob knew Mary would be waiting for his safe return. He wanted to go to her, but he was duty-bound to see his inheritance through with Weatherbee. Jacob knew he was the one who was to receive his uncle's inheritance.

Reaching down, Jacob stroked Buck's neck and said, "Buck, you're now the only one I can trust."

Jacob was melancholy throughout the rest of the day. He rode into the early evening and finally made camp. After unsaddling Buck and the pack mule, he turned them out to forage. He soon had a fire going, and reaching into his supplies, he pulled out biscuits, beans, and bacon.

Jacob finished his meal and reminisced about Mary. He thought of the plans they would make. Buck walked over to where Jacob was sitting and nuzzled his shoulder. Jacob reached up and stroked his neck.

Buck snorted and raised his head, with his ears forward. He seemed to be listening to approaching unseen visitors.

Jacob moved away from the fire, because Zed had taught him that a man never looks into the fire or he would become fire-blind and wouldn't be able to see anyone in the blackness of the night. Jacob quietly pulled out his revolver and crawled back into the shadows for protection. He edged around a large rock and saw two people slowly approaching his camp. He took careful aim at one of the figures waiting to see what they would do.

Jacob didn't dare pull the trigger, because they might be innocent travelers. Starlight penetrated the darkness, and he could see the strangers talking. Moccasin clad, Jacob crept silently, and kept low to the ground. He could now hear them speaking in low whispers in a language Jacob had never heard before. As Jacob moved forward, he mused to himself, "Either I am getting mighty good, or they sure are greenhorns."

The two strangers were both pointing at his fire. Jacob slowly crept behind them and put the gun barrel to the side of the short one's head.

He quietly said, "Put your hands up!"

Both of their hands went up instantly, and Jacob could see perspiration beading off the man's forehead, from the reflection of the firelight. Jacob moved the gun barrel to the back of the first one and commanded, "Move over to the fire."

They both obeyed and walked slowly into his camp.

Jacob reached over and grabbed the collar of the smaller man. He was just a scrawny kid. He removed the stranger's hat with his gun barrel to see his face, and in doing so, released a long strand of beautiful black hair that cascaded over his shoulders. This wasn't a boy! It was a girl!

The young woman had soft slanted eyes and a beautiful clear complexion. He removed the hat on the other person, and in doing so revealed an old man. They both were Chinese!

Jacob was more than surprised. It had been four years since he had seen any Chinese and that was in Boston. He wondered what they were doing in this part of the country.

Jacob didn't feel threatened so he lowered his gun and replaced it in his holster. Jacob's embarrassment was evident.

"Folks—Ma'am—I am so sorry. I didn't realize it was...ah...you."

The girl replied with sarcasm, "Just who were you expecting?"

Jacob squirmed, "No one special. I'm just real careful being out here with Indians in the area, I don't trust anyone unless I know who they are." Jacob talked directly to the girl, since she did all the talking he just assumed the old man didn't understand English. Embarrassed, Jacob tried to change the subject and asked her, "Where did you come from?"

She answered with an edge to her voice, "Grandfather and I were trying to get to California, where we have family. We came from New York and were traveling with a family on the Mormon Trail. They went on to Oregon, and we caught a ride with another family, until they turned off and went to another place. We have been walking on the road for three days."

Jacob didn't know if she was telling the truth or not. He said, "Three days! Have you had any food?"

She said, "We ran out of food two days ago and haven't found much to eat along the way. We meant you no harm. Grandfather didn't want to bother you, as it is our custom to serve others, rather than having someone serve us." She looked into his eyes and Jacob felt as if she could read his mind.

Turning his eyes away, and thoroughly flustered, Jacob apologized, "Please excuse my poor manners. My fire is yours, and whatever food I have, I'll be happy to share it with you."

The girl went on, "You know, Grandfather knew you were sneaking up behind him. He told me so before you showed your gun."

Snapping back, Jacob said, "Listen, no one in their right mind would come up on another man's camp without letting him know they were approaching. You could have gotten yourselves shot."

Smugly, she said, "My grandfather could have taken your gun away from you at any time."

Jacob laughed, "Excuse me, ma'am, but at his age your grandfather can't even run, let alone fight.!"

She glared at him and said nothing more. Then she began fixing the food that Jacob had provided.

Jacob felt frustrated. How could this young girl have gotten under his skin so easily? Trying to make peace, Jacob offered his bedroll to her. She turned her head as if disgusted with Jacob. Jacob listened as her grandfather spoke to her. With the bedroll still in his hand, the girl reached over, jerked it from his hand and coldly said, "Thank you!"

The sun had been up for nearly an hour, and Jacob still didn't want to awaken the girl. Her grandfather had been up at first light and had been busy gathering firewood. Jacob's saddle blanket had kept him warm during the night.

Jacob thought the girl would have at least shared his blanket with the old man, but he found him sleeping on the ground with nothing over him, even though it was cool during the night. The old man seemed refreshed and looked none less for the wear.

As Jacob put the coffee on, he noticed the girl was awake and staring at him.

She said pleasantly, "Good morning. Why did you let me sleep so long? I could have been up long ago to help."

Jacob looked down and said, "I figured that since you had walked all day that you had to be tired, and I thought you could use the rest."

Smiling, she said, "Thank you. You are very kind."

Jacob thought, *Very kind— Why the change, she wasn't that friendly last night!*

Soon the coffee was hot, and he handed a cup to the old man and the girl.

Jacob was a peacemaker and wanted to mend things with the girl. He asked, "What are your names?"

Pointing to her grandfather, the girl said, "His name is Chin Lee. He has lived in New York for the past ten years. I am Laura Lee, his granddaughter. When I was born, my parents gave me an American name. My parents died in a fire three years ago, and I have been living with my grandfather ever since. We are traveling to Yreka, California, where we have family."

Jacob said, "I'm sorry for last night. If you hadn't talked nonsense about your grandfather taking my gun, I wouldn't have gotten so angry."

Laura smiled and said, "That's alright. I would have felt the same if someone had said that to me. However, it is true. You would have stood no chance against Grandfather."

"You sure know how to get under my skin," he said. She smiled smugly and motioned for the old man to come over to where Jacob was standing. She spoke to him in Chinese, and he objected, shaking his head. She reached over and gently touched his arm and the old man nodded his head in agreement.

She led her grandfather over and stood him in front of Jacob and said, "Grandfather saw you sitting at your fire and knew you had a good heart. Now, please try and draw your gun on my grandfather."

Jacob's became impatient. He said frustrated, "The only time I draw my gun on someone is when I use it."

"It's Laura," she interjected.

Jacob continued, "Laura, I can draw my gun faster than your grandfather can blink."

"Sir," Laura said, "I don't even know your name." Teasing, she asked, "And what is your name anyway?"

Jacob thought, *How did I ever get mixed in with this girl?* Then he said with irritation, "My name is Jacob, Jacob Morgan."

"Please, Jacob Morgan, humor me and let me show you something. My grandfather has a gift."

Jacob thought, *Yeah, a crazy granddaughter.*

She went on, "Now draw your gun on Grandfather!"

Jacob knew she would never quit until she got her way. She was just like a dog chewing on a bone—she wouldn't leave it alone, she just kept chewing on it.

Irritated, Jacob said, "Okay, if it will make you happy. But I will take the caps from my gun so it won't fire!" Sarcastically, he added, "I wouldn't want to shoot a defenseless old man."

Jacob removed the caps from his revolver and re holstered it. He now stood in front of the old man and quickly reached for his gun. Before he could even raise his gun, the old man had his hand on his wrist.

Embarrassed, Jacob said, "Wait—wait a minute. Okay, let's try that again."

This time, Jacob concentrated and watched the old man's eyes. Zed had taught him to watch a man's eyes; he said you would know when your opponent was ready to make his move. With the speed of lightning, Jacob reached for his gun, but there was the old man's hand on his wrist again.

The old man looked at him in a humble way, as if to say, "I'm sorry." Then he turned and walked away.

Laura stepped in front of Jacob, shrugged her shoulders and said, "See, I told you so," and walked to the other side of the fire and sat down.

Jacob was humbled, to say the least. He had learned to fight Indian style, use a rapier, and do English boxing. Jacob was absolutely dumbfounded. So where did the old man's speed come from? And the worst part was, he had let an old man beat him.

Laura and her grandfather helped Jacob break camp and prepared to continue on their journey. Jacob told them he was going in the same direction, and invited them to travel with him. He said, "Laura, it's not safe for a young woman and an elderly man to travel alone."

Laura laughed. "Jacob, are you our knight in shining armor? Are you here to protect us?" she asked.

Jacob guffawed, "From what I've seen, I need to be protected by your grandfather! I have never seen hands move so fast." Now she laughed and leaned over and spoke to her grandfather. He looked at Jacob with a twinkle in his eyes, smiled, and nodded his head.

Jacob had more than one reason to spend his time with these newfound friends. He wanted to be taught what the old man knew. He quietly said, "Laura, I know you don't need my protection, but you do need my food. I am happy to share it with you, since I have plenty. Your grandfather knows something that I want to learn. What I want to know is, what did your grandfather do to have that type of speed? Anyone having that type of speed has to use it for self-defense. It was something I have never seen, and I made myself a promise long ago that I would learn all I could about defending myself and my family. So, can you teach me his technique? Maybe we can both help each other."

Laura was quiet for a moment, pondering Jacob's proposal. She reached over and touched her grandfather's arm and they stopped walking. She spoke softly to her grandfather. He turned and looked at Jacob for a long moment and then nodded his head in approval.

Jacob dismounted and walked beside them and throughout, Laura talked about Chinese methods of defense, compared to what Americans used. Laura criticized the self-defense used in America.

"When Americans fight, all they do is start swinging with their fists or grab something and use it as a club."

Laura went on to explain, "Martial arts in China, is referred to as kung fu. There are many different styles of fighting that have developed over many hundreds of years in China. We have techniques that mimic certain animals, like the tiger, the monkey, the bird, the bear, and the deer. These are called the Five Animal Plays."

Jacob listened intently and asked many questions about the different styles. His last question was, "How long would it take me to master this kung fu?"

Laura laughed and repeated the question to her grandfather. His eyes twinkled, and he chuckled as he spoke to Laura.

Laura replied, "Grandfather says that for you to learn the basics will take at least seven years, or maybe five years if you studied very hard and lived in China."

"Five years," exclaimed Jacob. "We only have a few weeks!"

Laughing again, Laura said teasingly, "Then, Jacob Morgan, I guess you will only have a few weeks to learn kung fu!"

As Laura continued to walk, she went on to explain, "Jacob, you do not understand. It has taken me thirteen of my seventeen years of life, practicing every day to get to the level I am at, and I am still learning. Grandfather was taught when he was very young by his father, who was taught by his father, and so on from father to son for many generations.

"The early Chinese Shaolin priests used their methods of defense at the Shaolin Monastery to protect themselves from bandits around 621 AD. You will never fully master kung fu." Laura stopped and turned to Jacob. She then said, "Grandfather says we will teach you what we can to help you in your self-defense."

Jacob had an idea and spoke up. "Laura, I know you are on your way to Yreka. I also have business there, but first I must go to San Francisco. Here is my proposal. I will give you funds and food so you will be able to make it to Yreka safely. Meanwhile, we will take our time to get there because I want to learn this new method as we cross over the Sierra Nevada Mountains. When we reach the other side, you can take the Siskiyou Trail to Yreka, and I will continue on to San Francisco and finish my business. When I am finished, I will find you in Yreka. This way we can help each other."

"We are out of food and we have no money," Laura said. "Grandfather will not take charity."

Jacob said, "It won't be charity. It will be payment for his teaching me."

She spoke with her grandfather—he agreed to Jacob's invitation.

The three stopped in the early afternoon to begin Jacob's training. Laura stood in front of Jacob and told him to try and hit her.

Jacob answered incredulously, "Are you crazy, Laura? I have never struck a woman before in my life."

She sarcastically said, "Are you listening, Jacob? I said try. You may try, but you will not succeed!"

Jacob chuckled. Little did she know about his knowledge of English boxing. Jacob remembered that Isaiah had once said that he threw one of the fastest punches he had ever seen. Jacob was quite confident of himself. Of course he could hit her! Well, she asked for it!

Out shot Jacob's right hand to connect with her chin. In an unbelievably swift movement, Laura had grabbed his hand, twisted it, and flipped Jacob onto his back.

Stunned, Jacob lay there in the dirt shaking his head, trying to clear away the cobwebs. He looked up at the old man, who was grinning and nodding his approval to Laura.

Jacob, though shaken, stood up and asked, "What was that? I didn't even see it coming!"

Laura smiled and said, "That, Jacob Morgan was kung fu!"

Laura would not show Jacob any further maneuvers. She assigned him exercises, which seemed to him like dancing. She demonstrated over and over the different moves, calling them the Five Animal Plays. Her hands and feet moved with a fluid rhythm, turning in different directions, while keeping in perfect balance. She moved her arms and feet as if dancing, imitating each animal move.

"Jacob," Laura said, "Watch carefully. I am now moving as a monkey moves."

Jacob concentrated and followed her precise movements.

"Very nice, Jacob," Laura replied. "You learn very fast."

Throughout the week, while walking the trail, Jacob would break away and ride Buck to a secluded area. Jacob couldn't practice and walk with them at the same time, so he let them continue their journey while he practiced over and over the dances he had been taught. After a few hours, he would catch up with Laura and her grandfather for additional training. Jacob did everything he could to master these new techniques.

Immigrant wagon trains slowly passed them each day, leaving the small group to themselves. They made their own secluded camp off the main trail. Jacob just wanted to be left alone, so he could learn this exciting new method of defense.

Early one morning, after two weeks of practicing every free moment he had. Jacob had strictly followed Laura's every move and command, Jacob balked and said, "Is this really necessary? I feel like a dancer. I have done this daily and I know all of the dances you have shown me, but how can this help in my self-defense?"

Irritated, Laura walked up to him and said, "Move like the tiger!"

Jacob moved slowly, not really caring. She knocked him down.

"Why did you do that?" he yelled, and got to his feet.

Again she said, "Move like the tiger, and faster."

Jacob complied, this time moving with faster speed as she moved aggressively toward him. His movement blocked her advance. She tried it again, and he again used the tiger play, and again blocked her advance.

She stopped and pointed her finger at him. "Jacob, there is a counter movement for every movement, for both attack and defense. If you will just listen, practice, and quit your complaining, you will learn much faster. Now, move like the monkey." She moved with precision and speed toward him, and he blocked her advance with his arm.

She yelled, "Use the bird."

Complying, he blocked her move with a kick of his leg.

"Concentrate, Jacob, and defend yourself. Use all of your moves. Mimic all of the animals," Laura yelled, while advancing toward Jacob.

For the next few minutes, Laura advanced and then retreated, and then Jacob became the attacker. Smiling, Laura said, "Very good, Jacob."

With a little pride, Jacob said, "Yes, I am getting good!" Then with a single movement unfamiliar to Jacob, she swept his feet out from under him and he landed with a thud on the ground.

Groaning, Jacob looked up. Laura smiled and smugly said, "No, Jacob, you are not getting good. You are still learning the basics. This training is vital. You cannot progress to the more advanced stages without first learning the basics of the Five Animal Plays. Now be patient, and soon there will be more."

Late that afternoon, after setting up camp, Grandfather spoke to Laura. Then she asked Jacob for his knife. Jacob handed his large Bowie knife to her, hilt first. She then placed it in her grandfather's hand, and he walked into a small grove of trees. Within the hour, Grandfather returned carrying two long sticks that he had cut and carved with Jacob's knife.

Handing him his knife, Laura said, "Grandfather feels it is time for you to learn self-defense with a stave." Handing him a long carved stick, she said, "These are called staves. They were used by the Shaolin monks as weapons of self-defense against bandits in China. Grandfather learned how to use the stave as a boy, when living in northern China. Grandfather says you must learn to control both the inside and the outside your body. Outside of the body, is using your hands, eyes, legs, and feet. These are the dances you have learned, and Grandfather will now teach you more. The next thing is to control the inside of your body, which includes your heart and your mind. It also includes controlling your breathing and your inner strength."

Laura then reached up and hit Jacob's chest with the palm of her hand, and said, "Jacob, it is important for you to have a strong body. Without strong, flexible muscles, you will not be able to defend yourself." She then pushed her fingers against his stomach and said, "You must learn to concentrate and use your breathing. By controlling your mind and body, they both become one."

Jacob scratched his head and said, "I didn't know you had to learn all of these things!" Laura said, "Now you can see why it takes years to learn. We will teach you only the basics. It will be up to you to practice every day. Always practice, and then your body will be ready when you need to defend your life!"

Jacob was amazed as the old man picked up one of the staves and started spinning it in his hand while dancing. He then balanced the stave in the crook of his arm, turning in circles and kicking up his feet in rhythm. Reversing his steps, Grandfather moved his arm and stave—together as one—and again kicked up his feet. Then he stopped.

After seeing Grandfather perform the different dances, Jacob was in total awe, and had great respect for Grandfather. The old man was incredible, to say the least. Laura spent the next two hours instructing Jacob on holding and using the stave correctly. In the late afternoon, after Jacob had practiced holding the stave, Laura showed him the new dance moves that went with using the stave. Jacob spent all of his spare time practicing his technique until late into the evening.

As Jacob sat by the fire eating his supper, he rehearsed in his mind the moves, using his hands, arms, and legs. Laura broke his concentration and said, "Grandfather told me he has watched you and perhaps in three or four years you could master some areas of kung fu."

Jacob laughed and said, "Thank you, Grandfather. Laura, please tell him that I really enjoy the animal dancing. I just don't know if my body can survive the beatings you give me when we practice!"

Laura teased Jacob and said, "In China, it is important for both husband and wife to know kung fu. That way they will have a harmonious relationship in their marriage. It is something they both can practice together."

Jacob, wanting to learn kung fu, had taken his time on getting to California, and on the morning of the seventh week on the trail, the time had come for them to part company. Laura and her grandfather prepared to continue on to Yreka, and Jacob had packed his mule and was ready to leave for his journey to San Francisco.

In his final training, Jacob stood in front of Laura with his stave and they both commenced circling. They both advanced toward each other, each striking hard and trying to hit the other. Every time Laura advanced, Jacob blocked her move and tried to strike her. It was fast and furious as both advanced and hit each other's stave with maximum force. When one person advanced, the other blocked, each trying to strike down the other with their moves.

At one point, Laura spun around with her stave and stuck Jacob's shoulder. He jerked back in pain and concentrated on finding a flaw in her move. He couldn't find any.

It frustrated him, and he threw his stave to the ground. He commenced using his bare hands and Laura followed. They both blocked with their hands and kicked with their feet. Jacob could feel his foot connect with Laura's shoulder, and then he struck her right hip. Laura was determined that Jacob's strikes would be returned with a vengeance. Jacob felt her feet connect with his body, as she struck like a tiger.

Circling, Jacob thought, *Sly as a fox*. Then with a new move he had thought up on his own, Jacob moved and struck with his foot. With extreme force, Laura landed on the ground with a thud.

Jacob stood over her and saw the look of shock on her face. He backed up and she said, "Where did that come from?"

Teasing, Jacob said, "It has been in our family for many years. I have saved it until today, especially for you."

Jacob heard genuine laughter, but it wasn't from Laura. He turned and saw Grandfather standing behind him, laughing so hard he had tears in his eyes. Laura started laughing with him, and then Jacob joined in.

By mid-morning, the sun was over the eastern ridges of the Sierra Nevada Mountains, and Jacob prepared to bid farewell to his friends. As Jacob stood in front of Laura and her Grandfather, the old man said something to Jacob in Chinese. Laura smiled and said, "Grandfather wants you to know that he has spent many years training pupils. He says that you are one of the best, especially for a white man from America."

Jacob put his hands together and bowed his head in respect to the old man. He had grown attached to his new friends and would miss them as he continued on to San Francisco, Jacob had learned much, but he also had a new respect for the Chinese people, not because he had learned kung fu, but because Laura and Chin Lee were kind and friendly to him. Reaching into his pocket, Jacob took out several gold coins, and placed them in Laura's hand. "Take these," Jacob said. "With the food I gave you and this money, your journey will be much easier. I will come and visit you when I finish my business in San Francisco."

Laura accepted the money with gratitude and lowered her head. She slowly reached up, and, placing her hand on his arm, she kissed him on the cheek. Smiling, she said, "Jacob, my grandfather and I will miss you!" She turned, and they continued on to Yreka.

Chapter 28
Fraud

Jacob watched as his two friends walked down the trail and headed north toward Yreka. They suddenly turned and waved back. He returned their wave and was grateful he could help them. Jacob gathered the reins and took a hold of the lead rope to the mule, stepped in the stirrup and climbed up into the saddle. Pausing to take one last look at his friends as they departed, he clucked to Buck and said, "Okay, Buck, you've had rest and it's time to move out. All I can say is it's good to be in the saddle again."

Jacob followed the California Trail and then turned south toward Sacramento. As he rode, Jacob passed hundreds of wagons winding their way slowly along the California Trail, all headed for the gold fields.

Gold had been found in Sacramento on January 24, 1848, at Sutter's Mill in Coloma, California. In all, over 300,000 people would come to the California Gold Rush. The people of the Sandwich Islands and Latin America were the first to arrive by sea in 1848. Those who had come in 1849 were called "forty-niners." Many prospectors had come from Washington and Oregon along the Siskiyou Trail. Thousands of people from the East traveled west following the Mormon Trail, and then continued on the California Trail to Sacramento.

Entering Sacramento, Jacob slowly maneuvered through the sea of merchants, with their wagons loaded with supplies, and prospectors headed for the gold fields

Jacob stopped at a general store and purchased additional food. He didn't trust anyone. He avoided strangers and spotted shysters everywhere who were trying to make an easy buck off unsuspecting emigrants. With his purchases completed, Jacob quickly rode out of Sacramento leading his mule. That night, he camped off the main trail in a secluded copse of trees, hoping that it would offer him safety.

The second day, after eating his morning meal, Jacob whistled for Buck to come. The stallion ran up to him, wanting to be saddled and on their way. Then Jacob gathered his mule and completed his packing.

Suddenly, Jacob felt the hair on the back of his neck come up. Buck warned him with a shrill whinny, and Jacob grabbed his rifle. He heard someone running away from his camp and jumped on Buck, following the sound of the retreating footsteps. When Jacob reached the road with rifle in hand, he glanced both ways. There he saw many people traveling in both directions, but could see no one running.

Jacob spoke out loud, asking, "Was that the other worthy recipient?"

Now, Jacob was even more vigilant. He stayed off the main roads until he finally crossed over the bay by ferry. By the end of the week, Jacob had carefully made his way back into San Francisco.

Jacob reminisced about his first visit to San Francisco, when he had gotten off the ship, *Brooklyn*, three years earlier. Much had changed in his life since then. Scanning the area, Jacob saw hundreds of new buildings, and improved roads. It was more congested with people than Sacramento. Numerous ships were anchored in the bay, laden with supplies, or letting passengers off into smaller boats to be taken ashore.

Jacob stayed at an inn on the outskirts of the city, some distance from Weatherbee's office. The inn was in a less traveled area, with its own livery stable. Jacob unpacked his supplies, stabled his animals, and relaxed for the evening.

The following morning, after a warm bath, haircut, and shave, Jacob put on his gentleman's clothing. He didn't want to ride Buck to the main district, because Benson had seen Buck and would recognize his horse immediately. So, he stabled Buck out of the city and rented another horse. He then proceeded to a men's haberdashery to buy a new wardrobe, including a top hat. After making his purchases, and changing into his new clothes, Jacob walked out of the shop and maneuvered through the sea of humanity. He was bumped hard by a pedestrian and almost knocked to the ground. There was no apology, just a grunt of disgust as the man hurried on. Jacob brushed it off and moved on about his business.

By mid-morning, Jacob had entered the business district, and after consulting with at least two dozen merchants, he came up with the names of two firms he felt comfortable with. Both were well known and respected, with reputations for honesty.

Jacob went to both of the establishments and observed the appearance of their buildings.

One building was well taken care of and in the heart of the business district, while the other building was unkempt in a rougher area of the city. The neatness of the building and its location reflected the type of attorneys that worked there. So, Jacob chose the firm of Pratt and Cole to consider as his solicitors.

They were attorneys and counselors-at-law, located in the Gothic Hall on the corner of Montgomery and Jackson Street. Jacob entered the large brick building and saw a pleasant-looking lady sitting behind a desk. She looked up, smiled, and asked. "May I help you, sir?"

Jacob reached up and took off his top hat. Then he said, "May I speak with either Mr. Pratt or Mr. Cole?"

The well-mannered receptionist asked if he had an appointment with either of the attorneys.

"No," replied Jacob.

"I am sorry, sir, but Mr. Pratt and Mr. Cole prefer their clients to make appointments."

"I understand. I am leaving in a few days and am looking for advice from an attorney before I leave. I need someone to represent my shipping lines and my gold mines in Yreka, California." Jacob paused for a moment and then calmly continued, "I understand if they are too busy. I will consult with another firm."

She spoke up quickly, and said, "Oh no, sir, since you are new in town and have to leave soon, I am sure they would be glad to speak with you. Would you like to see one or both of the attorneys?"

Jacob smiled kindly, and said, "If it wouldn't be an inconvenience, I would like to speak with both of them."

She smiled. Her face showed sincerity as she said, "Whom shall I say wants to see them?"

Jacob said, "Mr. Jacob Morgan of Boston."

She nodded to him and went into an adjoining room.

Jacob mused about how different this secretary was compared to Weatherbee's secretary, old 'Miss Pitchford'. This lady was very refreshing.

Jacob sat down in a comfortable leather chair, and in a few moments the office door opened. A stately looking man in his late forties approached Jacob. Jacob could see that the man was somewhat taken aback by Jacob's young age. He was expecting someone much older or someone with a more business-like appearance, and not a young man.

Jacob immediately reached out and before the man could speak said, "I am Jacob Morgan of Boston, and your name, sir?"

"I—I am Mr. Cole," Caught off guard, the attorney fumbled momentarily with his words. "Mr. Morgan, would you please come into our office? Mr. Pratt and I will be happy to meet with you."

Jacob followed Mr. Cole into his office. As they entered, another man stood up from his chair and extended his hand. "Mr. Morgan, I am Mr. Pratt. It is my pleasure to meet you."

Jacob could see the wisdom in this gentleman. He was one to not judge by mere appearance. Jacob immediately started the conversation. "Gentlemen, I can see by Mr. Cole's assessment of me that you are wondering why a young man, such as myself, would be seeking your advice and assistance. May I take a few moments to tell you my story?"

He explained his life story since he had left Boston and about his inheritance. He told them about living at Zed's ranch and spending two years with the Indians, including the death of his wife. Both men were enthralled with Jacob's story and sat on the very edge of their seats as he related his past three years' experience.

Now that he had their undivided attention, Jacob told them about his suspicions of Mr. Weatherbee. Jacob told about his run-in with Benson and their duel. He spoke of his concern about Mr. Weatherbee constantly referring to another worthy recipient.

Jacob related what he knew about Benson—that he had been in Boston and had said he knew his parents and that he was also from San Francisco.

"Benson said he was a cattle buyer from San Francisco." Jacob said. "No one had ever heard of a cattle buyer from there. Most cattle buyers were from Kansas, Texas, or other larger cities back East. My friend Zed and I felt he was a fraud, and we think he may have something going with Mr. Weatherbee."

Then, Jacob told them the sum of money he was to inherit.

Mr. Pratt let out a small gasp, and Mr. Cole let out a low whistle.

Jacob stood up. "Now gentlemen, do I have your cooperation?" Both men stood up grinning. Each man extended his hand and shook Jacob's hand with enthusiasm.

Smiling, Mr. Pratt said, "Mr. Morgan, I believe you could write a book on your adventures. That alone would make you wealthy."

Jacob laughed, "If I can just get you to look at my personal affairs concerning Weatherbee, that would be one adventure I would like to have over with!"

For the next week, Jacob kept a low profile and spent very little time in public. He wore his city clothes instead of his buckskins. If Benson was around, he didn't want to chance being recognized. He met at least three times with his new attorneys during the week and filled them in on all the necessary information concerning Mr. Weatherbee. He had moved Buck thirty miles from the city to make sure no one would find him.

Jacob rented a room across the street from Weatherbee's office and spent a considerable time watching the comings and goings. On the fourth day, Jacob saw a man walking toward Weatherbee's office that looked like Benson.

"Gotcha!" Jacob said as he watched the man near the office. It was Benson. He went directly into Weatherbee's office and was there for at least an hour. Jacob was now ready.

Jacob had hired Mr. John Ashley, who had worked for Pinkerton Detective Service, established in 1850. He was highly recommended by Cole and Pratt. John Ashley was one of their most experienced private detectives. He sat outside the building Jacob occupied, patiently waiting for Jacob's signal. He nonchalantly read the newspaper, keeping a watchful eye on Weatherbee's office.

As Benson exited, Jacob signaled. Ashley immediately followed Benson at a discrete distance through the business district and down to the wharf. Benson entered a saloon near the waterfront and sat with four men at a corner table.

Before entering the saloon, Ashley disheveled his hair and removed his jacket and tie. He then entered and sat at a table as close to Benson as he could without being noticed. Ashley ordered a beer, took out a deck of cards, and started playing solitaire. He talked out loud, mumbling while playing, as if intoxicated. No one paid him any attention.

He sat and listened intently to their conversation and found it very interesting! After half an hour, Benson got up and walked out, passing Ashley, who turned his head to avoid being noticed. After waiting a few moments, Ashley yelled a few obscenities at his cards, picked them up, and staggered out and he continued to follow Benson.

At Tattersalts' Livery Stable on the corner of Kearney and Pacific Street, Benson rented a horse. He rode to the wharf, where he boarded a ferry and waited to cross the bay. Ashley rented a horse at the same stable and followed Benson, where he also boarded the same ferry.

On the ferry, Ashley kept out of sight, hiding behind other travelers, carefully watching Benson. As the ferry crossed and docked, Benson mounted his horse and continued north along the coastal inland road for another ten miles. Ashley followed at a safe distance, mingling in with the many travelers traversing the busy road, while still keeping Benson in sight.

It was mid-afternoon before Benson turned off into a small ranch yard. Tying his horse at a hitching rail, he proceeded into the house. Ashley concealed his horse in a small grove of trees across the road; he counted six horses tied to the hitching rail next to the small barn. Unable to get closer without being seen, Ashley wrote down the description and location of the house and property.

It was an hour before Benson walked out the door, followed by five rough-looking men, all heavily armed. The group stood talking with Benson. Before Benson mounted his horse, he reached into his pocket and took out a large roll of bills, carefully counted out an unknown amount, and handed it to one of the men that Ashley assumed was their leader.

Taking his time traveling back to San Francisco, Benson stopped and looked around to see if he were being followed. There were numerous carriages and wagons along the road and people on foot coming and going. At one point, Ashley rode past Benson and turned his horse into a grove of trees in case Benson looked around and saw him. He then waited for Benson to pass and continued to follow him at a safe distance. Benson re-crossed on the ferry and arrived in San Francisco in the late afternoon. He turned in his horse at the livery stable, and then proceeded to Mr. Weatherbee's office, unaware that Ashley had been following him.

The following day, Ashley revisited the area where Benson had met with the five men. No one was at the farmhouse, so he made inquires with all the neighbors under the pretense of trying to locate his brother's residence. He said his brother was supposed to be living at that ranch house.

Late that afternoon, Ashley reported to Jacob and his attorneys with all he had learned about Benson.

Pratt questioned Ashley, "Now, you said that the neighbors reported that three of these five men were just out of prison and the fourth one was a well-known criminal. Is that correct?"

Ashley said, "That's what most all of the neighbors reported, some of them knew the men personally, but they didn't know anything about the fifth man."

Mr. Pratt asked, "What have you learned about the four men at the saloon?"

Ashley continued, "After I checked my sources, I found that the four men at the saloon have been known to shanghai men, and sell them to ship captains as slaves. I heard Benson say, that is what they planned to do with Jacob and make a tidy sum in the bargain.

"Whew," Cole blew out. "This is really getting interesting!"

Pratt raised his hands, and said, "I think we need to talk to the local police about this information!"

Jacob asked, "Can we trust them? I have a brother in Boston who is a constable, and he says that the constables who work the wharf will turn their heads at any foul play for a few coins."

Ashley nodded his agreement and said, "There are many here who also will look the other way for a token of appreciation. I know some city officials, who will help us discretely and get this riffraff off the streets. This will, of course, enhance their own careers."

Jacob looked glum. Thank goodness he had listened to Zed. He could have been shanghaied on some ship, and died out at sea.

"What information have you got on Mr. Weatherbee?" Jacob inquired.

"Great news!" smiled Mr. Cole. "We know the president of Weatherbee's bank. It is also your Uncle Zac's bank. It seems that your Uncle Zac had apprised the bank on the disbursement of all funds to you. However, Weatherbee had funds taken out in your behalf and at your behest."

Disbelieving, Jacob asked, "How could they do that? I didn't sign anything!"

"That's what's so interesting," replied Cole. "It seems they forged your signature from the agreement you signed at Weatherbee's when you agreed to the stipulations to your uncle's will. Listen to this, your Uncle Zac stipulated that the bank could not distribute over $5,000 a year without you being present. What a shrewd businessman your uncle was."

"Jacob," Mr. Cole continued, "we have found out that you have lost $15,000 so far to Weatherbee's scheme. However, if you are declared legally dead, then another 'worthy recipient' would be found."

Pratt interrupted, "And, of course, Weatherbee would find another 'worthy' recipient, since your late uncle is also dead. And that is where Mr. Samuel Benson comes in. When you are declared legally dead, he becomes the next worthy recipient, and Weatherbee continues to control the purse strings."

"Okay," said Jacob dejectedly, "so what do we need to do now?"

Over the next three weeks, Jacob, his two attorneys, and Ashley met with Captain Malachi Fallon, San Francisco's first captain and chief of police. Captain Fallon discussed the implementation of their plan.

Smiling at Jacob, Captain Fallon said, "The word on the street is that there is a large reward for the first person to locate a certain Jacob Morgan, dressed in buckskins, and riding a buckskin stallion. Everyone is hunting for a beautiful buckskin stallion but can't seem to locate him. I think, it was a good idea for you to hide your horse thirty miles from here. No one would think of looking that far out!"

Jacob stood up and said, "Captain Fallon, if it's all right with you, I want the opportunity of meeting Benson face-to-face in Weatherbee's office. I will follow him in and confront both him and Weatherbee. Both you and Ashley can stand at the back entrance listening to everything that is said. Benson reports to Weatherbee daily."

Captain Fallon said, "Jacob that could be dangerous. Can you take care of yourself?"

Cole broke in laughing and said, "Don't worry, Captain. If you knew what Jacob had done in the past, you would want him to watch over you!"

Fallon looked confused.

Jacob added, "Captain, I can take care of myself!

The next morning, Jacob checked the clock on the wall. It was 10:30 a.m. Waiting with him in the room across the street from Weatherbee's office was Captain Fallon and Ashley. Jacob was dressed in his buckskins and had his knife secured to the side of his leggings, with his colt holstered around his waist. All were ready to proceed as soon as Benson entered the office.

"Now don't be in too big of a hurry," Jacob teasingly said. "Be calm and listen for evidence. If there is some commotion, don't worry. I still have a score to settle with Samuel Benson, and I want to have a little fun while doing it."

Just then, Jacob looked up the street and saw Benson and another man walking at a fast pace in the direction of Weatherbee's office.

Ashley said, "The man behind Benson is one of the men from the wharf saloon."

As the two men hurriedly entered Weatherbee's office, Jacob whispered to the other two, "It's time to take some scalps," and he grinned.

The three split—the Captain and Ashley going to the back of Weatherbee's office and Jacob entering through the front door. Jacob paused outside the door of Weatherbee's office and mused out loud, "It was three years ago that I first stood at this door. And we will now see who the true recipient is."

As Jacob opened the door, there sat Miss Pitchford. She lifted her head and looked confused. Then recognition set in! She sat speechless, with her mouth agape.

She started to speak, but Jacob put his finger to his lips.

Whispering he said, "You will not speak. Do you understand?"

"Just who do you think you are?" she said, starting to raise her voice.

Jacob quickly put his hand over her mouth, pressed hard, and whispered in her ear, "Miss Pitchford, if you don't do as I say, I promise you that you will end up in jail this day!" Jacob continued in a soft voice, "At the back door of Mr. Weatherbee's office, is the captain of the police department, listening to their conversation. Now, if you don't want to cooperate, I will take you forcibly out of this office, and you will go to jail immediately. Is that understood?" Jacob said, glaring at her.

She choked back tears and nodded her head "yes."

Whispering, he said, "I will release my hand from your mouth. You will gather your personal belongings and leave this office immediately. Is that understood?"

Again, she nodded her head. Jacob released his hand from her mouth. She hastily grabbed her purse and was out the door and out of employment.

Jacob put his ear against the door.

"What do you mean he can't be found? Something is going on around here, and I don't like it," Weatherbee said.

Benson replied, "Don't worry. When he comes into town on his buckskin, we'll drug him and put him on a ship. They'll use him up for a few years, and then drop him off in the middle of the ocean."

"You have to find him before you can deliver him. From what I hear, he's not one to mess with," said Weatherbee in frustration. Taunting Benson, he went on. "Look what he did to you, and you were supposed to be the best."

"Just watch yer mouth, Weatherbee. When I see him again, I'll show him who the better man is. He just got me with a lucky punch. I'll have my chance when—"

Weatherbee cut him off, "You'll do as I say. I pay the bills around here, and if I say kill him, you kill him. If he goes on a ship, like many of the others, it will be all the more money for us. Just remember, I am in charge of this operation and I make all the decisions. If you play your cards the way I tell you, you will be the next recipient to all of Sherwood's inheritance, and we both will be wealthy men."

Jacob knocked on the door. In an angry tone, Weatherbee asked, "Yes, Miss Pitchford. It better be important!"

Jacob opened the door, and said, "I just thought I would drop in."

Weatherbee sat aghast when he saw Jacob. Benson let out a string of obscenities and lunged at Jacob. Jacob stepped aside and hit him on the side of the head with a glancing blow.

The seaman that had come in with Benson started swinging, and Jacob deftly moved aside and kicked him in his upper thigh. The man went down, grabbing his leg with a scream of pain. Benson grabbed Jacob from behind and tried to choke him. Jacob backed toward the wall, hitting Benson in the nose with the back of his head as he screamed and grabbed. The seaman rushed Jacob from behind and tried to pull him down.

There was a splintering of wood, as Captain Fallon and Ashley crashed through the back door and grabbed Weatherbee. Benson immediately ran out the front door and down the steps. The seaman had Jacob by the throat and was choking him. Jacob grasped each of his thumbs and pulled them forward, flipping the man over his head. The seaman landed hard on his back, and Ashley immediately had him in cuffs.

"Where's Benson?" yelled Jacob.

Ashley pointed to the front door, and Jacob followed in pursuit. Running out of the building, Jacob looked in all directions, but Benson was nowhere to be seen, he had escaped.

Before noon, the police had all four men from the saloon in custody and three of the five men at the farmhouse arrested. The men in the farmhouse were hired to find Jacob and kidnap him for service on a sailing vessel.

Benson was nowhere to be found. He had taken a horse from the livery stable and was said to be heading north toward Yreka.

Miss Pitchford was quite humble and very contrite when she was questioned by the police. After questioning her, Captain Fallon felt she didn't know anything nor was she involved in any of Weatherbee's business schemes.

After Captain Fallon had released Miss Pitchford, he explained to Jacob, "Weatherbee had embezzled over $60,000 from your inheritance. He has taken $15,000 from the bank and $45,000 in gold. He personally went to Yreka with a letter signed by your late uncle. He forged your uncle's signature, which gave him permission to collect the profits in gold from the mine owners."

Captain Fallon paused for a minute to let the news sink in. Then he continued, "We found an additional $20,000 in cash in his safe, plus he had an additional $23,000 in another bank account. It seems Mr. Weatherbee ran a very lucrative business in shanghaiing men for ships in the San Francisco Bay." Smiling, Captain Fallon then said, "Jacob, you will get all of your gold back, including the $15,000 that he embezzled from you." Taking a deep breath, he grinned and said, "Not bad for a day's work, huh?"

Jacob spent the next two days with his attorneys. All papers and deeds found in Weatherbee's safe that belonged to Jacob were changed back to his name and legally recorded. New bank accounts were opened, and Jacob gave his attorneys-power of attorney to handle his investments. Jacob's inheritance now included sailing vessels, gold mines, and other lucrative land investments made by his uncle Zac.

Two days later, Ashley and Jacob were asked to meet in Captain Fallon's office at the police headquarters. Upon arriving, they were directed into Fallon's personal office. After a few minutes, Fallon entered the room. He motioned for Ashley to bring him and Jacob up to date on his investigation.

Ashley turned to Jacob and said, "I've been tracking Benson, as you requested, and I found that he has gone to Yreka. He has friends in that area and most likely will ask for their help. He knows you'll show up sooner or later."

Captain Fallow interrupted and said, "Since we have no jurisdiction in that area, I have contacted the newly elected marshal of Yreka, Marshal Ely, and informed him that you are coming. He wants you to contact him as soon as you arrive."

Ashley continued, "Jacob, Benson knows he will never be your uncle's recipient now, and has nothing better to do than to take his revenge out on you."

Jacob's brother Isaiah's admonition again came to his mind: *Sly as a fox and wise as a badger.*

Chapter 29
Inheritance

Jacob crossed over the bay on a ferry with Buck and his pack mule. He now was a wealthy man. Stroking Buck's neck, he said, "Buck, you're still my most prized possession. I need to sell most of my holdings and clear up all business in Yreka. Then ole boy, we'll go back to Mary, and I'll settle down and raise a family."

Jacob rode the Siskiyou Trail up into northern California and then on to Yreka. He knew Benson would be waiting for any opportunity to kill him. He needed to be constantly alert and find allies who would work with him.

When gold was discovered in Yreka, Uncle Zac had grubstaked the first two prospectors who filed claims. They made Uncle Zac part owner in their mines, and made him a wealthy man.

Gold was first discovered in March of 1851.

By May 1851, the Gold Rush had created a boomtown, which was comprised of tents, shanties, and a few rough cabins. A baker had written "Bakery" on a sheet, and hung it backward over a hitching rail. The "B" was hidden, and all the miners could see was the word Yreka without the B. Thus the new miners thought the name of the town was Yreka—(bakery spelled backward without the "B".) The name stuck, and the boomtown became Yreka.

Jacob was told by his attorneys that Zac's cargo ships had been used to haul mining supplies to San Francisco. Then the mining supplies were shipped up to the gold fields in Yreka.

With the gold strike in full swing, there were more than one thousand Chinese workers in Yreka mining their own claims that first year. One section of the town was known as "Chinatown." Jacob was sure that some of the people there were relatives to Laura and her grandfather.

The influx of miners was so great that a county was formed in 1852 called Siskiyou County, with Yreka as the county seat.

Jacob entered at the south end of Yreka. He kept to the back roads and sidestreets to avoid being seen. There were literally hundreds of people on the streets. Many Chinese people led mules laden with supplies. Teamsters drove wagons heaped with goods pulled by several spans of horses. Deep ruts were formed in the road by wagons during the rainy season, and the mud would get so deep that it went halfway to a man's knees as he tried to cross the street.

Locating the marshal's office, Jacob met with Marshal Ely. The marshal welcomed Jacob and informed him that he had received information from Captain Fallon about Benson. Marshal Ely had already begun an investigation on the whereabouts of Samuel Benson but had not been able to locate him.

Jacob rented a room at the Metropolitan Hotel on Fourth and Lane Street and then stabled Buck and his mule at the livery stable. The next morning, Jacob ate an early breakfast at Mrs. Lowry's Cafe and saddled Buck to begin exploring the area.

There were many new brick and stone houses in the area. From the hotel owner, Jacob learned that there had been some devastating fires in the past that had burned one-third of Yreka due to all the wooden structures. To avoid that happening again, new buildings were built of brick and stone throughout the city.

By noon, Jacob was eighteen miles southeast of Yreka, approaching Fort Jones.

Fort Jones was built for protection against the Shasta and Modoc Indians. Captain Edward H. Fitzgerald was the commanding officer in charge of building the new fort. He chose Beaver Valley because there was adequate forage, water, and timber available. There were fifty-eight soldiers assigned under Fitzgerald's command. There were approximately two thousand Indians in the county. With the influx of miners, the Indians were being crowded out, as the miners staked out their hunting grounds for mining claims. The Indians had finally had enough and would not be pushed any further, so thus began a war, and soldiers were called in to protect the settlers.

From the papers taken from Weatherbee's safe by Jacob's attorneys, Jacob learned that Uncle Zac had grubstaked a Mr. O. Charles Wheelock in Fort Jones. Wheelock had discovered gold and now owned a trading post and a hotel. Jacob wanted to visit this man to see if he was aware of his uncle's death.

Jacob rode into Fort Jones, which was a small settlement with a few buildings scattered about. The area was heavily wooded on all sides. Located on the left side of the main road were Wheelock's hotel and trading post. One-half mile up the road was the fort, which was now under construction.

Jacob noticed that the trading post was busy. Horses and mules were tied to the hitching rail, and friendly Indians were standing about talking to each other.

As Jacob entered the trading post, he saw that the walls and floor were cluttered with mining equipment. On the wall behind the counter were rifles, colt dragoons, and boxes of powder, lead, and other miscellaneous items. Furs hung on pegs along one wall. A man and a woman were transacting business in the back of the post. At one end of the room were rolls of cotton fabric in a variety of colors. Jacob walked around, looking at the different types of merchandise used by the miners in the area. After two busy hours, everyone had finally left. Then, Jacob walked to the front counter.

A well-built man in his late forties approached Jacob. Looking at Jacob, he said, "You sure remind me of someone."

"And who might that be?" asked Jacob.

The man smiled and said, "And you speak just like him—for a mountain man he sure was learned."

Jacob smiled and said, "Might his name be Zachariah Sherwood?"

Stunned, the man looked again and said, "Are you any relation to Zac?"

Nodding his head, Jacob said, "Yes, sir. I am his nephew, Jacob Morgan."

The man, smiling, extended his hand and said, "I am Charles Wheelock, your uncle's partner. I owe everything to him. How is your Uncle Zac?"

Shaking his hand, Jacob lowered his head and said, "He died from consumption a few years ago."

Charles's smile vanished, and he said sadly, "I'm very sorry. You couldn't find a better, more honest man than your Uncle Zac."

"Thank you," Jacob said.

"Martha," Charles yelled to the back, "please come up here. I want you to meet Zac Sherwood's nephew."

In a few moments, a pleasant-looking woman walked out of the back to meet Jacob. She radiated warmth as she smiled. Charles said, "This young man is Jacob Morgan, Zac's kin. Jacob tells me Zac passed away a few years ago."

Jacob could see the surprise registered on her face. He saw the pain, as she reached out her hand and taking Jacob's said, "I am so sorry. Zac was a good friend to us." Continuing, she said, "My name is Martha. I am Charles's wife."

"Martha, my pleasure," said Jacob, releasing her hand.

Pausing for a moment, she reflected, "I remember now." Looking at Charles she said, "Remember, when Zac told us about his nephew that lived in Boston. It was his desire that he come west and join him." Reaching over and touching Jacob's arm, Martha said, "We were just about to sit down for our meal, Jacob. Would you please join us? We would love to hear about you and your uncle."

During their meal, Jacob told of the letter he had received from Uncle Zac's attorney and about his inheritance. He talked about the time he spent with Zed and their experiences with the Indians. When he finished, Jacob realized they had been captivated by his story. Jacob blushed and said, "I'm sorry. I didn't mean to talk so much."

Laughing, Martha said, "Jacob, you have had such a colorful life over the past three years. You ought to write a book.

With that remark, Charles stood immediately and walked to the back of the post. He returned and handed Jacob a heavy leather pouch. He said, "This is your Uncle Zac's share of our business. As we earn more, we will make sure you get it. Business has been very good, and we owe it all to your uncle."

Jacob hefted the leather pouch. It was heavy. "How much is in here?" asked Jacob.

Smiling, Charles said. "There's just over $3,000 in gold coins."

"Whew!" said Jacob. Surprised, he said, "I really don't feel comfortable taking this from you folks; after all, you dealt directly with my Uncle Zac—"

Martha interrupted him and said, "Jacob, we made an agreement with your uncle. We would not have these funds if it hadn't been for your uncle's trust in Charles and me."

Jacob said, "Here's my agreement with you fine folks. As of today, you have completed your obligations to my late Uncle Zac. I know this is what Uncle Zac would want. This is the least I can do for you."

Tears filled Martha's eyes, and she said, "Jacob you are just like your uncle. We thank you."

Riding back to Yreka, Jacob felt wonderfully at peace with himself. He wondered if feeling this good was because he had helped people. If so, he wanted to do it more often.

Riding to the livery stable, Jacob heard Marshal Ely call out to him. "Jacob, can you come to my office?" Jacob nodded his head and quickly took care of Buck and complied.

The marshal was sitting at his desk as Jacob entered the office. He motioned for him to take a seat. Finishing the paperwork on his desk, Marshal Ely said, "Thanks for coming. I wanted to let you know that this Benson was seen this morning by one of my deputies. He had two other men with him but the deputy lost them. Also, I had an inquiry yesterday from a Chinese girl who came in asking if you had arrived yet. She told me to tell you where you could find her. Is there a problem?"

Jacob smiled and told Marshal Ely about their meeting along the California Trail.

Marshal Ely remarked, "We have over a thousand Chinese in this area. They all are hard workers and share their claims with each other. During the winter, they live in boarding houses or wherever they can find housing because they don't do well in cold weather."

Putting his boots on his desk, and leaning back in his chair, Ely went on. "It's been my experience that where there is a Chinatown, the 'Tong' shows up."

Jacob was puzzled and asked, "What is the 'Tong'?"

Marshal Ely took his boots off the desk and pulled his chair closer to Jacob. He explained, "The 'Tong' is a bunch of thugs who take money from the poor working Chinese for protection."

"Protection!" Jacob said. "Protection from what?"

Marshal Ely laughed sarcastically. "From the guys who collect the money. In other words, if you don't want your head bashed in, you pay them not to do it!"

Jacob was shocked. "Is this a problem here in Yreka?" he asked.

Now Marshal Ely sat back in his chair and replied, "If it isn't now, I think it will be soon. Jacob, I could use your help." Jacob listened. "I want you to talk with the Lee family, and if there is a problem, please let me know. We would like to keep this area free from the 'Tong.' We have enough problems without having them here."

Jacob said, "I'll do my best. Where can I find the Lee family?"

Soon, Jacob was walking toward a boarding house located on the north side of Yreka.

Laura was just coming out of the door when she saw Jacob. "Jacob," she yelled, raising her hand to hail him. She ran and stood in front of him, beaming. "It is so good to see you, Jacob. Grandfather and I have been worried about you."

Jacob smiled, reached down, and gave her a hug. Releasing her, he asked, "How is your grandfather? Did you have enough money for your trip?"

Laughing, Laura said, "Grandfather is doing well, and Jacob, you gave us far too much money. We still have much of it left. Grandfather wants me to return the rest of it back to you."

Jacob looked at her and said, "I have missed you both also. I have practiced my dances daily, and I want you keep the money. The lessons were worth every gold piece I gave you."

They walked to an upper room in the boarding house, and there, sitting cross-legged on the floor, was Grandfather. He looked up, smiled, and then said, "Jacob, you come back"

Jacob went over and embraced the old man and thought, *This feels like family.*

Late into the afternoon, Jacob, Laura, and Grandfather sat talking. Laura interpreted as they conversed. Jacob looked at Grandfather confused and said, "Laura, I think Grandfather understands more than he lets on. I can see it in his eyes."

Laughing, Laura said, "There are many things Grandfather does not understand, but Jacob, you are right, he does understand much. Grandfather says he can learn much more by listening when others think he cannot understand."

Jacob laughed and said, "I knew it. I knew it. I sensed it when we were on the trail."

"Grandfather," Jacob said, "you are sly, like the dance animals—especially the tiger."

To Jacob's surprise, Grandfather said, "I listen good. I learn much." Now all of them laughed.

As he was getting ready to leave, Jacob approached them with his errand from Marshal Ely. "Laura, do you know Marshal Ely?"

Laura shrugged her shoulders and said, "Only a little. I asked him two days ago if he had seen you."

Jacob went on, "Marshal Ely was concerned about the Chinese Tong. Are you aware of them? Are they now in this area?"

Grandfather raised his hand as if wanting to be heard. "Yes, they come here past two weeks."

Laura interrupted and said, "Jacob, they are very bad men. They charge the Chinese workers for protection."

"And is that protection from the beatings they would give to them if they didn't pay?" asked Jacob.

Laura lowered her head and said, "Yes. We can't do anything about it. There is only Grandfather and myself. They are powerful and the Chinese boss has a very large Chinese man who does the beating. They won't come after grandfather and me because we don't have any gold claims. It is our relatives with the mining claims whom they hurt. Our family doesn't know how to take care of themselves, so they have to pay for this protection."

Later that evening, Jacob lay on his bed, trying to come up with a solution for the Chinese miners. Then he got up, and sat at the desk in his room, and while shuffling through his papers, he located the second miner's name. Weatherbee had come to Yreka a year before and collected $15,000 in gold from the prospector that Uncle Zac had grubstaked.

Early the next morning, Jacob rode north along the Klamath River to Cottonwood Flat. Jacob was looking for John Thomas. After searching all morning, he finally located him at Rich Gulch. When Jacob rode up, two men were working a sluice box that was carrying water down to wash the gravel. Behind them, next to the hill, sat two tents. Jacob supposed one was used for supplies and the other for sleeping. Claims were being worked on by other miners in every direction. A crude sign at the front of the property read, "Thomas Claim."

Both men hailed Jacob as he dismounted and tied Buck to a tree. As Jacob walked over to the men, one man asked, "Can we help you?"

Jacob replied, "I am looking for a Mr. John Thomas."

A short, stocky man said, "I'm Thomas. What can I do for you?"

Smiling, Jacob said, "I am Jacob Morgan, nephew to Zac Sherwood."

Smiling, John reached out his hand and said, "Any kin of Zac Sherwood's is always welcome in my camp. You look just like him." Pointing to the other man he went on, "This here is Bill Jenkins. He's helpin' me on my claim. I haven't seen yer Uncle Zac for a few years now. How is he?"

Jacob looked at him and said, "Uncle Zac died of consumption a few years back."

John looked incredulous and said, "Died! That's impossible. His attorney came to me a year ago and said yer uncle was doing fine. He came and got yer uncle's share of the gold."

Jacob walked over and sat on a tree stump. Frowning, he said, "Yes, that was Clarence Weatherbee. He is now in jail." Jacob went on to explain that he was Zac's legitimate heir, and Weatherbee had been embezzling Uncle Zac's gold and everything else he had.

John frowned and said, "I didn't like that Weatherbee none, but he had a signed affidavit, so I gave him the gold. He told me he would be back in six months for another share of Zac's gold. So that's the reason I haven't see him? Serves him right!"

Jacob laughed, and then John stood up and said, "Yer Uncle Zac was a good man. He grubstaked me and was very generous with his money. Ole Zac told me I was his old-age pension."

Turning, he went into his tent. A moment later he came out with a large pouch in his hand. Hefting the pouch up and down in his right hand as if trying to determine its weight, John said as he handed it to Jacob, "This here's yer uncle's share of my earnings. Don't know how much is here, but must be over $3,000 worth of gold."

"Whew!" whistled Jacob. "I appreciate your honesty in working with my uncle. I have a deal for you."

John raised his eyebrows and asked, "A deal?"

"Yes," replied Jacob. "As of today, your agreement with my uncle is ended. This claim is yours, free and clear."

John asked, "What's the catch, Jacob?"

"Finding someone who is honest is very rare these days. So, because you're so honest, I release you from your agreement with my uncle. I think Uncle Zac would have wanted it that way."

Completely caught off guard, John looked at Jacob and said, "Are you sure?"

"Absolutely," said Jacob, and he extended his hand to seal their agreement.

John, laughing, said, "Well then, the least I can do is to offer you a meal."

Later, as Jacob sat eating with the two men, he said, "I need to ask you a few questions about some of the miners."

"I'll tell you anything you want to know," said John.

Jacob went on, "It's about the Chinese miners. Are you familiar with them?"

Bill spoke up, "There are quite a few of them in this area. They mostly keep to themselves and are very hard workers. They are so skinny. I can't understand how they can work so hard. When they first came in, all they owned was carried in a large sack attached to a pole over their shoulders."

"What's your interest in them?" asked John.

Jacob commented on Marshal Ely's concern with the Chinese Tong.

John spoke up, "About two weeks ago, we heard that two Chinese men had arrived in the area. One was an older man, and the other was a big man with a long ponytail braid. They visited the claims and scared most of the Chinese miners half to death."

Jacob asked, "Do you know where they can be found?"

"Nope," replied John. "But wherever the Chinese live, I think you'll find them."

Jacob rode back to Yreka, and as he turned up Main Street, the hair went up on the back of his neck again. He slid off Buck and pulled his gun as he ran to the side of a building. He slowly examined every shadow and window in the area.

Jacob noticed a dark shadow on the side of a building at the end of a small alley. It looked like it was a man trying to conceal himself behind a large barrel. Marshal Ely and his deputy were just coming out of his office when Jacob darted across the street and pointed his gun toward the alley.

The marshal and his deputy drew their guns and proceeded cautiously toward the alley. The marshal quickly glanced around the corner. All he saw was a large barrel at the end. No one was there.

The marshal started to walk forward, when Jacob grabbed his arm and pulled him back. Whispering, Jacob said, "Behind the barrel."

Marshal Ely said, "Don't think so."

Still the hair stood up on the back of Jacob's neck. Jacob pulled the marshal back and said, "Let me try something." He pointed his gun, and fired twice into the barrel. Its contents poured out and a man jumped out, and fired at the corner where Jacob had been standing.

Splinters of wood hit Jacob's face as he pulled back. Now Marshal Ely jumped forward and fired three shots and his deputy fired two.

Yelling loudly, the marshal said, "This is Marshal Ely. Come out or we will open fire!"

A groan was heard, and Marshal Ely quickly glanced around the corner and saw a man lying next to the barrel, with his rifle alongside him. The man had been shot in his leg and his side was bleeding profusely. Half of Yreka had heard the shooting, and soon a large crowd was gathered.

Someone yelled, "Get the doc!"

Marshal Ely and his deputy carried the man out from the dark alley. "Does anyone know this man?" asked the marshal.

No one spoke up. Within a few minutes, a doctor came running up and knelt next to the man. Examining him, the doctor said, "He'll live."

Ely said, "A couple of you boys grab him and carry him over to the jailhouse where doc can work on him." Four men hurriedly lifted the wounded man and carried him to the jail, while the doctor followed.

In the marshal's office, Jacob sat on a chair next to the desk. "Jacob, thanks for not getting me killed. I owe you," said the marshal.

Smiling, Jacob said, "I'm just glad it was him and not one of us."

Having an opportune moment to talk to the marshal, Jacob said, "You remember asking me about the Chinese Tong?" The marshal nodded his head. Jacob said, "Today I learned that the Tong is in the area, and they are collecting protection money from the Chinese miners. They've been here for the past two weeks. There is an older man and one big man with a long braided pony tail."

Marshal Ely sat, listening intently. "Just where can I find these men?" asked Ely.

Jacob said, "They are ruthless in collecting their protection money. I don't think you'll get anyone to testify because they are all too scared. We need to find another way get them," replied Jacob.

Just then, the doctor walked out from the cell and said, "You can talk to him now. I took out the bullet in his leg. The other bullet went clean through, just below his ribs. He'll be fine as long as he doesn't get infection."

As the marshal and Jacob entered the cell, the older man lying on the cot moaned in pain. The marshal touched his shoulder and asked, "What's yer name?"

The man made no reply. Jacob winked at the marshal and said, "Just let him be. Pass the word, and they'll lynch him like the last one. It'll save the town the expense of a trial."

The marshal nodded, and said, "That's a good idea. Everyone sure enjoyed that hanging." Then they started to walk out.

"Wait a minute!" the man said. "Are you serious about the hanging?"

"You bet," replied Marshal Ely. "Maybe you heard about it. Some guy shot a man and the miners got him. He fought like a cougar, but they hung him anyway. Only problem was that he didn't die right away. Took him about fifteen minutes before that rope finally choked him." Marshal Ely looked at Jacob and winked and then said, "One thing I can't control is a mob of lynchers, especially when they're my friends."

He turned to go out of the cell, and the man said, "I don't want to be hung. What do you want me to tell ya?"

Marshal Ely said, "First of all, what's your name?"

"George Merritt."

"Okay, Mr. Merritt, why were you gunning for Jacob?"

Merritt didn't say anything.

Jacob said, "Did Benson pay you to do it?"

A look of surprised came over Merritt, as if he didn't know what to say.

Jacob continued, "Did you know that Benson is wanted in San Francisco? If you are one of his accomplices, that means you also will hang."

A look of terror came over Merritt and he said, "I met Benson two months ago, but I never killed no buddy. I was only supposed to wound you so Benson could personally take care of you."

This gave Jacob an idea. Walking out of the cell, Jacob explained his plan to the marshal. Smiling, the marshal readily agreed and said, "Jacob, I think it just might work."

Within the hour, Jacob had a bandage around his head and one over his right shoulder. The marshal put the word out that a man had been shot, and his name was Jacob Morgan. Two men carried Jacob to his hotel room. One deputy was assigned to sit outside of his room. Jacob would be the decoy, while they waited for Benson to come looking for him.

For two days, Jacob stayed in his room on the first floor with a deputy on guard. Each day, the deputy made it a point to go for lunch and dinner at the same time.

The second evening arrived, and the guard tapped lightly on Jacob's door three times, indicating that he would be gone. Covers and extra blankets were heaped together on Jacob's bed to make it look like he was there sleeping. Fifteen minutes later, Jacob heard soft footsteps along the hall. Standing behind the door, Jacob saw the knob turn slowly and the door inched open.

A harsh voice said, "This is for you, Morgan." The man had a rapier in his hand and thrust it into the bed sheets. As he did, he suddenly realized there was no substance under the quilts.

"Welcome home, Benson. I have been waiting for you." Jacob hit Benson's wrist, knocking the rapier away. Jacob turned Benson around and said, "My turn now," and Jacob hit him. Benson went over the bed and was up lunging at Jacob. A right fist caught Jacob in the side of his neck. He went down in pain. Benson jumped on him, and continued hitting Jacob's head with his fists and screaming.

Jacob rolled over the bed with Benson on him. He managed to knee Benson in the groin, and Benson let out a howl. They continued to struggle and crashed backward out the window on to the ground. Jacob rolled and quickly got to his feet. The Marshal and his deputy immediately took hold of Benson and prepared to handcuff him.

Benson screamed and cursed at Jacob, "Let me at him! Let me at him! I'll kill him," he ranted. Addressing the Marshall, Jacob said, "Let this be a private fight between Benson and me. This will be his last chance to avenge himself before he goes to jail."

The Marshall could see the hate and contempt Benson had for Jacob. He asked, "Are you sure?" Jacob nodded his head.

There was still daylight, and the townspeople had quickly gathered to see what the commotion was all about. The deputy released Benson, and both men began to circled each other. As Benson circled around Jacob he suddenly bent down and pulled a knife from his boot.

Someone yelled, "Knife!"

The deputy drew his gun and pointed it at Benson, Jacob held up his hand and said, "It's okay. I can handle this."

To Jacob's left, standing in the crowd, were Laura and Grandfather. Catching Grandfather's eye, Jacob saw him nodding his approval.

Benson was waiting for Jacob to make a mistake.

Jacob began to move effortlessly into a tiger dance, anticipating Benson's first move. As Benson moved closer to Jacob, his knife hand suddenly thrust out toward Jacob's stomach. Jacob moved back and with a sweep of his right foot, he caught Benson's wrist and knocked the knife to the ground.

Benson lunged forward, trying to knee Jacob's groin. Jacob pivoted and used a combination of kung fu and English boxing, as he toyed with Benson. Benson suddenly kicked Jacob on his right hip, knocking him down. Seeing, his chance, Benson rushed forward and tried to stomp Jacob's face. Seeing the foot coming, Jacob rolled to his side and Benson's foot barely missed.

Jacob grabbed Benson's foot and twisted hard. Benson went down, and Jacob quickly scrambled to his feet. Jacob cautiously moved in a circle, dancing the tiger play again, as he waited for Benson to get on his feet.

As Benson slowly got to his feet, Jacob said, "Let's see what you've got."

Jacob changed to English boxing and struck with his right fist, snapping Benson's head back and splitting his lower lip. Jacob, spinning on the monkey play, struck Benson on the side of his head with his left foot and then used his right foot to knock him down.

Benson got up and again came in swinging. Jacob blocked his punch and hit him in his stomach. Benson gasped for air and staggered back. Jacob moved in and struck Benson with a left to his head and then a right that put a two-inch gash over Benson's left cheek.

Benson swung, hitting Jacob on the right side of his chin, knocking him back. Jacob momentarily saw darkness, and shook his head, trying to recover. Jacob moved in, and with a right uppercut, created a large cut on Benson's chin. Jacob backed away, letting Benson catch his breath.

Screaming and shouting obscenities, Benson reached down and grabbed a handful of dirt and threw it at Jacob's eyes. Jacob pivoted on his left foot and let the dirt pass harmlessly away from him. Jacob glared at his nemesis and said, "Now, Benson, let's get this over with." He hit the raging Benson with two more blows to his face. Then with his own kung fu move, he swept with his right foot, and Benson fell to the ground unconscious.

Gasping for air and wet with sweat and grime, Jacob felt a hand on his shoulder. It was Marshal Ely. Smiling, he said, "Nice work, Jacob. My deputy will put Benson in jail. Then I'll contact Captain Fallon, and next week we'll transport Benson back to San Francisco. I'm sure he'll hang. Is there anything else I can help you with?"

Jacob paused a moment, trying to catch his breath, and said, "Yes, I'll have two Chinese prisoners you can take along with you. Give me at least four days."

Chapter 30
Chinese Tong

"We've got to catch them with the money and prove they were collecting the money for protection," the Marshal said, as he sat in at his desk the following morning. Jacob, Laura, and her grandfather sat alongside of the marshal's desk, with two deputies leaning against the wall.

Marshal Ely emphasized, "If we're going to make these charges stick, then we need positive proof. All they would need is for some slick attorney to get them off for some mistake we make." He stood up and continued, "The reason I wanted to meet with everyone this morning is to find a way that we can put these two Chinese thugs out of business for good."

The marshal turned to Laura and said, "Jacob has told me about you and your grandfather. He said members of your family, along with other Chinese miners, have to pay protection money. Is that correct?"

Laura nodded her head and said, "Yes. The bully is an older man from China. The authorities were after him there for doing the same thing. He left China before they had a chance to arrest him, and he has now hired this cruel giant to collect for him in America."

The Marshal said, "I need to catch them in the very act of collecting, and then we can put them both away. From what I hear, that big Chinese brute would be hard to take down. It may take a dozen men to subdue him."

Jacob spoke, "Marshal, as you know, there are many small log houses and a few boarding houses that are filled only with Chinese miners. Some of these log houses are on the north side of town. Laura told me that all the Chinese miners fear the Tong. As the miners work their claims, the Tong come and force the workers to pay with their gold for protection or they are beaten."

Jacob said, "Laura informed me that the Chinese miners have dug tunnels under their places of lodging in town. They dig these tunnels from the inside of their houses at night, and then work their claims during the day. This way they can keep their gold because the Tong are not aware of these tunnels."

A look of surprise came over the Marshal's face, and he asked, "Are you sure of this Jacob?"

Jacob nodded his head and answered, "Yes. However, I don't think this will go on much longer because eventually the Tong will find out."

Laura said, "The Tong live in the boarding houses with the miners so they can keep an eye on the miners."

Marshal Ely nodded his head in understanding. "I heard a rumor that there were tunnels, but I didn't believe it. If some of their tunnels infringe on another person's claim, that could mean trouble."

Laura said, "We have just become aware of this from our family. We have been told that everyone is very careful not to go on another person's claim."

Marshal Ely then shrugged his shoulders and said, "We'll have to deal with that issue some other time. But right now, our main problem is the Tong. What are the names of these two men?"

Laura said, "The name of the Chinese boss is Chaoxiang and his helper, the giant, is called Changpu. They both are very dangerous."

Jacob said, "Why don't we have some of the Chinese miners' let it leak out to the Tong that tunnels are being dug under their houses. Then when the Tong comes to collect, we will be waiting."

"You and whose army?" asked the Marshal. "Have you seen the size of that brute? He must weigh at least four hundred pounds. It'll take at least a dozen men to subdue him."

The word was leaked out by a couple of the Chinese miners to Chaoxiang that some of the Chinese were digging tunnels from their homes and others were living in boarding houses where they kept their share of the gold.

It was a quiet Sunday morning, and many of the Chinese workers had taken the day off to take care of their personal needs. Laura felt sure that Chaoxiang would make his move that day.

Before noon, a buckboard pulled by a single horse arrived in front of the boarding house. Chaoxiang and his thug, Changpu got out of the wagon and walked upstairs into the boarding house. A few minutes later there was a commotion inside. A Chinese man was thrown through a window, landing in a heap on the ground below.

Marshal Ely was waiting with ten deputies in the livery stable across the street. A deputy was sent over to move the horse and carriage to prevent them from escaping. The deputies walked quietly toward the boarding house with great apprehension. Their signal given was when the Chinese miners had paid Chaoxiang, they would run outside indicating the funds had been exchanged.

Jacob, Laura, and Grandfather watched from a distance as the group of lawmen approached and waited for their signal. Marshal Ely walked over to the man who had been thrown out of the window and checked him for a pulse. He was dead. Now it was more than extortion; it was also murder. From the boarding house, there came yelling and screaming. Three Chinese workers burst through the door running for their lives, with Changpu close behind them.

The Marshal's orders were they were not to shoot unless they feared for their lives. As each of the deputies looked at the large Chinese thug, they all drew their guns. The marshal shouted, "I said don't shoot them. We need to have them stand trial."

Changpu turned and saw the ten officers. He grinned and headed immediately in their direction. One of the deputies ran from behind and tackled the giant. As he fell, all of the deputies dove in on top of him, swinging their fists as hard as they could. Within a few moments, deputies were flying in all directions. Jacob looked at Laura and said, "I think they could use some help?"

Laura nodded. She looked at Grandfather, and he said, "I get Chaoxiang. You help the marshal."

Jacob ran as fast as he could. He knew lives depended on his and Laura's skills. As he neared Changpu, he jumped, feet first in the air, and connected with the upper back of the giant. The force sent the thug sprawling forward on the ground.

As the brute lay sprawled on the ground he saw Jacob. He shouted what Jacob figured were obscenities in Chinese and got up and came running at him, reaching out with his boulder-size fists ready for action. Jacob quickly avoided the giant, and with a swift kick of his right foot, he struck the giant's knee and sent him down on his back. Now all the more enraged, and uninjured, the giant circled slowly around Jacob.

Suddenly, Laura landed a blow to Changpu on the back of his head. He went down and forward in a tucked position and came up and connected his fist with Jacob's left shoulder. The blow sent Jacob flying and he rolled over twice before coming to a stop. Then Laura ran and leaped into the air kicking the giant directly in his face. He grabbed for her, but she pivoted on her foot and struck him on the side of his head with her other foot.

Jacob came from behind, and grabbed Changpu around his neck, trying to choke him down. The brute went down to his knees, and grabbed Jacob by his head, and flipped him over onto his back. The giant lunged forward, trying to stomp on Jacob's head. In a daze, Jacob saw the giant battling it out with Laura. He had to give her credit, she could move, but it was clear she was no match for this evil man. If Changpu got his hands on her, he would crush the life out of her in seconds.

Laura connected with Changpu's head and did a backward somersault, barely escaping his grasp. She kicked and connected with Changpu's midsection. He grabbed her leg, throwing her to the ground. At that moment, eight deputies came forward trying to subdue the Goliath, but he flung them away as if they were rag dolls.

Changpu reached down and grabbed Laura by her throat. Grinning, he picked her up with both hands and held her out in front of him and with great satisfaction began squeezing the life out of her.

Jacob had to make sure that Changpu would never use his huge hands to hurt anyone again. Drawing his gun, he ran forward and aimed directly at Changpu's wrists and fired. The bullet shattered the bones in both wrists. Screaming in pain, he dropped Laura and she crumpled to the ground holding her throat and gasping for breath.

Marshal Ely now calmly walked up to the giant and cuffed his bleeding wrists. Changpu' was finished,;

Two of the deputies were down with broken ribs. The rest only had bruises and a few cuts. Laura called for Grandfather. From the side of the building appeared Chaoxiang, his hair was messed up, and he had cuts and bruises on his face. Grandfather walked behind him, and smiling, he pushed him over to the marshal. With both men handcuffed, Marshal Ely escorted them to jail.

That evening, there was a big celebration among the Chinese workers with Chaoxiang's and Changpu's arrest. Marshal Ely was praised by the whole town for getting rid of the Tong.

As Jacob walked down Main Street, the marshal motioned for Jacob to join him. "Jacob," He said, "Let me buy you a drink." As they walked into the Arcade Saloon, the owner, James Wheeler, and his partner, W. R. Taylor, greeted him.

"Marshal, we sure thank you for a job well done," James said.

Marshal Ely replied, pointing toward Jacob, "I couldn't have been done without Jacob's help."

"Well, Jacob, what are your plans now?" asked Marshal Ely.

Jacob said, "I'll be leaving in a couple days for the Utah Territory. Marshal Ely chuckled, "Then I guess it wouldn't do me any good to ask you to stay and work for me?"

Jacob smiled and shook his head. "Sorry, Marshal, There is someone I need to see."

It was late when Jacob said his good-byes to Laura and Grandfather. He gave them enough funds to live comfortably for many years to come. Grandfather objected, but Jacob would forever be in their debt for all that they had taught him.

Jacob went to the livery stable to give Buck an extra portion of oats, because they had a long ride ahead of them. There was a quarter moon and a warm summer breeze gently blowing over Yreka. In the morning, Jacob would be off to see Zed and then off to the Windslow Ranch to see Mary.

Chapter 31
His Nemesis

It was close to midnight when Jacob finally started across the street to his hotel room when he sensed danger because the hair on the back of his neck was standing up. The lights from the saloon windows revealed a lone man standing in the middle of the street, wearing all black clothing and a black hood.

"What do you want?" asked Jacob warily.

The man replied, "I have been watching you ever since you got off the ship Brooklyn over three years ago. I have been waiting for my chance to become the worthy recipient." He walked slowly toward Jacob without out a sound. He was light on his feet, and when he got closer he started to circle him.

Jacob went on the defense and faced him, and matched him step for step. The man in black said, "You need to thank me. I'm the one who stopped Lone Wolf from killing you in the Dakotas. I didn't want him to take my chance for revenge against you. If Zed hadn't been there, I would have killed you myself."

The man paused for a moment and then continued, "Remember that feeling you had when you were searching for Weatherbee's office? You ran trying to hide from me." He laughed and continued, "I saw how you rushed into his office.

The man in black moved slowly and continued to watch Jacob carefully with each move. "I also followed you when you were riding your horse into that canyon. I was going to kill you, but you didn't have your rifle, so I let you live because you were still a city boy, and I only fight with men. Are you a man, or are you still a boy, Jacob Morgan?"

Jacob was infuriated. This was the man who had caused his hair to come up on the back of his neck so many times.

The man continued. "Remember, Graff? He's still hunting for you and wants to kill you. He won't have the pleasure, because I will do it for him." Laughing menacingly, he then said, "I will get all of Zachariah Sherwood's inheritance, and you will get nothing!"

The man in black taunted Jacob as he continued to slowly circle around him. The dark figure continued, "Another thing, Jacob, you should never cock your weapon when someone is trying to enter your cave. Thank you. That foolish mistake saved my life. That clicking sound warned me that you were armed, and I was prepared to kill you then, but I am a patient man, as you can see. I have stalked you over the past three years."

Jacob's heart raced, and he thought, *So this is the man who has made my life so miserable so many times over the years.* Then Jacob calmly said, "I want to thank you for your help."

"My help?" questioned the hooded man.

"Yes," replied Jacob. "You have helped me learn to face my fears and to become a man. You'll never know the heartaches or sorrows I have felt. At least, I now can meet my greatest fear. And now, I don't fear you, because I can see you."

"Well, now that you see me, you shall see that I am the most worthy recipient." He continued, crouching down as he slowly closed the circle and whispered, "Jacob Morgan, are you prepared to die?"

In a low, menacing voice, Jacob said, "We will see who the worthy recipient will be." Jacob could see his last remark caught the man off guard. Jacob continued, "Now I become the hunter and you have become the hunted."

Circling closer Jacob extended his right hand and motioned for his hooded nemesis to come forward. Jacob was in charge. This was his battle. He had prepared himself, and he was now ready to make war on his nemesis.

Running at the man, Jacob prepared to kick out with his right foot. His hooded opponent anticipated his every move and pivoted on his foot so he was out of striking distance.

"Oh, so you thought you would try and kick me. Poor move, Jacob. I could see it in your eyes," the man said, laughing. He was again taunting Jacob.

Jacob thought, *This time I will be the fox and the badger.*

Then the man took a kung fu fighting stance. Jacob countered every move as the man struck over and over. Then Jacob went on the offense. He pivoted on his feet, using the tiger and monkey dance, striking and hitting the man on the side of his head. The hooded man was surprised. He paused for a moment, shaking his head,

With a sarcastic laugh, he said, "Jacob, you are doing better." In a quick pivoting movement, the man struck out with his right foot, connecting with Jacob's head. The lights flashed and Jacob felt a blinding pain. He shook his head, trying to clear away the cobwebs.

Jacob could see the man nodding his head in satisfaction. "So, I hurt you," he said, and added, "Did the little city boy feel pain?"

Without giving the man any warning, Jacob changed tactics and went into the English boxing mode. He struck with his right fist, connecting with the man's jaw. He moved in and gave two solid hits to the man's stomach. Jacob heard a whoosh of air. Jacob stepped back and followed with a sweep of his left foot. It caught the man on the right side of his head, and he went down.

Quickly rolling, the man in black came up, standing on his two feet he moved cautiously, and he changed to English boxing as well. He suddenly jabbed with his left hand and Jacob blocked him. The man hit Jacob with his right fist, knocking him down. Jacob slowly got up, a little dazed. The man suddenly did a sweep with his right foot, and it caught Jacob on the left side of his face. The force sent him tumbling head over heels.

Jacob lay on the ground and shook his head, trying to clear away the dizziness. Never had he been caught this much off guard. *Who was this man, and where did he come from?* Jacob asked himself. *Is he another Benson?*

As if reading his thoughts, the man said. "Benson—he was a fool. He thought he was good with a rapier, but he was too sure of himself and look where he is now."

Walking to the side of the building, the hooded man reached over and picked up two staves. He asked, "Are you still a little dazed by my last move, city boy?"

Throwing one stave to Jacob, the lone man in black circled him with the other stave in his hand. He advanced quickly, and before Jacob could block, he had hit Jacob on the side of the neck and then on his shoulder.

The man laughed and said, "Concentrate on what you've been taught, Jacob. I've been paid well to follow you over the past three years."

To throw Jacob off track, the hooded man said, "By the way, Jacob, did you know that Isaiah and I are good friends?"

He then moved again toward Jacob, attempting to strike him with his stave. Jacob blocked his thrust and used his stave to hit his opponent twice.

The hooded man laughed in derision and changed the subject. "When your detective, Mr. Ashley, followed Benson to the saloon and listened to the four men at the table, I walked in and sat at a table right next to him. I saw and heard everything. He was so busy playing the drunk that he wasn't aware he was also being followed. When Ashley pursued Benson and got on the ferry to cross the bay, I stood right behind him, watching his every move. He wasn't even aware." The hooded man paused as if in thought and he continued, "Jacob, your fancy, Mr. Ashley didn't know it, but I followed him ten miles out of San Francisco too. He was so busy following Benson that he didn't even know I was behind him."

Now the hooded man reversed his direction and spoke further. "The word was out to hunt for a man in buckskins riding a buckskin stallion. They hunted all over, but I knew your horse was thirty miles outside San Francisco. I wanted to see you get Weatherbee. He deserved it. It will make it so much easier for me to collect my inheritance. All I need to do is to let them know my name."

Suddenly, throwing his stave down, he lunged and hit Jacob on the side of his head with his left fist.

Jacob fell backward and immediately rolled onto his feet. "Very good," the man said. "I guess you have been learning kung fu from Laura Lee and her grandfather, Chin Lee."

Jacob asked incredulously, "Who are you, and how do you know these things?"

Laughing in a taunting tone, the hooded man said, "You never knew who I was. I was around you many times and you didn't even know. While you were walking out of the men's haberdashery, I bumped into you, trying to knock you down. You didn't even realize it was me.

Jacob, you were so foolish. You don't deserve to be the recipient, but I do. The money will be all mine."

It was into the early morning hours on the streets of Yreka, and no one had interrupted them in their fight to the death, as the two circled cautiously around each other. *Will I have to kill this man?* Jacob asked himself. *Yes, if I have to, but first I will find out who he is, and find out who else is involved in this plot. It has to be more than just one man.*

Jacob moved with determination to put this man down and suddenly remembered his special move he had learned on his own. He moved forward and stumbled purposely. As he did, he rolled and with his right foot, swept the man's feet out from under him. His move completely caught the man off guard. The man in black went down and, as he started to get up, Jacob hit him with his right fist on the left side of his head. He went down with a groan, and Jacob grabbed his hood and started to yank it off.

The man in black came to and grasped Jacob by the throat, squeezing tightly. Jacob, putting both hands together, forced his hands quickly up between the man's wrists and broke his handhold. Jacob reached forward and held the man by the back of his head and pulled it forward. Thrusting his head upward, Jacob struck the man on the bridge of his nose. The attacker screamed in pain and pulled back.

Jacob again swept with his right foot. It connected solidly with the man's head. Down he went on his back, groaning. As he started to get up, Jacob hit him again on the side of his jaw and then again in succession. The hooded man went down, and as he started to get up, Jacob did a sweep with his right foot that connected with the side of the man's head, knocking him down and he was out cold.

Not waiting for his nemesis to wake up, Jacob crawled on his hands and knees and grabbed the man by his shirt and rolled him over on his back. Now with firm resolve, Jacob said, "Now I will see who my real nemesis is."

Jacob yanked off the hood to reveal the man's face. What the light from the saloon window revealed, stunned Jacob. He couldn't speak. He just sat there staring—it couldn't be. No, he must be dreaming.

It was Uncle Zac!

Jacob collected his thoughts and patted his uncle's face, trying to revive him, but he really felt like slapping him.

"Uncle Zac, Uncle Zac, wake up. Is it really you? What's going on?" Jacob said.

There was a groan, and Uncle Zac slowly opened his eyes as he tried to focus. He muttered something that Jacob couldn't understand and then blacked out again. Jacob stood up and went over to the horse trough next to a building. He plunged his handkerchief into the water and carried it back to where Uncle Zac lay and put it on his face.

Kneeling down, Jacob cradled his uncle's head and bathed his face with the wet cloth while wiping away the blood from his face. Jacob wanted to drag his uncle's sorry carcass over to the water trough and throw him in. Zac suddenly opened his eyes and blinked, trying to focus on his surroundings

He groaned and tried to move, and slowly shook his head trying to clear the cobwebs away. He looked up at Jacob. and with a weak smile said, "Hello Jacob," As Jacob looked at the blood smeared face of his uncle, he had very little compassion for the man who had been his nemesis for the past three years.

"Uncle Zac, I thought you were dead. Even Zed thought you were dead."

Zac reached for Jacob's hand and said, "Help me up, Nephew" Jacob pulled his uncle to his feet. Zac said weakly, "Let's go to your hotel room and talk. Then I can clean myself up."

In Jacob's hotel room, Zac took a deep breath and submerged his face in the wash basin, trying to revive himself. One eye was already swollen and shut as he wiped the blood from his nose and face. With swollen lips, he grimaced at Jacob and began to offer an explanation for his actions for the last three years. Zac began, "Jacob, I was dead."

Jacob didn't understand. "Uncle Zac, you have to do better than that. Explain why you put on this ruse these past three years.

"Jacob, I mean it. I was really dead, not physically, but mentally. I had all the money I needed, but I wasn't alive. I wanted family." He looked at Jacob and continued, "Do you understand that blood is thicker than water? You were of my blood. You were the only one who

I ever got along with and who would accept me as I was. I had no wife, no children, and no family.

"Remember when I came to Boston to visit? Everyone shunned me as if I had some kind of plague. You were the only one who had anything to do with me. I thought the family would change with time. I kept thinking that each time I visited them they would change. But it was you, Jacob, who accepted me for what I was. There was no judgment, only acceptance. When I talked about my Indian wife and my living with the Sioux tribe they wouldn't even listen. Many of our family members are so self-righteous. They judge people by the color of their skin and not by what's in their hearts."

Jacob sat on the bed quietly listening.

Moving to get more comfortable, Uncle Zac continued, "They all considered me to be a worthless vagabond. They judged me because of my buckskin clothes. Little did any of them know that I could have bought any of them a hundred times over. But, I wasn't there to buy any of them, or to show off my wealth, I was there to give my love and be loved as family. Jacob, you were the only one who paid me any attention."

Uncle Zac sat and stared off into space for a long moment. He said nothing, as if his mind were miles away. Then slowly, he said, "Jacob, I loved my squaw, Warm Hands. She was a lot like your White Fawn; she was kind and gentle. Our family's love in Boston only went to those they chose to love. It wasn't universal for anyone, their love was so narrow that they missed the greater things of this world. Can you understand any of this, Jacob?" asked Uncle Zac.

Jacob slowly nodded his head and said, "Yes, Uncle Zac. I really can."

Uncle Zac then stood up and paced back and forth in the small room. He started again, "Jacob, I've spent years at sea learning about other cultures. There are wonderful people in this world. How did you feel about Laura and Mr. Lee? Weren't they great? Didn't you feel like they were family? Also, how did you feel about Chief Two Clouds and Dancing Light? They loved you like a son, and they didn't judge you by your color, but by the life you lived. As you know, Jacob, there are really a lot of wonderful people in this world, and I wanted to give you the opportunity to find life for yourself."

Jacob asked, "Why didn't you come to see me?"

A painful expression crossed Uncle Zac's face. "Believe it or not, Jacob, I had been in Boston many times over the years, and saw you from a distance. I wanted to see you so many times, but your parents forbade me. They said I was putting ideas into your head that would cause you to want a life outside of Boston. Your parents already had your life planned out, but you and your apron strings needed to be cut so you could be your own man."

Zac went over to the water basin and submersed the towel back in the water and then wrung it out. He painfully applied in to his face and continued. "As you know, Jacob, I have done very well over the years in my investing with shipping. Your parents thought I was a failure in everything I did. As you now realize, you are the proud owner of quite a few investments I have accumulated over the years." Leaning over closer to Jacob, Zac said softly, "Listen to me, Jacob. The things I have accumulated are only things. There is more to life than just things. There are people to know, and people to love. You loved White Fawn, and you came to love the Sioux people."

Zac in a whisper said, "Jacob, I was near you at all times, but you never knew it. I visited with my friend, Chief Two Clouds after you left, and explained everything and why I did what I did. Both Two Clouds and Dancing Light were not only amused, but they approved of what I had done. They love you as their own son and only wished that their White Fawn could have lived to provide you with many sons and daughters."

Zac lay back on the side of the bed to ease his pain. He carefully licked his swollen lips and moved his jaw back and forth before continuing. "Jacob, I had to devise a plan where you would be able to become a man on your own, without interference from your parents. So, I cut the apron strings the only way I could. I devised a plan, faked my death, and left you my inheritance. There were conditions for you to follow. Your becoming a man was the most important thing I wanted for you. I saw more in you than my sister and your father ever did." Zac looked at Jacob apprehensively and said, "I hope you can forgive me, but that's why I did it."

Without giving Jacob a chance to respond, Zac smiled and said, "I had the opportunity to talk with Captain Richardson, and he was very pleased with you as well. He got a chuckle over the trick I was playing on you. He said you could serve as a member of his crew on his ship any time, and even as an officer if you wanted."

"Did you ever tell Zed?" Jacob asked.

Lowering his head, Zac said, "Not until a couple of months ago. I sent him a long letter telling him the whole story. I want to go back and visit with him. I never could have completed this adventure without his help. I told Zed I was sick. He wanted to come to me, but I told him by the time he came it would be too late. I sent him a letter telling him that I had given everything to you on condition that you spent time with him for two years and with the Sioux Indians for one year. I even bought a spot of ground for a grave and had it dug. I actually had a headstone made. I knew that Zed would come to my grave, and he did."

Jacob asked, "Did you know Zed got married?"

A big smile came over Zac's swollen face, and he said, "You don't say. Tell me all about it."

Jacob eagerly told Zac about Rosa and then about Mary. The anger was starting to leave Jacob. He was beginning to understand why his uncle had hatched this maddening scheme—he had done it all for him. Uncle Zac had given all he had, and Jacob had most certainly become the true recipient.

Zac again stood up and walked back and forth to ease some of his pain. He got another wet cloth, applied it to his head, and continued. "Jacob, I was with you all the way. I couldn't come to the ranch where your Mary was, but I did learn about your run-in with the two Brawn brothers you about killed. Served them right for beating up Billy. I also met the seven Indians you had talked to in the grove while you were with Mary. You are one gutsy guy, Jacob. They laughed and told me all of the things they had heard about you. Talk about a reputation, Jacob, I'm real proud to have you as my nephew. You remind me of myself."

Zac then placed his hands on Jacob's shoulders and looked seriously into his eyes. Then he said, "Jacob, there is one more thing I think you need to be concerned about."

Jacob stiffened, looked into his uncle's eyes, and asked, "What are you talking about, Uncle Zac?"

Uncle Zac motioned for him to sit on the bed. Jacob reluctantly sat and asked, "What's the problem?"

"It's Graff," Uncle Zac said, with a worried look on his face. "Both he and his partners are hunting for you. The word among the mountain men is that Graff is willing to pay for information on your whereabouts. They plan on killing you because they figure you cheated them when Buck won the contest. I think you should be aware because at sometime or at some place you will meet up with them, and if you're not careful, it could mean your life. I know them personally, and they are vile men. Killing you would only bring them pleasure."

Uncle Zac smiled and slapped Jacob on his shoulder. "Well, Jacob, that will be another day and time. The important thing is that you have finally found me, yer long lost dead uncle."

Jacob smiled, but deep down he was worried about his future. The thought crossed his mind *:sly as a fox and wise as a badger.* He would always keep his wits about him, no matter where he went or what he did. He would constantly be on alert for anyone or for any enemy.

Jacob slowly smiled. Looking at his uncle, he took in a deep breath and said, "Well, Uncle Zac, what are your plans now?"

"Well, Jacob, my nephew, you have all of my money, so maybe I can work for you," he said laughing.

Jacob immediately said, "No, Uncle Zac, what I have is really yours."

Uncle Zac held up his hands and sternly said, "Jacob, what you have, you earned by yourself. You followed all of my requests and now it's all yours." He tried to wink and said, "I actually have more money. I never put all my eggs in one basket."

Considering Jacob's question, Zac thoughtfully said, "I think I'll try my hand at ranching. I've always wanted to be a cattle man."

Jacob walked over, put his hand on his uncle's shoulder, and smiling, he said, "Uncle Zac, I have an idea that I think we can both agree on. I want to buy a large ranch, and I need a partner I can trust. I have your money, and now it's my time to serve you." Jacob had a twinkle in his eye and said, "And, I have a woman waiting for me, and I also saw a beautiful school teacher that is a young widow. When I saw her, I actually thought of you. I really think you need to check her out. She is a real beauty."

Jacob looked intently at his uncle and sincerely said, "Uncle Zac, you need to trust my judgment on this one, she is one fine woman."

Then laughing, Jacob said, "It's about time you settled down and stayed close to me."

"Ah, like on the same ranch," said Zac, grinning.

Jacob extended his hand and said, "That sounds great. Is it a deal?"

Zac reached out and gripped Jacob's hand and said, "I couldn't think of anyone I would rather spend my time with than my favorite nephew." And then uncle and nephew gingerly embraced.

Author's Notes

The story and the characters in the book are for the most part fictional. However, where possible, I weaved actual places and peoples' names into my novel. Here are some of the actual places and people:

- Boston 1850—the Massachusetts Bank is the correct name of the bank.
- The ship *Brooklyn* sailed in 1847 with a large group of Mormons. The problems that Jacob experienced were actual problems the Mormons experienced on their journey.
- The captain of the ship *Brooklyn* was named Captain Richardson. He was also part owner.
- The historical information about San Francisco was correct. There were only 1,000 people. Then after the gold rush of 1850, it soon had a population of over 25,000. The total amount of people that went to California for the gold rush was over 300,000 people.
- The information used in training Buck was information I got from my Grandfather Cooper. He had a horse that would crush people as they entered his stall. After grandfather used the board with the nails, the horse never crowded anyone again.
- The information I reported on the Sioux tribe was from research. I also gathered some of it from reading *Undaunted Courage,* by Stephen E. Ambrose.
- The names of the attorneys, Cole and Pratt, were actual attorneys. The address of where their office was located in San Francisco was correct as well.

Author's Notes

- Tattersalts' Livery Stable was located on the corner of Kearney and Pacific Street.
- Jacob stayed at the Metropolitan Hotel on Fourth and Lane Street in Yreka, a real place.
- In 1851, during the Gold Rush, Mrs. Lowry's Cafe fed the miners.
- There were approximately 2,000 Indians in the Siskiyou County in 1851. They were the Modoc and Shasta Indians.
- In March of 1851, Abraham Thompson, while taking his mules to Scott Valley from southern Oregon, stopped to rest near a ravine called Black Gulch. As Abraham and his friend let their mules graze and eat the grass, Thompson noticed something glittering when a mule pulled up the roots of the grass. Upon further investigation, he discovered it was gold.
- Within six weeks of Abraham's discovery, 2,000 miners arrived in Yreka for the big gold rush.
- Fort Jones is factual. Captain Edward H. Fitzgerald was in charge of building a new fort. He chose Beaver Valley because there was adequate forage for the animals along with water and timber available for buildings and enclosures. There were fifty-eight soldiers under Captain Fitzgerald's command. They were used as escorts for the arriving wagon trains. Captain Ulysses S. Grant was posted to Fort Jones, but was AWOL. He never reported for duty.
- The names of the mines were actual names, and I used the names of miners who owned the mines and claims.
- There were over 1,000 Chinese workers. They did have two Chinatowns.
- The information given on kung fu was taken from Wikipedia.
- The two people who Uncle Zac grubstaked were real names. They were miners and had claims. O. C. Wheelock's was the owner of the trading post and hotel in Fort Jones. John Thomas was at Rich Gulch. Bill Jenkins was also an actual miner in that area.
- The old mining town of Cottonwood was on Cottonwood Flat.
- The Chinese Tong was real in areas where there was Chinese business. I do not know if they were present in Yreka in the 1850s. But they were well known in San Francisco's Chinatown.

Author's Notes

- Box social lunches were popular in those years. I was told by my grandparents of box lunch socials being held at schoolhouses in their day.
- The Indians did gather together to hunt camas and form large buffalo hunts. All of that information can be obtained online.
- Throughout the early years, Yreka suffered from many devastating fires, thus many buildings were made of stone or brick.
- Marshal Ely was elected marshal in Yreka in 1854.

The information used in this novel is written to help you enjoy and relax while reading it. I tried to paint exact pictures of what I thought it was like. I wanted to lighten hearts and keep my story clean where anyone, at any age, could just sit back and enjoy it.

I hope you enjoy it.

Terrance M. Cooper, Author
I would enjoy hearing from you.
doctmcooper@yahoo.com
Please visit my website: doctmcooper.com

About the Author

Doc Terrance M. Cooper, was raised on a farm in Cooperville, Michigan, and drove teams of horses by the time he was nine years old. He enjoyed riding his own horse, Cherokee, everywhere in the countryside until he joined the Marine Corps in 1959. After he got out of the Marine Corps, he spent two and one half years in Samoa as a missionary for his church. He returned to the States and immediately entered college. When he finished college, he entered Palmer College of Chiropractic in Davenport, Iowa, in 1966, and graduated in 1970.

In 1970 he went on a blind date and met his wife, Julie Ann. He saw her twice, and on the third date, he proposed to her and she accepted. They were married three months later.

They have been married forty-five years, and have six children, thirty grandchildren, and two great-grandchildren.

In 1985, he moved his family to Hornbrook, California, to an 800-acre ranch, where they raised kids, quarter horses, and cows. He opened a chiropractic office in Yreka and became fascinated by the early history of Siskiyou County. He enjoyed taking his wife and children to the Marble Mountain Wilderness where they packed in by horseback and camped and fished.

Doc then moved to Roosevelt, Utah, in the Uinta Basin where he continued his chiropractic practice, bought a smaller ranch, and continued raising kids, horses, and cows. Their family consisted of six children—two boys and four girls. As a family they would pack in the Uinta Mountains and camp and fish. They participated on many cattle roundups with neighbors in the area. Their daughters were the most avid riders. Their small ranch stock consisted of eighteen pair of mother cows, their calves, and ten horses. As a family they would have a yearly round-up, where they would brand, tag the ears, and inoculate the stock. The family did everything else that went with ranch life. And, yes, they even ate Rocky Mountain Oysters.

Scan to visit

www.doctmcooper.com